About Winter of the Wolf

The Wild Hunt Legacy: Book 2

Erotic paranormal ménage romance

I have read all of Cherise's books (several times over) and never been disappointed, but I have to say that Winter of the Wolf was one of my favorites. Magic and mystery abound with two tortured, lonely bad boys and an equally wounded heart in our heroine

~ You Gotta Read Reviews

After years in foster care, Breanne Gallagher has the stable life she's always wanted, living with her foster-sister, working as a chef, enjoying her comfortable routines. Then one devastating night, a hellish creature invades her apartment and shatters her fragile existence. Shifting between monster and man, it slaughters her foster sister and assaults Bree. Alone, wounded, her beloved home tainted by gruesome memories, Bree flees to a tiny wilderness town, following her only clue to her past.

Shapeshifting warriors, Zeb and Shay move from one pack to another, hunting the hellhounds which prey on their kind. Assigned to Cold Creek, they take over management of a decrepit fishing lodge for their "human" cover. Their first renter is a pretty human female who trembles at the sight of them—yet stands her ground. Furious at the hurt they see in her eyes, the protective nomads are drawn into helping her. Although no shapeshifter is ever attracted to a human, her scent is oddly compelling, and her ferocious determination to conquer her fears ignites longings neither loner ever expected to face.

Bree is healing, learning to shoot the biggest pistol she can find, and overcoming her fears, especially of the two deadly, disconcertingly attractive hunters. Her life is getting back on track…until she tries to save a little girl from a hellhound and discovers that everything she knows about herself is false.

There are not many authors that know how to write such an emotional story but Cherise Sinclair is a master at it. She brings you into her wondrous worlds, filled with wonderful characters, and never lets the reader go until she is good and ready.

~ Just Erotic Romance Reviews

Want to be notified of the next release?

Sent only on release day, Cherise's newsletters contain freebies, excerpts, and articles.

Sign up at:

www.CheriseSinclair.com/NewsletterForm

Winter of the Wolf

The Wild Hunt Legacy 2

Cherise Sinclair

VanScoy Publishing Group

Acknowledgements

I want to extend my profound appreciation to the following people:

To my editor Jacy Mackin for her keen eye.

To the Erotic Romance Authors who helped kick-start the opening chapters and will kept me rewriting until something made sense. And my gratitude for the cheering during good times and handholding during the bad.

A special shoutout goes to Bianca Sommerland and Cari Silverwood for the first read-through of this baby and for helping the plot to stand up on its little legs.

To my beta readers who went above and beyond the call of critiquing duty: Monette Michaels, mistress of the phrase "tighten this"; Fiona Campbell for your help with language inconsistencies, Rosie Moewe for your help with blurbs; and Carol Ann MacKay for your incredibly keen eye.

To the fantastic readers and writers who keep me company on my Facebook page. Your cheerful (and occasionally perverted) humor makes life so much more fun.

To those of you who demanded that a certain rough cahir get his happy ending, Zeb said to tell y'all: *thank you*! (Well, he included a four-letter word or two for emphasis, but that's what he meant.)

To my patient and loving family. You tolerate my snarls during deadlines, lure me out of my cave with popcorn and movies, and make Diet Coke runs to keep me alive. I love you all so, so much.

Chapter One

Seattle ~ Dark of the Moon

I WON, I won, I won! As Breanne Gallagher drove into the parking lot of her apartment complex, excitement fizzed in her veins like champagne. Her five tiered, chocolate praline cake had taken first place at the competition for Northwest pastry chefs. She bounced up and down, grinning like an idiot.

Even more incredible—two of the finest downtown Seattle restaurants had indicated their interest in hiring her. Not that she'd accept, because, hey, she had everything she needed right here. The restaurant where she'd worked for years was in the top ratings and close to where she and her foster-sister, Ashley, lived. She finally had the stable life she's always wanted and planned to keep it that way.

But she could certainly hit her boss up for a raise.

After parking near the end of the lot, she opened her car door. Industrial tech music hammered down from one of the three buildings in the complex, overwhelming the traffic noise from the nearby I-5 freeway. Her mood dimmed as she stood, letting her eyes adjust to the darkness. With a couple of lights out and no moon in the sky, the far end of the parking lot was creepy as heck. Pulling her coat closed against the moist winter air, she hurried toward her apartment building.

Nearing the better-lighted area, Bree slowed and glanced around, but didn't see Ashley's bright yellow car. But she should be home soon, and then they could celebrate. *Because I won!* Spirits rising again, she did a victory dance down the center. *I rule!* As she twirled around, a car entered the lot, the headlights painfully bright. With a squeak of alarm, she jumped out of the way and tripped on a parked motorcycle. She landed hard, scraping her hands and knees on the rough pavement.

Face flaming with embarrassment, she knelt and tried to catch her breath. Blood trickled down her burning palms. Wow, way to crash off the victory pedestal.

"You okay?" Someone took her hand and lifted her to her feet.

"Fine." Bree looked up. Wow, the man was huge, well over six feet tall, and he smelled like a garbage can filled with rotting oranges and chicken carcasses. *Ew.* Pulling her bleeding hand out of his, she backed away hastily. "Well. Thanks for the help."

The doublewide door to the building opened, spilling out a wash of light and a handful of teenaged girls, Bree hastily pushed past them, glancing back as she stepped inside.

He was staring at her, his eyes a brownish-red—the color of dried blood. A chill ran up her spine as he lifted his hand to his face and licked his palm. As she headed down the hallway, she heard his voice, as greasy as cold bacon. "Well, well, well."

SHE MADE A batch of chocolate chip cookies, the best cure for unsettled emotions. Since Ashley still wasn't home, Bree pulled out her memento box for company. She smiled at the pictures of the Edwards and Petersons, her favorite foster families, then scowled at one of Mr. Harvey, *the pervert.* A shame she hadn't had a black belt then or she'd have snapped his *thing* off. Turning the picture face down, she moved on to the ribbons from cooking contests.

With a sigh of sadness, she stroked the photo of a short, wiry man at a karate tournament. Sensei had been the closest person she'd ever had to a father. He'd have been proud of her today. *I miss you.*

Realizing her trip down memory lane wasn't helping, she gathered up a handful of shelled nuts from a bag in the kitchen. The apartment door was on the left side of the living room. She went the other direction, through the sliding glass door and out to the landscaped grounds. The cold chilled her bare feet as she ran across the grass to a big maple tree illuminated by decorative solar lights. Standing on her tiptoes, she scattered the food along a low branch. "Here you go, Tinkerbelle."

Chittering happily, the little thing she called a tree fairy scampered down the trunk. Bree had to laugh. It—she—was the size of a Barbie doll, almost ethereally pale, with intense green eyes. No wings though, so it wasn't really a fairy.

Close enough. Bree laughed as Tinkerbelle tried to pick up an almond bigger than her hands.

"Hey, Bree, are you there?" Her roommate, Ashley Carrigan, stood in the door, the wind whipping her red hair back over her shoulders.

"Over here."

"Woohoo, girl. I saw on the news. You won!" With her long-legged stride, Ash crossed the yard and gave Bree a jubilant hug. "Congratulations!"

Bree basked in the glow. Nothing was better than having someone to share the good and the bad. "Thanks, sis."

Ash stepped back and glanced at the tree, obviously seeing the nuts. "Are you feeding that nonexistent thing again?"

"Sure. Imaginary creatures get hungry in the winter." Bree grinned as her roommate squinted up at the tree. In all the years since they'd met in a foster home, Ash had never seen any of the beings—but she always tried.

"You know, with your imagination, you should write children's books."

"Uh-huh. With your blindness, maybe you should get glasses." Unfortunately, that was a poor defense since no one except Bree ever saw the fairy things that lived in trees and flowers. Or the tiny trolls in the gutters. Or the shimmering beings in Puget Sound that looked like fish with faces. Why, darn it? Why was she the only one to see them?

But it didn't matter. The little creatures added light and wonder to her world, and had since before she could remember. "So, why don't—"

Tinkerbelle sniffed the air, dropped the almond, and leaped into the darkness of the higher branches.

Had something spooked her? Bree glanced around but saw nothing. The small grassy area wasn't a popular place on a damp winter night. "Let's head back. My feet are going numb."

As they walked toward the open glass door, Ashley frowned. "How much time did you spend creating that winning masterpiece anyway? You look pooped."

"Not that long. I'm fine." Only she wasn't, and it wasn't because of the time spent cooking. No matter how much or how little she did, she was always tired. Her doctor thought she had chronic fatigue syndrome, although he admitted that her symptoms didn't quite fit. "Probably a lack of chocolate. I made cookies, so it's all good."

The apartment enfolded Bree in warmth, and she wiggled her chilled toes in the carpet. The room felt cozy, decorated in sunny colors with cheerful flowering plants to offset the Seattle gloom. Tired or not, she had a good life—a wonderful foster-sister, a good job, and a happy place to live.

"I stopped and got a bottle of wine and a couple of movies to help celebrate." Ash shook her head. "I figured you'd be too tired to want to go out…and what's the point in taking you out to eat after you spend all day in a restaurant?"

"Sounds perfect. What did you get?"

"For me, Runaway Bride. For you, Lethal Weapon 4." Ashley narrowed her gray eyes. "But if you start critiquing the karate stuff, I'm turning it off."

"I'll be good." Besides, most of the fun of pointing out the mistakes had disappeared when Sensei had died. The ache of grief squeezed her chest again. After pulling her off the streets, he'd set her on her path to independence. Why couldn't he have lived long enough to see her flourish? Bree pushed the sadness away. Tonight was about celebration, not mourning.

"Get those cookies, and I'll put in the movie," Ash said. "Which one first?"

"Let's start with the interesting one—the one with action. And I don't mean sex, okay?"

She fetched the cookies from the kitchen, inhaling the sweet fragrance.

Shriek! Screams and gunshots split the air, and Bree jumped, almost dropping the plate. "Darn that kid! He must have volume at max." The young man in the adjacent apartment was addicted to slasher movies.

"Men and their loud toys." Ash snorted. She slid Bree's mementos to one side to clear space for the food, then nodded at a silver-disked bracelet and a crumpled photo of a couple holding a very young Breanne. "You still got those, huh?"

"Hey, they're my heritage, right?" Other people got antique china and photo albums and precious furniture, but the picture and bracelet were all she'd possessed when a ranger had found her lost in a forest at the age of three.

Ash tapped the photo. "You know, if you blew this up, you might be able to get an ID on your parents. The Internet has all sorts of customizable search engines now."

As the noise from next door diminished slightly, Bree sat on the couch and poured wine. "Nah. Either they're dead or didn't want me. Why bother?"

"Maybe you just got lost, and they've been looking for you. Wanting to take you home." Ashley's father was in jail, her mother OD'd, so she'd set her heart on Bree's parents being wonderful and rich and loving, like out of some Disney movie.

Ash didn't get it that Disney created fantasies as fake as the idea that Bree's parents had given a darn about her. "Couldn't have searched that hard. It's been over twenty years." Bree shook her head. "Besides, who needs them? You're my family. And I have the perfect home right here."

"Well...I wanted to talk to you about that." Ashley picked up the glass of wine, spinning it around and around in her hands.

The last time Ash had looked that flustered, she'd confessed to slamming the oven door, causing Bree's dessert soufflé to collapse. Bree set the remote down. "What's wrong?"

"My boss talked to me today. They're opening a division in San Diego." Ash's face lit with pride and excitement. "He asked me to head the software section."

"San Diego? B-but you live here." *I live here.*

The glow in Ashley's face faded slightly. "You'll come with me, right? We'll get an apartment and—"

"No." Move away? Bree rose, wrapping her arms around herself. "This is home. Here." *This apartment. This city. My job.*

"Jesus, Mary, and Joseph, we've lived in this building forever. You've worked at that restaurant for even longer. You could be a chef anywhere. Don't you ever want to see or do something else?"

"No." Bree opened the sliding glass door, breathing in the chill air. "I moved enough when I was little." Foster home to foster home, new families, new neighborhoods, new schools. Different foods, strange routines, unfamiliar beds. Nothing had ever stayed the same.

"But..." Ashley bit her lip. "I'm *tired* of the rain. I want to live somewhere sunny. I want you to come too."

Bree shook her head. The very thought of leaving made her sick. This was her home. "I-I can't. Moving is your dream." But how could she survive the loneliness if her foster-sister left?

"Dammit, Bree, you—" Ash's words were drowned out by a cinematic explosion from the adjoining apartment.

Bree closed the sliding door and paused. Something moved across the landscaped grounds. Four-legged and bigger than a dog. A bear? In Seattle? The tiny hairs on the back of her neck rose.

"What's wrong?" Ashley joined her.

"I think there's a—"

The huge black form headed for the apartment, picking up speed.

"Get back!" Bree backpedaled, pulling Ash with her.

To her shock, the animal charged straight at the patio door. It wouldn't; it *did*. Glass shattered with a horrendous crash as the beast burst through.

Ash screamed, high and shrill, frozen directly in the bear's path.

"No!" Bree shoved a chair in front of the bear and darted behind the couch, yanking Ash along. Heart pounding, she turned toward the... *That's no bear.*

Oh, God, what is that thing?

Evil red-brown eyes stared at her. The size of a grizzly, but armored like a dinosaur with bony spiked plates. A shark-like head displayed massive pointed teeth. The stench of it was like raw meat left in the garbage for days. Worse.

She stood petrified for a moment, cold chills running down her spine.

It took a step forward.

Her mind screamed: *run away, run away*. But she wouldn't—couldn't—turn her back on it. She took a slow step back. Keeping her gaze on the creature, she slid her hand up the wall and yanked the *bokken* from the rack. The familiar grip of the wooden practice sword felt comforting in her hands.

Ash had no weapon, no training. "Go get help," Bree ordered under her breath. "Hurry!"

"But—"

"*Go.*"

As Ash moved away, Bree jumped forward, waving her sword as a diversion. "Beat it! Get out of here." Keeping eye contact, she inched backwards. *Come after me, beast. Follow me.*

The sound of the unlocking deadbolt *snicked* loud in the room. The creature's head turned, and it charged toward Ash.

"No!" With all her strength, Bree bashed the sword on its skull. The wooden blade splintered. Broke.

Not slowing at all, the creature shouldered past, knocking her backwards. She slammed into the wall with a hard thud.

Head spinning, she regained her feet and saw it leap at Ashley.

The monster hit, biting Ash's shoulder, pulling her to the ground, savaging her. Her screams almost drowned out its ghastly snarls.

"Noooo." Terrified, frantic, Bree flung herself across the room. "Get off her!" She spun, kicking the beast in the stomach. Pain blasted through her foot. The creature barely rocked.

"Ash, run!"

The monster's massive head whipped around and gore-covered teeth snapped at Bree's ankle, spattering her jeans with saliva and blood. Ashley's blood.

Bree jumped back, expecting Ash to stand. To get through the door. Why wasn't she moving? She darted a glance behind the beast and froze. Unable to move. To think.

Ash's neck was ripped—ripped away. Blood everywhere. Her gray eyes were open. Blank. *Oh Ash.* Bree took a step forward. *No no no. This can't happen. Oh please, no.* Her breath hitched.

The monster watched her, mouth open as if laughing.

When the creature sniffed at the pool of blood beside Ashley's body, rage roared in Bree's head. *Kill it, kill it, kill it.* Yet terror shook her bones until she couldn't breathe.

Lapping at the blood, it stood between her and the apartment's front door.

Get a knife. Her pulse pounded in her ears as she backpedaled quickly into the kitchen. But the monster followed, red-brown eyes never leaving her face. Like thick smoke, the sense of evil choked her. Clicking sounds made her look down. The beast had massive claws—each one bigger than a finger. Oh God.

Can I kill it?

Slimy pink drool dripped from its mouth onto her tile floor as it stopped, trapping her in the kitchen.

Her back bumped the counter. She reached behind her, and her hand found the knife rack. Not that one. Or that. Her fingers closed on the butcher knife. With a deep breath, then another, she tried to push the fear to one side like at a martial arts tournament. Didn't work.

Hit it where? The wooden sword had splintered in her hand. The spiked plating on its back looked too thick. The neck?

The monster lunged at her.

She dodged sideways, aimed the knife toward its throat— and the blade skidded across the plates, catching in the grooves. The head whipped around. *Heck!*

She yanked her hand away, and its teeth closed on emptiness with an ugly snap.

Was she stupid? Get help. She screamed, loud and shrill,

screamed again. And then the thing was on her. She slashed at its neck. The shock jarred her hand. The blade broke off at the hilt.

"No!" She chopped at its neck with the edge of her hand. Her hand bounced off, bleeding from the sharp points of the plates. She could break concrete—but not this thing? "*Why don't you die?*"

Vaulting up and over, she cut her palms on its spiky armor, but landed behind it. She slammed a kick into its leg. A bone in her foot fractured. The sound and the pain were nauseating, and she staggered back.

The hellish creature spun. Jaws clamped onto her arm, and it whipped her around like a land-borne shark. She hit the counter, grunted in pain, and punched at its eyes. Too protected, too recessed in the armor.

The jaws tightened on her arm. Pain burst through her, and her knees buckled. She struggled, a helpless mouse, as it dragged her across the floor to the living room. With a jerk of its head, the monster flung her across the room.

Free. She rolled over and sprang away, one arm limp at her side.

With a savage growl, the animal jumped on her, driving her face into the floor. Claws dug into her back. The rotten stench closed her throat. *I'm going to die.* The inevitability beat at her.

Its teeth ripped into her flesh, tearing at her shoulder.

It hurts, oh God, it hurts. She screamed, twisting onto her back to kick at it. Her feet hit uselessly, like hammering on a tank.

Suddenly it backed away. She tried to stand and failed. Her hand skidded in the blood soaking the carpet. *My blood.* She gritted her teeth, tears smearing her vision. *Where was—*

The beast blurred and turned into a person. A man.

No. She sucked in a breath, trying to get her eyes to focus.

It was the guy from the parking lot. Naked. His thick hairless chest was streaked with gore. Blood dripped from his mouth and chin. He licked his lips. "You are like nothing I've ever had." His voice was oily. "I knew I tasted something...extra in your blood. What are you? Where did you come from?"

His head tilted, and a cruel smile grew on his face. He crooned, "Are there more like you?" Pink-tinged drool rolled down his chin as he stared down at her.

She shuddered. Her fingers curled into the carpet, and she tried to inch away.

"You look human." He wiped his blood-spattered cheek, sniffed, then ran his tongue over his palm. "Mmm. You don't smell different, but I've never, ever, tasted anything like this before."

She raised her feet to kick at him, to keep him away. One arm wouldn't lift, and she was losing blood fast.

He took a step forward.

"Bastard!" She snap-kicked his knee.

He hissed in pain and blurred into the creature. With a vicious snarl, the beast lunged at her. Teeth punched through her jeans, ripping into her thigh, and her screams echoed in the room. Oh God, why did no one come?

Her eyes lost focus and then he was a man again, licking his lips. Laughing. "The taste of you is just—fucking great." He loomed over her, huge and evil. "Killing you tonight would be a waste." He glanced at Ashley's body. "I can feed on her. But first..."

His hand slid down his stomach to his cock—horribly erect—and wrapped around it.

Ailill Ridge, Rainier Territory ~ Dark of the Moon

ONLY A FEW hours remained before dawn, and the small mountain town of Ailill Ridge was silent. Thick clouds had blotted out the stars in the moonless night, but the cold wind off Mt. Rainier brought the stench of evil—rotting flesh mixed with a nauseating tang like molding oranges. The scent came from the front of a one-story house, and Zebulon Damron paused in the shadow of an oak, searching for any movement.

The hellhound was close. Zeb would have his fight tonight even if his patrol-partner Shay reached the demon-dog first. Not even Shay could kill a hellhound alone, though the obsessed idiot would probably try.

He felt the touch of the God of the Hunt. Power poured into his cahir's body like wine into a glass, gifting him with far more than a normal shifter's strength.

AFTER SKIRTING THE patches of snow that might betray him, he edged around the corner of the house. Thorns from a rose bush scraped across his neck, and he froze, silently cursing all females and their vicious plants. The smell of fresh blood would alert the hellhound to his presence.

He checked his weapons. Sheathed on his right hip: stiletto for the demon-dog's eyes, double-edged dagger for its belly. Left hip: pistol for the eyes—although bullets were almost worthless. Be nice if cahirs had as few vulnerabilities as hellhounds.

So where was it? He risked a quick check of the narrow side yard. *Good evening, hellhound.* Its front paws on the planter box, the demon scum peered through the window.

Zeb slid his blade from the sheath strapped to his right thigh. The tiny vulnerable area of the beast's stomach was exposed. If he could get to it before—

With a heave of its heavily muscled hindquarters, the hellhound smashed through the glass. Fuck.

"Shay. Inside!" Zeb roared to his partner in the front yard. After sheathing his knife, he dove through the window. The splintered glass edging the sides scraped along his leather-covered shoulders. Dammit, just once he'd like to enter a house by the door. Somersaulting to his feet, Zeb pulled his dagger and spun in a circle. Empty living room.

A woman shrieked, the sound so filled with horror that a chill ran up Zeb's spine. *Had my sister screamed like that?* He shoved the thought away.

Glass shattered as Shay sprang through the front window, his wolf form as hefty as his human one. His paws scrambled for purchase on the tile floor.

His partner right behind him, Zeb sprinted down the hallway. They burst into the bedroom together, the well-practiced move possible only because Shay always fought as a wolf.

Zeb preferred to have a knife or pistol in hand.

Shay went left; Zeb right. In the center, the hellhound stalked the female cowering to the right of the door. She was a shifter, and the scent of fear poured from her—the demonhound would gorge on that emotion like a grizzly on a new-killed deer.

The hellhound's attention turned, and Zeb braced himself. This one was normal-sized—waist-high and bigger than any wolf, wrapped in bulletproof plating like a fucking dinosaur. It snarled, and the bony pointed muzzle displayed razor-sharp fangs.

Zeb snarled back, cursing silently. So much for surprise.

The beast stepped forward, bear-like claws clicking on the hardwood floor.

"By Herne, you are an ugly one." He checked Shay who would attack from the rear, the diversion allowing Zeb to drop, roll half under his quarry, and slice down the narrow leathery part of its gut.

Sometimes it worked.

Zeb glanced at the female and realized she wasn't overweight, but pregnant. The knowledge sent his protective instincts skyrocketing. After checking the hellhound, he moved forward a couple of steps, leaving room between him and the wall, then caught her gaze and glanced behind him. *Run that way, little female, so I can keep you safe.*

Despite her terror, she gave him an infinitesimal nod.

Satisfied, he returned his attention to the demon scum's eyes. The red in its pupils widened with rage. It would charge soon.

With a loud snarl, Shay darted in. His jaw clamped on the hellhound's hind leg, jaw working to penetrate the overlapping plates.

The hellhound bellowed and spun

Zeb crouched to spring forward—

Trying to flee, the woman tripped, falling against Zeb's legs from behind. He staggered, dropping to one knee as she scrambled to her feet and through the door.

From the other side of the room, Shay yelped. His body thudded loudly against the wall. Silence.

"Fuck!" Strategy gone, Zeb charged the creature savaging his partner. His leather tore as he rammed into its spiky shoulder, knocking it back a step. He reached down, trying to stab the gut. His blade scraped over the plating, caught the narrow leathery strip down the belly, and made a shallow slice.

He'd barely scratched the fucking tank. Zeb scrambled away. Too slow.

The hellhound's jaws ripped a chunk from his right arm in a flash of hellish pain.

Fuck. As it spun completely around, Zeb dove away. The demon-dog charged forward, one hind leg weaker. Shay must have managed to bite through the shallower plates there.

Zeb braced himself as it advanced. Not going to survive this one. One-on-one with a hellhound was suicide. *So be it.* But the creature would finish Shay off, so he had to kill it. *Had to.* Maybe the hallway would give him a chance to use his pistol.

He dodged the first attack and risked a glance sideways. His partner's leg was awash in blood, but the big wolf was trying to rise. Alive, thank the Mother.

Darting for the door, Zeb yanked out his revolver. The hellhound's claws scraped on the floor as it followed.

Halfway down the hall, Zeb spun. He aimed—the recessed eyes were the only place a bullet was effective—and fired again and again.

But the attacking demon scum tipped its head down, so the bullets splatted off the armored head and ricocheted off the wall.

Useless. He back-pedaled, but the hellhound hit him hard. As Zeb landed on his back, the creature lunged for his throat. Weapons flying, Zeb grabbed its neck to hold the jaws away. He kicked sideways to spin his torso out of reach of the claws.

The hellhound tried to shake off his grip. Twisting and lunging. Over and over.

Fuck. It couldn't reach his throat...yet...but Zeb couldn't use his knife. Stalemate, and he knew damn well which of them would tire sooner. If he hadn't had a cahir's extra strength from the God of the Hunt, Herne, he'd be dead by now. The muscles of his arms started to spasm.

His death shone in the red-brown eyes.

His stiletto was still sheathed. Could he stab its eye as it tore his throat out? *Can't...can't let it kill Shay.*

The jaws inched closer, the stench foul.

"You know, it really wants a taste of you." With a lurching movement, Shay pulled Zeb's stiletto from his hip sheath and buried it in the demon-dog's eye.

Its roar filled the room, and the creature collapsed onto Zeb, knocking the wind out of him.

Shuddering, it died, changing to human a second later. A very dead, very naked male. Oversized, like all hellhounds.

Zeb shoved the body off and staggered to his feet. The hallway spun around him. He bent, hands on knees to catch his breath. Just taking a breath hurt as if an iron trap had closed on his chest. Must have cracked a rib. His arm bled; his hands weren't much better and hurt worse.

He waited for his partner's low howl, to start the song of victory over a hellhound. Over death. Nothing. He painfully straightened. "Shay?"

"Sorry I was slow," his partner managed before toppling to the floor.

Fuck, fuck, fuck. Throat tight, Zeb dropped to his knees. Still in human form and naked, Shay had bites, gouges, ripped flesh down his right hip and leg. Blood flowed sluggishly over his pale skin.

Gut twisting, Zeb ripped a bed sheet and bound up the worst of Shay's wounds. His eyes kept blurring with memories of his brothers and sister—his littermates. How their flesh had been torn away from the bones, how blood had pooled around them.

Shay would live. But with no healer in the area, he'd hurt for a fucking long time. Once again, guilt swept over Zeb. *My fault.* Hadn't thought ahead, hadn't dodged the woman, should have moved faster.

Hands shaking, he holstered his weapon and sheathed his knives. With a grunt of pain, he carefully lifted his partner.

The cold night air stung his skin. The starlight blurred and cleared as he staggered down the small street. After a minute, he raised his face to the moonless sky and howled his song of victory and death, of lingering grief for his family. Of loneliness.

Chapter Two

Seattle ~ First quarter moon

A WEEK AFTER the attack, Bree entered her apartment and snapped the deadbolt. Leaning her forehead against the door, she tried to steel herself to move. Criminy, she hurt. Her leg, her shoulder, her arm—her wounds burned as if the thing's teeth were ripping at them all over again. As the pain eased, she pulled in a slow breath, smelling the harsh odor of industrial cleaners. *Okay, I can do this.*

She slowly turned, terrified of what she'd see. But there was no body, no gore, no pools of blood.

The glass door had been repaired. The beige carpet was new. The knots in her shoulders eased. Of course, the landlord had had the place cleaned up, and the police had already told her that the murderer had taken Ashley's body. The knowledge sent a shudder through her.

Seeing the bloody paw prints, the cops had decided the killer had brought a dog with him. They certainly didn't buy her story of a monster that changed into a man. Although the detectives, doctor, nurses, and counselors had been very sympathetic, she knew no sane person could possibly believe her. She didn't blame them, but how could the police find the creature if they didn't realize what they were looking for?

Hauling in a deep breath, she forced herself away from the door—after rechecking the deadbolt three times. Not that a lock was much use. After all, the sliding door had been closed last week, and the beast had charged right through the glass. Thank God, Mrs. Johnson had been walking her terrier and noticed the shattered glass, or Bree would have bled to death.

But help hadn't arrived soon enough to prevent Ash's death or soon enough to keep the monster from... Bree's stomach turned over, and she barely made it to the toilet. She vomited over and over until she was empty. Bile burned her mouth, and she crumpled on the cold tile like a used towel.

Used—that was the word. She'd been *used*. She scrambled for the toilet again.

When the dry heaving finally ended, she fell back against the tub, clammy sweat drying on her skin. She'd avoided thinking about it, but she had to face reality. She'd been attacked, savaged, bitten, torn up by a...creature, and then she'd been— She swallowed. Swallowed again. *Raped.*

After rinsing her mouth, she headed for the kitchen on wobbly legs. A diet cola erased the last traces of sickness from her mouth, and the caffeine refueled her flagging energy. Nightmares had stolen her sleep. She hadn't been able to eat. A bitter laugh broke from her—at least she was clean, considering how many showers she was taking, day and night. But no matter how hard she washed, she still smelled him on her skin.

She wasn't pregnant, at least. Living on the street had taught her a few lessons. *1: Life isn't safe. 2: Having children by accident is stupid.* She'd been on birth control pills since she was able to obtain them, and the hospital had given her extra medications as part of the hospital's post...assault...protocol.

Holding the cola, she sank down on the couch and noticed that someone had picked up her spilled memory box. On top was the photo of her with the people everyone assumed were her parents. "*You know, if you blew this up, you might be able to get an ID on your parents.*" The memory of Ash's voice was so clear that Bree looked around, but the apartment was empty. Would always be empty.

All that was left in these rooms was horror. A sob lodged in her chest, hurting, trying to break free. Everything she'd worked for—her beautiful stable world—was shattered. *I want it back. My Ashley, my home, everything. Please, God, put it back.* With a tearing feeling, the sob broke loose. Pushing her face against the cushion, she cried, the anguished sounds ripping her sore throat.

Eventually, she regained control. Wiping tears from her cheeks, she pulled in a shuddering breath. What's done was done. Time to deal with it. Taking a determined sip of cola, she straightened her shoulders and started making plans.

First of all, she couldn't live here anymore. When her lips quivered, she firmed them immediately. No more tears. She'd have to find a different apartment somewhere in Seattle. She could keep everything else the same—her job, her city. Just a new apartment. With luck, she could find a place that was several stories up and that had security.

And if the monster could get through those precautions? A shiver ran through her. She'd used her fists, her feet, even the sword and knife. Nothing had worked. Bree wrapped her arms around herself, gritting her teeth as the movement tugged on the stitches in her arm and shoulder.

If fists, feet, or blades wouldn't work, she'd find something better. A pistol. Would a bullet go through those bony spikes? Putting her fingers together, she pointed at the glass door. "Bang, bang, bang."

Even the *pretend* recoil made her drop the imaginary gun and grab her shoulder. "Ooow." But...a pistol would work. Her spirits lifted. She could shoot the monster. Over and over. Until it was just bloody bits.

As she leaned back, her arm and shoulder throbbed viciously. Unfortunately, owning a pistol wouldn't help if she couldn't shoot it. She needed to find someplace safe to live until she finished healing. Getting out of Seattle would probably be the best idea. With a sigh, she set her finger on the faces in the photograph. The creature had said she was something different, wondered if she were human and if there were more like her.

Are there more like me? No one else ever saw the flower-fairies. What if she'd inherited something from her mother or father? Would they know about this monster? She'd never cared about trying to find her parents—so loving that they'd managed to lose her. But if she had to leave the city while she healed, she might as well try to find some answers as well. Her eyes burned with fresh tears. *Look, Ash, I'm going to look for my parents just as you wanted.*

She blinked hard and raised her chin. There—she had a recipe for the next few weeks. Get out of the city. Find parents. Heal up. And buy the biggest darn pistol she could lift.

Ailill Ridge, Rainier Territory ~ First quarter moon

"YOU'RE THROWING US OUT?" Blindsided by the announcement, Zeb stared in disbelief at the Cosantir—Herne's appointed guardian and ruler of Rainier Territory. When Pete Wendell had summoned him and Shay to his house for a meeting, Zeb hadn't thought much about it. He'd figured the two-bit local bar owner had griped to pudgy Pete about the chairs he'd busted up in a fight last weekend.

But this… A hollow spot formed in his gut.

"Throw you out?" Pete rested his hands on the kitchen table and widened his eyes in assumed shock. "Of course not. It's simply that the Cosantir of North Cascades Territory needs cahirs who know how to kill hellhounds. You and Shay are the most experienced here."

Beside Zeb, Shay made a derogatory noise. "This area still has and will always have hellhounds. So with your usual impeccable logic, you're sending away your most experienced cahirs?"

Zeb pulled in a slow, painful breath. He'd been doing okay here. Not like in Banff Territory where the alpha and beta had been so aggressive that he'd gotten into fights every few days.

Pete's hands closed into fists. "My own cahirs can handle any problems here. Since I shut down the fishing camp, you two are out of jobs. There's nothing keeping you in my territory. You don't have family or friends, not even among your wolf pack."

True. Zeb didn't make friends. Didn't have family. Didn't belong anywhere. He tried to ignore the hollowness growing inside. "I can guess why you want *me* to leave." He glanced at the beautiful blonde seated in the living room.

Gretchen's lips turned up in a tiny smirk. She might be gorgeous, but her self-absorption and vindictiveness made her the most unappealing female he'd ever met. He wouldn't waste his time mating with such as her.

His gaze on her, Zeb said, "I had her once, and she wanted more." She never spoke to him normally, but when in heat, her instincts ruled. "I didn't."

She turned dark red, mouth twisting with anger.

Zeb kept his voice even despite his growing rage. "But why send Shay away?"

Shay leaned back, dwarfing his chair with his oversized frame. His expression turned hard. "Your brother put you up to it, I'd bet. As alpha of the pack, Roger should be able to dominate me, but he can't."

Pete reddened at the insult—a Cosantir wasn't supposed to be swayed by relatives or females. Then his mouth flattened into an ugly line. "You don't have to move to the Cascades. You two can go where you want. But you're not welcome in my territory. In my house. At my table."

Even through Zeb's fury, he saw the Cosantir clearly. No power glimmered around his body showing that the god, Herne, supported him. This wasn't a true Cosantir's Judgment. He and Shay could fight this. If they wanted to. He glanced at his patrol-partner.

Shay's eyes were the cold blue-gray of a winter mountain lake as he shrugged. "Let the hellhounds have them. I never liked this territory...or house...or table anyway."

Zeb rose and helped Shay to his feet. As his partner limped from the room, Zeb's temper slipped. He slammed his fists on the table, splitting the wood down the center.

The sound of it falling and Pete's cursing accompanied him out the door.

Chapter Three

Cold Creek, North Cascades Territory

A T LEAST PACKING hadn't taken long, Shay O'Donnell thought the next day. All their belongings fit in the back of Zeb's truck. *Pitiful.*

As Zeb turned into the parking lot of the Wild Hunt Tavern, Shay gritted his teeth. His leg ached as if the hellhound's teeth were grinding into it, and his skin itched from the long drive. Damn metal. Be nice if they'd invent plastic vehicles.

Fun week. No healer for his wounds, only a few days of recovery, then kicked out of the territory. Unfortunately, they'd probably be back on the road within the hour, especially if their reputations preceded them.

Far too often, he was more dominant than a territory's pack leader. Even though he'd side-step actual challenges, irritated alphas meant unsettled packs and dominance struggles. Then there was his patrol partner. Scarred. Bitter. Hell, Zeb scared almost everybody—except during Gatherings when the females in heat flocked to the strongest males.

So fine, they'd go through the motions, get rejected, and then figure out what to do. Probably go separate ways since Zeb gave new meaning to the lone wolf designation.

Shay glanced at his partner's dark face. Rigid spine, tight

shoulders, the acrid scent of tension. No shifter could live alone forever, especially a wolf. How many rejections could the male take before he broke and went feral?

How many can I take? But with his bond to the God of the Hunt, he couldn't turn feral. Just lonely.

Shay slid out of the truck and held onto the door, studying the area as he waited for the pain to recede.

Like Ailill Ridge, the Cold Creek population supposedly contained more Daonain—shifters—than humans. It looked like a pretty place, the town cupped in the palm of the mountains, in much the same way that the forest curved around the two-story log tavern. The air held a frosty bite, sweetened by the fragrance of pine forests and a hint of cedar wood smoke.

"Ready?" Zeb's black eyes were cynical.

"Let's get this over with."

The scent of beer and roasted peanuts filled the dimly lit tavern. Across a wealth of scattered tables and chairs, a long, dark oak bar dominated the back wall like a scene from a western movie. The late afternoon hour meant the room was mostly empty. Two shifter females sat at the bar. One was beautifully curvy, and Shay gave her an appreciative look.

Three humans played pool in an alcove to the right, and upon seeing Zeb, they gathered into a protective cluster like a herd of prey. In the left corner, a cahir-sized man was drinking a beer.

"Where's the Cosantir?" Shay asked.

Zeb nodded at the black-haired bartender.

"Him?" But damned if the male wasn't surrounded by the thin shimmer of Herne's power. The bartender caught Shay's gaze and tilted his head toward the corner table where the lone man sat.

As Zeb and Shay approached, the beer-drinker stood and held out a hand. "I'm Alec McGregor. Good to see you again, cahir," he said to Zeb with an easy grin.

The corner of Zeb's mouth pulled up in his version of a smile. "Likewise, cahir."

As protectors of the clan, cahirs tended to be huge. Alec was typical—around six-five, heavily muscled, bearing Herne's blade-shaped blue mark on his cheek. He turned to Shay and held out his hand. "And you're Shay O'Donnell."

Shay nodded. Alec's grip was firm without any testosterone-driven display of strength.

Approaching with a tray of drinks, the Cosantir had the distinctive prowl of a werecat. Only a couple of inches shorter than Shay and slightly less broad of shoulder, he was as muscled as any cahir. And, unlike their old Cosantir, this one's power flowed in a luminescent aura around him.

"Sit, cahirs." He set a mug of dark beer by Zeb and a mug of light in front of Shay.

Shay glanced at Zeb and caught the cynical acknowledgement. The Cosantir had done his research if he knew the type of beer they drank—in which case, he'd also know how little he'd want them in his area. Hell.

Well, since Herne wasn't calling Shay in any specific direction, he could go anywhere. Maybe Zeb would be interested in visiting the Rockies. The hellhounds were thick around there.

"I am Calum McGregor," the Cosantir said.

"McGregor?" Shay asked, glancing at lighter complexion of Alec *McGregor.*

Calum nodded. "Alec's my littermate." He took a seat and steepled his fingers on the table. "I've talked with people about you and have decided—"

Shay held up his hand. Why draw this out? He caught the resignation in Zeb's black eyes and leaned forward. "Let's not waste time on amenities, Cosantir. I realize you didn't know who Pete would send until too late to call us off. We'll finish our drinks—and I thank you for them—and get out of your territory."

Alec laughed and shook his head.

"I think not. Be silent, and drink your beer." The Cosantir didn't raise his voice, but the order was so compelling that Shay took a swallow before he realized it.

"Cosan—" Shay started. Seeing the darkening of the Cosantir's gray gaze, he shut his mouth. Zeb had mentioned meeting this guy at some Gathering, said he was deadly. Shay leaned back in his chair.

Zeb's glance held a hint of amusement.

Alec tilted his glass in apparent approval of Shay's show of self-preservation, and Shay growled at him.

"I know your Cosantir did not enjoy having you in his territory. You're both overly inclined to fight. *You* may not start them, but dominance fights follow you around"—Calum's gaze rested on Shay before turning to Zeb—" and *you* frighten humans and shifters alike."

Shay shrugged and sipped his beer. Nothing like getting lectured before being pitched out on one's ear.

Calum said mildly. "I doubt those traits will cause a problem in my area."

Shay blinked, replayed the words, and lowered his glass. Hope glimmered inside him. "You want us to stay?"

"Exactly so. I was pleased when your Cosantir indicated you were leaving his territory. You're the very ones I'd hoped for."

"Why?"

Alec leaned forward. "We've got at least one hellhound in the area, maybe more. We lost a young male two moons ago, a female last month." He and his brother exchanged glances, their grief and fury obvious. Protective shifters, both of them. Nice to see.

Alec continued. "Aside from me, there's only a couple of other cahirs in our territory—Owen and Ben. None of us have experience with finding hellhounds, let alone killing them. You two are the best I've heard of."

A compliment? How long since he'd had one of those?

Alec rubbed his ear and smiled slowly. "My lifemate says there are three words that have an irresistible effect on her."

Shay stared. By Herne's antlers, what did his mate have to do with this? "I can guess. She wants the *'I love you'* words?"

The Cosantir tilted his head, drawing Shay's gaze back. With a bladelike smile, he said, "No, cahir, not the *'I love you'* words. These words"—he paused—"we *need* you."

The phrase hit Shay like a gut punch and silenced him utterly.

Zeb looked as stunned. He met Shay's gaze, looking as defenseless as Shay had ever seen the dangerous wolf, but after a second, he nodded.

Shay cleared his throat. "If you need us, then you've got us."

ALEC AND CALUM accompanied them out to the truck. As Zeb opened the door and slid behind the wheel, he felt as if he'd stepped onto a talus slope and lost his footing. Yet, maybe...maybe this would work, at least for a time. Calum was known as a good Cosantir. Open-minded. Fair.

Calum gripped the door before Zeb could close it. "One final detail. While in my territory, you live together. Under one roof."

Zeb's jaw dropped open as something washed through him that tasted like fear. "I live alone."

"You used to live alone. Now you don't." The Cosantir leveled a hard stare at Zeb. "I've found wolves function better if they're around other wolves. If you prefer to join someone else, that would be acceptable. Gerhard Schmidt is the alpha in this territory if you need help."

Shay scowled and said what Zeb was thinking. "This type of

decree is made by the pack alpha. For a Cosantir, especially a werecat, to presume is—"

"*Presumptuous*," Calum said with a slight smile. "I do know that. Nonetheless, the *decree* is not negotiable." Not waiting for an answer, he strode back to his tavern.

"Fuck. I knew this was too good to be true." Shay hit the back of his head against the neck rest and glared at the bar. "You know, if we both took him on, we'd—"

"Die. Messily." Zeb was inclined to try anyway. But no. "Even when Pete calls on Herne in a ritual, he doesn't receive that much power."

"Yeah, McGregor looks like a walking light bulb." Shay frowned. "A competent Cosantir would be a change. I liked him except for this living together bullshit."

"Uh-huh." Zeb wanted to go further, but the words didn't come. Words never came. He'd spent too many years as a wolf before returning to civilization. Fuck, he couldn't do this.

Shay waited a beat, then shook his head. "Okay, asshole, I'll say it. You think we can share a house? Without killing each other?"

"I've never..." He'd been alone since he was thirteen, when his uncle and littermates had died. He blinked away the wash of grief and guilt. By Herne, he didn't want anyone in his den. Didn't need anyone.

Shay waited.

It'd been over two years since Shay had been called to Rainier Territory. Two years that they'd been assigned together as partners—perhaps the only decision Pete had ever gotten right.

Zeb clenched the steering wheel until his knuckles turned white. He trusted Shay with his life. Could he make it work? Fuck. His throat tightened, and his raspy voice came out sounding raw. "I'll give it a shot."

Shay gave him a keen glance, but said only, "Good enough."

Zeb started the engine and then turned it off. "Where the fuck are we going?"

Even as Shay barked a laugh, Zeb saw Alec leaning against a truck, waiting for their response to the Cosantir's ruling.

Now he came over. He didn't ask what they'd decided, probably didn't have to. "You two have a place in mind?"

"No." Zeb barely kept from growling at him.

"Good. Calum and I had an idea."

"Why am I not surprised?" Shay snapped.

Grinning, Alec motioned to his battered pickup. "Follow me, and we'll see if you agree."

Zeb trailed the other vehicle to the road. Less than a tenth of a mile farther out of town, they turned left at a sign indicating "WILDWOOD LODGE" and headed straight into the pine forest.

The dirt road was poorly kept with foot-deep ruts. As the truck bounced, he caught the scent of pain.

Shay had turned pale and was bracing his injured leg.

Zeb slowed, easing around the potholes.

"I'm good." Although tendons stood out on his square jaw, Shay jerked his chin at Alec's disappearing pickup. "Keep going."

Hell would freeze over before the idiot complained of pain.

Zeb scowled. It sucked that Ailill Ridge hadn't had a healer. Instead, their wounds had had to close up the slow way. Zeb was doing all right, but Shay's injuries had been ugly. Unfortunately, even if a healer lived in Cold Creek, it was too late now.

A massive two-story log cabin—the design much like that of the tavern—came into sight, and Zeb parked beside Alec's vehicle. Just past the building, the road narrowed, and tiny lanes branched off to small rustic cabins. The Wildwood Lodge. Good name.

Zeb jumped from the pickup. He hauled in a breath, letting

the crisp pine air erase the stench of truck fumes and Shay's pain-filled sweat. Cold Creek was definitely deeper in the wilderness than Ailill Ridge. Turning in a circle, he caught whiffs of deer and fox and the bitter mineral scent of dwarves. "Your mountains smell good."

Alec's voice drifted out the front door of the building. "They're your mountains now too. Get your asses in here and tell me what you think."

Zeb slammed the truck door shut, trying to control his temper. He'd liked the werecat when they'd met at a Gathering last fall. But the scent of Shay's pain had abraded his nerves, his arm hurt, and, fuck it, knowing he'd have to live with someone made him feel like cornered prey.

If McGregor wasn't careful, he was going to get his face smashed in. Back stiff, Zeb followed Shay into the lodge.

Alec glanced at Zeb, then moved away to lean against a wall.

Pulling in a slow breath, Zeb looked around. Stale air indicated the place had been closed for a time. The lower floor was mostly open with well-polished hardwood floors and large windows. To the left was a small reception desk with an office behind it. Farther down was a sitting area around a glass-fronted fireplace. On the right was another space with couches and game tables and books.

He trailed Alec and Shay to the back. A TV room and a weight room were on the left. The center of the rear was a dining area with assorted tables—obviously, the place could be used as a bed and breakfast. The right held a country kitchen with a round oak table. The scent of lemon and soap indicated someone had cleaned recently, but he spotted no signs of a resident brownie, so the task had been done by human or shifter.

The place felt...good. The muscles in Zeb's chest loosened, letting him breathe deeper.

Speaking for the first time, Alec said, "The second floor has six bedrooms and three baths." He pointed to the wide stairs dividing the front from the back.

"Big place," Shay grunted. His color hadn't improved, and Zeb took a step toward him.

Alec's gaze drifted from Shay's face to his leg, and then the cahir dropped into a leather chair beside the fireplace. "Let me tell you what we were thinking." He paused, obviously not going to continue until they were seated. Until *Shay* was seated.

Manipulative werecat. Zeb was starting to like him. He chose one of the couches.

Shay frowned before taking the other couch. His muffled sigh of relief was followed by a scowl at his own weakness. "Talk," he said to Alec.

"We heard you two managed a small fishing camp for the Rainier clan. Reports are it had lost money until you arrived."

Zeb nodded. And that asshole Pete had decreased the clan income by closing it down.

Alec continued, "This place made money when it was open. Almost a hundred percent occupancy during the summer. In winter, there are always a few diehard fishermen, and shifters book a day or two when they come into town each month for the Gatherings."

The Cosantir wanted them to run the place? Zeb could get his teeth into that idea.

"The owner made a good living—not fancy, but good," Alec said. "James died last fall with no heirs, so the lodge went into the Cosantir's care. He suggests you give it a shot. Manage it yourselves. The paperwork for the lodge's bank account is in the office—there's enough to get you up and running. When you start making a profit, pay ten percent into the North Cascades funds."

Zeb managed to keep his face impassive, but his hand closed on the couch arm. "We wouldn't work for you?"

Alec grinned. "Calum says you're too independent to make good employees."

"Damn," Shay said. "Is your Cosantir psychic?"

"Worse," Alec said soberly. "He was a lawyer."

Zeb let out a laugh before glancing at his patrol-partner and giving a short nod. Despite Pete's continual orders, Shay had handled the business end at the Rainier camp; the decision would be mostly his.

"I'm not into long-term arrangements." Shay frowned, his fingers tracing the scar of the oathbound on his cheek. "I made a vow to Herne to kill hellhounds. When He calls, I go."

"Understood," Alec said.

Jaw set, Shay considered. "Fine. We'll take it and see how it goes."

"Good." Alec glanced at his watch and winced. "I'd help you unload, but my shift starts in ten minutes. I'll be back tomorrow to discuss hellhounds."

He'd reached the entrance when Zeb asked, "What work do you do?"

Alec's grin was wicked. "I'm the county sheriff." He walked out and closed the door.

Staring at the door, Zeb thought about his bar fight not even two weeks ago. And when he and Shay had brawled through downtown Ailill Ridge, busting a street light and a planter. And when he'd tossed a shifter through a window during a Gathering fracas.

Any idiot could avoid human law enforcement. But a werecat sheriff who was also a cahir? "We're screwed."

Chapter Four

Cold Creek, North Cascades Territory

WELL, I'M HERE. After deciding to leave Seattle four days ago, Bree had started her search for her parents. After enlarging the photo, she managed to decipher the sign on a building in the background—the "Wild Hunt" tavern. The only bar of that name in the entire United States was in this tiny town nestled deep in the Cascades.

As she steered her Toyota out of Cold Creek, she stared. There was the bar! Her parents had actually been there. Oh, wow. She braked, then sighed and kept driving. Investigate later. First, she needed a place to stay.

About a block or so past the tavern, she spotted a sign for the Wildwood Lodge. She'd hoped to stay at the downtown bed and breakfast, but it'd closed for repairs during the off-season. *Murphy's Law strikes again.* The B&B's owner said the lodge was newly reopened, and maybe there'd be a cabin available.

Maybe. She pulled in an exhausted breath. If she didn't find a place to stay, she'd probably break down and bawl like a baby.

She turned left onto a tiny dirt road. As the car squeaked and complained about every muddy rut, her hands tightened on the wheel. Gritting her teeth, she tried to dredge up some enthusiasm. *Look at me.* Miss Never-been-out-of-the-city was going to stay in a wilderness lodge. Woohoo. But it was impossible to ignore the wailing voice inside her: *I don't want to be here. I want to go home.*

After parking the car in front of the lodge, she crossed her arms on the steering wheel and lay her head down. So tired. Her eyes burned. The raw wounds on her arm, back, and leg ached from the jostling and long hours in the car.

She slid out and closed the door, feeling as if she were shutting the door on her past as well. But as she breathed in the icy-scented air and the early afternoon sun warmed her shoulders, her spirits lifted. Patches of snow were melting into miniature streams, as if to please the tiny fairy peeking at her from an overhanging branch. Behind the lodge and the cabins, the slope rose into ever-higher foothills and glacier-covered mountains.

She climbed the steps to the porch. Unsure whether to enter, she tapped on the closed door.

"Hold on." A man's voice.

A minute later, the door opened. The guy was huge, well over six feet tall and built like a football player—one who'd taken far too many steroids.

Feeling the blood drain from her face, Bree hastily took a step back. Her stomach twisted uneasily. Yesterday, when she'd picked up her paycheck at the restaurant, she'd discovered that big men now made her...skittish. Way skittish.

And this guy's appearance went with his size. He had a lean battered face. A hard jaw with a cleft in it. He practically oozed testosterone. She tensed, waiting for him to advance on her.

"Can I help you?" He didn't move.

Her surge of adrenaline drained away, leaving her exhausted and chilled. "Yes." She mustered her determination. "I'd like to rent a cabin. Do you have any available, and can I see one?"

His gaze lingered on her body, and she stiffened, until she noticed his attention was on her white-knuckled hands.

His eyes narrowed, but he answered easily, "Yes, we have one available and yes, you can see it." When he smiled, laugh lines crinkled around his blue-gray eyes, and she relaxed.

He reached back inside the lodge and lifted a key ring off a nail. "The previous owner died a few months ago, and the lodge has been closed. Since we only took over two days ago, we're not functioning as smoothly as we will be. I'm Shay O'Donnell." His deep voice was velvet smooth and oddly calming. He nodded his head at the tiny dirt road continuing past the lodge. "There are cabins all up and down the lane, but we've only finished setting the first one to rights. How many in your party?"

"Just me."

"That'll work then. It's a one bedroom." He limped across the porch and down the steps, obviously trying not to favor his right leg.

Well, at least his handicap would slow him down if he tried to grab her. "How'd you get hurt?" She flushed. Nosy. "I'm sorry."

"No problem. I had a run-in with something large and fast. I lost." He sounded pretty pissed off about the losing part.

Her mind immediately jumped to a monster. *Ah, no, Bree, don't be stupid.* A bear? She glanced at the trees that could hide about anything. Or maybe he'd just had a nice normal car accident.

"How about you?" he asked.

Darn. But fair was fair. "Same thing." Definitely large and fast; definitely lost the battle. She forced her breathing to stay smooth and ignored his curious look.

They turned onto the lane off the dirt road. Surrounded by forest, the log cabin appeared tiny under the giant trees. "Hansel and Gretel's place?" she murmured.

"The hu—the fairy tale, right?" His slow smile erased the lines of pain beside his mouth. How old was he? In his thirties?

Shaggy brown hair fell over his forehead and curled along his collar in back, but she didn't see any gray in it. He was pretty beat-up though. A prizefighter's face. His nose had been broken at least once. Two blue-tinted scars marked a tanned cheekbone—one shaped like a knife, the other a primitive sketch of antlers. Fine parallel scars ran across his jaw. A quiver of unease ran through her. How had he collected so much damage?

He opened the door, motioned her in, and waited as she wandered around.

The style was rustic. She walked through the "living room" which consisted of a brown and green couch and two worn leather chairs by a glass-fronted woodstove. Near the back was a sorry excuse for a kitchen and a small round table with three chairs. The bathroom was at the back left, tiny but clean, with dark green towels.

To the front left, the bedroom had a queen-sized bed with a beautiful handmade quilt, a dresser, and a bedside table. There was no closet to search for bogeymen. One less place to worry about.

The entrance and back doors were heavy oak. The front window was large and…she looked closer. It had metal bars on the inside, hinged so they'd open inward.

Her mind replayed how easily the monster had come through the glass door. She spun, checked the other windows, then went into the bedroom. All the windows had bars. Maybe the landlord really had run into a bear. But she'd prefer bears to monsters any day. She turned. "I'll take—"

He stood inside the bedroom, his big frame blocking the door.

She choked and backed up so fast her shoulders banged into the wall. Pain flamed across her wounded shoulder and arm, and her legs wobbled. Heart hammering, she raised her fists and squared her stance. Darned if she'd go through life afraid of everything and everyone. Not again. Been there, done that, have the black belt as an answer.

He breathed in, and his nostrils flared as he studied her. "Relax, *a leannan*. I don't go around attacking females." He stepped back and went into the living room.

She huffed out a shaky breath and sagged against the wall. *I need a gun.* Of course, shooting the landlord would mean no bed tonight, and she really wanted a place to stay.

If he'd rent her anything now. He probably thought she was crazy. She walked out of the bedroom and saw him leaning on the far wall. "I'm sorry. Too much caffeine makes me jumpy," she said.

"I've heard it can do that." His expression said he didn't believe a word of it.

"Why do you have metal bars on the windows?"

"When the cabins are empty, critters can be a problem."

Critters. She shivered.

Eyes the color of a winter sky studied her. "Too much caffeine, huh," he said in a dry voice.

SHE SIGNED THE rental papers and handed over a check. God, three weeks sounded like such a long, long time to be away. After taking an ibuprofen—she'd really hit that wall hard—she showered and had to force herself to stop scrubbing. Would there ever come a time she didn't smell that creature's stench on her skin? Didn't feel soiled?

After unpacking, she lay on the bed, trying to relax and failing miserably. This wasn't her place. It was all wrong. She wanted to go home. *Not happening, so get over it, Bree.*

Then again, she'd never had a home as a kid, so maybe she'd skipped the homesick stage and needed to go through it now. Her lips curved in a wry smile. Naptime would be good right about now, too.

But she couldn't keep from staring at the metal bars on the window. They looked easy to open from inside, so could someone—something—open one from outside?

Unable to shake the thought, she raised the window, then went outside. Stretching her arm past the window and bars, she tried to reach the clasp that would let her push the bars open. Couldn't. She put her face against the glass to check how far her fingers fell short.

"If you're breaking in, try the door. It's open." The man's voice sounded like gravel.

She spun and bumped into the cabin wall. Pain ripped through her shoulder. Darn it. Bracing her feet, she raised her fists and got a look at the person.

Her spine chilled as if gripped in an icy hand. Willing her lungs to work again, she stared at him. The man was even taller than her landlord, and one cheek had the same knife-like blue mark. Sinister white scars marked his neck. His forearms. His powerful hands. His eyes were so dark a brown they were almost black with a terrifying coldness—like there was no human home in there.

The guy looked like he killed puppies for fun.

"I'm not breaking in," she said, trying not to act like a petrified rabbit. Slowly, she eased away from the wall and lowered her fists. "This is my cabin."

Straight black hair reached past his shoulders, and he had the dusky complexion of someone of mixed Native American descent. His brows lifted. "We have a renter?"

We? Please say this cruel-looking character wasn't her landlord. He wasn't anything like Shay. Well, other than being seriously huge. Shay'd been pretty nice, all in all; this guy looked like he could rip apart a bear. With his bare hands. "Shay rented me this cabin." *Not you.*

"I'm Zeb Damron. Shay and I run this place together." He loomed over her—far too much like her nightmares—and held out his hand. "You got a name?"

"Breanne Gallagher." She gritted her teeth. *I am fine. I am. I can touch him.* She'd been through this fear as a teen after Mr. Harvey tried to force her. She just had to gut it out again. So when his scarred-up, callused hand engulfed hers, she squeezed hard, trying to crush his bones and show him what a tough bitch she was.

His expression didn't change. "I make you nervous." There wasn't a shadow of a doubt in his voice, but no triumph either. Just a flat statement.

She jerked her hand away. "Well—"

"Don't lie." His nostrils flared. "Or would terrified be a better word?"

Definitely. Her teeth gritted together. "Maybe I just don't like pushy guys." *Oh yeah, Bree, piss off the huge landlord.*

The corner of his mouth turned up slightly. "Sorry."

"I—" How had he gone from scaring her to making her feel rude? "You... There's no one around—" *Good going, dummy, point out how isolated this is.* "You're big. And a guy."

"No male would harm a female," he said, his wording uncannily like Shay's. His dark brows drew together, his eyes intent. "You don't believe that."

"I know it's not true." *The weight on her, pinning her down.* A shudder ran through her.

He folded his arms over his chest and studied her. The rolled-up sleeves of his flannel shirt displayed wrists as thick as her upper arms. "Little female, if you are bothered by a male, tell me. I'll take care of him for you." His cheek creased. "Part of the Wildwood service."

He was serious. He was really serious. How could a man scare her spitless and make her feel safe at the same time? But he smelled of clean pine forests and nothing like the monster. She managed almost a smile. "Um. Right. Thank you."

He nodded and moved back into the forest. Silently.

ZEB WALKED INTO the lodge and sniffed. The scent of beef and onion filling the air was enough to make a hungry wolf howl. He found Shay in the kitchen, stirring something in a Crockpot. Every counter was covered with vegetable peelings, meat, and dirty dishes.

Zeb tried not to wince. "Supper?"

"Aye. I found the grocery store. Tiny place in the center of town. And you're cooking tomorrow, *a mhac.*"

Zeb growled. Shay'd grown up in one of the more isolated Daonain villages that still clung to the older ways and languages. Over the last two years, Zeb had learned a few words. "I'm not your fucking son."

Son, my ass. Typical dominant wolf, going all paternalistic. He needed a pack to babysit, not a partner. "You're not even ten years older than me."

Shay snorted. "I feel older. By the way, I rented out the next-door cabin."

"Met her. Pretty little human. Scared though." She'd triggered every protective instinct in his body—only it had been him she was afraid of. Zeb checked the fridge. Shay had bought dark and light beer. Good male. He grabbed one of each and took a chair at the kitchen table, pushing away the scattered newspapers. Beer or not, having a person in his living space was weird. And this messy mongrel? Fuck.

"Definitely scared." After putting the lid on the pot, Shay sat down and rested his injured leg on an adjacent chair. "She acted like a trapped mouse when I blocked a door in the cabin."

The dark malty beer was cold with a smooth bite. "Huh.

Figured it was me. I told her that."

"Zeb, you have all the tact of a dwarf."

Now that hurt. Dwarves were the rudest of all the Other-Folk, even worse than gnomes. "She said I was big and that the cabin was isolated. At least she didn't run away screaming." Zeb sipped his beer. Yeah, he'd seen terror in those big blue eyes, but she'd stood her ground. She'd even raised those little fists. Admirable.

Shay's brows drew together. "Isolated? Could she be afraid of *males*?"

"Maybe. She moved as if she was damaged, smelled of fresh blood, and not the moon cycle type. Then again, she's female—they're not designed to be understood." He never spent time with females outside of Gathering night.

"Aye. And human. Their mating patterns are strange." Shay rubbed his chin. "We should find out if she has a reason to worry. Wouldn't want some asshole coming here and bothering our first renter."

"You do the finding out. I'll instruct the male on manners."

"I'll talk, and we both beat the shit out of him."

Zeb scowled. Shrugged. Whatever. As long as he didn't have to try to quiz her. Tact wasn't on his short list of talents.

Shay set his drink down. "Supper's still got a while to cook. Let's do some scouting."

Be good to know what to expect before the next new moon. Most of the snow was gone, but tracks might remain in the wet dirt. Hellhounds were heavy. "Your leg up for it?"

"By Herne's hooves, do I look like I need a momma?"

They stripped and went out the side door into an area concealed by trees and bushes. The previous owner had been a careful Daonain.

The first quarter moon was high in the black sky. Carrying the chill of snow-capped peaks, the wind swirled the brush and made the bare tree limbs clatter. Zeb *trawsfurred* to his animal form, feeling the gift of the Mother's love run through him, hearing the siren song of the wild. He flicked his ears forward to catch the rustling of tiny animals in the dead grass, the slow flapping of an owl overhead. Shay's scent mingled with the fainter ones of deer and cougar drifting down from the mountain.

Shay shifted as well, turning into a big-boned, heavy wolf with light silver-gray fur.

Zeb glimpsed yellow light through the bushes, showing the little human was still awake. Good thing he'd barred her cabin windows. She'd be safe. Then again, hellhounds preferred shifters to humans, so she'd be ignored as long as it caught a shifter scent first.

Shay barked, getting his attention, and loped into the forest. Zeb followed.

ON MONDAY, BREE sat on a bench and scoped out Cold Creek. The mountain town was a friendly little place, she decided. The traffic lanes were separated by fancifully landscaped islands that ran down the center of each street. The iron benches, antique streetlights, and tall trees on the rectangular, plaza-like spaces gave the town a sit-down-and-stay-awhile atmosphere.

Life was slower here. No one rushed—they strolled and stopped to chat with friends. And apparently, they walked, since only two or three cars were parked on each block. She shook her head, feeling like a foreigner.

Last night the lack of traffic noise had unsettled her more than the owl hooting and rustling noises outside her window. Then her cabin had been freezing when she got up, even colder than the time it had snowed in the city.

She bit her lip as a solid lump of homesickness settled in her stomach. *I want my apartment with my own stuff—my cooking things, my books, my comfy bed piled high with bright pillows and soft, soft sheets. And I want to go to work and create pies and cakes that make people happy.*

Wrapping her arms around herself, she rocked back and forth. *I want Ashley. I want my friends.* Eric would miss her—she always babysat him on Sunday afternoons. Would he think she'd forgotten him?

Under one of the leafless trees, two toddlers were ignoring their mother to play in a puddle of melted snow. Bree sighed, her heart aching, wishing she had a couple like them. Like little Eric. But the chances for that were slim and getting slimmer. No man had interested her—ever—and now just the thought of having sex gave her the shakes.

Wasn't being scared fun?

With a sigh, she straightened her spine, recognizing the cold feeling deep inside her. That and the headaches, the weird bursts of tears and laughter, and the sudden fears were uncomfortable, but she'd experienced the feelings before and knew they'd eventually fade. She'd survived an almost-rape as a teen; she'd survive now and be all the stronger for it. One more verse; same as the first.

As part of her cure back then, Sensei had taught her to defend herself. Time to do the same now, only she needed something more effective than fists. Ignoring the throbbing in her leg, she headed across the street.

Old-fashioned with a wood floor and redolent with the scents of metal and oil, the small hardware store could have fit into a corner of a Wal-Mart. A counter on one side held sporting goods and weapons, and she bent over it, trying to figure out what to get.

The young clerk edged closer, obviously itching to help, and she appealed to him. "I want a pistol. Something big that could stop a"—*monster*—"bear."

"*You* want a weapon?" His eyes widened before he caught himself. "Oh. Right. Let me show you what we've got."

He lined up pistols on the countertop, and she settled on a .50 cal Desert Eagle. It was impressively huge.

"There's a five day waiting period before you can take it home." He tucked the pistol back in the box.

"I know." Or she'd have bought a pistol in Seattle. "Um." She glanced at his name badge. "Warren, I don't know anything about shooting. Is there a gun range where I could learn?"

"Not in Cold Creek. People around here use rifles, not pistols. Well, the sheriff carries a handgun."

She shook her head. She'd had her fill of law enforcement buttheads.

He brightened. "Hey, there's the two new ca—um, two new men who just moved here. Both of them use pistols for hunting...stuff. They're good from what I hear. Really good."

Well, that was a glowing recommendation. "Wonderful. What're their names?"

"Shay and Zack or Z...Z-something. They run the Wildwood Lodge."

Bree gulped, and her anticipation flattened as if Mr. *Z-something* had put his oversized boot on it.

Chapter Five

A GOOD NIGHT'S sleep and a day of lounging about had done wonders for Bree. Her iPod and Elvis kept her company as she dusted and cleaned to the bouncy refrain of "You ain't nothin' but a hound dog."

But the cabin wasn't big, and now she was bored out of her mind. No friends, no job. She couldn't even exercise until she healed some more. *Pfft.*

She glanced at the photo and bracelet on the coffee table. Time to go on a parental search.

After a shower—her third of the day—Bree pulled on a sweatshirt and tucked the picture into her jeans. Smoke from the woodstove still wafted from the chimney as she stepped outside. After a glance at her car, she headed down the snowy dirt road on foot. The walk would do her leg good, and it was a pretty day. A gentle snowfall had stopped mid-afternoon, leaving the sky a wondrous blue and the air crisp. The trees swayed in the light wind. Snow dusted from the taller drifts, tickling her cheeks with cold kisses.

When she reached the end of the short Wildwood road, her injured thigh had started to burn. She slowed her pace, grinning as she spotted a wingless fairy peeking at her from a tree hole. The forest had a whole bunch more of them than Seattle did.

To the right, a bird screeched in alarm and whirred out of a tall oak. Bree spun around and froze.

A giant dog stepped out of the bushes onto the road.

When the beast's jaws opened, displaying long, sharp fangs, her skin went cold. *No no no, not again.* She took a step back, her heart thudding against her ribcage.

It stopped, and its plumy tail waved.

Fear sweat rolled down Bree's back as she stared at the animal. Then she let out a sigh. It had fur. A dog's face. *Way to panic, idiot.* This wasn't any horrendous bony-plated monster, but just a dog with fluffy fur, pretty yellow-brown eyes, and a waving tail. A wagging tail was good, even she knew that. Not that she'd met many big dogs in apartment complex-land.

Maybe I can pet it. She held her hand out. "Look at you. Aren't you pretty?"

The thick silver-gray fur down its back shaded to tawny on the sides and… Oh, it was holding one leg up. "Are you hurt, baby?" She knelt in the road. "Can I see?"

He—and he was definitely a he, she noticed—whined slightly and padded over to her. Criminy, he was really big. Big and shaggy, but anyone could see he was giving her a distinctive doggy smile.

She petted him, ruffled his fur, and scratched under his chin until silvery dog hair covered her dark blue sweatshirt. Gradually, she eased him around until she could assess his leg. The fur there was etched with puckered red lines, but nothing was open. "Bet that hurt, but I guess it's too late to haul you to a vet to get looked at, huh, buddy."

He shoved his nose under her arm, demanding more petting. She laughed and complied. "You ain't nothin' but a hound dog, all right. And a sweetie. None of my foster homes had dogs." After that, living on the streets and then an apartment meant no furbabies for her. "So, Elvis." She grinned at him, pleased with giving him a name. "Come by my cabin tonight, and I'll share some steak with you."

To her startled delight, his tail whipped back and forth, and he barked once before trotting into the forest.

A few minutes later, she stood in the parking lot for the Wild Hunt. She pulled the old photo from her pocket and held it up. The two-story log-style building hadn't changed a bit in twenty-some years. A thrill ran through her. Her mom and dad stood right there, holding her. For a moment, they seemed very real.

She pushed the feeling aside. Over the years, their importance had diminished. More than anything, she just wanted to fit in somewhere. Have a home. Not be a weird person who saw invisible creatures.

The door of the tavern was heavy and took an effort to open. As she stepped inside, her shoulder and arm ached in time with her leg, and all of her was exhausted. Only twenty-six years old, and she was already over the hill.

Taking a moment, she glanced around. The round oak tables were spotlessly clean; the sconces gleamed, as did the long mirror on the far wall. Popcorn and roasted peanuts provided a comforting fragrance, and the country twang wafting from the jukebox completed the picture. Two thumbs up for the perfect tavern ambiance.

Even better, the people matched the decor. T-shirts, flannel shirts, jeans, down vests. Definitely more casual than the city, but not in a bad way, and far more pleasant than a Seattle meat market. So, where to start asking questions?

Maybe the bartender? She crossed the room and slid onto a barstool.

When the bartender walked over, she frowned. Were all the men around here over six feet? Wasn't the average height supposed to be five-ten? His white shirt showed off a dark complexion and a lean musculature. He wasn't as huge as her two landlords, but still... Maybe they all chopped wood in their spare time.

"What may I get you to drink?" His faint English accent and chiseled features didn't quite match the country decor, and neither did the shoulder-length black hair tied back with a band.

"A diet cola, please."

A minute later, he set a full glass in front of her.

"If you could..." She held out her battered photo. "I think the picture was taken in front of your tavern."

He took the photo, glanced at it, and a black eyebrow quirked up. "This is quite old."

"At least twenty-three years, I think." That had been her best guess, considering her social worker said she was around three when found. "Any chance you recognize the people in it?"

"I regret not." He turned the photo over and smiled faintly at the purple scribbles on the back. "The child would be you?"

"Mmmhmm. I'm hoping someone in Cold Creek knows who the adults are."

By his sympathetic expression, he understood and was tactful enough not to ask more. "Some people have lived here for forty or fifty years. You might try Joe Thorson at the bookstore or Albert Baty at the grocery."

"Thank you. I'll do that." She took the picture back, feeling deflated. Had she really thought she could wave it in the air, and someone would rush up saying, *my long lost daughter has returned to me.* Her parents had probably just stopped for a drink on the way to somewhere else. Still, it was a starting point. Tomorrow she'd go into Cold Creek.

"I don't remember seeing you in here before." The bartender studied her as he wiped away a spot on the gleaming bartop. "Are you staying in town?"

"She rented a cabin." Zeb slid onto a stool beside her.

She spun around so fast, she almost tipped her cola over. With her heart doing a dance inside her ribcage, she edged off her barstool, putting distance between them. And then she planted her feet. "Next time make some noise or something, would you?"

But she was angrier with herself than him. She had to get over these make-like-a-mouse responses.

"Sorry." Eyes the color of darkest chocolate studied her. "You want me to sit over there?" He jerked his chin at the end of the bar.

Yes. "No. You're fine." She inhaled and started to relax. The monster in Seattle had smelled like rotting meat but Zeb had a clean, intriguing scent like the forest behind her cabin. She forced herself back onto the stool, carefully ignoring how wide his shoulders were.

"Is there a problem?" the bartender asked Zeb, his tone icy. When Zeb didn't answer, he glanced at her. "Miss?"

"Why are all the men in this place so darned tall? And big?" she asked without thinking.

Zeb snorted.

"I believe there is something in the water," the bartender said without a trace of a smile. He drew a beer for Zeb, then returned his attention to Bree. "I'm Calum. Please call me if there is anything I can get you." He tilted his head toward Zeb and added, "However, I fear I cannot make him shorter."

She had to grin. "Thanks." And wasn't that a pity? If Zeb was smaller—say about five feet seven—she might find the nerve to request pistol lessons.

As Calum headed away, a short, brunette walked up to the barmaid station and slapped the bar. "Hey, bartender-person, four darks and a light."

Calum turned, his brows drawing together into a daunting expression. "Victoria? What are you doing here? Where's

Rosie?"

The barmaid didn't appear intimidated in the least. "Her daughter went into labor. She won't be in tonight."

"You already put in a full shift as deputy."

She glanced around the room. "No problem. There aren't many people—" Her gaze lit on Zeb, and she flushed from her low neckline to her forehead.

ZEB'S SMILE OF recognition froze as the little female he'd almost mated at the fall Gathering turned bright red. From behind the bar, a furious snarl came from the Cosantir.

Oh, fuck. Zeb eased off the stool and backed away. He turned his head. Not good—the Cosantir's eyes had turned the color of night.

Zeb spoke carefully. "Vicki, the Cosantir is upset."

She glanced at the bartender, and her jaw dropped. "Fuck! Um, Calum? It... I just wasn't expecting..." She looked at Zeb helplessly.

"Calum," Zeb said softly. "Our only meeting was at a Gathering. She doesn't want me." He held his hand out to Vicki. "Give me your hand. Slowly."

Her small fingers were the size of Breanne's, he noticed. When he raised her arm, he saw two *lifemating* bracelets. She was bonded to two males, and apparently, one was Calum.

Her wrists had been bare last fall. New ties meant unstable mates. Hoping he wouldn't get his throat ripped out, he pressed a kiss to her wrist, heard another low snarl.

Not even bothering to check the scent, he held her arm out to her mate. "No attraction. Just a Gathering."

Leaning over the bar, Calum took the woman's wrist in his hand, bent, and inhaled. Stilled. Cradling her hand, he closed his eyes, taking deep, slow breaths. Seconds passed. When he opened his eyes, his irises had returned to dark gray.

Zeb pulled in a relieved breath and tried to unknot his muscles.

"Forgive me, cahir," Calum said. He kissed his mate's fingers before releasing her. "I overreacted."

"New mates." Zeb shrugged. "If I didn't like being a step from death, I wouldn't be a cahir."

Calum winced, then turned his gaze to his lifemate. "Victoria, if I might speak to you in the kitchen for a moment?" He headed that way without waiting.

"Fucking A, that was freaky." Vicki pushed her long brown hair back and smiled at Zeb. "Sorry. I heard about new cahirs coming, but I didn't realize one was you. Last fall was my first and only Gathering, so I'm still…" She flushed again. "Hell. Welcome to Cold Creek?"

"Thanks." Zeb jerked his head toward the kitchen. "Go, before he comes out after you."

"No shit. The bastard would, too."

Zeb watched as she was snagged by her mate before she barely got through the kitchen door. Little as she was, she almost disappeared within Calum's embrace.

Chuckling inside, Zeb lifted his beer and sucked down a hefty swallow. A shame Vicki had already bonded to Calum and Alec when he met her; she'd have been a delight to mate.

Come to think of it, the moon was full tomorrow. There would be a Gathering.

A noise recalled him to the present. He glanced down at the female next to him.

Her eyes were so big and blue that looking in them was like falling into a mountain lake. "Was he going to attack you?"

Oh, fuck, they'd done this show in front of a *human*. Talk about indiscreet. How to fix this? Talking fast was Shay's job. "Ah, his…wife and I had a previous"—*almost mating*—

"encounter. "She and Calum haven't been"—*lifebound*—"married long, and he still gets jealous quickly." The type of jealous where he'd gut a man and leave his intestines strewn across the floor.

"No kidding." She sipped her drink, and then those blue eyes fixed on him like spotlights on a police car. "What does kaheer and ko-san-something mean?"

"Local slang." When the bar door opened, Zeb turned, hoping for a diversion. Alec. That would work.

Still in uniform, the sheriff crossed the room with a wave for the females playing pool. Just a friendly cop with the stalking stride of a werecat. The two women watched with open appreciation.

Alec stopped beside Zeb. "Ca—" With a glance at Breanne, he smoothly revised to, "Shall we sit at a table?"

"Good plan." Go where they could talk without censoring their language for a human.

"Let me get a drink." Alec frowned at the lack of a bartender, looked toward the kitchen, and his eyebrows rose. "I have to say, the service in this place has gone sadly downhill in the last few months."

Zeb followed his gaze. Calum had one arm around his mate's waist, the other on her ass, and was kissing her as if it was Gathering night and she was in heat. He snorted.

When Breanne laughed, Alec gave her an easy smile. "Are you new to town?"

Zeb frowned and moved closer to the little female.

"There's *definitely* something in the water," she murmured, her gaze going from Alec to Zeb. "Breanne Gallagher, and I'm renting a cabin at the Wildwood." After a slight hesitation, she held out her hand.

She hadn't volunteered to shake hands with Zeb yesterday.

"Alec McGregor. Welcome to Cold Creek. If there's anything I can do to help you settle in, let me know."

"Thank you."

Alec grinned at Zeb and went behind the bar to fetch his own drink.

When Zeb started to move away, Breanne reached out. After a moment, she actually touched his arm. "I—ah, I actually wanted to talk to you. About learning how to shoot a gun."

"You? Why would a *female* want a weapon?"

She rolled her eyes. "And here I thought dinosaurs went extinct. Target shooting is my new hobby, and I need lessons."

"No."

"Men." Hair tangled and lips swollen, Vicki walked over and grinned at Breanne. "Can't live with 'em, but if you have a weapon, at least you can shoot them."

"My thought exactly." Breanne gave Zeb an annoyed look, then bit her lower lip between white, even teeth.

Soft-looking lips. Pink and—

"If I don't get lessons," she said, "I'll probably shoot myself in the foot."

"I've heard Zeb is damned accurate," Vicki offered. "Couldn't ask for a better instructor."

What the fuck was the Cosantir's mate doing? Didn't someone say she was hell on wheels in a fight and with weapons? Why was she tossing him to this—this blue-eyed human?

Breanne gave him an appealing look, still biting her lip.

Those lips just begged for a man's mouth. *But she's human.* He scowled.

She flinched and took a step back, the scent of fear in the air. "Never mind. I'll find someone else."

He should be used to being disliked, and fuck, he didn't care if he scared males. But it hurt to know he terrified little females. "You get your pistol," Zeb growled, even more pissed off when she took another step away from him. "I will, at least, show you how to miss your foot."

Her scent still held a hint of fear, but when she smiled at him, he had to close his eyes against her appeal. Fuck. Vicki might have given him a push, but he was the one offering up his own throat. To a human.

Chapter Six

Cold Creek, North Cascades Territory ~ Full moon

BREE HAD WOKEN a couple of hours before dawn, unable to sleep any longer. Grumbling, she pulled on her clothes.

After a glance at the wall heater, she grabbed a log from the basket, knelt by the still-warm woodstove, and opened the door. Live coals remained under the white ashes.

A flurry of sparks rose as something in the coals moved. A lizard-like head rose, and black beady eyes glinted at her.

Bree fell backwards onto her butt, yelping as the impact jarred her wounds. The thing stared at her, wiggled its reptilelike body, and settled down.

Whoa. She stared back. Almost the same size as the wingless fairies, but jeez, she'd never seen any of them in a fire. It didn't seem evil, not like the monster. Or a cockroach. In fact, it was almost cute, in a reptilian sort of way with luminous scales that glowed as red as the coals. Its head turned toward the log she'd dropped, and it squirmed again.

"You want more fire?" she asked slowly.

A very enthusiastic wiggle.

"When did my life get so weird?" She set the log on the coals beside the lizard-thing. The wood ignited quickly, sending up pretty yellow flames. Bree watched the lizard as its long tail flickered back and forth. How could anything live there?

But it leaped into the fire and spiraled in the flames as if with a lover. After shooting up the stovepipe in a fountain of sparks, it dived back into the coals, as playful as a dolphin in the waves. A flame-dancer. Grinning, Bree leaned back to enjoy the show.

Eventually, her leg announced it needed to be stretched, and she rose to her feet. "Sorry, buddy, I need to get moving."

The lizard-thing responded with an impertinent lash of its tail as she closed the glass door.

She prowled around her slowly warming cabin and scowled at the ill-equipped kitchen. Why hadn't she packed some of her copper-bottomed pots and pans? And a few knives. Her herbs. She shook her head. Might as well be cooking over a campfire— at least that would have the benefit of a smoky flavor. Did lizard-things visit campfires? Were they like flower-fairies in that only she could see them?

"I wish I knew if these things really exist, or if I need to be locked up," she muttered. To settle herself, she put on Leonard Cohen for some moody music, made coffee, started some bread, and set the dough to rise.

Inventiveness at an end, she walked a circle around the place—*cabin fever, anyone?*—and noticed the blue curtains at the front of the cabin glowed. She peeked through them. The light came from the full moon. Well, duh, no wonder she was twitchy. She always got restless and achy at full moons. Like her friends with PMS—something else she'd never experienced.

PMS. *Criminy, I almost forgot.* She went into the bathroom to rummage through her toiletries bag. Dang dang dang. No birth control packets remained, and she'd taken the last pill yesterday. Her mail order pharmacy would have already shipped her next three months, so the box probably sat in her apartment mailbox. By the time she could get it forwarded here, her cycle would be all screwed up.

She might as well go off the pills for a month, then restart them in Seattle with her next period. Not even dawn, and the day was going downhill.

After pulling on her jacket, she stepped onto the porch and let the frigid air shock the temper out of her. Leaning against the rough porch post, she stretched her throbbing leg and looked around at the night.

The huge, golden moon hung over the western mountains, and the light was so heavy it seemed to reverberate in her bones. Around her, the forest talked to itself—bare branches creaking, a gurgle from the unfrozen center of the creek, the rustle of animals. That skittering sound in the dry brush—what would that be?

A small chittering made her look up in time to see a tiny body disappear into a tree trunk hole. Guess she'd made enough noise to wake up a fairy. Could her parents see them? God, she had to figure out who she was and where she came from.

At least her first goal was on its way to being accomplished. She'd bought a pistol. And she'd found an instructor. One that scared her to death, with his Vin Diesel, *I-prefer-to-slaughter-people-rather-than-talk-to-them* attitude. But slaughter was exactly what she needed to learn. And quickly too.

In three weeks, she'd have to return to Seattle and pack up her apartment. What if the monster found her again? *"I'll be back for another taste,"* it had whispered before she passed out. She swallowed against the urge to vomit. Pushed away the need to shower and scrub and scrub and scrub.

Slow breaths. Feel the clean air. Watch the beautiful moon slide behind the mountains.

As her stomach settled, she heard voices. A woman's laughter. Bree glanced down the narrow road to her left. The lodge was dark and quiet. Maybe she was hearing people at the tavern?

As the crow flew, it would be about a block or so away, and she'd noticed how clearly sound carried in the quiet mountains. But weren't bars supposed to close at two a.m.?

Sounded like fun though. She sat down on the single porch step and listened. Men and women calling goodbyes, car doors slamming. She'd missed the sound of people. After being surrounded in a busy restaurant every day, she found the cabin awfully lonely.

The faint crunch of boots on snow made Bree stiffen.

Zeb and Shay walked down the road, two huge men who moved as gracefully as animals. They really were gorgeous. Ashley would have flirted herself silly with Shay. Bree sighed, feeling very alone. *I miss you, Ash.*

At the lodge, Zeb lifted his head as if he were sniffing the air and said something. Shay looked toward her. As his partner went into the lodge, Shay headed toward Bree's cabin.

A shiver of nervousness ran up her spine, and she rose. Suddenly, the night seemed far too empty, and she had the urge to run inside and lock the door.

His gait silent in the wet dirt, he strolled closer. "You're either up early or you haven't been to bed. Problems?" The moon behind him left his face in shadow and seemed to make his body bigger than it really was. His shoulders blotted out an entire mountain range.

She smothered a gulp. "No. I just couldn't sleep. Were you at a party over there?" She nodded toward the Wild Hunt.

When he leaned against the porch post, she relaxed. He'd turned so she could see his face, the curve of his lips, the strong jaw. Not a man-monster stinking of rotting meat; just a powerful man with the soapy fragrance of a recent shower.

"We went for a while," he agreed. "Why can't you sleep? Is something wrong with the cabin?"

She laughed. A true innkeeper. "Not at all. I was listening to the woods, trying to figure out what I'm hearing. Not that I can tell—I've never been away from Seattle before."

"A city girl. Let's see if I can help." He tipped his head to listen, and then pointed toward the road. "There's a skunk over there."

Bree leaned forward. "Where?"

Shay moved behind her, extending his arm along her line of sight. "By the big patch of snow."

A small black and white animal waddled along the tree line, tail arching in the air. "Oh, it is! I think I saw him before."

The chuckle was deep and smooth. "Good eyes, a leannan, he lives around here. This spring, he'll invite a new female to his den each night." He set a hand on her shoulder and turned her slightly. "A doe is in the brush."

Squinting, she made out a brown shadow and the movement of a head. The deer stepped onto the road and into the moonlight so gracefully it took her breath away. "She's beautiful."

"Yes." His hand still rested on her shoulder, very warm, very big, and she could feel his breath on her neck, the heat from his body on her back.

When she tried to edge away, his arm came around her waist, pulling her back against a hard chest. "Shhh, look to your right."

Her need to escape disappeared when a small animal—a dog?—trotted across the lodge clearing. Its coat flashed with red in the moonlight. "What is it?"

"Fox."

"Wow." As the fox disappeared, Bree realized her position. The man's arm crossed her stomach like an iron bar, and his hand gripped her hip, holding her in place. Her breathing hitched. She pulled away, almost surprised when he released her. She retreated a step, and her nervousness dissipated when he didn't move. She smiled at him. "That was awesome. How do you see them so well?"

"Experience." The corners of his eyes crinkled. "I enjoy sharing my forest."

"I don't know how to thank you." Maybe she should make him a pie or—

"A leannan, it's done like this." One finger tilted her chin up, and he brushed his lips across hers. Firm yet velvety soft. Just the slightest lingering. He'd moved back and stepped completely off the porch before she had a chance to panic. He gave her his slow smile. "That's how a female thanks a male." He turned and strode away.

Pressing a hand to her tingling lips, she tried to summon the willpower to call him a pompous jerk. She couldn't. Deep inside her, heat flickered to life—something she'd never felt before.

Chapter Seven

ON SUNDAY, FOUR nights after the Gathering, Shay walked into the Wild Hunt for the Cosantir's meeting. The tavern was already noisy with shifters seated at tables and lined along the walls.

Late. He scowled over his shoulder at Zeb. The anti-social mongrel had stalled, hoping Shay would go without him.

In front of his bar, Calum talked with people at the nearest tables. After nodding at the few people he'd already met, Shay chose an unobtrusive position in the rear. As cahirs, he and Zeb were much larger than other males, and only werebears liked being stared at.

"If I could have your attention." When Calum's quiet voice cut across the conversations like fangs through a soft rabbit, people stilled. "After the deaths of Chris Anderson and Nancy Ming, I requested two more cahirs for our territory." He nodded toward the back. "Daonain, welcome Seamus O'Donnell, known as Shay, and Zebulon Damron, known as Zeb. Both wolves."

After the applause and welcoming calls ended, the Cosantir continued. "It's not common knowledge, but they've each killed more hellhounds than any other cahir."

We have? After the first few, he'd lost count.

"They know their business," Calum said. "That business is

what they will discuss tonight."

Zeb grunted like someone had hit him. "Fuck."

"Shay." Calum's gaze targeted him. "Tell the Daonain about hellhounds. Assume we know nothing. Better you sound patronizing than we miss vital information."

As Shay straightened, Zeb said under his breath, "Better you than me."

Shay shrugged. He didn't mind talking, but where should he start? "Fae shapeshifters and humans interbred creating us, the Daonain.

"Hellhounds are more of a mixture. First, an insane Fae-shifter in reptile form mated with a demon." He snorted. Talk about disgusting sex. "The offspring raped a human female creating the first hellhound—a mix of demon, Fae, and human."

Many in the crowd looked appalled.

"Like us, hellhounds have animal and human forms. Unlike us, in human form, they can occasionally impregnate humans. The hellhounds would die out otherwise, since only males are birthed."

Murmurs told him some information was new to them. Being isolated, the Cold Creek residents had been lucky so far. But now civilization encroached, and where humans went, demonkin followed. "In both forms, the hellhounds smell like rotting meat—"

"And moldy oranges," Zeb added.

"Tell us about their forms," urged the older female who owned the diner.

Shay set a foot on an empty chair and leaned his forearms on his thigh. "The light-hating demon heritage means a hellhound only trawsfurs to animal on new moon. It will *always* shift at least once that night.

The room went silent. An old guy with as many scars as Zeb growled, "They don't attack if it's not the dark of the moon?"

"In hellhound form. In human form, they'll rape, assault, or murder at any time at night." His mouth tightened as he remembered one sickening night when he'd been too late to save a small boy. "Demonkin feed off violent emotions. In animal form, it craves flesh. Although humans are good fodder, a shifter is like heroin, and the magic in our blood incites them to madness." He stopped, his well-worn grief a dull ache as he remembered how his brothers had been torn apart. "It won't bother to attack a human if it scents a shifter."

"That means they could be living in our town. Could be anyone." A middle-aged female's shrill voice escalated to hysteria. The scent of fear rose. Shay saw Calum straighten.

"No." Zeb's flat, hard response silenced the room. "Use the brains the Mother gifted you. We can scent them in both their forms."

Several shifters eased back in their chairs.

Surprisingly, Zeb continued. "They need the anonymity of cities. A hellhound is born from rape. Around twenty, it first shifts and demon instincts take over. Since they don't associate with each other, they don't know their own history." He frowned at Shay, obviously annoyed he'd been sucked into speaking.

"And you were doing so well," Shay said, earning himself a dark look. "Once a hellhound discovers a tasty shifter community, it will return each new moon. Other nights of the month, one might show up in human form." He stopped, unable to think of anything to add.

"Good background, cahirs." Calum's gaze pinned Zeb like a cat's unsheathed claws. "Zebulon, what should our people do to protect themselves?"

For a moment, Shay thought Zeb would refuse.

But as Calum stood, waiting with the patience of a feline at a birdfeeder, Zeb gave in...and wasn't that fun to see?

"Heavy iron bars on your windows with the fastenings deep into the frame. Reinforce the doors. As human, a hellhound is as powerful as a cahir. It's far stronger in demon form." He glanced at Shay.

Shay said, "We've been refitting the cabins. Visit the Wildwood if you want examples." He smiled sweetly at Zeb, forcing him to continue.

"Check strangers in town. Get close enough to smell them," Zeb bit out.

Heads nodded.

"One-on-one, you can't win a fight." Zeb rubbed his face, unconsciously drawing attention to the scars. "Dark of the moon is the most dangerous time. Just stay the fuck home." Limit reached, Zeb crossed his arms over his chest and scowled at Calum.

To his credit, Calum didn't laugh, but announced, "Official meeting's over. You can stay and ask questions."

When Zeb growled like a caged wolf, Shay slapped his arm. "Not bad, *a mhac*. Let's mingle."

That earned him another growl.

Unlike the jaded citizens of Rainier Territory, the shifters here were embarrassingly grateful for both the information and the presence of Zeb and Shay. They were thanked so many times that Zeb's dark face acquired a reddish hue.

One lanky woman carrying the scent of furniture polish shouldered through the crowd to ask, "What about children? Sometimes they're out after dark, visiting friends and such."

Zeb raised his voice. "Listen up."

Silence.

"A hellhound's demon form has bullet-proof plating. The only vulnerable areas are its eyes or a narrow patch on its gut. You can't win a fight with one."

Shay's belly tightened. Children were so fragile. "Never let them outside on the dark moon. Otherwise, make sure they're escorted by several well-armed adults."

Shay inclined his head at Zeb as conversations started again. "Damned if you're not good at this. You take point for speaking engagements from now on."

"Fuck you." His black gaze promised Shay a fist in the face.

Grinning, Shay glanced around for more questions. Instead, he saw three men stalk across the room preceded by a wave of testosterone. Pretty obvious who they were.

His mouth tightened. He didn't have the time or interest to dick around with some alpha wolf on a power trip.

The one in the lead was about six-one, over two hundred pounds, and stank of hostility. His receding light brown hair had been buzz cut. From the similarity in beefy facial features and builds, the other two were his littermates. The pack alpha didn't halt until he was well within Shay's personal space. Trying for dominance.

Good luck, alpha-hole. A normal wolf had two choices when meeting an alpha. Drop the gaze to acknowledge him as dominant. Or challenge.

Shay stepped back. Didn't drop his gaze.

As the alpha tried to puzzle out what that meant, Shay heard an amused snort from behind him. Zeb had moved up to guard his back. Damned if that didn't feel good.

The alpha pushed out his chest. "I'm Gerhard Schmidt. These are my brothers Dieter and Klaus." The two betas glared at Shay. Probably in their sixties, not that he could tell since shifters didn't look old until after ninety.

"Good to meet you," Shay said pleasantly. "When's the next run?"

Gerhard moved closer, getting up in Shay's face, his aggression a foul stench.

By Herne's giant balls, this sucked. His dominant instincts

demanded he flatten the pushy cur. But even if he wasn't oathbound, he didn't want to be alpha. Never again. "Gerhard, I'm not interested in games. Don't push me and I won't" *close my jaws over your throat* "push you."

Gerhard slid sideways to circle him.

As the hair on his nape rose, Shay started to turn—never allow an enemy in the rear—then realized he didn't have to. The heat from Zeb's body warmed his shoulders. Back to back.

He heard the pack leader stop in front of Zeb and knew Gerhard got no satisfaction there. Zeb submitted to no one, and very few were willing to risk the death in his eyes. The Rainier alpha had dealt carefully with Zeb.

But he'd never stopped trying to dominate Shay.

Shay saw Calum watching, but Cosantirs didn't interfere in pack politics.

Gerhard finished his stiff-legged circling and faced Shay again. "The pack hunts the day before full moon." Gerhard was stupid enough to add, "We'll give you a few lessons in manners next time."

"I enjoy learning." And he and his co-instructors—pain and blood—always ended up being the ones teaching etiquette.

With a last scowl, Gerhard stalked away, followed by his littermates.

As Zeb stepped up beside him, Shay said, "That went well, don't you think?"

"You ever met an alpha you didn't piss off?"

"The older, smarter ones don't get proddy." Shay rubbed his face. "But why do they focus on me and not you? You don't submit any more than I do."

"I don't give off alpha vibes, and you were born to lead." Zeb's eyes glinted with amusement before he turned serious. "You should be a—"

"I want a beer." Shay walked away. He'd been an alpha. Had a pack…and he'd led it right into death.

Chapter Eight

ON MONDAY, A little over a week after arriving, Bree parked her car downtown. As she slid out, a rip in the ancient plastic seat cover sliced her finger. "Ow!"

Just what she needed—another injury. With a grunt of annoyance, she stuck her finger in her mouth. Tracing torn skin with her tongue, she tasted the metallic tang.

The monster had liked her blood. Said it was different. Why? The lab work from her regular physicals always came back normal. She was O positive. So what was special about her blood? Would her parents know?

The bartender had suggested she visit the bookstore and grocery. She glanced at one unembellished sign, "*BOOKS*," and grinned. The owner probably didn't like fancy French sauces or intricate desserts either.

Inside the store, a gray-haired man was attaching iron bars inside the display window. Were wild animals really a problem in the downtown area? She started to speak, then smiled at a sudden realization. Zeb would eventually look like this older man—tough as leather, scarred to heck and gone, still a little scary.

The man nodded at her. No greeting. Yeah, definitely like Zeb.

Fine, she'd be the polite one. "Hello."

The sigh was almost, but not quite, inaudible. "Miss, can I help you?"

"Calum at the Wild Hunt suggested I stop in here." She pulled the photo from her denim purse and handed it to him. "Would you know these people? The picture was taken around twenty-three years ago."

When he held the photo up, his hands and arms were covered by so many thin white lines it looked as if he'd picked blackberries every day of his life. What would cause such scarring?

He shook his head. "Sorry."

"Neither one lived in Cold Creek?"

"No, and I've been here close to fifty years."

Oh. Her hopes fell like over-yeasted rolls, leaving her sagging inside. "Well, thank you for looking."

"No problem."

As tears welled, she hastily turned and ran into a hard body.

Too tall, too big. *The monster. His horrible touch, foul odor, the way he ripped*—Bree punched out blindly.

The monster caught her arms in a merciless grip.

"No!" She tried to yank away and couldn't. *Oh God.* Her gasping brought her a scent like thick mountain forests. So very masculine and clean.

"Easy, little human, easy," the deep voice said.

Not the creature. She sagged in the ruthless grasp.

THE SOFT LITTLE human went limp in his hands like a captured rabbit, and her panic-filled blue eyes filled with relief. "Zeb."

His name on her lips was strangely satisfying. "Little female," he acknowledged.

As her legs recovered, her chin lifted and her spine turned straight as a young pine. "Sorry. Guess I had too much caffeine."

Shay'd mentioned her explanation. He bent far enough to murmur in her ear, "Shay didn't buy that excuse, and neither do I."

When her face turned pink, he felt a trickle of amusement. She didn't look scared of him now.

Still holding her arms, he nodded to the bookstore owner. "Thorson."

"You come to give me a hand installing this sh—stuff?" The old man's scowl was belied by the amusement in his eyes.

"Aye."

"Well, I'll let you get to work," Breanne said. She pulled away and walked toward the bookshelves.

Mesmerizing little thing. All golden hair and curves. Zeb watched her a second, then turned toward the preparation Thorson had done. "Good start." He picked up the drill.

As they finished the first set of bars and started on the second, Zeb's gaze kept sliding to Breanne. He liked the way her full breasts stretched her shirt when she reached for a book, the way her jeans cupped her round ass.

A screwdriver smacked his knuckles, and Thorson growled, "She's pretty, but human. It's not good to break their hearts."

Zeb nodded. All too true, and not usually a problem. Humans didn't attract Daonain any more than bears attracted coyotes. But her scent, although human, was oddly pleasing.

As Zeb worked, a male entered the bookstore with two boys not yet past the bumbling puppy stage. Their red shoes were no longer than his fingers. Cute. They raced through the store toward the back.

Lot of excitement for books. As the man followed, Zeb stepped away from the window to look. The right corner held short book-laden shelves, a tiny table, and a wooden box of colorful toys.

Zeb glanced at Thorson. "You like kids?"

"Keep the children busy, and the parents have time to purchase books." The grizzled werecat's mouth tipped up at their laughter. "Calum's mate suggested it, probably so she could come in and play with the cubs."

"Females are sneaky." He could smell Breanne on his hands: woman, vanilla, and strawberry, like a feminine dessert.

A thud came from the back. A child's high-pitched scream.

Zeb spun. One of the boys lay on the floor, holding his knee.

"Tyler, hey, it's okay." The father frantically patted the boy's shoulder. The cub kept screaming.

Every instinct in Zeb cried out to help, but with his battered face, he'd scare the boy further. He watched helplessly.

Breanne walked out of the stacks. After setting her books on the floor, she sat beside the pup. "Oh, you got a boo-boo," she said, her pretty voice almost a croon.

The screaming stopped as Tyler stared at her with big eyes, fat tears spilling down his cheeks.

"Let me see?" She rolled up his jeans and frowned at the knee. "Oh look, no nasty blood. Maybe a kiss would make it better?" She arched her brows.

Lower lip poking out, the little boy nodded solemnly, and Breanne bent to place a smacking kiss on the knee. "There you go. Now you'd better sit with me while the magic works." Winking at the father, she pulled the kid into her lap.

As the father eased onto to a tiny chair, Breanne rocked Tyler, murmuring tales of clumsy rabbits and foolish mice. A hiccup or two later, the kid was quiet, leaning against her chest, sucking his thumb.

"Amazing," Thorson muttered. "Last time that mischief-maker got hurt, Brady had to carry him to his mother before he'd settle down."

"Likes women."

Thorson snorted. "What male doesn't?"

But Breanne's appeal was more than just being female. Her smile, her eyes, her whole body projected comfort so strongly Zeb felt it from across the room. When the other boy snuggled up to her side, she wrapped an arm around him also.

"Thank you," the father said and smiled with an appreciation that had nothing to do with her comforting manner.

Zeb growled under his breath.

"My pleasure." Breanne didn't even look at the man, and Zeb felt marginally better. "I haven't had a kid-fix for a while now. You have beautiful children." She kissed the top of each little head before whispering to them, "Did you guys look in the box? I saw a really scary dinosaur in there. I almost screamed."

Two heads popped up, and the children ran to dig through the box of toys. "Here!" The hurt one scrambled back to lay the dinosaur in her lap like a well-trained pup, staring up at her for approval.

"Oh no! Is it going to growl at me?" She waggled it with such a tiny provocative growl that Zeb hardened.

Not a human. I'm not attracted to a human. He turned to concentrate on his work.

He heard one child say, "My name is Luke. Who are you?"

"Breanne—but since I like you, you can call me, Bree. That's what my friends call me."

Bree, huh.

After playing a few minutes longer, she came to the front to purchase several books and a postcard of Cold Creek from the counter rack. She stopped beside Zeb on her way out. "I'm picking up my pistol today."

"Mmmhmm." Her fragrance eroded his control, and he ran a finger down her cheek. Her skin was as soft and smooth as he'd thought.

She backed away as if he'd bitten her, eyes wide

with…bewilderment. Her scent held only a trace of fear.

Want more.

Thorson cleared his throat. "Time's a wasting, cub."

Cub? Zeb curled his lip at the old werecat, then with a grunt of frustration, stepped back from the female.

AS BREE WAITED for the clerk to open the box containing her gun, the door to the hardware store opened.

When Zeb stalked in, she took an involuntary step back. Black flannel shirt, black jeans, black eyes and hair. Mr. Deadly himself. He glanced at Warren, and the young man retreated behind the counter. The dark gaze settled on her. "Show me what you chose."

Warren shoved the Desert Eagle across the counter. When Zeb picked it up, the huge weapon looked like a perfect fit for his oversized hand. He hefted the weapon, played with the slidey thing, and checked the sights before handing it to her. "Point it at the wall."

She edged away and had to remind herself they weren't alone. He was trying to help. Her shoulder wound pulled painfully as she struggled to aim the heavy pistol. The barrel wavered like a flag in a high wind.

"Use the slide on top."

She managed to pull the slide back, although it almost snapped shut onto her palm.

He turned a black frown on Warren, making the kid gulp. "Herne's hooves, if a female insists on a pistol, give her one she can manage. The kickback on this will bust her face. Show me your revolvers."

"She wanted a big pistol. I didn't think about…" Warren's gaze measured her. "I've never sold a weapon to a female. She's awful little, isn't she?" Despite Bree's scowl, Warren forgot his nervousness in the challenge. He considered the array of pistols under the glass counter, then pulled one out. "Try this. A Smith & Wesson. Lighter but it can shoot .357 magnums."

Zeb weighed the pistol and nodded. He plucked the Eagle out of her grip, replacing it with the revolver.

She pointed it at the wall and dry-fired. There was an obvious difference, especially when holding the thing out at arm's length.

Zeb grunted his approval. "Start her on .38 specials. She can work up to the .357s."

Bree handed Warren the revolver. "I guess that's what I'll do."

"I'll add ear plugs too." Warren started piling boxes on the counter.

Bree smiled at Zeb. "Thank you. I'm glad you were here."

Arms crossed over his massive chest, he returned to frowning. "Why the fuck do you need a weapon?"

Because a knife didn't work. Her fingers still held the memory of her butcher knife breaking against the monster's bony plating. She swallowed. Forcing words through her tight throat gave them a snap she hadn't intended. "That's really none of your business."

His eyes narrowed before he nodded. "First lesson at ten tomorrow." He glanced at Warren. "You got ax handles somewhere? Mine busted."

"Yes, sir. Give me a sec, and I'll show you." After Warren put a hefty dent in Bree's credit card tab, he handed over her monster killer and motioned to Zeb.

As the men headed for the rear, Bree escaped out the front. Whew. Guns made her nervous; Zeb even more so. Yet, his very reluctance to teach her was reassuring. If he were after her…body…he'd want a reason to spend time with her.

She shook her head. The most scary-looking guy she'd ever

met, and she felt as if he'd protect her. *Confused much, Bree?*

I obviously need chocolate. The tiny grocery store was right there, and even if the cabin's oven wasn't up to her standards, chocolate chip cookies were impossible to ruin.

"Hey, Breanne."

She turned at the sound of her name.

Vicki strode across the street with a blonde teen trailing in her wake. "We didn't get a formal intro before. I'm Vicki. How do you like Cold Creek?"

"Bree. And I'm enjoying the quiet."

"Well, then stay away from this noisy one," Vicki slung an arm around the girl. "Bree, this is my daughter, Jamie. Well, technically, she's Calum's baby, but she's mine now too. Jamie, Bree's staying at the Wildwood Cabins."

"It's nice to meet you, Jamie." Bree blinked. Considering Calum's black hair and dark complexion, his fair-skinned, blue-eyed *baby* looked more like she should be a child of Bree's. A pang ran through her. *I'd like children.*

"Hi." Jamie studied her. "You're here to fish?"

"No, I just needed a break from the city." Bree hesitated, but the more people that knew of her quest, the more likely she'd succeed. "I'm hunting for information about my parents."

The girl's eyes widened slightly, and freckles crinkled over her nose. "You lost your parents?"

"Or they lost me."

The hardware store door slammed.

"Hey, Zeb," Vicki greeted.

Zeb nodded at her, frowned at Bree, and glanced at Jamie. The girl backed away, sliding behind her mother.

The man's face tightened. He walked away, without saying a word.

Vicki looked over her shoulder. "Why're you hiding back there?"

"Well, duh, MomVee, the guy's really scary. Didn't you notice?"

"Not really." Vicki watched him for a moment. "He's big and scarred up, and… Okay, I can see how you might think scary, but he's also—I don't know—vulnerable or something."

Bree stared at her. "And you pet rattlesnakes in your spare time, right?"

Vicki snorted. "That's me. Are you starting to get cabin fever yet?"

"Well…" *Yes.*

"Come to the tavern tonight. I'll buy you a drink. Fair warning though—if the place gets busy, Calum's liable to put you to work as a barmaid."

Bree grinned. When she was sixteen and Sensei decided she had no calling for martial arts, he'd finagled her a job at a restaurant. She'd not only found her true calling, but also had paid for culinary school by waitressing. "I'd love it."

Chapter Nine

A T THE OUTSKIRTS of Cold Creek that night, Zeb impatiently waited for Alec to catch up. Although his fur warded off
the misty cold, the snow wedged in the pads of his paws was
uncomfortable as hell. He was ready for a warm tavern and a
beer.

He heard the pines swaying, a sprite rustling into her tree-
hole for the night...and then a faint padding as the oversized
cougar stalked out from behind a house. The cougar's paws were
the size of dinner plates, and Zeb braced himself—just in case—
then almost laughed. Was this how the little human felt when he
was around?

With a lash of his tail, Alec pounced on a wayward leaf like a
kitten would, obviously to put Zeb at ease.

Fucking observant sheriff. Zeb headed into the forest, sniffing as he went. Normal scents. Deer. Weasel. Hare. Catching a
trace of something foul, he put his nose down, moving slowly,
working the air. *There.* A huge footprint. The heavy claw marks
were bigger than a grizzly's. He whined to catch Alec's attention.

The cougar joined him, brushing against his shoulder. Sniffing, studying. A low snarl.

A few minutes later in the cave, Zeb shifted to human, tied
his hair back, and donned the clothing he'd left in a niche in the

rock wall. Nice setup here. The hidden tunnel under the tavern let shifters enter the forest without the risk of a human stumbling over a pile of clothes.

After Alec pulled on his sheriff's uniform and combed his fingers through his sandy brown hair, he nodded at Zeb. "A good night's work."

"The tracks were old, but it'll be back at new moon."

"We'll be ready this time." Alec's voice was grim. The Cascade Territory's head cahir had taken the loss of life in his territory personally. Zeb had discovered Alec's easy-going attitude overlay a steel core and a logical mind. Now the cop knew what to smell for, he'd be watching for new tracks like a winter-starved weasel.

Alec motioned toward the stairs. "C'mon, I'll buy you a beer."

The sheriff is buying me a drink, not trying to lock me up. Amused, he followed Alec upstairs through the concealed door in a closet, out a private room, down a hall, and into the main tavern itself. The place had filled while they ranged the forest, and a wave of scents hit Zeb like a blow: beer, wine, perfumes, cologne, sweat. The country music might be good, but the babble of too fucking many people drowned it out.

"Pretty full tonight." Alec stopped at the bar and checked his watch. "I need to get back, see what damage Jenkins has done to the town."

"Want us tomorrow?" Shay should have finished the bookkeeping by then and be in a better mood. Earlier, he'd discovered the previous owner's "records" were receipts stuffed in a drawer, and the constant growling from the office had driven Zeb out of the lodge. After years of lone wolfing, he wasn't fucking ready to have a fucking roommate.

"Tomorrow, yes. Same time and we'll meet here again. That way I can get a beer." Alec slapped him on the shoulder, shocking the hell out of Zeb. People didn't touch him. Too big, too mean looking. This cahir didn't seem to notice.

After holding up one finger to his littermate behind the bar, Alec strode away.

Zeb leaned an elbow on the bartop and studied the crowd. Noticing three dwarves at the out-of-the-way corner table, he bowed his head politely and received the same in return.

The Cosantir's mate, Vicki, was working as a barmaid again, although she was one of Alec's deputies, as well. When Zeb had met her at a Gathering, she'd been overwhelmed by her first heat. Now she was laughing and trading insults with the customers. He was pleased to see she'd adjusted and found her place.

A sweet voice caught his attention. Carrying a small tray she could use one-handed, Bree was taking drink orders. As she wove her way around the tables, her sunny hair gleamed in the light from the wall sconces. The wavy tangle stopped just above her waist, drawing attention to the way her jeans cupped her round ass. An inch or two taller than Vicki, she was even curvier and totally appealing. Fuck.

Others had noticed, as well. She was collecting interested looks from the entire male population of the bar, even Daonain. But, true to form, humans started the trouble. Drunk, human, and male spelled *pain in the ass*, and the center table held four PITAs.

One latched onto Bree's arm tightly enough she couldn't jerk away without spilling the drinks. Another had the effrontery to grab her ass.

Taller than everyone in the room, Zeb had a clear view. He started to push his way through the crowd.

She scowled and snapped something, but the human males only laughed. And then, she pivoted and planted her foot into the ass-toucher's stomach. Man and chair went over backwards, skidding a few feet until coming to rest against the adjacent table.

She hadn't even spilled a drink.

She turned toward the other male. He snatched his hand from her arm. With a swing of her blonde hair, she moved away as if she'd never been stopped.

Fucking amazing. Zeb adjusted his jeans around a disconcerting hard-on and returned to the bar.

Calum was waiting for him. "Could you do me the favor of taking out the trash? Just the two. Politeness is not required. The others may stay."

"With pleasure, Co—Calum."

As he moved away, he heard Calum murmur, "I rather thought so…"

At the PITAs' table, Zeb stopped beside the worm who'd grabbed Breanne's arm.

"Yeah? What?" the human said.

Zeb bent and spoke quietly, "The owner says, '*leave.*' I *really* hope you stay."

The guy was out the door before Zeb straightened. Well, fuck. Talk about ruining his fun. The other human had regained his chair. Hand on his gut, he still looked green.

Zeb's lips twitched. Bree had some power in that kick.

One more piece of garbage to dispose of. He grabbed the asshole by his shirt collar and dragged him like a deer carcass across the room. With a flick of his wrist, he tossed the trash out the door and paused to make sure he wouldn't come back in. Apparently, the human had urgent business elsewhere. Pity.

Zeb glanced at the other two at the table. They held up their hands as if he'd drawn a pistol. So he nodded. When he returned to the bar, his spot was empty of encroachers.

Calum set a dark beer in front of him. "From Alec. And that was nice work. Thank you." He'd returned to drawing drinks before Zeb processed what he'd said. It was fucking strange to be thanked for having a good time.

The beer was cold and malty, and somehow the tavern had taken on a pleasant atmosphere.

A few minutes later, Bree halted beside Zeb. After setting her tray on the bar, she grinned up at him, her eyes dancing with humor.

His breath stopped in his throat, and heat surged through him. The little female was deadly when she directed that smile at a male. *For fuck's sake, she's human.* He didn't realize he'd frowned until she took a step back.

He tried not to let it hurt.

Then her chin rose, and she forced herself to regain the distance she'd retreated. Brave little female. Her lips curved up again as she said, "When Calum told me the garbage would be removed, I thought he meant bussing the tables. Then I saw you—" Her laugh reminded him of bubbly water in a rocky creek.

"Anyway, thank you," she finished.

Without thinking, he rubbed his knuckles down her cheek, and she stilled, staring at him like a sparrow spotting a bobcat. Damn. He set his hand back on the bar. "You handled the problem. I just did disposal."

"Very neatly too." Although her words were light, her expression had turned cautious. She watched his hand as if it might fly up and strike her.

"Little female." He waited until her gaze met his. "You weren't afraid when you took on two drunks." He knew what she smelled like when she was afraid—exactly the scent he caught now. "There's only one of me, yet you are frightened."

She started to shake her head in denial.

"Don't lie."

"Fine." Her glare was diminished by the hint of terror in her eyes. "They were little—no, they weren't," she corrected.

"You're just so very big. And unfriendly. And you loom over me."

She turned to grab her tray off the bar and stopped.

Holding the drink orders off her tray, Calum was watching them. He tilted his head at Bree. "I regret again, he would be difficult to cut down to size."

The double meaning didn't escape Zeb, and he lifted his beer in acknowledgment.

As the Cosantir moved away, leafing through the tickets, Bree glanced up at Zeb. "I can't decide. Does he like you or not?"

"Damned if I can tell." Zeb looked into her big blue eyes and deliberately rubbed a knuckle up and down her soft cheek. Why did he feel the need to get her accustomed to his hands on her?

He watched her stiffen and over-ride her instinct to retreat. Gutsy little human. He asked, "Got suggestions on how to make friends with people?"

"I'll think about it." She knocked his hand away from her face in a skillful move. "In fact, I'll make you a nice long list."

AN HOUR LATER in the tavern kitchen, Bree reluctantly pulled on her jacket and headed toward the door. It had been so fun to be back in the midst of people, surrounded by conversation and laughter. But now she'd been sent home like a baby. Jeez.

Earlier, Calum had seen her limping and told her to take a break. She'd tried for a few minutes, but sitting while Vicki worked had been impossible. Unfortunately, when Bree had handed him a new pile of orders, Calum had thanked her, taken her tray away, and ordered her to leave.

She glanced back. Yes, he was watching to make sure she obeyed.

Fine. I'm going. And maybe he was right. Her thigh throbbed as if teeth were biting at it. And even though she'd used her good arm to carry the tray, her wounded one ached. So did her shoulder. *Overdone it a little, dummy?*

As the door closed behind her, shutting off the babble of voices, she took a slow breath of cold night air. Up above, fat stars dotted the black sky. In the east, white-topped mountain peaks gleamed in the waning moonlight. Seattle was beautiful, but it had never grabbed her throat like this.

Smiling, she set out along the side of the building toward the shortcut she'd discovered earlier. Fishermen staying at the lodge had made a bee-line trail through the woods to the tavern.

As she moved away from the lit windows, unease crept up her spine. She'd walked over in the dusk, not thinking about how dark it would be on the walk home. Where was that darn four-footed Elvis when she needed him?

A huge man stepped out of the shadows.

Terror stopped her breathing. Every instinct said *flee*—but the door was too far. She lurched backwards, bringing up her guard. As her bad leg quivered with her weight, sickness balled in her belly, knowing what would come.

The monster didn't move, but gave a long-suffering sigh. "You gonna threaten me every time we meet?" He stepped into a pool of light. Black hair, wide shoulders, a corner of his mouth tipped-up. *Zeb.*

Relief melted her bones, and she sagged against the log wall. "I'm sorry. I didn't see you standing there."

"Weak apology."

Her hands were shaking. "It was an explanation, not an apology."

"Uh-huh." He wrapped his fingers around her arm and tugged her forward. Effortlessly. "Let's go."

"What do you mean? Go?"

He nodded at the crowded parking lot. "No car. Means you walked." The pressure of his hand on her low back kept her moving.

She started walking so he'd have no excuse to leave his hand there—right above her butt. "Did you wait for me?"

"The night isn't safe." He looked down, the moonlight turning his scars white. "Especially for little females."

"Oh." He'd wanted to protect her? She frowned, realizing she was starting to get used to him—mostly. "I appreciate it."

He sure didn't talk much, but his presence on the block-long path was oddly reassuring. Okay, a lot reassuring. Even a monster might think twice before taking him on.

But he walked way too fast, considering the moon-dappled darkness. When she tripped on a tree root and stumbled, he grabbed her arms. Fear shot through her at the feel of his powerful hands, but set her on her feet, released her without a word, and waited.

After a minute, when her heart had withdrawn from her throat, she managed, "Thank you."

He grunted his answer, but curtailed his long stride to her shorter one...the most gallant rude man she'd ever met. Did he even know how to talk to a woman?

Her nervousness flipped into humor. "So, have you lived in Cold Creek all your life? Are you from this area?"

His brows drew together, and he scowled at her in disbelief—*you want me to talk?*

Stifling a laugh, she raised her eyebrows and waited.

"Shay and I just moved here." He paused and added, "I grew up in the Canadian mountains."

Mountain man fit him well, but she couldn't imagine him as a child. "Is your family still there?"

The muscles of his face tightened to rival the hardness of granite. "No family."

Her heart softened with pity. "Me, neither."

"No luck with your picture?"

"No. Nobody's ever seen them." No family. All alone now. Grief slid through her. *I miss you so much, Ashley.*

They walked another minute in silence, then his hand on her arm stopped her. He pointed and whispered, "Bobcat."

With gray-brown fur and black-tufted ears, it looked like a cat on steroids. "It's so pretty."

He actually grinned, a brief flash of white teeth in his dark face. Her heart hitched. For a second she saw him, not as a huge protector or a threat, but a man. Not a gorgeous one…but devastatingly masculine.

Swallowing hard, she started walking again. Faster.

The shortcut ended on Wildwood's dirt road by the lodge. He didn't speak as they went past the lodge and turned onto the narrower road to her cabin.

After unlocking her door, she started in, only to be blocked by a muscular arm.

"Wait." Zeb stalked through the cabin, checking any hiding places. When he returned to where she stood in the door, he nodded. "Good night, little female."

"Don't call me that," she said.

He touched her cheek with his knuckles again, an infinitely gentle slide that set her nerve ends quivering. "But you are." His gaze ran from her toes to the top of her head, leaving heat behind. "Definitely little."

He inhaled, and a crease appeared in his cheek. "Very female."

He bent and brushed his lips across hers. "Very soft." His mouth moved over hers again, so lightly, not taking, but coaxing until she leaned into him, lost in the feel of the firm lips against her own.

She jerked back. What was she thinking? "Um." She gave

him a wary look.

His expression unreadable, he ran his finger over her damp lower lip. "Goodnight, little female." He walked out, shutting the door quietly behind him.

She stared after him and jumped at a loud thump.

"*Lock* it."

She did.

For the first time in three weeks, she slept the entire night.

Chapter Ten

THE MID-DAY SUN was bright and clear as Shay rolled down the windows of his truck, hoping the brisk air would chill his temper before he reached the lodge. Cold Creek was too small to avoid Gerhard, but if the alpha-hole bared his fangs at Shay one more time, he'd be spitting teeth for a month.

No, dammit, punching him was a bad plan, since the alpha would take it as a challenge. *Be polite, furface.* Shay growled in frustration and turned onto the dirt road. Most of the items on his checklist were completed: spare linens stocked, a new refrigerator in the back of the truck for cabin five, a routine test ordered on the well water, septic pumping done. The Wildwood business was coming together nicely.

After parking at the side of the lodge, he jumped out, itching as if ants had crawled into his clothes. Damned metal truck. He scratched his chest, wishing he could trawsfur and roll in the dirt.

As he stepped onto the porch, the distinctive crack of a pistol split the mountain silence. Shay stiffened. The sound had come from behind the cabins, somewhere in the forest. Another shot. Two more. Someone either was in trouble or was hunting in posted territory.

He glanced toward Breanne's cabin, feeling a quiver of unease. Her car was there, but no one moved inside.

Best go investigate. With luck, the shooter would be a tres-passer, and he'd have a valid target for his frustration. He strode through the lodge, out the side door, started to pull off his shirt, then stopped. Running around as a wolf might get him peppered with bullets. With a grunt of annoyance, he stayed human and headed into the forest.

Three more shots. Shay broke into a run.

A few minutes later, he sniffed the air. Not trespassers—Breanne and Zeb. He slowed as he reached a clearing, then stopped to watch.

Their backs were to him. Zeb fired a few shots, all hitting the hand-drawn paper target, before handing the pistol to Breanne. Shay lifted his eyebrows. Shooting lessons? The thought of an armed female was unsettling, but maybe humans did that sort of thing.

His partner had set up a decent firing range. A massive tree had toppled sideways and created a hollowed-out area in the slope that would stop any stray bullets. Zeb's jacket and a backpack with a gun case and boxes of bullets lay nearby.

Silently, Shay watched as Zeb demonstrated the proper stance. Frowning in concentration, Breanne copied the position like a cub imitating its mama.

No need to disturb the lesson. Shay started to head back when the breeze shifted.

Zeb sniffed and turned. "Hey."

Breanne spun around, pointing the pistol at Shay's chest.

He hastily stepped behind the tree next to him.

Zeb pushed her arm down and tugged the revolver from her hand. "Don't point unless you're going to kill. Kill the bad guys, not your landlord."

She bit her lip and nodded, then gave Shay a tentative smile. "I'm sorry. What are you doing up here?"

"Heard the gunfire." He came forward. "Nice shooting, Zeb."

Zeb shrugged off the compliment and returned to instructing. "Sight with both eyes. Breathe out. Squeeze gently, like you'd stroke a male's balls." His lips quirked.

"Oh well, sure," Breanne muttered. Her pale skin pinkened.

Was anything more attractive than a blushing female? Shay barked a laugh.

She heard. Her finger yanked on the trigger viciously, snapping a shot out, before she looked straight at Shay. "Stroke it like that?"

Zeb glanced over, amusement in his eyes.

"Hell, a leannan." Shay shook his head. "You'd have me walking bow-legged for a week."

Even though her flush increased to a deep red, she laughed. Low and melodic, the sound ran up his spine with a gentle caress.

Obviously affected the same way, Zeb cleared his throat. "Keep shooting."

Too intrigued to leave, Shay grabbed some earplugs from the packet on the ground. Shoulder against a tree trunk, he put them in, blotting out the irritated chatter of a wood pixie above him.

That was a very focused female. Each suggestion Zeb made was implemented immediately with fierce determination. Her aim continued to improve until she hit the target more times than not.

After about fifteen minutes, Zeb checked the sun. "Time's up. I promised Alec I'd pa"—he glanced at Breanne and amended—"buy him a beer. Shay can watch you."

"No."

"I have time." Shay couldn't think of anything more fun, in fact.

"Little female, mind what Shay says." Zeb tapped one finger against her chin and got a frown. After grabbing his jacket, he jogged down the trail toward the lodge.

Lower lip between her teeth, Breanne looked forlorn for a second, then straightened her shoulders. Shay could almost hear her saying, *I'm not scared.* Ignoring him completely, she reloaded and fired until her revolver emptied.

He moved closer once her weapon was empty. He wasn't about to frighten a skittish female with a loaded gun, especially considering the way she reacted to Zeb's *stroking balls* joke. He laughed silently. When he was playing Elvis, he'd discovered she had a wry sense of humor. One he liked. But sometimes he forgot she didn't know him in human form. "Hold for a moment."

She looked at him.

"Focus on the target, a leannan. The front tip of your gun should be fuzzy."

As she raised the pistol, her gaze changed from the barrel to the target. "Got it." Her next shots were all on the paper, although scattered.

"Better."

Her grin lit her face. After setting the pistol down, she pulled off her jean jacket. Her bright red sweater hugged high, firm breasts, and Shay's mouth went dry.

He yanked his gaze away. What the hell was wrong with him? She was human. Only a desperate male shifter—one who couldn't win a Daonain female—would mate with a human.

She pushed her sweater sleeves up and raised the revolver again.

Keeping his attention off her softer assets, Shay studied her arms. She had some good muscle tone, except... He walked around to her right side and scowled at the pink-red marks above her wrist. "What happened?"

Breanne grimaced. "Um. Something bigger and faster than me. I'm healing though."

Outraged to think something would attack a female, Shay moved closer. "That must have hurt." Without thinking, he took her arm and turned it to expose the underside. Serrated markings, dimpling of the skin where a human doctor had stitched the tissue together. Pink and fragile. Probably less than a month old. "What bit you?"

She pulled her elbow out of his grasp. "I'm not exactly sure. It happened too fast." She aimed the pistol and fired savagely. Again and again until the hammer clicked on an empty cartridge.

"Not bad," Shay said absently, trying to think of all the animals with jaws that large. Not a hellhound—it wouldn't leave a victim alive. A dog? A bear? "Did your biter also take a chunk out of your leg? Is that why you limp?"

Her face whitened, but her fingers were steady as she reloaded the pistol. "That's why."

Shay stepped back and let her work. In all his years, he'd never seen a female like this. Enough fear to fill a lake and a mountain of determination to match it. "You've started pulling to the left," he remarked. "Take your stance."

She assumed the posture she'd been taught—perfectly. But her aim was getting worse. Not because of her arm injury, he decided. But her alignment was off. He closed his hands over her shoulders.

She yelped and jerked away, but too late. He'd felt the gouges in the muscle.

"It got your shoulder too?" he said gently. Rage swept through him with the need to tear apart whatever had done such damage to a female. *This* female.

"Yeah."

"Give me the pistol." He held out his hand and, after a second, she complied. He unloaded, ignoring the protest in her eyes. "You're done for today, lass. Any more and you'll damage those muscles."

"But...I need to practice. I need to. They're my muscles, anyway."

She had the biggest blue eyes he'd ever seen, and by Herne's hooves, it was hard to say no. "You can shoot every day. But not this long."

"I don't even know how long this was."

"Look." He tucked his arm around her waist and turned her to face the target. After an initial startle, she allowed the contact. No scent of fear, just female fragrance with a hint of vanilla. He'd enjoyed holding her the morning after the Gathering, and her lips had been sweet.

What the hell was wrong with him? Human, remember? He let her go—*bad wolf*—and pointed to the target. "See the holes where you started shooting and where you started improving. But this last round? Your aim slid off to the left as you started to hurt."

She huffed out a breath. "You're right."

"Of course I am." He grinned at her and caught a responding smile. "When your aim starts to veer, then quit. You'll be able to go longer each day."

She sighed. "Okay. That sounds okay."

With his free hand, he pushed her silky hair behind her ear and let his fingers trail down her neck. Silky skin, warm and damp with a female's compelling fragrance. The tiny freckles scattered across her nose and cheeks cried out to be licked.

Human. She's human. He stepped away. Then took another step for good measure. "Let's go."

At midnight, Zeb headed back to the cave. He'd patrolled the eastern half of town, Shay the west. He'd found nothing new, but they wouldn't relax. With the moon in the last quarter, they had only a week before the deadly dark night.

Under the Wild Hunt, he shifted and dressed, grumbling about the Cosantir's latest order—to report in after each patrol.

"*How else will I know if you get yourself killed?*" Calum had asked and then amended, "*I'd prefer to know if one of you is missing before I check my territory after closing.*" A chilling reminder that—how a Cosantir's tie to Herne let him locate any shifter within his domain.

Scowling, Zeb climbed the steps to the closet, through the locked room, and into the hallway. He liked this competent Cosantir—one who gave a damn about his people and his cahirs—but sometimes he felt as if he was on a leash.

Living in an overcrowded den didn't help. If he'd been dumped into a house with anyone but Shay, he'd have torn his fucking throat out by now. If Shay gave him any more crap, he'd do it anyway. Messy, bossy, talkative mutt.

The babble of the people as Zeb entered the bar room made him flinch. The country music was loud, the place jam-packed. Saturday. He'd forgotten it was the weekend. Fucking Cosantir's orders.

He growled, and people melted from his path like sheep from a mountain lion. That only pissed him off more.

A college-aged brat had taken Zeb's preferred spot at the end of the bar—the one where his back wasn't turned to the door. The kid glanced over, paled, and backed away. Zeb didn't quite sneer.

Calum worked his way down, filling orders as he came. Seemed strange to have a Cosantir doing something so menial, but running a bar would be a fine way of keeping track of everything in town. Sneaky werecat.

Calum handed him a dark beer and raised his voice to be heard over the noise. "Problems?"

"All quiet."

"In that case, refrain from terrifying my customers."

Zeb snorted. "I scare everybody. What—"

"No, Zebulon." Calum gave him a level look. "Cahirs can be intimidating, yes. However, when you stalk in here as if you'd enjoy gutting someone, then you frighten people. Control that."

He moved away, leaving Zeb glaring at his back. Or what? Fucking arrogant bast—

"What's the problem?" Shay stepped into the respectful space everyone else had left. "You look like you got a paw stuck in a trap."

Every place he went, some asshole was talking at him. "Fuck that. If I want your opinion, I'll beat it out of you."

"By the God's balls." Shay thumped his bottle of beer down. "You and what army?"

That did it. Zeb snarled and punched his fucking roommate right in his loud mouth, knocking him back against the other customers. Satisfaction blasted through him. That's what the healer ordered. No Herne-aided strength, just fists.

Shay wiped his lip, glanced at the blood on his hand, and scowled. His hands fisted; his knuckles cracked with hard pops to accompany the country music. "Been a while."

"Too fucking long."

Shay feinted to Zeb's head, then delivered a solid punch to his gut. Zeb absorbed the pain with a grunt and nailed Shay across the cheekbone. The crowd scattered with shouts and screams. A chair hit the floor.

Shay roared, and the battle was on.

BREE STARED AT the two men, toe-to-toe, slugging each other. When one of Shay's punches sent Zeb crashing backwards into a table, she flinched.

"Oh, hell, are they rehearsing for *Battle of the Titans*?" Vicki set her tray on an empty table. "Well, let's break it up."

"Us? Are you insane?"

"Barmaid/bouncer. That's my job description."

"Not mine. I just help out for fun." Bree heard a deep, raspy roar. *Zeb*. Customers shouted. A woman screamed. "Vicki, they're huge. Your husband won't let you—"

"You think?" Vicki nodded at the bar. Calum jerked his head at the fighters in a very clear order. Laughing, Vicki strode toward the fighting.

"Oh heavens. Why can't they be normal-sized guys?" Bree pressed a hand to her churning stomach. How could she fight men the size of the monster? *I don't want to*. Her pistol was in her purse in the kitchen. Could she just shoot the idiots?

She hurried after Vicki. She couldn't let her friend do this alone, but if her heart pounded through her ribs, there'd be bones all over the floor, and Vicki'd have to clean them up.

As she pushed past the crowd, she saw Zeb kick Shay halfway across the room.

"Perfect. You take Zeb. I got Shay," Vicki directed.

Bree winced. *Oh thanks*. Shay might have been reasonable. Taking on Zeb was sheer suicide. She pushed her fear down into her gut. Okay, fine, she'd fought big guys before—lots of them—and won. Her black belt hadn't been earned by sitting home knitting.

As Zeb stalked after his opponent, Bree slid into his path, stance balanced and ready. "No fighting in the bar." Two points for her—her voice hadn't squeaked.

He didn't answer, just gripped her shoulder to push her aside.

She slapped his hand away and stayed in front of him.

"Move, little human," he growled, wiping the blood from his face.

Human? What kind of derogatory term was that? "I'm not

little," she growled back, "and I'm not moving."

He grabbed her shirtfront faster than she could block. With no apparent effort, he lifted her off her feet like an errant puppy and set her to one side. She brought her fists down on his forearm, broke his hold, and planted herself in his path again.

"Fuck, you're stubborn." He gave her a lethal look. "I could hurt you. Badly."

The whiplash of fear made her mad. She glared back. "I'd do my best to hurt you. Badly."

He exhaled loudly and glanced over her head at someone behind her. "You got a problem too?"

Easing sideways, Bree followed his gaze.

Hands on hips, Vicki blocked Shay who had the same frustrated expression as Zeb. "Are you finished?" Vicki asked Shay.

"Hell." Shay looked at Zeb. "Are we done?"

Zeb cupped Bree's face with a battered hand. His thumb traced her lips so very gently that a tingle shimmered through her. "Guess we're done," he murmured.

Shay tugged on Vicki's hair, then limped over to Bree. "Brave little warrior, aren't you?" He tucked her disheveled hair behind her ear before turning to Zeb. "Most fun I've had in weeks. C'mon, I'll buy you a beer."

Bree stared as the two guys walked to the bar, side by side. Around her, people set tables and chairs in place and picked up spilled drinks. A few muttered about *damned cay-heers*, whatever that meant. She shook her head. "They try to kill each other and now they're best friends?"

"Guys. Assholes. No difference."

As Bree followed Vicki to the bar, Calum smiled and set out their working drinks. Diet cola for Bree, water for Vicki. "Efficiently done. Thank you."

Even as the compliment sang through her, Bree narrowed her eyes. "Seems like a man would worry about his wife getting hurt."

"My mate could take those two with one arm tied behind her back," he said mildly. "Even without the unfair advantage." At a hail from a customer, he moved down the bar.

"What advantage?" Bree asked Vicki.

"Being female." Vicki drank some water, glanced over at Zeb and Shay. "Any shif—um, around here, most men would die before they'd hurt a woman. As long as we were obstinate enough to stay in their way, they couldn't fight. But if Calum had intervened, the guys would have happily turned it into a three-way brawl." She sighed. "It would've been more fun if they'd thrown a punch or two."

"Jeez, you're as crazy as they are." Bree frowned at the bartender. "I'm not sure whether to be horrified or impressed that he'd risk you."

"Calum uses all his resources, even me. It's one of the reasons I love the overbearing bastard."

Calum apparently heard. His eyes turned darker as he gave his wife a look that should have been x-rated. Even weirder, she could swear she heard Vicki purr.

Bree suppressed a sigh. What she wouldn't give for some man to look at her as if she was his whole world.

Chapter Eleven

*H*EART POUNDING, BREE *tore out of the house, gagging at the taste of blood. Mr. Harvey had tried to force his thing into her mouth and she'd bit it. Her scalp hurt from where he'd gripped her hair. She reached the end of the block and turned. She couldn't go back. No one would ever believe a fifteen-year-old over a foster parent.*

Bree startled awake, heart pounding, then felt a brush of fur against her arm and the warmth of a furry body against her side. Elvis was sprawled beside her on the smooth boulder in the forest glade. She relaxed.

Over the past few days, the amber-eyed dog had joined her on most of her lazy-paced hikes. His limp was almost gone now. And she was healing as well, both mentally and physically. She slept late every morning, read books from BOOKS, and quizzed the townspeople about her photo. Unfortunately, no one remembered her parents.

Afternoons, she practiced her shooting—and was getting better. Even though Shay had cut the target in half, she could still hit it, although she was nowhere near as accurate as the men were. Wasn't it a shame she couldn't bring them back to Seattle for protection? *Hi, guys. Would you help me pack…and if a nonexistent monster crashes through the door, you please kill it. Oh, and bring your guns. You'll need them.* She rolled her eyes, imagining their reaction.

No, she'd return to Seattle by herself. But she wasn't stupid. She'd stay in a hotel while she searched for an apartment. Then maybe she'd give herself a giant moving-out party so she could pack and load her stuff surrounded by people. With luck, the noise would drown out her memories of Ash's laughing, scolding voice. Of her screams. *Of my screams.*

Her shudder attracted Elvis's attention, and then he was licking her face and neck, washing away her grief, and making her giggle as she tried to fend him off. "Ew, dog spit. That's just gross."

He gave her a canine grin, tongue lolling out, totally unrepentant.

"It's late, buddy. We'd better head back."

After a final swipe of his tongue over her chin, he jumped off the boulder and started down the trail.

Following behind him, she grinned. The bossy dog never let her go in front...which might be a good thing. "You know, I'd probably have gotten lost if you hadn't been with me."

His tail wagged with his obvious agreement.

"But that's not true anymore." Stopping for a moment, she looked around. Yes, she recognized this trail. "Not my fault. I never hiked before. Actually, I'd never left Seattle before this trip. Isn't that weird?"

The dog tilted its ears back. Best listener she'd ever met.

"I was scared to leave the city." Her hiking boots thudded as she crossed the wooden footbridge. Sunlight glinted off the creek and melted the ice along the banks. "I was found in the woods somewhere—at least that's what the social worker said, and I get nightmares about being lost."

As the wind rustled through the evergreens, the branches sighed. The creek gurgled and sang, and in the sky, a lonely eagle cried out. The damp green scent of the forest filled the air, seasoned with the tang of snow. "Who knew mountains were so magnificent?"

A few minutes later, she smiled at the sight of her cabin. No, it wasn't home, but it had been a good sanctuary. Hearing thuds, she walked around the side of the building to the front. Elvis followed.

Coat discarded on the ground, Zeb transferred a load of firewood from a wheelbarrow onto her porch. As he hefted several pieces, his muscular biceps and shoulders bulged. The neck of his flannel shirt was open, displaying the scars that ran down his neck onto his chest. So many scars.

Bree shivered and cleared her dry throat. "Thanks for the wood."

He nodded, then raised one eyebrow at the dog. "Got a pal?"

Odd how reassuring it was to have Elvis next to her, even if Zeb didn't scare her anymore. Much. She hugged the dog, got her face licked, and laughed. "Elvis is a darling. Do you know who owns him?"

"Elvis?" Zeb snorted a laugh. "Nobody owns that noisy mutt. Keep him—but you should probably neuter him."

The dog showed its fangs and growled at Zeb.

Bree's mouth dropped open.

Even more startling—Zeb actually grinned.

THE NEXT EVENING, Bree walked a circle around her table. The display of cones and twigs looked appropriate and rustic with the heavy stoneware.

Three place settings.

Her cold hands trembled as she straightened a napkin. Dinner was almost ready, the table prepared. Now she had to invite the guests. She put a hand on her quivering stomach. Two huge men. She glanced longingly at her purse by the door, but wearing her pistol to supper would probably be rude.

Honestly, Bree. Get over yourself. She stiffened her spine. If she couldn't even have a couple of guys over—no matter how tall— then how did she expect to return to a city filled with men?

Zeb and Shay had been kind. And hey, they'd each given her a kiss—if those little brushes could be called kisses. It was odd that after she got past being startled, she'd actually wanted more. She snorted. Like more kissing would happen if she ran screaming for the woods.

So—next step. *Desensitization.* That's what an allergic friend had called it when the doc injected her with increasingly higher doses of ragweed. If the method worked, eventually she'd stop being frightened of humongous guys.

Okay, then. After yanking on her coat, she hurried over to the lodge and pounded on the door.

She squeaked when it jerked open.

"What the fuck is—oh." Zeb looked down, and a glint of humor lit those dark chocolate-colored eyes. "Little female, you knock like someone much bigger."

"Are you ever going to stop calling me little female?"

He studied her for an interminable minute, his gaze starting at her feet and moving up her body in a way that made her catch her breath. Heat flooded her cheeks.

"No."

She blinked. "No what?"

"No, I'm not going to stop calling you little female."

When Shay appeared in the doorway behind Zeb, the two together looked like they'd need the side of the house removed for easy access. "Is Zeb bothering you? Should I beat on him?"

"You two did enough fighting the other night. Was Calum angry?"

Shay tilted his head. "Does he get mad?"

"He does," Zeb said. "Don't go there."

Bree remembered her first visit to the bar and how Calum's gray eyes had turned black.

"He wasn't upset about the fight. Just wanted us to fix what we broke," Shay said.

"You here for a reason?" Zeb crossed his arms over his chest. Not into small talk, was he?

"My vacation time is over. I'm leaving Saturday," Bree said awkwardly.

"That's a shame." Shay studied her. "Why do you—"

"I cooked a pot of spaghetti," she interrupted hastily. No questions, please. "To thank you for the stuff you've done for me. You know, firewood and shooting lessons and repairs. Escort services. Stuff."

Shay leaned a shoulder against the doorjamb, his smile slow. "You want to feed us; we're there."

Zeb just nodded, his gaze flat and watchful again.

"Uh. Good. Dinner's in twenty minutes." As she walked away, she felt their eyes on her back. *Walk slower. Don't act like a kitten fleeing from a dog.* They didn't need to know her heart was bruising her rib cage.

BEING HUMAN, THE female had never seen cahirs eat, Zeb realized, enjoying her surprise when he and Shay polished off the salad, garlic bread, and an entire pot of spaghetti. The stuff from a can never tasted like *this*. With the scents of food, wood smoke, and female, the cabin smelled like what he imagined a home would.

Since Shay kept the conversation rolling despite Bree's nervousness, Zeb could eat and enjoy the scenery. The little female was definitely worth looking at, even if she was human.

After telling them to stay put, she started clearing the table. Every time she turned, her long hair rippled with different colors. Some strands were the color of sunshine, some as white as the glaciers on Rainier. Fascinating. His hair was black and...black.

Shay leaned forward and said in a low voice, "If you keep watching her like she's a breakfast rabbit, I'll smash your face."

"You and what pack?" Not his fault that he remembered the feel of her lips, her scent. Her blue sweater looked softer than a wolf's downy undercoat and cupped her full breasts in a way that stirred his cock. They'd be heavy, would fill his palms, would taste like—dammit, why in Herne's name was he so attracted to her? Humans were nice enough, but not for sex. He'd known a few males who'd fuck anything, but he wasn't one of them.

Yet she pulled at him—her scent, her body, even her personality. Especially her personality.

She wanted to take care of everyone, from cuddling the children in the bookstore to feeding him and Shay. And she had to be the most stubborn, bravest little female he'd ever met. When her rounded chin came up and her lips compressed, she wouldn't budge from a decision. Especially when it came to shooting that fucking pistol.

Or stopping a fight. The little human had moved with the sureness of a cat. Considering how easily she'd broken his hold and the graceful way she'd kicked the grabby human, she knew some sort of fighting skill.

Calum's mate moved in that manner too...and a year ago, Vicki had been human also. What was wrong with human males that their females must learn to fight and handle firearms?

"You leave on Saturday. For Seattle?" he asked, even as a pang hit him at the thought.

She hesitated, then her chin came up. "Yes."

"Is that why you bought a pistol?" He caught the faint scent of her fear, arousing every protective instinct in his body.

"Cities are dangerous. Women sometimes need to defend

themselves."

So whatever had made her afraid, had happened in Seattle. The gutsy human was going back to face it. Admirable. But why the hell had she been hurt in the first place? Why was no male protecting her? Someone this sweet must have males fighting for her favor. "I don't think—"

"True," Shay broke in, giving him a shut-up-or-I'll-put-my-fangs-in-your-neck look. "You don't."

Bree laughed, her fear scent dissipating. "You two are so funny. How in the world did you end up partners?"

"Well…" Shay leaned back in his chair. "Zeb worked at a fishing camp. He's excellent at maintenance and repairs, but the owner wanted someone to handle promotion and business."

In other words, someone who wouldn't scare the fishermen away. Zeb's mouth tightened.

A delicate hand covered his. Bree glared at Shay, then looked at Zeb with gentle blue eyes as clear as a mountain lake. "That stuff is overrated. I like people who don't lie or make things sound better than they really are."

She defended him? His gaze met Shay's, sharing both the humor and the disbelief…but the warmth he felt at her words he'd keep to himself.

He realized she'd asked something. "What?"

"Do you guys like chocolate? I made brownies."

Zeb stared at her. *Brownies are born, not made.* "You can't—"

"Hell yes, we like chocolate," Shay interrupted. As Bree headed for the kitchen corner, he said under his breath, "Humans have a chewy cake they call brownies. She didn't mean OtherFolk."

Food? Did they eat desserts called *dwarf* and *pixie* as well? That was just wrong.

Nonetheless, Zeb took one of the dark squares. The chocolate burst in his mouth like a mountain springtime, and he growled his pleasure before taking another.

When Breanne laughed and pushed the plate closer to him, he caught sight of the scars on her arm. He wrapped his fingers around her tiny wrist.

"Zeb?" She tried to tug away.

"Shay said you were hurt. I will look." Holding her firmly, he slid her loose sleeve up to expose ugly bite marks on her fair skin. The scars were as wide as some of his. "What did this?" Couldn't be a hellhound or she wouldn't be alive. Whatever had savaged her, he'd enjoy killing it.

She yanked away and pulled her sleeve down. "You have less manners than a—a—"

"I've heard that." He ignored Shay's chuckle. "Answer me."

She shot him an icy glare.

He waited.

The sound she made was almost a growl and absurdly arousing. "Fine. A dog—a very big dog. Okay?"

The way her voice trembled made him want to pull her into his arms and surround her with safety. He knew better—she'd run from him.

"Is it dead?" Shay asked harshly.

A haunted look filled her eyes. "It got away."

I want to kill it. He couldn't. Tracking would be impossible in a city of concrete and metal and far too many bodies. He eyed the way she fingered her sleeve. Still upset. Unhappy. He'd done that. "Sorry, Bree."

Surprised, she looked up. "You've never used my name before."

Shay laughed. "Got you pegged, doesn't she?"

With an effort, Zeb pulled his gaze from hers and searched for a diversion. A photo lay on the coffee table. He walked over to look, needing to escape his growing awareness of her as a female. Perhaps it was good she was leaving.

The picture was the one she'd shown to Thorson.

Shay followed. "You were a pretty toddler, a leannan."

She had dimples when she smiled. "Thank you. Now tell me, what does *a leannan* mean?"

"It's something like sweetheart or darling," Zeb said. Apparently, Shay wasn't immune to the breakfast bunny either, and yet, the knowledge didn't raise Zeb's hackles.

"Darling. That's almost as patronizing as little female." Bree frowned at Shay who shot an evil look at Zeb.

As Zeb set the photo down, he saw a *lifemating* bracelet. Silver discs progressed from a thin crescent moon to a full circle and back down. Magic-enhanced silver wires between them ensured the band would change sizes during a trawsfur. How had a human come by it? "You find this around here?"

"No. I've had it, oh, forever." She gave him a smile as fragile as the bracelet. "I was abandoned and only had these two things."

Perhaps a human had found the bracelet and given it to the pup as a toy? But the photo was of the Wild Hunt, implying a tie to the Daonain.

She wasn't of the clan though. She carried no shifter scent, and she was far past the age when a Daonain begins to trawsfur. Perhaps her parents knew some shifters.

"You were lost in a forest when they found you," Shay said.

"Why, yes. How did you know?" Breanne asked.

Shay winced. Apparently, Breanne had talked to her doggie friend. What else had *Elvis* learned?

"I thought that's what Zeb meant," Shay answered in an innocent voice.

Her eyes narrowed.

Someone pounded on the door.

When Bree startled, Zeb instinctively moved between her and the entrance.

Shay took point and answered the door. "Evening, Alec."

Alec was still in his sheriff's uniform. "I couldn't find you at the lodge, and I heard voices here. I thought we were meeting at eleven."

Zeb glanced at the sky, visible through the doorway. Late.

"Sorry. We lost track of time," Shay said. "Our renter stuffed us like geese for the slaughter."

Shay returned to Bree and held out his hand. After a second, she put her fingers into his grasp. "Thank you, Breanne. It was the best meal I've had in a long time."

"You're welcome. Thank you for all the help."

Before she could pull away, Shay drew her hand to his lips and kissed her palm so slowly and thoroughly that a flush rose in her cheeks.

As Shay joined Alec, Zeb took his place. Unable to resist pushing her limits himself, he cupped her cheek. Silky smooth and pale. The little female was like peach tree wood, delicate grained, but incredibly durable. "I also thank you." He paused. "Bree."

Her breath hitched.

Pleasure rippled through him, for along with the faint scent of fear, he caught something more elusive—a whiff of arousal.

Chapter Twelve

Cold Creek, North Cascades Territory ~ Dark of the moon

MY LAST NIGHT *here*. Her three weeks had flown by, and tomorrow, she'd leave for home. Only she didn't have a home any longer, did she? Melancholy shadowing her, Bree stood in her doorway, staring into the night. No moon ruled the sky, and darkness reigned. The cabin echoed with emptiness.

Faint country music wafted from The Wild Hunt like an invitation. She stepped into the cabin to get her coat and purse. The tavern would have people and noise. Just what she needed.

A few minutes later, she pulled into the half-empty parking lot. Strange—the place was usually packed on a Friday night. As she grabbed her purse and slid out of the car, Boot Scootin' Boogie drifted through the air unchallenged by loud voices.

No matter. Calum and probably Vicki would be there. Maybe Shay and Zeb also, since the lodge was dark.

The thought of the two men made her smile. Shay had kissed her palm, and the look in his eyes had said he'd wanted to do more. Lots more. Just thinking about him set off a tugging deep in her lower half, a...wanting.

Not only him either. The memory of how Zeb had cupped her face in his big hand seemed to heat up the chill night.

Bad Bree. How could she be attracted to both Shay *and* his partner? But she was. Her arms wrapped around herself as she remembered the way Zeb's dark, dark eyes would glint with amusement, how a corner of his mouth would curl up, almost against his will, at something she'd said. She wanted him to wrap those muscular arms around her.

She stared at the tavern, shocked to realize that for the first time, she was actually *interested* in guys...like a perfectly normal woman. Jeez, this was so amazing.

Delighted with herself, she spun in the pale glow of the streetlight, then stopped at a sound from the right.

A small figure trotted across the road with something in her arms. Blonde hair glinted in the parking lot lights. Slender. Young. Vicki's daughter.

Zipping up her sweatshirt, Bree walked toward her. "Jamie, what are you doing out here?"

The girl stopped, so revved up that she hummed like a race-car engine. "Hey, Bree." She was holding a squirming puppy. "I heard something crying, and I snuck out. Some tourist must have tossed him in the ditch." She giggled as the fuzzball energetically licked her chin. "Isn't he cute?"

Bree fondled the downy soft ears. "He's adorable." She glanced at the ditch, then the second floor where Vicki said they lived. "You heard him from up there?"

"I've got good ears." Jamie shifted her weight with a nervous glance at the tavern. "I need to get inside. We're not supposed to go out after dark tonight, and if Daddy finds out, I'll be doing dishes for a month."

We? "Scoot." Hopefully the girl wouldn't get into trouble for her good deed.

As Jamie trotted toward the private gate at the right of the building, Bree headed for the bar. Her anticipation started to rise. Would Zeb or Sh—

A terrified scream split the night air. A yelp of pain.

Bree spun and broke into a run. "Jamie? Jamie!"

There she was—sprawled on the ground, trying to stand. The puppy cowered against her legs.

"Are you okay?"

"I saw something. Something awful." Jamie regained her feet and snatched up the dog. She turned in a circle, her young face twisted with fear.

As Bree searched the darkness, she smelled it. Decaying meat, rotten orange peels. *The monster.* Her heart slammed into overdrive.

Had it followed her from Seattle?

A rustling noise came from the right, barely audible over the country music. Probably no one inside had heard the kid scream. Undoubtedly, the monster had.

Quietly, despite her trembling hands, Bree slid the pistol from her bag. "Come here, Jamie. Now." She dropped her purse and shoved the kid behind her. The memory of doing the same with Ashley stabbed at her, but a spark of anger burned away some fear. This time...this time, she'd kill the thing.

"Bree," Jamie whispered. "It's—"

"Shhh. You run..." Bree paused. The creature had attacked Ashley first. Did running incite it? "Wait till it charges me. Then you run. And scream for help." Step by step, she backed them toward the tavern. *Please, God, let me get the child close enough to get in the door.*

"It's a hellhound." Jamie pressed closer. "I don't think—"

The leafless bushes at the lot's edge rustled, and the monster stepped out. Huge. Bony plates. Eyes the color of dried blood.

It is—it really is the monster. Bree's hands turned cold and numb, and she gasped for air, not finding any. As her body remembered the horrific pain, every nerve shrieked for her to flee. Screams echoed in her memory. She spun...and bumped into Jamie.

A child. Can't run. She fought the constriction in her lungs. *I have a weapon.*

The monster advanced a few steps, red-brown eyes focused on them. But it seemed smaller. Thinner.

It *was* smaller. Not the same creature? There were more?

With a vicious snarl, the hellhound trotted across the lot toward them.

Bree took a step forward and snapped, "Run, Jamie!"

Don't let it look at the girl. As Jamie fled, screaming shrilly, Bree aimed. She pulled the trigger three times. Bullets hit the creature along the head and shoulders. Dull thuds. A ping as something hit the concrete. Why wasn't it bleeding? Dying?

Terror iced her belly as the creature advanced, step by step. She couldn't stop it. The shark-shaped head turned toward Jamie.

No no no. You can't have her. Bree charged and pulled the trigger. If she could divert it long enough…

Even as the pistol clicked on empty, the creature veered toward the child.

Bree rammed into its shoulder. It staggered back a step, then turned.

Jaws closed over her forearm. Its teeth punched through her sweatshirt, through her skin, into her flesh. Pain ripped up her arm. *Hurts; it hurts.* As her vision fogged, her knees buckled.

Something barreled into the creature.

It released her and whirled.

Bree gasped. "No, Jamie!" But it wasn't the kid.

Zeb had hit it. On his hands and knees, he tried to dodge, but the hellhound grabbed his leg. He grunted in pain.

No! Arm burning like fire, Bree scrambled to her feet.

Elvis darted from the darkness and attacked from the rear. The big dog's growls filled the air.

With a snarl, the monster dropped Zeb and whipped

around.

Elvis jumped away—too slow. He yelped as the monster caught him, shook, and flung him across the concrete.

Zeb rolled to his feet, pulling a pistol from a tied-down holster. "Hey!"

The monster turned, and Zeb fired. The bullets thudded dully. Some were deflected off the plating, shattering the concrete.

"Fuck." With a growl, Zeb pulled a knife from a hip sheath and planted his feet.

An uncontrollable scream rose in Bree's throat. His knife wouldn't work. It would break as hers had. The men had no idea what this was.

The monster charged Zeb.

Snatching her revolver off the ground, Bree threw it, then gravel as well. "Get away from him!"

It veered toward her…

Elvis attacked again. The monster snapped around and ripped at the dog's furry neck. Elvis gave a pained, gut-wrenching whine.

Zeb lunged forward in a low dive, hit the pavement on his shoulder, and rolled onto his back. Half-under the monster, he punched his knife up into the beast's belly.

In. The knife went in. Bree stared as Zeb slashed toward the monster's back legs, gutting it like a chicken.

Dark blood gushed. Everywhere. Snarling continuously, the creature staggered. Fell. It landed heavily on Zeb, and he cursed.

As the rust-colored eyes filled with emptiness, Bree panted. Would it get up? In movies, monsters always came back to life.

It didn't move. And Zeb was alive, swearing and trying to shove out from under the thing.

Elvis. His furry body lay unmoving.

"No. No, this can't happen." Tears blurring her eyes, Bree

ran to him. Not Elvis. Not another death. Oh please. She fell to her knees beside the dog. He whined. Still alive. She hugged him with her uninjured arm. "You saved us. Please be okay."

But blood poured from his gashed flesh, warm over her chilled fingers. Too much blood.

Choking on sobs, she tried to check how badly he was hurt, but the lot was too dark and kept getting darker. She heard people running, yelling. Getting closer, even as the noise slowly faded...

SHAY! ZEB TRIED to see over the hellhound's body, but fucking plating pinned his legs against the concrete.

The sound Shay had made rang in his ears. And Bree—where was she? Sweating with fear, Zeb shoved at the hellhound, ripping his leathers, then his skin on the sharp points of the armor. Finally, it shuddered and died, shifting back to its lighter human form.

"Fucking demon scum." Zeb pushed the corpse off and staggered to his feet. Pain blazed down his leg as he half-ran, half-limped to Shay.

Find Bree too. How the hell had she gotten hurt? In a town of shifters, no hellhound would attack a human. It should have gone straight for Calum's werecat kid.

When Zeb reached Bree and Shay, he tried to kneel. His leg buckled, and his knees impacted the pavement in a blast of agony. "Fuck!" Teeth clenched, he slid closer.

Bree was out cold, lying half across the wolf.

"Dammit, little female." His chest tightened as he remembered how she'd deliberately drawn the hellhound's attention. So appallingly gutsy. He gently moved her off of Shay, so he could check their wounds.

His gut clenched. Blood everywhere, from both of them: matting the fur on Shay's shoulder and neck, drenching Bree's pale blue sleeve with darkness. Fuck, where was he supposed to start?

The weaker human. He tore her sweatshirt sleeve away. By the God of the Hunt. Her arm looked like she'd shoved it in a wood chipper. Delicate female skin—wrong to see it damaged. The scent of blood filled the air. Too late. Again, too late.

He pressed his palm over her wounds, trying to staunch the terrifyingly fast flow of blood.

People were coming, at long fucking last. Three cahirs ran across the parking lot from the direction of the road. More people poured from the tavern, and he realized the fight had lasted only a minute or so.

Spotting Calum and his daughter in the lead, Zeb yelled, "Get medical supplies!"

"I will," the Cosantir's cub yipped. "I'll get them." She spun around, dashing back to the bar.

Calum reached them first and simply ripped the sleeve off his white shirt. He knelt beside Shay and used the fabric as a bandage, putting pressure against the wolf's neck wound.

Shay didn't make a sound.

Dammit, Shay. Zeb found it hard to breathe. "Is he…?"

"He's alive." Calum motioned one of the cahirs over. "Owen, Donal returned yesterday. Get him up here."

"Aye, Cosantir." Owen pulled a cell phone from his pocket.

In a lower voice, Calum ordered the other cahir, "Ben, get the humans out of here before the healer arrives."

"Will do, Cosantir."

"We heard screaming." Alec dropped down beside Zeb, scowled at his leg and Bree's arm. "There's a mess."

The Cosantir's cub skidded to a stop. "Daddy, here's the stuff." Choking with sobs, she laid a metal box on the ground.

"Thank you, Jamie. Now go back in the tavern." Calum silenced her protest with a glance. As she left, he flipped up the lid of the medical kit with one hand and handed Zeb dressing supplies. "Tend your leg."

As Zeb took the gauze, Calum said, "Alec, see to the girl."

Every territorial instinct in Zeb objected. *Mine.* Biting back his protest, he started wrapping his leg.

Alec pulled supplies from the box and pressed a handful of gauze to Bree's arm. She moaned, rousing enough to pull away.

With a snarl, Shay scrambled to his feet and snapped at Alec.

The cop snatched his hand back. "By the God, Shay."

Shoulder and neck streaming blood, Shay positioned himself over Bree and growled.

"Shay, stop it." Relief lightened Zeb's voice—his partner was alive.

When Alec tried to touch Bree, Shay growled again. "Well, that's helpful," Alec said, holding the useless bandages. "You'd think he was her mate."

"So it seems," Calum said.

The other two cahirs were still moving people away. Headlights streamed down the road as the parking lot emptied of cars. Despite shaking hands, Zeb finally knotted the fucking dressing on his leg. Bree was bleeding. He must—

"Zebulon."

"Cosantir?"

"Take the dressings and bind up Breanne's arm. Shay might permit *you* to touch her."

Finally able to do as he needed, Zeb snatched the gauze pads and rolls from Alec. He shoved a wad of gauze against Shay's ripped up neck and curved his hand over it, holding it here. With his shoulder, he nudged the wolf sideways. "Move, dummy."

As the wolf eased over, Zeb used the gauze in his free hand to put pressure on the mess the hellhound had made of Bree's arm.

Her cry of pain broke Zeb's heart.

Shay snarled, and he snarled back. "You bite me and I'll break your fucking teeth."

With a low whine, Shay leaned against Zeb's side, and the warmth was comforting. But Bree's bleeding didn't slow, and the gauze Zeb held on Shay's neck was already blood-soaked. Fuck. Would the idiot let someone care for the wound on his shoulder?

A car roared into the lot and screeched to a halt a few feet away.

"Thank the Mother," Alec muttered.

As the lanky driver dashed over, Zeb spotted a silvery crescent-moon on his cheekbone—the mark of a healer—and he echoed Alec's sentiment.

Shay growled weakly as the man approached.

Zeb huffed an exasperated breath. "That's the healer, and by Herne's big balls, you need one." Quickly. Not even a cahir could bleed forever.

A human would have even less time. He looked up at the Cosantir. "What about Bree?"

"An ambulance is on the way from the valley. Keep pressure on her arm." Calum's eyes were dark with frustrated anger as he walked over to speak with Owen. Zeb understood. But a Cosantir's power didn't include the ability to snuff out hellhounds.

That was a cahir's job. Zeb's guilt increased.

"This is the new cahir, right?" The healer knelt and reached for Shay.

The wolf twisted. With his nose, he nudged the healer's hand toward Bree.

"She's not Daonain, Shay," Alec said. "The healer can't help her."

Shay growled at Alec, then whined at Zeb.

Did Shay think she was a shifter? Not possible. She had a human scent. Yet the hellhound had attacked her, not Jamie. With the scent of a Daonain in the area, the demon-dog shouldn't have wasted a moment on a human. Zeb stared at Bree, tracking the elusive thought, trying not to panic at how much blood Bree and Shay were losing. *Maybe...maybe.* "Cosantir?"

Calum returned and gripped Zeb's shoulder with a pulse of power. "Cahir, what do you require?"

He tried to speak quickly, yet make sense. "I think... As a child, she was found with a lifemating bracelet."

"Was she now?" Calum murmured. "Go on."

"The hellhound attacked her instead of going after Jamie. And Shay..."

Despite the blood loss and the tremors shaking his body, the wolf still tried to guard Bree.

"That's not how a shifter acts toward a human," Zeb finished, trying to keep pressure on Shay's neck and instill strength into his partner through his touch. Fuck, the stubborn mongrel was going to bleed to death in front of them all.

"No. It isn't." Calum took a knee beside Zeb, caught his gaze, and held it. "How do *you* feel toward Breanne, Zebulon?"

"Like Shay." Insanely protective didn't even come close.

"So." The Cosantir considered only a second. "Donal, try to heal the girl first. Let's see if you succeed."

"But..." Donal's silver-gray eyes showed his protest.

The Cosantir tilted his head in a silent command.

"As you will, Cosantir." Taking Zeb's place, Donal pulled the gauze back, hissing as the damage to Bree's arm was revealed. He glanced at Calum in obvious disapproval of wasting time, then bent his dark head and set his hands around the wound.

Zeb pulled Shay closer so he could put pressure on his

shoulder wound as well. And he watched.

Magic shimmered the air as the Mother's soothing power moved through the healer. The bleeding slowed. Zeb held his breath as if a noise would start the flow again.

The healer pushed the white tendons together, and the cords fused. Stayed. He moved to the muscles, layer by layer. His touch was slow, careful, thorough. Finally, he slid the pieces of skin together, like a jigsaw puzzle, and then only fragile pink lines remained to show Bree had been hurt.

Shay's tail thumped the ground.

"By the Mother," Zeb whispered. "She's one of us."

"Now the wolf," the healer said, using his forearm to wipe the sweat from his brow. He motioned Zeb away from Shay.

Zeb moved back gladly. A healer. Shay would live.

"One of us? That answers a question or two," Alec commented.

"And raises more," Calum said dryly. "She doesn't smell like a shifter, and I don't sense her as one either. If she were thirteen, this would make sense, but she's far too old to never have trawsfurred."

From the pain in his leg, Zeb knew he'd fall if he tried to stand. Instead, he scraped across the concrete to the little female. As her eyes fluttered open, he couldn't keep from gathering her up. Small and soft and so fucking brave.

His hand on Shay's neck, Donal glanced over his shoulder. "Cosantir, no matter how old, that female is a shifter, and she's got major problems."

"...*IS A SHIFTER*..."

Bree heard a man's voice as she wakened. She started to panic, then remembered: the monster was dead. Zeb had killed it.

Warmth surrounded her. The roar of pain in her arm had died to an aching noise.

After a moment, she realized someone had her on his lap. Her cheek lay against a solid chest—a man's chest. His heartbeat thudded in her ear.

When she tried to sit up, she heard a rumble of denial, and the arms tightened. "Stay put, little female."

"Zeb?" She tilted her head, but saw only his corded neck and the strong, clean line of his jaw. As he held her firmly against him, he rubbed her back in slow, comforting strokes.

She sighed as exhaustion blurred her mind. Everyone was alive, but no—they were hurt. She jerked upright, and Zeb grunted in pain.

"S-sorry," she stammered. His leg—the monster had bitten him. He was bleeding while she sat all comfy on his lap. Was he insane? "Let me up. I need to check your leg. And Elvis too."

"Shhh." He snuggled her closer, and his long hair brushed against her cheeks in a soothing kiss. "I'm okay. Donal's taking care of…Elvis."

She should check anyway. From Sensei's classes, she'd learned men never admitted to being hurt. She tried to get up, despite Zeb's hold, but the effort only made her muscles tremble. "Why do I feel so weak?"

"A healing uses some of your own energy. You'll be tired for a while."

"A what?"

"Dammit, lie down." A man's voice.

Bree lifted her head. People everywhere. Calum and Alec, others.

Elvis stood in front of her and Zeb, facing away. A tall, dark-haired man was coaxing the dog to lie down, but Elvis didn't move. He was guarding them.

"Fuck, Shay," Zeb said and tried to rise with her in his arms.

"Let me up." Struggling against Zeb's hold, Bree looked for Shay. He could help with Elvis.

With a grunt of exasperation, the stranger turned to Calum. "Cosantir, he's too agitated to cooperate. The humans are gone. Shift him back."

"Seamus." Calum grabbed the loose skin on the dog's neck, holding Elvis despite his effort to pull away. His voice deepened, vibrated like the lowest key on a church organ. "*Trawsfur.*"

The dog blurred as if a mist had surrounded him, and then Shay appeared on hands and knees. Naked. No dog.

"No!" The monster had changed like that. In her apartment. To a man. And then... Panic swept through Bree, and she struggled against Zeb's merciless hold. "Let me go!"

"Shhh." His deep rough voice anchored her against waves of terror. "That's Shay. You know Shay. He'd never hurt you, Bree."

She shuddered in a breath. Shay. Not a monster.

His shoulder was a ghastly, mangled mess. His neck was worse. Like Elvis's had been.

Tears burned her eyes and spilled down her cheeks. "He's bleeding. We need to help him."

"The healer will."

Alec laid a blanket on the ground beside Shay. "Here, cahir. Onto this."

Still on hands and knees, arms shaking, Shay didn't move. His steel-blue eyes were glazed as he looked at her and Zeb.

"She's all right," Zeb said. "Get your fucking ass on the blanket and let the healer work."

Shay shook the hair out of his eyes, staring at her.

"I'm okay," she whispered.

With a low groan, Shay collapsed sideways. The white blanket started to turn red.

"'Bout time." The dark-haired guy knelt and put his hands

right into the open neck wound. Shay's face contorted in pain.

Bree struggled. "No, he's hurting him. What's he *doing*?"

Shay didn't make a sound although the muscles in his jaw corded tight.

"Shhh. It's okay," Zeb murmured. His arms caged her.

She strained against his embrace and—

Shay's bleeding slowed. When the man's fingers nudged the gaping edges closer, the flesh remained together.

She blinked, shook her head. Dreaming? A dog turns into Shay? A person makes bleeding stop? How was he *doing* that?

The man sagged, his face turning pale. His shoulders heaved as he gasped for breath.

Calum grasped his collar and tugged until he no longer touched Shay. "Stop before you damage yourself, Donal."

"I can—"

"You cannot." Calum glanced at his brother. "Alec, find some women Donal has mated with—"

Alec grinned. "Ahead of you, *brawd*. I already called a couple. Should be here any minute."

"He's speaking English, but he's not making sense," Bree whispered fuzzily to Zeb.

He made a low sound, almost a laugh, and actually nuzzled her hair.

A car turned into the lot, and a woman jumped out. No coat. Her shirt misbuttoned. When Donal beckoned to her, she dropped to her knees, embracing him from the back. Donal revived as if the woman was water in a desert. Leaning forward, he set his hands around the ripped flesh on Shay's shoulder.

Bree could only watch in fascination.

After another minute, Shay pulled away. The wound was mostly closed. No longer bleeding. "Enough, Healer. Help Zeb before you exhaust your strength." Mouth set in determination, he pushed himself to a sitting position on the blanket.

After studying Shay for a moment, the healer nodded. "Trade places with your brother then."

"He's not—" Shay started. Stopped.

The healer gave him a steady look. "Most brothers share a womb. Some, instead, share life and blood and death."

Shay's head turned, and he stared at Zeb with an unreadable expression. Pain and exhaustion and...something else. "Well." His voice was husky, strained. "Guess you're right."

Bree realized Zeb had stopped breathing. His muscles were rigid.

Shay let Alec pull him to his feet. Taking a step forward, he looked down at Bree. And Zeb. "*A bhràthair*, give Bree to me and let the healer tend you."

Silence.

Zeb's chest expanded as he pulled in a slow breath. His voice sounded as if he'd swallowed gravel. "Brother."

Shay's shoulders relaxed. Still staring at Zeb, he lifted Bree into his arms.

As Zeb was helped onto the blanket by the healer, Shay settled onto the pavement, adjusting her in his lap.

She felt his cheek rest on the top of her head for a moment. "By the God, you scared me, Breanne," he murmured. "I'll yell at you later."

Okay. She leaned against his shoulder, soaking up the warmth of his body. Shudders ran through her, and yet, as with Zeb, she felt safer than she'd felt...ever.

I'm sitting on a naked man who was a dog a few minutes ago.

It didn't seem to matter. Exhaustion swept over her and dragged her back into the depths.

HOURS LATER IN Breanne's cabin, Shay watched her sleep. By Herne's hooves, she'd come so close to dying. Her tiny freckles stood out on a pure white face. Needing to reassure himself she was alive, he brushed his knuckles over her cheek. Warm.

She was going to be all right.

With a groan of exhaustion, he walked out into the main room.

Legs stretched out in front of him, beer in hand, Zeb rested in a chair and stared at the fire in the small woodstove.

My *brother*. When he concentrated, Shay could feel the link to Zeb, warming the deep places inside. He'd shared the same tie to his littermates before they'd died. This bond might have been there a while, but the healer's recognition had brought it into the light.

He wasn't alone in this world any longer. "Mo bhràthair." *My brother.*

Zeb lifted his head, and the acknowledgement showed in his eyes. Not that the gruff wolf would say anything.

Not that anything needed to be said.

Shay pulled a battered leather chair closer to the woodstove and imitated Zeb's position, noticing a cold beer for him on the end table. Soothed by the crackle of the fire, he watched a salamander dance in the flames. His bones felt filled with lead, the familiar aftermath of a healing, and his partly healed wounds and bruises ached. Didn't matter though. Not when they were all alive.

Might not have been. If he and Zeb hadn't already been headed back to report in, Breanne and Jamie would be dead. If Breanne hadn't been insanely brave and diverted the hellhound's attention, he and Zeb would have died. If a healer hadn't been available, they all might have returned to the Mother.

He touched his shoulder and neck—tender, but intact. No additional scars this time. If the Mother graced a shifter with her touch, she didn't leave scars. Just warmth and love. What would it be like to be a healer and have that sensation moving through you? He shook his head and opened his beer.

Zeb glanced at Shay's neck, then his own leg. "Cold Creek's smaller than Ailill Ridge, but has a healer."

Odd how their thoughts often followed the same trail. "If you were a healer, who would you choose for your Cosantir? Calum or Pete?"

"Good point." Zeb turned his gaze back to the fire. "She's a shifter."

"Explains the lifemating bracelet."

"I don't get the bracelet being on a cub."

"My mother let us wear hers. Just for a minute. It gives you a sense of the Mother, almost like when you trawsfur." Smiling at the memory, Shay glanced at his new brother. Had Zeb's mother never shared? Or perhaps she'd not been lifemated. Not all mothers were.

"You figure she wore the bracelet when her parents were killed."

"Seems like. Car accident. Hellhound. Avalanche. She may never find out what happened." Shay glanced at the bedroom, his ears tuned to her slow breathing.

"Rough way to start a life." Zeb drank some beer, then his rare grin appeared. "When she wakes up, *Elvis* might end up neutered."

Shay winced. "By the God, she's going to be upset." He'd first accompanied her as a wolf because she'd worried him. So weak, but determined to push herself up the trails. But after she grew stronger, he went simply because he liked her company. Liked seeing her increasing delight in the forest.

"Yep." Zeb leaned his head back, his face in shadow. "She's a shifter, *brawd*. We going to do anything about that?"

It took a second for Shay to get past being called *brother* before he comprehended what Zeb had asked. *Did they want to try to win her as their mate?* "I—no." The taste in Shay's mouth turned bitter. "You could pursue her, but I can't. No female would want me for a mate."

"Oathbound?"

"Aye." Shay rubbed his jaw, searching for words. "When Cosantirs send requests for help with hellhounds, I can pick and choose like you do. But if Herne summons me to a location, I have to obey. My mate would have to follow, and everywhere I'm sent, the hellhounds are the worst. She'd never be safe. I'm oathbound until death, and face it, my life won't be long. What female would tolerate that?"

In the two years they'd been partners, Zeb had never asked about Shay's past. Now the question lurked in his silence.

Shay owed his brother the truth. "I'd led my pack for only a year, then I lost a member to a hellhound." Mason had been scrawny teenager with green eyes. The hellhound had left very little behind. Shay'd been furious that something—whatever it was—had killed one of his wolves. "Although the pup's blood was still warm, the elders advised against going after the creature. They'd heard of hellhounds." Shay gave a bitter laugh. "I ignored them. I took the males, and we trailed it. My brothers and I led."

He'd seen the hellhound and charged. So stupid. "It caught me, shook me like a rat, and threw me into a tree." Shay's throat tightened, but he forced the words out. "By the time, I roused, my brothers were dead."

"A hellhound let you live?" Zeb asked incredulously.

"Dawn was close. The fighting delayed the hellhound, and it fled…too late. The sun caught it, forced it to human form, and my wolves tore it apart."

"Lucky timing."

"Aye." The demonkin could have killed his whole pack. "When I saw…" Peter and Thomas had died in agony because they'd tried to save his worthless hide. With his littermates gone, only the need for vengeance had remained for Shay. "I gave the pack to a wiser wolf and offered Herne my oath in return for making me a cahir." A cahir possessed the size and strength to fight hellhounds. He leaned his head back.

Although the fire had died to coals and a chill crept around the edges of the room, Shay felt the warmth of the brother-bond inside him. The thought of losing it was hard, but he forced the words out. "Eventually, Herne will summon me to the next territory that needs me." Into the loud silence, he added, "If you want Breanne, you should stay here."

Zeb turned, his face unreadable. "You dumping me? *Brawd?*" Pain threaded his voice.

"By the God, no. Not willingly."

"My place is at your side, asshole." Yet Zeb glanced at the bedroom door, and his unhappiness matched Shay's.

Breanne was special, pulling at Shay in ways he'd never felt before. But she deserved a life. Trying to win her, to see if she'd choose them, mustn't happen. The knowledge joined the ache in his bones.

But at least, when he left here, it would be with his brother. Shay pulled in a slow breath. "Then we travel together."

"Fucking right." Zeb opened the door of the woodstove and tossed a log on the dying coals. As the wood caught fire, the salamander rose to twirl and dance in the golden flames.

Chapter Thirteen

WAKING UP SUCKED. Bree's head hurt. Everything hurt. And there was an excessive amount of sunlight coming through the window. She squinted at it in annoyance.

Shay slept in a chair beside her bed. The lines beside his mouth had deepened, and he looked as tired as she felt. When she stirred, he woke immediately. "Look who's back among the living." He leaned forward to stroke her hair off her face. His hand was gentle, and she pressed her cheek against his warm palm, needing the comfort.

Where had that lost feeling come from? As she pushed up in the bed, her arm flared with pain.

"Hold on." He stood. Hands around her waist, he effortlessly lifted her to a sitting position. His face was so close she could see the dark gray circle around his blue irises. "Better?" he murmured, eyes intent.

Far too aware of the strength of his hands, she couldn't move, couldn't look away. "Uh. Yes?"

His lips curved. After he resumed his seat, he leaned forward and set his elbows on his knees. The sleeves of his blue and green flannel shirt were rolled up, showing off the thick muscles of his forearms and his golden tan.

He was tanned all over, she knew, because she'd seen him

naked last night. She shook her head. *Right. Dreaming, Bree.*

"Breanne?"

She frowned. "Why are you here?" *In my bedroom?*

"You were hurt pretty badly. The healer closed the wounds on your arm, but he didn't like the way you passed out later. We were worried."

Healer. Hurt. A chill swept up her spine as she stared down at her bloody, ripped sweatshirt. Her arm—the right arm had ugly, lumpy red scars from a month ago. Her left forearm had areas of fragile pink skin, but was perfectly smooth. "That wasn't a dream?" she whispered, her chest tightening.

A monster. Her hands clenched. *In the bushes, the smell, Jamie screaming.* "A creature attacked us." *The pain as teeth tore through her clothes, her skin. Her terror for Zeb. Elvis bleeding everywhere. Calum taking the dog's...*

She stiffened. Calum had grabbed Elvis's neck and then Shay had appeared. "Oh my God, you're a dog. Elvis." Her voice squeaked. "It's a dream, right?" He didn't even have a beard—how could have fur?

"No dream, a leannan."

Zeb walked into the bedroom, carrying a steaming cup. Even though he scowled at her, he made her feel awfully female. And exposed.

She pulled her covers higher and stuck her chin out. "What?"

"You attacked a hellhound," he growled. "Are you fucking nuts?"

"Oh, well, next time I'll let it kill a little girl." Jamie would have died just like Ashley had. *Torn apart.* The memory lodged in her chest and choked her. She turned her face toward the wall, blinking hard.

"Breanne?" Shay's deep voice was gentle.

But he'd transformed, just like the thing in her apartment.

And then, the creature-man had… She swallowed. *Don't think of that.*

Everything about last night felt warped, like when she'd read the original fairy tales—the ones that didn't have happy endings, and little boys and girls get killed. Or cooked by the bad witch. Eaten by the wolf.

A chill ran down her spine as she stared at Zeb, then Shay. *I don't know these people at all.* Shay had turned into a dog. "Out," she said. "Both of you. Get out."

"But—" Shay protested.

She pointed her finger at the door, shivering at the thought they might not leave.

Stalking away, Shay shoved past Zeb. "Nice going, dumbass."

"We'll talk later, little female." Zeb's hard gaze was a woolen blanket of attention, prickly, yet warm. "About last night. And about what happened in your city that still upsets you so much." He set the cup on the bedside stand with a thump and left, closing the door behind him.

She waited, half-expecting their return. A minute passed.

Her hand shook as she picked up the drink. She sniffed it suspiciously. Broth. Well, if they wanted her dead, they'd had the opportunity last night. When she swallowed some, wonderful heat slid all the way to her stomach.

After another sip, she tried to think. She'd been attacked by a monster—a *hellhound*—only not the same one as in Seattle. There were more. She shivered. The city one still lived. But she had a gun now.

Only…her bullets hadn't worked. Her eyes squeezed shut as she remembered firing her revolver. The hellhound had kept coming. *I have no defense against it at all.*

As her hand shook, broth sloshed over the cup sides. Wait. Zeb had knifed the creature, and it died. So a monster could be killed. It *could*.

She drank more broth to fortify herself, then examined her bitten arm. She'd been bleeding badly, but now only pink lines remained. Zeb didn't limp today. No bandages showed on Shay's neck. That silvery-eyed man really had done some new-age healing thing. She studied her arm and smiled. *Actually, I'm totally okay with this kind of healing.*

But definitely not the other stuff when Elvis had turned into Shay. She scowled. There was no way that she'd believe it. Uh-uh. Besides, she'd seen the dog and Shay at the same time. Hadn't she? She bit her lip. Zeb had made a joke about neutering, and Elvis had growled. The dog had listened to her, tilting its head, as if it understood. God, she'd told Elvis all sorts of stuff about her past.

Had she stumbled into a fairy-tale—or a nightmare? She wrapped her arms around her pillow. This world held monsters, dogs that were people, and men who could push flesh back together. *This is so not my life. I want to go back to my city, my job, my apartment. My home.* Her desire died as she remembered Seattle had a monster.

She pulled in a quivery breath. Okay then, fine. The only way to get through this was one step at a time. Like following a new recipe. She grimaced. Her first loaf of bread had been harder than the concrete blocks she broke in karate. Recipes don't always work.

So Shay turned into a dog. She stiffened. A dog? Or a wolf? Was he a werewolf? Her heart started to race. Was she going to turn into a creature too? *No no no.* Her hands fisted in the covers. But he hadn't bitten her. Her panting slowed. She'd been alone with him on long, long hikes, and he had never hurt her.

Last night, he'd attacked the monster. Tried to save her.

Her hands slowly unclenched. Werewolf or not, she owed the dog and Zeb her life. Her mouth tightened. And they darned well owed her a whole lot of answers.

As she tossed the covers back, she saw the blood on her sweatshirt. Her skin started to crawl. The monster had hurt her. "It only bit me," she whispered, "nothing else." Her self-reassurance didn't help. She was unclean. Soiled, inside and out. She could smell the stench on her body. *I need a shower.*

When she stood, the walls danced and spun. Her stomach twisted uneasily. She felt horrible, even worse than after the first hellhound's attack although it had done much more damage.

What's wrong with me?

IN THE MAIN cabin space with Zeb, Shay waited through the sounds of the shower and the rustling noises in the bedroom. The door opened.

Using the doorframe for support, Breanne paused. She'd changed into jeans and a loose dark green sweater. The way her full breasts moved beneath it showed she hadn't put on a bra. Shay tried not to notice. Unsuccessfully.

Dead pale, she still assessed the room like a warrior. He and Zeb both started to rise, but she shook her head at them. Her gait lacked her usual grace, and he had to grit his teeth not to help. As slow as an arthritic elder, she lowered herself into the armchair.

"I have questions for you two." The beauty of her voice defeated her attempt at sounding firm. By the God, she was pretty.

Zeb handed her a soda he'd fetched from the lodge. When she stared at the can as if it were a scorpion, he scowled. "We're guys. We don't do diet."

"Well. Thank you." She sipped, staring at the glass door of the woodstove. Another salamander had joined the first, and they chased each other into the stovepipe. When her gaze followed their movements, Shay realized she actually saw the OtherFolk. Like a Daonain, she had the Sight.

After hauling in a slow breath, she fixed Shay with a frown. "Did you turn into a dog and go hiking with me?"

"Well, that's blunt," Shay muttered. Damned if she didn't make him feel like he'd been blasted rude or something, so his answer was equally brusque. "Yes."

She blinked, then her dimples appeared. "Guess I deserved that. Sorry."

By Herne's hooves, her ability to laugh at herself drew him as strongly as her courage.

She drank more of her soda. "Can you guys explain what's going on? Please?"

Zeb's glance said the cowardly mutt was giving Shay that task.

At least Calum had ordered them to tell Breanne everything, and he didn't have to try to evade the truth. "We're called shifters or Daonain. We're descended from Fae shapeshifters. And you're one of us."

She went white.

Zeb glared at him.

Okay, maybe he'd gone too fast. "I do turn into—"

She held up her hand to pause him, and he could see her mind working. The female was so logical, it was scary. "You said *us*. You're not the only one who turns into a dog?"

Shay sighed. "Enough insults. I'm a wolf, not a damned pet."

"A werewolf? Like you bite people?"

"Fucking human movies." Zeb scowled. "No. We don't."

Her pretty blue eyes focused on Zeb like cop car spotlights. "You're a werewolf too?"

"Yes."

"And you think I'm a werewolf?"

Damn, she was calm. Shay smiled before he saw how her hands had wrapped, white-knuckled around the can. Not calm. *Controlled.* He said gently, "We know you're a shifter because our kind of healing doesn't work on humans. So yes, you should be able to change into an animal—cat, bear, or wolf."

"Werecat?" She blinked. "Like a Persian or Siamese?"

Zeb choked on his beer.

"More like a mountain lion." Shay added, "Calum, Alec, and Vicki are werecats."

Her eyes widened. "Vicki? No. No way. You gave me drugs." Bree tried to rise, but failed. "That's why I'm so weak. You gave me drugs and I dreamed—"

FIRM KNOCKING SILENCED Bree. She closed her eyes, trying not to scream or go into real hysterics. Vicki? Some sort of cat? Either Bree was going crazy or they'd drugged her. *I want a better set of drugs.*

Zeb answered the door. His deep voice rasped, "Cosantir."

Coatless, in a long-sleeved black shirt and black jeans, Calum stepped in. She scowled as he walked—no, *prowled*—across the room, like a cat or something.

She shook her head. *Last chance to hang on to reality, Bree. Next stop, a locked facility.* Then again, even nuthouses needed good chefs.

"Did you come to help explain?" she asked Calum.

"Not exactly." He assessed her with steel gray eyes. "I came to assign Seamus and Zebulon to act as your mentors." He glanced at the two men. "She needs to trawsfur without delay."

"Why the rush?" Shay asked.

"We restock our magic stores when we shift. Her healing depleted the scant magic she possessed. Donal thinks if she doesn't shift soon, she won't survive." He frowned at Bree. "Actually, he was shocked you're alive at all."

"Oh." Rather than terror, she felt relief. Was this why she'd grown weaker each month? But she could think about that later. Right now... What kind of weird stuff was Calum talking about?

Zeb and Shay watched her, as if she were a shook-up soda ready to explode.

"Listen, whatever a mentor does, I want a woman, like Vicki. Who are you to 'assign' me anything anyway?" She tried again to rise. Her legs failed. Shivering, she wrapped her arms around herself.

"Vicki has been a shifter less than a year, not long enough to mentor anyone. The only Daonain you've spent time with are Seamus and Zebulon." Calum's lips turned up in a faint smile. "I'm the one who will try to push you into your first trawsfur."

Zeb's head turned quickly. "She can't shift on her own?"

"Donal doesn't think so or she would have by now. Once the door is opened, she should be able to return. Opening it the first time might be difficult." Calum's eyes darkened ominously. "Shay, explain what will happen. Now. She's weakening as we talk."

"Am not—" Bree protested.

Ignoring her objections, Shay picked her up like a doll and sat with her in his lap. Even as her mind jittered, her body relaxed. He was warm, and she was so very cold.

"Listen." Shay pulled her closer until she heard his voice rumbling in his chest. "When a shifter hits puberty, the door to the wild—that's the way to becoming an animal—appears in our mind. Small door off in the back."

"You're being weird." *Door in my head. Next he'll tell me there's this big bridge in Seattle for sale...*

"Close your eyes and imagine yourself turning in circles. Look for it."

She lifted her head to give him an incredulous look, but he simply waited. Fine. She shut her eyes, imagined spinning like a blender blade. *No, Bree, they're not joking. Take this seriously.* She really looked and felt goosebumps creep up her arms. "There's something. I'm not sure it's a door—it's awfully dark." She opened her eyes in time to see Zeb's mouth flatten. "What?"

He glanced at Calum. "The Cosantir will help you open it."

His tight voice scared her. "I don't think I want—"

"The alternative is death." Shay shook her slightly to emphasize his words. "Now, once you're through—and the first time is a hell of a shock—you turn and locate that door in your head. You've got to come back through it to be human again. Calum can't do that for you, right, Cosantir?"

"I cannot. To push you into a shift is risky. If I intervene and draw you back before you've made a connection to the door, you might lose the way entirely. A shifter must trawsfur to stay alive."

"So once you're on four legs, you find your door. Then we'll go run in the forest." Shay squeezed her shoulder. "Breanne, being your animal is a wondrous thing. There's nothing as beautiful." His words were convincing, the look in his eyes more so.

Zeb's gaze met hers to say the same.

Her breathing wasn't under her control anymore, and her brain felt fuzzy. Worse, Calum was right. She could feel herself sagging, like a doll with the stuffing leaking out.

Calum opened the back door and waited.

"Okay," she whispered.

Zeb plucked her from Shay's arms and carried her outside. When he set her on her trembling legs, his iron-hard arm around her waist kept her upright. The cold wet ground chilled her bare feet. "I need shoes. A jacket."

"No, you don't. First lesson." Shay faced her. "Take off your clothes. Animals don't have fingers, and you'll rip your clothes trying to get them off." He demonstrated with a shocking lack of modesty and stood before her completely naked. God, he was gorgeous. The hard planes of his chest muscles rippled when he moved.

Then her eyes seemed to cross. To blur. He disappeared, and a fluffy dog—no, a wolf—took his place.

"Elvis?"

He padded over to sit at her feet.

"That's amazing." Stalling for time, she bent to stroke his soft fur. *Terrifying.*

When she straightened, Zeb said, "Strip, little female." Without waiting, he one-handedly tugged her sweater over her head.

She gasped and tried to cover her naked breasts. His arm held her steady as he unzipped her jeans. Paused. "Everything, Bree."

Shay had said that, but... *Me?* Naked in front of Calum and Zeb.

He waited. Calum did the same, obviously content to let her so-called mentors handle her.

Whining, Shay pawed at her bare feet so carefully she barely felt the scrape of his claws.

"Okay, fine." Her fingers shook as she pushed her jeans off her hips and let them fall around her ankles. Zeb held her up as she stepped out of them. She tried to pretend it was nothing. But the last time she'd been naked in front of a man, the monster had... A chill ran through her.

"Bree." Zeb lifted her chin and forced her to meet his black gaze. "Stay here. This is a shifting lesson, nothing else."

His piercing stare drew her back into the present. "Right." She endeavored a smile and whispered, "Thanks."

A crease appeared in his cheek although his lips stayed straight. "Cosantir. Now would be good."

Silently, Calum appeared at her other side. Zeb didn't move

away, and his closeness was a comfort. Calum curved his hand around her nape, gripping firmly. "Look at me."

She stared at the buttons of his shirt.

"*Now*, Breanne." The order couldn't be refused. She lifted her gaze and was trapped as his eyes turned from gray to an unfathomable black. She trembled, frozen in place.

"*Trawsfur*," he said, his voice cold and deep. In a wide-open stream of electricity, energy poured into her, lifting every hair on her body. The dark door in her mind quaked, and pain seared her veins as it slammed open.

She felt herself shoved through that space, tingling all over. *Falling.* She landed on her hands and knees, yelled in outrage, and heard a yelp. She was—her fingers were gone. She stared down at thin fur-covered legs and paws. Her paws. In the dirt. Oh. My. God.

A glowing warmth rose through her, brushing away the uncomfortable tingling, and filling her with soft energy. The feeling was like Thanksgiving when she'd cooked for friends. Rain poured down outside, but her home was filled with fragrant scents and laughter. Here on the edge of the wilderness forest, she felt that again. *Love. Belonging.*

As it faded, she shook her head and felt her ears flap. Like a dog.

"A werewolf, then," Calum said.

Panting with nervousness, she looked up. Zeb towered over her, and she tried to back up. Her way-too-many legs tangled, and she staggered sideways.

"Easy, little female." Zeb squatted and rubbed his hand along her cheek. As everything inside her hummed with pleasure, she edged closer, sniffing. He smelled really, really good.

"Bree," he said.

At the base of her spine, something quivered. Moved. A *tail.* She had a tail. Amazing. If she concentrated, it actually—

"*Bree.*"

She looked at him, and wow, her tail moved back and forth all on its own.

"Find the fucking door." Zeb's dark eyes crackled with intensity.

With an effort, she blocked out everything and looked into her own mind. Well, hey. The door was all big and shiny and even glowed a little.

"You find it?"

She wagged her tail.

"Good girl." His voice was a shivery, growly sound. "When it's time, open the door and step through. You clear on that, little female?"

She wagged her tail and looked around again. So much to see.

Zeb was undressing.

Shay, still a dog—no, a wolf—paced forward. His muzzle touched hers, then he stalked around her, sniffing, before standing in front of her again.

God, he smelled wonderful too, like power and mountains with a musky elusive scent. She trembled, and her tongue flicked out to lick his muzzle. Like it was something she should do.

He licked her back, making her tail wag uncontrollably.

She'd missed seeing Zeb without clothes—and wasn't that an interesting regret?—but he'd already turned into a wolf. With almost black fur, he was taller, yet more streamlined than Shay. If it were possible, Zeb looked even more deadly as a wolf.

He, too, walked around her, sniffing. His shoulder bumped against hers, giving her a feel for how much heavier and more powerful he was, and making something quiver deep inside her.

She whined.

Shay's head turned toward Calum.

Although the darkness was gone from his eyes, the air

around Calum rippled like waves rising from an overheated oven. He smiled at her. "You did well, Breanne. Listen to your mentors and enjoy your first trawsfur."

Even on four legs, Shay loomed over her. He licked her muzzle, and her attention snapped to him. With a low bark, he bounded away, heading into the forest. Zeb followed to the edge of the trees and looked back.

With a sharp yip she couldn't contain, Bree leaped after them, trying not to look down. Four legs…I have four legs.

Chapter Fourteen

*A*CK! BREE YELPED as her shoes fell off her hind paws. Her sweater bunched up, tangling her front legs.

She whined, trying not to panic as her own clothes trapped her. Shivering, she held still. The scents of the house—wood smoke, hazelnut coffee, herbal soap from the shower—washed over her. The breeze coming in the windows brought the fragrance of pine and snow. The mountains were calling her. She took a step in that direction and halted as her jeans slid off her haunches.

Door, door, where's the darned door? Time expanded to eternity before she found it and mentally opened it. She stepped through…and was on her hands and knees in the middle of her cabin. As the magical tingles danced over her skin, she bowed her head. Sweat chilled her forehead. Well, wasn't that fun?

After a couple of deep breaths, she pushed to her feet and wiggled her jeans up. *Werewolf am I? Not a very competent one.* How come the movies made it look so easy? With a resigned laugh, she adjusted the bra that had bunched under her arms. Maybe she should go without underwear until she got the hang of this stuff. She'd already popped into wolfy form twice today.

She glanced wistfully at the back door, but Shay and Zeb said she couldn't run the forest without one of them along. Not yet.

"Babysitters. At my age." She brushed her hands off and combed her hair back. "Huge babysitters, no less." After dropping onto the couch, she put her feet on the hand-hewn coffee table.

Shocking revelations or not, she physically felt great. How long had it been since she was healthy? Truly alive? Would she have slowly faded away to death in Seattle? She bit her lip. Apparently. But now, she was going to live, only…she was a werewolf. *I don't munch on people though. Ew.* And she hadn't trawsfurred into something grotesque like in the movies.

Last night in the cabin, Shay had called her over to the bathroom door mirror. Zeb had padded in to stand beside her. She'd looked so delicate next to him. Her fur was glimmery and pale as moonlight on her sides and legs. A darker gray streak ran down her back and marked her ears. Her cheek and neck fur was pure white. Really, she made a prettier wolf than a woman.

A wolf. *Jeez. I'm accepting this really well, aren't I?*

Now if she could only figure out what came next. Last night, the men had started to answer her questions, but she'd fallen asleep right there on the couch. One of them must have carried her to the bed and tucked her in. They sure held her a lot. The memory of Zeb's hard arms and his rumbling voice made her melt inside. And with Shay, so big he almost engulfed her, she felt small and fragile, and so, so safe. Did they see her as a woman or just another chore?

How did she want them to see her?

She shook her head. One thing at a time. Meantime, she had to learn to manage this wolfy shape. How to differentiate all the kazillion scents. Keep the legs moving in an organized manner—which she could mostly do, if she didn't think about it. Manage the weird maneuver of turning one ear forward and one back. She grinned. That was so cool.

How long would she be in Cold Creek? Should she, maybe, stay? The momentary hope startled her, then terrified her. *This isn't my place. Not at all. I have to go back to Seattle. That's my home.* But how did a shifter survive in a city? She frowned. What would the joggers in Discovery Park say if a wolf joined them...?

THE SUN WAS high overhead when Zeb turned and headed back down the mountain at a trot. Bree had kept up well; her endurance had improved over the last four days.

She was a damned fast little wolf—as long as she didn't overthink and get her legs tangled up. He tipped an ear to the rear, listening to the rhythm of her paws on the trail. She stayed close. The icy wind off the glaciers whipped through his fur, a welcome coolness after the hard run they'd finished, but wafting her scent to him. She'd had an appealing scent before; now, with the wild tang of a shifter added in, it was almost irresistible.

The wind veered and brought him the scent of a rat in the tangle of dead branches ahead. He let Bree catch up, then lifted his muzzle and sniffed.

She needed to learn to deal with prey, and a rodent was a good place to start. As she caught the scent, he stepped back to let her handle it.

She waited for the tiny betraying rustle, then pounced. She had the rat in her jaws. A crunch and whipping motion broke its neck. Good. She'd completed her first hunt, no matter how short. Her first taste of warm blood.

Instincts took over, and she had the rodent half-eaten before her brain caught up. And then she backed away from the carcass as if a bee had stung her nose. A second later, she was human. On her knees, she stared at the mess and scrubbed her hands over her face. She looked at the streaks of blood on her palms and her nose wrinkled.

Fuck, was she going to panic? Worried, he trawsfurred.

"Oh jeez, I ate a rat." She looked at him with horrified eyes. "I killed it and ate it. *Ewww*."

Something inside him tickled, increased to uncontrollable, and then he burst into laughter. She glared at him, making it worse, until he put his hands on his knees and just roared.

Her lips curved up reluctantly. "I've never heard you laugh like that. But it's not funny."

"It's just lunch." He considered and added, "I'd rather have field mice though. Crunchier—like popcorn."

She gave him a revolted look and swallowed hard.

Zeb tried to suppress another wave of laughter. By the God, he hadn't laughed that hard in...ever. He leaned against a tree and watched her. Pretty little female, her hair shining gold in the sunlight and tiny nose wrinkled in disgust. Usually she was pink from embarrassment, but now her skin was an even creamy color. Her breasts were beautifully large with nipples the same color as her lips. His hands twitched with the need to touch. "You still hungry?"

Her gaze averted from the bloody mess, she shook her head. "I may never eat again."

He nodded and shifted to a wolf, pausing long enough to finish off the rat. Nice appetizer—although from the way the little wolf's ears flattened, she probably wouldn't invite him to lunch now.

BREE FOLLOWED ZEB across the small creek toward her cabin. Her muscles felt warm and happy from the run. Lifting her nose, she checked the air. Wood smoke from the lodge, the lingering fragrance of oatmeal from breakfast, a rodent-something from the corner bush. Even as her ears pricked forward, she told herself, no more rats. *Ever. Ew.*

As she shifted to human, the wind whipped around her body, making her far too aware of her lack of clothes. Apparently, shifters didn't worry about the nakedness stuff. But she did. She put a hand on the doorknob, intent on getting into the jeans and shirt she'd left right inside.

"Wait, Bree."

She turned.

Still naked, Zeb walked over, close enough that his heat radiated to her through the chilling afternoon air. His skin held a dark fragrance, overwhelmingly masculine.

She took a step back and bumped into the closed door. "Um. What?"

Muscles rippled along his arms and shoulders as he set one hand on the wall and leaned on it. Under black chest hair, scars ran over his skin in various patterns—and her belly clenched as she realized some must be from hellhound claws.

He'd said he and Shay fought the monsters, that they were *cay-heers*, cahirs, who guarded the Daonain. She'd have to ask more about that...sometime.

Lower down, his stomach had those six-pack muscles the men liked to boast about, and his guy package was—she jerked her gaze back up. Heat flooded her cheeks.

He didn't say anything, but his expression had changed to that of a man looking at a woman he wanted.

"Um, did you want something?" Duh, bad way to phrase that. "To tell me something?"

He studied her face, making her even more nervous. "Don't forget tonight. The alpha is holding a run to introduce you to the pack."

"I remember." A social event. A bunch of wolfy shifters out for a night jog. Only, she'd be naked if she trawsfurred. A shiver of unease ran through her. "The alpha is, like, boss wolf?"

The corner of his mouth turned up. "Just like. His name's

Gerhard.

German? One of the waitresses had been German. A real sweetie. And a pack sounded nice. Like an instant family. She missed having women around. But there would be men she didn't know. "Will they...bother me? The men?" Make advances. Rape?

When he lightly rubbed his knuckles over her cheek, the sensation tingled through her. "No. We don't have enough females. You are cherished. Protected."

"What about s-sex?"

"You ever going to tell me what happened?"

Never. She shook her head.

His mouth tightened, then he said, "For sex, a female must want it or nothing happens."

Was he joking? "Fine, then there should be no problem." Too aware of how close he was, she tried to push him back. Under her palm, his skin stretched tightly over rock-hard chest muscles. He felt so warm. She snatched her hand back. "I don't like men. I'm gay."

His nostrils flared, and amusement lightened his eyes. "No, you're not."

"Oh, like you w-would know." Her voice cracked.

"I can smell your interest, little female."

Her heart was pounding. "I'm not interested in you."

"Don't lie."

"I—"

He kissed her. A light brushing of his warm lips against hers. He paused and did it again, leaning closer.

As the silky hair on his chest feathered against her breasts, she caught her breath. "Get back."

"No." He cupped her face in his powerful hands and took her lips, then her mouth, plunging his tongue in to take possession.

She shivered, unnerved by the disconcerting sensations running through her. Her skin felt sensitive, tight, wanting to be touched…and he did.

As his tongue explored her mouth, he stroked his hands up her bare waist and ribs. His thumbs grazed the sides of her breasts.

Her breath caught in her throat as her bones melted like butter in a hot pan.

He took the kiss deeper before he pulled back. "Not interested, huh." His voice had deepened to a rasp.

"I—" Oh God, she could feel dampness on her inner thighs. She looked toward the forest. *Run run run.*

He put his thumb under her chin to tilt her face up. To force her to look at him. When his eyes caught hers, the ground under her bare feet shifted. "You're not gay, Bree." He ran a hand down her arm, and his fingers closed around her wrist. Firmly.

"Zeb. Wait."

"If a female is interested, her scent changes." His long hair brushed over her arm as he lifted her wrist to his face and sniffed. "A male can smell it."

"On her wrist?" Get real.

"On skin. Anywhere. We're part-animal—scent is important." His lips quirked. "But, rather than sniffing asses, we settle for wrists. More polite, don't you think?"

The thought of his head going anywhere near her groin made her quiver inside. "Uh. Yes. Polite is good."

His other hand still rested on her ribs, his thumb stroking gently over the side of her breast, making heat flare in her low belly. His gaze showed his satisfaction. "Your mind may not want me, little female, but your body does."

After running one finger over her dampened lower lip, he took a few steps back, blurred, and shifted into his dark wolf. He glanced over his shoulder with gray-brown eyes, then loped into the forest.

The air brushed across her skin, startlingly cold after the heat of his body. Her bones felt as if they'd turned to custard, and she sagged against the door. Her breasts ached as if her skin had shrunk. So this was what arousal felt like. *God help me.*

Chapter Fifteen

A PACK RUN was a party on four legs, Bree thought, as she happily trotted along near the rear. They'd hunted a deer earlier, shared the spoils, and as long as she didn't think about eating raw bloody meat, it had tasted wonderful. Deer tartare—far better than rat.

The pack turned, flowing across the slope. Her blood sang in her veins as she breathed in the cold night air, scenting the different wolves, her shoulder brushing against the others. A feeling of belonging grew in her, filling the hollow spaces in her heart.

The pack stopped on a ridge overlooking the forest. An owl slowly flapped over the dark trees. Drifts of snow glinted white in the moonlight.

The alpha wolf, Gerhard, barked twice before lifting his nose and giving a long slow howl. His brothers, Klaus and Dieter, joined in, then the rest of the wolves. Bree caught the dark fragrance of Zeb and the crisper scent of Shay as they moved up beside her. Shay's muzzle lifted, and his howl was resonant and beautiful. Zeb joined him, his voice deeper and rougher.

Compelled, Bree tried. A bark first, then the song caught her, pulling her with it, higher, beautiful. The quarter moon shone down, silvering the dark and light fur. If she'd been in human form, she'd have cried for the beauty. Instead, she sank into the whole. *I'm alive, and here is where I belong.*

As the howls faded away, the alpha trotted down the slope, wending his way back into the forest. The pack streamed behind him.

Bree began to follow, then realized Zeb and Shay hadn't moved. As Zeb sniffed the air, Bree imitated him and caught a foul scent. *Hellhound.* The fur on her ruff rose, even as a fearful whine escaped her.

Shay started in the direction of the scent, but hesitated. He looked at Zeb, then her. As if he'd spoken, she knew he'd told Zeb to stay with her. But, what if there was a hellhound close?

She shifted, pleased at how easy it was. "Don't you dare go by yourself. Take the pack."

Shay's ears went back and he growled. For a second, he scared her. Then he shook his head as if to dislodge a fly and looked like her sweet Elvis again.

Boy, oh boy, he sure didn't like the idea of taking the pack after a hellhound. But he couldn't handle a monster by himself. If he got hurt because of her… She turned to Zeb. "You both go. I'll hang out with the others."

Shay didn't move.

She sighed. "I'll stay on the trail with the slow wolves." Although running with the younger ones was more fun. She was faster than most of them.

No movement.

Bree crossed her arms over her breasts, startled at the feeling of naked skin. "Zeb said that this is your *cay-heer* job. So go to it."

Shay's ears flattened—Mr. Bossy didn't like taking orders—then his tail waved slightly.

And she scores a win! Grinning, Bree shifted.

As if telling her to be careful, Zeb shouldered her and licked her muzzle in a way that made her insides quiver.

Taking his place, Shay nipped her ear in admonishment and licked her nose. His scent wrapped around her like a blanket of arousal.

Whoa, she needed to get away from them before she melted like snow in the sun. With a yip, she dashed after the pack.

After catching up, she took a place in the rear with the older wolves. The lovely song from the ridge still hummed in her veins as they wound through the mountains, climbed a steep trail, and crested into an open area. The wolves formed a circle, and Bree joined the cluster of females.

Overhead, clouds skittered in front of the quarter moon, and shadows slid across the dark dead grasses. The pack was silent. So what would happen now? Bree's tail drooped with her uncertainty. Darn it, she liked things to be consistent. Routine. Or at *least* to know what was planned.

The alpha stepped into the center of the circle and shifted to human. The rest of the wolves followed suit. Except for Bree. Naked in a crowd? Not happening.

Gerhard walked over, a large man with a dark red complexion and a thick gut. "*Trawsfur.*"

She felt an internal push, a need to obey, reminiscent of when she was five and a foster parent gave her an order. Although she realized she could resist Gerhard's command, everyone else was in human form. Maybe she was being rude. With a feeling of resentment, she trawsfurred, then stood and stepped back behind the other women. Gerhard wasn't as intimidating as Shay and Zeb, but he was still a big man. And really naked.

He returned to the center of the clearing. "Wolves," he said, his coarse voice disturbing the beauty of the night. "We have a new female—unattached. Breanne, step forward." He held his hand out as if he expected her to walk forward and take it.

Dream on, buddy. She raised her hand. "Hey, everyone."

Gerhard's brows drew together.

"Move." A big woman shoved, and Bree staggered forward, trying to find her footing. Jeez. Several feet into the center of the clearing, she recovered and clasped her hands in front of herself. Her sense of belonging had disappeared, leaving her empty.

The alpha glanced at her, not as if she were a female, but a duty. "You're staying alone in a cabin at the lodge. Tomorrow, you move into the pack house until you find a mate."

She stared at him. She'd heard he and his two brothers lived in the pack house with a varying population of other wolves. *Polite. Be polite, Bree.* "Thank you for the offer, but I'm perfectly happy where I'm at."

"Wolves don't live alone, especially females." His face turned darker red, and he crossed his arms over his bull-like chest. "This isn't a choice."

She could see the pot starting to boil over, knew she couldn't stop it. No way could she live with a bunch of strange men, especially big ones like him and his brothers. "I'm sor—"

Again, she felt the compulsion to obey—the creeptoid was doing some weird mental thing. Her desire to be polite disappeared. She glared at him. "No."

In her restaurant, the head chef always walked away from an argument. Now she understood why. They can't argue if you're not here. Ignoring disbelieving murmurs, she pushed through the crowd and headed for the trail. When she escaped into the trees, she took a breath of relief. *Way to play nice with the wolfies, Bree.*

Too shaken to shift, she slowed to consider her options. Navigating the steep path in the dark with rubbery legs would be suicide. Even worse, she wasn't real clear on where home was. *If I go straight downhill, eventually, I'll find Cold Creek. I hope.*

Footsteps sounded above her, and one of Gerhard's brothers—Klaus—ran down the trail. In the shadowy light, he seemed to smile. "Good, I won't have to exert myself after all." He glanced behind him, up the slope. The pack wasn't in sight. "So, Breanne, is it? There's something you need to realize…" He pointed down the trail.

She turned to look—and his fist slammed into her face. The skin over her cheekbone split. Pain seared through her like fire. Arms windmilling, she staggered back…and off the trail, down the steep, rocky slope.

Falling. Rocks gashed her back and sides, hit her head. Her skin scraped, tore, as she grabbed for something, anything. Nothing slowed her fall. *Please.*

She smashed into a massive tree, and the impact knocked the air from her lungs. Head spinning, she gasped for air. The sound of someone coming after her made her try to rise.

"Oh, did the mouthy bitch fall down?" Klaus yanked her to her feet. With one hand fisted in her hair, the other around her arm, he forced her up the slope. Struggling for breath, head whirling, she couldn't fight.

"We're going back to the meeting. You're going to do exactly what Gerhard says." He yanked her hair, and his ugly laugh turned her stomach. "If you don't, your next fall will be off a cliff. New shifter. Clumsy. No one will think twice."

"You wouldn't."

"Oh, I would. I have."

The gloating tone in his voice convinced her. Don't answer. She'd tell Zeb and Shay. They'd—

"It's your word against mine, bitch. If your cahir friends show their fangs, my brother will kick them out of the territory." Hearing his slimy laugh was more nauseating than eating rat, and she swallowed bile.

With a painful grip on her arm, he dragged her up the trail, through the crowd, and into the center of the meeting.

Gerhard—she thought, although her vision kept doubling up—stopped in mid-sentence. "Klaus, what happened?"

"Your new wolf fell off the trail. Good thing I found her."

"Fell?" Gerhard's voice turned expressionless. "I glad you saved her, Klaus." He looked at her. "Did you change your mind?"

Trickles of blood ran down her forehead, her calf, her shoulder. Pain from the fall was beginning to blossom…everywhere. Her ribs stabbed with every painful gasp for air. Even so, she tried to pull away, and Klaus's grip tightened.

Self-preservation said she should agree to his demands. She couldn't. "No." Her voice shook worse than her legs, and she forced it to steady. "There won't be a problem. I'll leave your stupid territory."

The fingers around her arm dug in painfully.

"A new shifter can't leave until the Cosantir permits," Gerhard said. "That'll be a few months at least."

"I don't give a hoot."

"The fall must have confused her, Gerhard. I'll take her back to the tavern for you." Klaus's ugly voice and hostile scent scraped over her nerves. He tried to pull her back through the crowd.

He'll kill me this time. As fear-induced adrenaline cleared Bree's head, she could almost see Sensei's frown. He'd never quit; he had never let her quit. Within the heart of one breath, she found her center.

"Poor girl, she—"

Whirling, she kicked Klaus's shin. He yelled and his grip loosened. She ripped free. Standing close enough her blurred vision wasn't a problem, she punched him in the face. Cartilage crunched under her knuckles—his nose.

As he staggered back, she snap-kicked his knee, making him roar.

The sight of wavery figures converging on their fight distracted her, and Klaus fisted her in the ribs, knocking her to her knees. Pain washed over her in fiery waves. Struggling to regain her breath, she felt caught in a nightmare, surrounded by enemies with no one to save her.

WHEN SHAY REACHED the rear of the pack, he realized his partner had paused under a tree to snatch up a wayward mouse. From the few facts Zeb had shared, he'd stayed as a wolf for years after losing his family. Not only had he managed to live alone without going feral, but—Shay grinned—he'd learned to never pass up a snack.

Shay's smile faded. He and Zeb had found the demonkin's tracks. They needed to talk with Calum and Alec. The scent wasn't familiar, which meant the territory still had a hellhound in it.

With a glance around, he saw everyone was in human form, so he shifted. Shouting sounded from the front along with the smack of flesh on flesh. Probably the young males playing dominance games. He smelled healthy sweat. Anger.

Then, even as a woman yelled, "No! Leave her alone," Shay caught Breanne's fear-laden scent. Something inside him twisted and burst with anger. He couldn't see her. His snarl ripped out.

In the center of the circle, Gerhard turned. Their eyes met.

Shay started shoving through the crowd.

The alpha yelled a command, and males deliberately blocked Shay's path. By the God, they'd regret that. He grabbed the first by one arm and threw him at the next in his path. Stepping around them, he flattened a skinny male who got in his way.

Zeb's roar came from the rear and someone screeched. A male yelled, then shouted in pain. As Zeb appeared, the remaining obstacles melted out of their way.

When he reached the center, Shay saw Breanne on her hands and knees. Four males surrounded her, like wolves on a downed deer. Gerhard stood nearby.

Shay dove forward, trawsfurring in midair, landing as a wolf. Ears back, hackles raised, he placed himself in front of Breanne, taking up a guard position.

One of Gerhard's brothers retreated, as did the two other males. Klaus remained, his features distorted with rage. Blood smeared his face and dripped off his chin.

Zeb stepped between him and Shay. "Try me, scat-head."

Klaus scowled, but backed up a step in token retreat. Zeb watched, his scent acrid with anger.

When no one moved for seconds, Shay shifted and knelt beside Breanne. She was bleeding from scores of gashes and scratches, and red blotches of broken blood vessels showed on her fair skin. Eyes glazed, she didn't see him as she tried to stand. But she was alive, thank the God.

His fury edged down a whisker, far enough to restrain it. Anger still ruled his brother. "Zeb." He nodded toward Breanne. *Guard her while I talk.*

Zeb understood. He inhaled slowly, visibly fighting for control, and moved to stand behind her. She pushed up onto her knees but his hand on her shoulder kept her from rising.

When she swung at him, Zeb leaned over, speaking in her ear. A sigh shuddered through her, and her hand closed over his, gripping tightly.

Shay rose and faced the alpha, striving to keep his voice even. Non-threatening. "What is going on?"

Gerhard's usually ruddy face was almost purple. "She attacked Klaus. He tried to help her, and she hit him. She's feral."

Idiot. "She's no more feral than you are." Shay glanced at Klaus, saw the tension in the shifter's muscles. "I can see which of them looks more damaged. What did you do to her?"

"Nothing. She lost her temper. Stomped away and fell off the trail," Gerhard said. "Klaus found her and brought her back. And she punched him, broke his nose."

"That doesn't sound like Breanne," Shay said. *You mangy curs are lying.* "What made her angry?"

"I ordered her to move into the pack house. She refused." The alpha's expression was stubborn. "A female cannot live alone. It's pack law."

"Your pack law is a farce."

The wolves' shocked gasps told Shay that he'd gone too far. He didn't give a damn. He and Zeb had been kicked out of their last territory; what was one more? Zeb's low growl agreed.

Gerhard snarled. "You and your br—"

"Breanne was raised human. Before last week, she didn't even know the Daonain existed. You expect her to know pack law?" As Shay turned in a circle, gazes were averted in shame. The two men who weren't Gerhard's brothers slid into the crowd.

"She's just a little wolf," Shay said softly. "And she's afraid of males. Your actions tonight have increased that fear."

A muttering ran through the pack like a wind whispering in the pines.

Blood surged into Gerhard's face. "She can't live alone. She—"

"She knows me and Zeb and has lived next door to us for a month. She can move into the lodge until she finds someone she likes better."

Breanne didn't speak.

Shay glanced back to check her response, but the sight infuriated him again. "By the Mother's grace, *look* at her." Cuts, bruises, gashes. "She's barely recovered from saving the Cosantir's daughter."

Gerhard stiffened, reminded that he'd better tread carefully.

Shay glanced at Zeb—his brother was close to losing control and tearing a few males to bits. Time to step back. "If you care about this little member of your pack, alpha, let her stay where she can thrive." He managed to put hint of plea into his words, although the concession tasted foul.

Gerhard crossed his arms. "Is she going to refuse to live with you? If so…" The gleam in his eyes showed he hoped she'd give him cause to force her compliance.

Heedless of Gerhard and his brothers, Shay knelt beside Breanne. Zeb straightened, taking guard.

Breanne's eyes had cleared. She met his gaze.

"Did you hear Gerhard?" Shay asked.

She didn't speak, although tears of pain ran down her cheeks. What kind of female learned to take that much pain silently?

He struggled not to pull her into his arms. "Will you stay with me and Zeb for now?"

Her mouth tightened. She was going to refuse.

He touched her cheek, felt her flinch, and leaned closer to whisper, "He's an asshole, but he's right that wolves don't live alone. It's bad for us, a leannan. That's why Calum makes Zeb and me share a house."

Trembles shook her body as she thought. "Okay." She took a slow breath and her voice steadied. "For now. Until I can leave this horrible place."

Her voice was loud enough that everyone heard. More frowns appeared. Once a new shifter achieved adequate control, she could go where she wanted. Pack rarely left their territory, but this little female knew there was a whole world out there.

Shay stroked her hair before standing. He held Gerhard's gaze until the alpha agreed, "She can live with you. For now."

"C'mon, little female. It's to the healer for you." Despite the anger coming off him in waves, Zeb lifted her into his arms very,

very gently. "Bad week. First you get ripped up fighting a hellhound." He shot a deadly glare at Gerhard. "Then the alpha tries to finish the job."

The pack was totally silent.

ONCE AWAY FROM the other males—and with Bree safely in his arms—Zeb regained control of his temper. Farther down the trail in a level spot, he set Bree on her feet. "If we carry you, it'll take a long time to get back."

"I can walk." The stubborn little female took two shaky steps before her knees buckled.

"By Herne, that wasn't what I meant." When he caught her, his hands slipped on her blood. His temper surged, and he took a step upslope. "I'll kill them."

"No, a bhràthair." Shay's voice was mild, though his fury scented the wind. "Don't challenge him. You'd make a lousy alpha."

"Better than that cur." Then Zeb sighed in agreement He'd go crazy if all those people looked to him to lead them. "Fine."

Shay touched Bree's cheek. "Trawsfur to wolf. Four legs work better than two, your fur will keep you warm, and we'll get off the mountain more quickly. Can you do that?"

She considered. Her chin lifted with determination, before she blurred into her wolf. Blood streaked her light fur and her tail drooped, but she followed Shay without a whine.

Zeb's chest ached as he remembered how the small wolf had danced in happiness an hour earlier.

Her stubborn determination took her almost all the way down the mountain. When her strength gave out, he and Shay took turns carrying her. Something inside him was soothed to have her in his arms safe where he could protect her.

Finally, they reached the cave under the Wild Hunt. After

dressing and wrapping Bree in a blanket, Shay drove them to the healer's house on Cumberland Street—swearing in Gaelic the entire way.

Donal O'Connor opened the door, dressed only in a pair of sweat pants. "Don't you know it's late?" He frowned at the sight of Bree. "Thought I'd healed her. Now what?"

Bree opened her eyes, saw the healer, and her curvy body stiffened. "No," she said in a thin voice, all the melody gone. "I don't want him to touch me."

Donal snorted. "Females." He stepped back so they could enter. "Now you know why I'm not lifemated."

In his youth, Zeb would have agreed. "Where do you want her?"

"I get a feeling the medical room would be a mistake." Donal pulled on a gray sweatshirt as he led the way into the living room.

The room had an arched ceiling and was the size of one of their cabins. With the chairs and couch in evergreen colors and a deep brown carpet over a hardwood floor, the room held the comfort of a summer forest. "Nice."

"Thank you." Donal pointed to the couch. "Put her there."

Zeb set her down gently.

"No. I don't want this." Bree struggled to stand.

"Stubborn female." Yet he welcomed the excuse to keep her in his arms. He scooped her back up and took her place on the cushions, holding her in his lap.

The way she relaxed against him pleased the hell out of him.

Donal shook his head. "Never seen anyone less willing to be healed. What did I do?"

"You were born with a dick," Shay answered. He took a place behind the couch, leaning over Zeb's shoulder. "Have at it, Healer."

When Donal pulled back the blanket to expose Bree's arms

and shoulders, he hissed at the bruises and gashes and cuts. "You boys play rough. If this is how you get your rocks off, don't come back here again."

The fucking dunghead thought he and Shay had… With a snarl, Zeb started to stand, but Shay held him back.

"Wasn't us, Donal," Shay said. "She disagreed with the alpha. Apparently she ran from the pack and fell off a trail."

Donal grunted his disgust. "Makes me glad I'm a werecat—we answer to only the Cosantir." He met Zeb's eyes. "Sorry. I jumped too fast. Wouldn't have happened, except last year, a human male moved here, and he liked to beat his mate into jelly."

"I'd have killed him." Zeb's arms tightened around the little female until she squirmed. He loosened his hold.

"My first inclination as well, but not allowed for healers." Donal opened an elaborately carved armoire filled with medical supplies.

"Doesn't sound like it's still going on." Shay reached over Zeb's shoulder to stroke Bree's hair. "What happened?"

"They'd been in town a week when Angie dragged the female here. She was human, so I couldn't heal her, but I bandaged what I could. She had uneven bones, old scars as well as new, but refused to talk about it." Donal dropped gauze onto a tray. "The sheriff and Cosantir would have found out soon enough, but I dropped a hint. Not much, but Alec's quick on the uptake." He added tape as well. "He assigned his mate—she's a deputy—to check things out. I don't know what Vicki saw, but she lost her temper and beat the crap out of the guy."

Zeb gave an amused snort. The sheriff's werecat mate was a good match for the cahir. "She get in trouble?"

"Alec stood there and watched." Donal grinned. "And laughed."

Zeb shifted Bree and nuzzled her hair. The scents of vanilla and the haunting wild fragrance of a shifter female were buried under that of blood and pain. He needed someone to punch. "Is the asshole still in town?"

"Nah. He left that day. Alec found a local human to take the woman to her relatives." Donal set the tray filled with gauze, saline, and antibiotic ointment on the coffee table. Down on one knee, he tugged on the blanket around Bree.

Zeb felt Bree rouse.

"NO." BREE SHOVED the stranger's hand away, her heart starting to speed. Pain reverberated through her body, blurring everything together—Klaus hitting her, men surrounding her, the hellhound's teeth, the monster-man pushing her down and...

Panic flooded her veins, drowning her ability to think. "Don't touch me." She tried to hide, burying her head against Zeb's hard chest. He was safe. He and Shay had saved her. "Please, no."

"Little female," Zeb's rumbling voice filled the air. "Some of those marks will leave scars. Might affect your mobility. Let Donal work."

The blanket shook with her trembling. She knew she was acting like a whipped dog, only her mind couldn't seem to get in front of the fear.

Shay sat down, his hip next to her outstretched legs. He took her hands in his big ones. "Lass, do you think we'd let Donal hurt you?" His eyes were a grave blue-gray. "Can you not trust us?"

She turned to stare at Donal, her thoughts splintering into fragments. Her chest heaved as she tried to get her breath.

"Donal, start with something less...intimate." Shay paused and then ordered, "Heal her back first."

Despite her protests, Zeb firmly pulled the blanket down and repositioned her so her face was in the hollow of his shoulder, her breasts against his chest. His hair was long enough to hide part of her face, and he smelled of forests and safety. Shay still held her hands, his fingers warm, an anchor as much as a restraint.

The stranger touched her.

"Noooo." Pain burst through her when his fingers entered an open area on her shoulder. A hot tingling swamped her senses. She whimpered.

"Shhh." Zeb's arms tightened around her. "You're safe, Bree. Shhh."

The man's hands moved. A burn. Tingling. She struggled, trying to get away.

He pulled the blanket lower, and she whined like a hurt dog. "Sorry, girl, but this one's bleeding. Looks like you hit a rock."

She'd fallen because Klaus had backhanded her. Knocked her down. She opened her mouth, then remembered he'd said he'd kill her if she told.

Shay and Zeb won't let him.

But he'd said Gerhard would exile them. Could the alpha do that? The healer's palm flattened over her side and what felt like a cracked rib. She winced as he pressed as if to push the prickly tingles deeper.

"I've wondered why you don't take over the pack, Shay. You're dominant," the healer said, as if he was chatting instead of touching her. His hand settled on her arm, his finger tracing a painful gash.

"I'm oathbound." Shay squeezed her fingers, diverting her. "I don't stay anywhere long—Herne sends me where the hellhounds are."

"Rough life," Donal said. "Turn her, Zeb. I need to do the front."

She tried to pull her hands free to cling to Zeb, but Shay held tight and Zeb ruthlessly turned her around. As Shay knelt to hold her arms to her sides, the healer pushed the blanket down to her waist, exposing her breasts.

Unable to look at him, she scrunched her eyes shut. Her tears burned her cheeks, and Zeb made a sound as if she'd kicked him.

"Easy, girl. It's not that bad," the Healer muttered.

Bree felt a touch on her breast. Like a downpour, panic sheeted over her. "No!" She fought the hands restraining her, touching her. The monster was everywhere; she couldn't escape.

Forever...it seemed forever until she could hear over the screaming in her head and the roar of her pulse. Zeb's rough voice had mixed together with Shay's resonant deep one: "We've got you. You're safe. No one will hurt you." As their words registered, she went limp, exhausted. Panting.

"Damn, she really doesn't want this," Donal said. "I'd say leave her front, but there's a couple that would make ugly scars, and at least another busted rib. Breanne, I'm sorry, I'll be as fast as I can."

Shay took her wrists, holding them in one hand. He set his palm on her cheek and turned her face to his. His voice deepened, demanding her attention. "Look at me." Her gaze met his intense one, and he kept her eyes pinned to his. "It'll be over soon, a leannan."

"Move this out of my way," Donal muttered. Someone's hand cupped her left breast and lifted it. She whimpered.

Zeb whispered, "It's me, little female, my hand."

Shay's eyes were full of pain, and she tried to get control of herself. "I'm sorry," she whispered. "I can't..." She shuddered, her hands trapped, her body trapped, hands on her body, the feeling too much like—

"I've seen this a couple times before," the healer said, his anger obvious. "With human females who'd been assaulted."

"Raped," Zeb growled.

"Yes," Donal's voice was almost the same snarl. "One more and we're done. Only one more, Breanne." Fingers touching her again, pain and burning across the top of one breast.

"Were you raped, Bree?" Zeb asked.

When she gulped, her stomach twisting, Shay snarled, "Dammit, Zeb."

But the healer knew anyway. A shudder ran through her as she managed a nod.

She realized the sound in her ear was Zeb growling, low and deep. A matching rumble came from Shay. Why the sounds didn't terrify her seemed to make no sense.

"There—done." Donal sighed. "Give me a second to get out of punching range and let her up."

Shay gave a weak laugh and released her hands. A second later, he had the blanket closed around her.

Zeb shifted her to a more comfortable position on his lap.

"Let me go," she whispered.

"In a second. You were…" He laid his cheek on top of her head, his arms very gentle around her. "I need to feel you're all right."

Under his words, she heard such fury and sorrow that her eyes filled. She let him cradle her against his chest. Why did it help to have him so upset?

Shay rejoined them on the couch, stroking her hair as if she were a puppy. "If we'd stayed with the pack, this wouldn't have happened. I could have talked Gerhard around. She wouldn't have run away and fallen."

Zeb's arms tightened as if he agreed, but he said instead, "Not your fault, brawd. You were going to send me with her, remember? And I've probably have punched Gerhard just for fun."

Shay snorted. "Too true."

At the armoire, Donal was putting his supplies away. He

glanced over his shoulder. "Doesn't interfering with an alpha's judgment get you driven from the territory? You guys lone wolves now?"

Bree struggled to sit up, panic mingling with shame. "He won't make you leave, will he?"

Shay tugged her hair lightly, a smile lightening his eyes. "You weren't following the last part of that, were you?"

"It's blurry."

"We're not exiled, Breanne.

I can't tell them about Klaus. If they attacked the alpha's brother—and they would—then Gerhard would kick them out. She couldn't do that to them.

"Why'd she run from the pack?" Donal dropped into a chair.

"He ordered her to live in the pack house. After that—seems like she had a problem with the alpha's brother. What happened, Breanne?" Shay asked.

Can't tell the truth. Can't get them exiled. "He tried to keep me from leaving again," she said. "I didn't like it."

Zeb snorted. "You busted the scat-head's nose. Nice job."

"I think the pack was shocked at how fast everything blew up," Shay said. "We got Gerhard to back off, and she'll be living with us."

"Good plan," Donal said. "She doesn't need any more grief."

Bree managed to look at the healer, seeing the long, lean body, the honesty in his stern silvery-gray eyes. He had a scar over his cheekbone, like Shay and Zeb, only his was a crescent, like a new moon. She met his gaze. "Thank you."

Donal's eyes softened. "You're very welcome. I'm glad I was still in town." He glanced at Zeb and Shay. "Take her home, cahirs. She's had a bad day."

IN THE LODGE, they settled the little female into an upstairs bedroom. She snuggled under the covers like a pup, and her whispered *thank you* made Zeb's chest ache. So little and so hurt. And he hadn't protected her.

As Zeb entered the living room, Shay handed over a beer.

Zeb unscrewed the top, took a big swallow, and sank down in the chair closest to the fireplace. "Fuck."

"No shit." Shay took the couch and put his feet on the coffee table.

"You find out who raped her, so we can kill him."

"Better stalk that carefully and not right away." Shay's mouth flattened into a line. "But, we'll get the information from her sooner or later."

Zeb tipped his beer in a salute. "We're on the same trail, brawd."

"You ready for another problem?"

Fuck no. "What?"

"Her reaction to being touched. She's afraid of men. Been raped. How's she going to deal with a Gathering? She didn't grow up a shifter, and she hasn't a clue what's going to happen."

"Oh, fuck. Like Calum's mate." This was past bad, going into nightmare time. "Last fall was her first Gather. It overwhelmed her, and she's a tough female." He ran his fingers through his hair, remembering how he'd stepped back, let her settle.

"So's our little wolf." A slow smile grew on Shay's face. "She did a great job on reshaping Klaus's nose."

Zeb felt a glow at the memory. Bree had a wicked punch. "Yeah."

"Guts or not, she's liable to panic at the Gathering. We need to do something."

"Us?" Zeb felt his own panic rise.

"She trusts us. We can touch her. Maybe we can get her past some of that fear."

"I've been trying to keep my distance." Except for this morning. Her breasts had rubbed against his chest; her mouth had been soft, sweet. Giving.

Even as Zeb's cock hardened, his gut clenched. He wasn't sure he'd survive if she returned to being afraid of him.

"We have, what?" Shay paused, calculating. "Only a week to get her past this."

"Fuck."

Chapter Sixteen

A KNOCK ON the door woke Bree, and with a groan, she sat up in bed and stared around. *Not my room.* As the memory of the previous evening returned, she chilled. *Klaus hitting her, pain, falling down the hill, the men around her...*

But Zeb had held her and carried her. Shay had stroked her hair, talked her out of the panic. Funny how his gaze and firm voice had held her as securely as Zeb's arms had.

Another louder knock made her jump.

"Come in."

Shay opened the door. "Breanne, Calum has..." His eyes warmed.

What? "I—jeez." She yanked the covers up to her chin and glared at him.

"A *leannan*, I've seen you without clothes before." The sun lines at the corners of his eyes deepened. "But it's always enjoyable."

Heat crept up her face. "You knocked for a reason?"

"'Fraid so. Calum ordered our presence. All three of us. Preferably soon."

Would she have time for a shower? Wait. Just why was she jumping out of bed because Calum said to anyway? "Shay?"

He came in and sat on her bed, crowding into her space,

which wasn't like him at all. The blankets stymied her attempt to edge away.

The laughter in his eyes showed he knew exactly how nervous he made her. "Did you have a question?"

"Um." Question? Oh, right. "Who is Calum? Everybody jumps when he says anything, and you guys call him a Cosan-something. Why did he have to be the one to make me shift instead of you or Zeb?"

"I forget sometimes how little you know. Zeb and I aren't very good teachers."

She shrugged. "I keep forgetting to ask." Because she'd been so entranced with turning into a wolfy.

"The mountain ranges are divided into territories. Each one has a guardian over it. A Cosantir."

Cosantir. "So Calum is kinda in charge. But—"

Shay put his hand on her knee to stop her. Even through the blanket, she felt the heat of his palm. Why did her skin seem to beg for more? More touch, more heat.

"Not *kinda.*" His thumb stroked back and forth. "A Cosantir is appointed by Herne—the God—and he gets powers to go with the job."

Her mouth twisted. "Like Gerhard?"

"More. Gerhard's power comes from the pack. A Cosantir's powers come from Herne." His eyes narrowed as he thought. "A Cosantir always knows what shifters are in his territory and where they are. He's the only one who can force a trawsfur."

Her skepticism took a step back. She'd definitely experienced that *I'll-make-you-shift* talent.

"In his territory, he's…what did my grandsir call it? High, low, and middle justice? He can banish a shifter or kill one with a touch.

"Get real." The Cosantir was starting to sound like a TV evangelist. Miracles performed every night at seven o'clock.

Riiight. "And God's-gift to the earth spends his days tending bar?"

Shay grinned. "Actually, he was a lawyer before Herne made him Cosantir, and from what Alec says, Calum was pretty pissed-off about being drafted."

A *lawyer?* "I don't think I'll ever understand this place."

"You will, Breanne, you will." He ran a finger over her bare shoulder, sending a shiver through her. "Go easy today. Healers don't fix minor damages. You'll be sore for a couple of days."

No kidding. She felt like she'd fallen off a mountain and hit every stone on the way down. Oh wait. She *had.* "I'll take it easy."

"Good answer, little wolf. I enjoy being obeyed." Shay leaned over and teasingly kissed her. Before she could pull away, he nibbled her lower lip and sent heat rushing through her. His firm lips demanded more, and hers softened under the swift assault.

He pulled back and was off the bed before she could punch him. And she might have if her brain hadn't turned to mush. "Shay," she warned, tasting peppermint on her lips.

"Breanne." His blue-gray eyes were as level as his voice. "I enjoyed that—" He inhaled through his nose and gave her a wicked grin. "And so did you, lass."

She stared as the door closed behind him. A week ago, she'd been exhilarated because she'd felt like a woman, because she'd responded to him and Zeb. *But I don't want any more changes. Not now.*

This heat and the need streaming through her body was definitely a change.

After a minute, she shook her head. Meeting. Must move. Lacking clothes, she wrapped a quilt around herself and headed for the bathroom at the end of the hall.

In front of the mirror, she dropped the blanket and got a

glimpse of the cuts and bruises covering her body. Nausea churned her stomach, and she hastily stepped into the shower. As hot water poured over her, she washed, trying to erase the memory of being naked. Being touched. Klaus's grip had felt like that of the monster. *I'm dirty. Ugly.* She could smell the hellhound's stench on her, and she scrubbed harder.

When the water turned pink, she realized what she was doing. Blood trickled from her cuts and scratches. *Stop, Bree. Stop.* Tears burned her eyes as despair filled her. She'd thought she was getting better. Despite the heat of the shower, she felt cold inside.

After forcing herself to shut off the water, she got out. The mirror displayed how many scrapes she'd reopened. What a mess. A colorful mess too. Although the healed cuts were a tender pink-red, dark red and purple bruises had blossomed over her arms and shoulders, ribs, back, and legs. She fingered her puffy cheek and winced at the soreness.

I don't like this place. Or any place with people like Klaus in it. He'd made a pleased sound when he'd hit her. Sick jerk.

When the pack had been running and singing, she'd felt as if she belonged. But not any more. How soon could she leave?

She gingerly patted herself dry. Gerhard had said the Cosantir decided that. So today, she'd make Calum understand she'd be here another week at the most. She'd learn whatever she needed and avoid Klaus.

A week. That meant her time with Shay and Zeb was limited as well. The empty feeling that swept through her was disconcerting. When had she grown so attached to them?

With a sigh, she wrapped the towel around herself. After pushing her wet hair back, she opened the bathroom door and ran right into Zeb. She squeaked.

His chuckle sounded like rocks grating together. He held out jeans, a sweater, and underwear. "From your cabin."

"Thank you." She smiled up at him, and her breathing stopped.

His eyes were molten darkness as his gaze slowly dropped from her face to her bare shoulders to where the towel barely covered her breasts. "You're all pink, little female," he murmured, handing her the clothing.

When her hands were full, he stroked his callused fingers down her neck and across one shoulder. He turned his hand over to brush his knuckles over the tops of her breasts. His skin was so warm, and an answering heat pooled in her lower half.

"Do you need help getting dressed?" he asked. His index finger curved under the edge of the towel between her breasts.

Her mouth dropped open, then she fled back into the bathroom, slamming the door in his face. Her hands shook as she dressed in the jeans and cashmere sweater he'd brought. She couldn't get past how he'd looked at her. Touched her. He didn't make her feel dirty, but he'd woken a funny...anxious...feeling deep in her stomach. Not scary though. Not quite.

A thump on the door made her jump. "Let's go, female."

On the walk to the tavern, Bree listened to the men idly discuss which cabins needed more repairs, what the weather would be, who was patrolling for hellhounds.

Hellhounds. Plural. She ignored the coldness in the pit of her stomach and firmed her voice. "Zeb, when I shot at the hellhound, my bullets bounced off. What are those creatures made of anyway?"

"A kind of bony plating."

Shay added, "A paleontologist said some dinosaurs had plating as good as body armor. Hellhounds do too." He patted his stomach. "A strip down their belly is the only place not armored."

No wonder her blade had broken. She frowned at Zeb. "When you were under it, you stabbed it with a knife. Why not use your pistol?"

"Good way to die," Zeb said.

Now there was an informative answer. She gave him a dirty look.

"Two reasons. First: the angle's wrong to hit the heart," Shay explained, taking pity on her. "Ripping downward with a knife will slice through a big artery, but bullets can miss it, and you don't have time to keep trying. If a hellhound doesn't die fast, it kills the cahir."

She swallowed hard. Zeb could so easily have died. "The other reason?"

"Bullets usually embed in the armor, but sometimes will bounce off," Shay said, a hint of humor in his eyes. "If you're underneath and miss the strip, the belly plating means you're liable to eat your own bullet."

Jeez. "You two looked like an acrobat team. How many have you killed?"

"With Shay? Around a dozen," Zeb said absently.

The lack of air made her clutch his arm. "So many?"

"Some before we got together." Shay tugged her hair. "Zeb and I hunt them, remember? And looks like there's still one around Cold Creek."

The blood drained from her head.

"Easy, little female." Zeb put his arm over her shoulder and the heat of his body melted some of the chill. She concentrated on inhaling slowly, on feeling the warmth of Zeb against her, the hardness of his body, on watching Shay move ahead of them, all power and skill.

"Hey, have you seen the gnome under cabin seven?" Shay asked lightly.

She tried to smile at him, knowing he'd changed the subject for her. And Zeb, antisocial Zeb, kept her snuggled against his side the rest of the way.

At the tavern, Shay opened the door and motioned her inside. She stopped for a second to let her eyes adjust, after the brightness of the outside. The jukebox was turned down low, and the place was almost empty except for a couple of truckers at the bar.

Calum spotted them and nodded at a table near the front window. After she and the men had sat down, he arrived with a tray of drinks and handed them out.

Bree studied him over the rim of her diet cola. So, he was like the king in the area? Admittedly, the man seemed quite authoritative. But still…

He met her look with a slight smile before turning to Shay and Zeb. "I heard about last night. I'm pleased Breanne will stay with you."

Shay nodded.

Calum looked at her. "I wanted to speak to you about your future."

"Excellent idea." She set her glass down. Gerhard had said the Cosantir wouldn't let her leave. She'd just see about that.

Before she could speak, he continued, "New shifters, no matter their age, are taught by the old ones. Like you, Victoria became a shifter as an adult and lacked the knowledge we normally gain in childhood. She's at Elder Village now, getting lessons in Daonain history and customs."

"Oh. I was wondering where she'd gone. I miss her."

"As do I. Normally, I'd send you to the village to get formally recognized, if nothing else. But I cannot spare Shay or Zeb, and you're not ready to be parted from your mentors. I'll get you there in a month or two."

"A month or two?" She stared at him. Gerhard had been right? How long did they think she'd be here?

He nodded at Shay and Zeb. "I'd like the Elders to recognize you two as well. Once the other cahirs are trained, one of you can travel up with Breanne, meet them, and return. Later, the other can go and bring her back. Then I can do a proper introduction to the clan here."

Bree pursed her lips. He was certainly free with planning her life. Too bad. She didn't want to go to some village and meet new people. The ones here were bad enough. "Listen, Calum, I don't want to go—"

"Breanne," he interrupted. "This is a tradition and requirement for new shifters. Unfortunately, our Elders are just that—elderly—and they cannot travel to meet you. It would be a courtesy if you would accommodate them."

Heck, saying no would make her sound inconsiderate to old people. "You're sneakier than I thought."

His eyes glinted with amusement. "Thank you. Meantime, you have lessons to learn here."

He was *not* going to run right over her, the big jerk. "You act as if I'm staying here, and I'm not. I need to get back to Seattle." The restaurant wouldn't hold her job forever.

"Your life is here for the foreseeable future. After your lessons are complete and you've achieved control, you may go wherever you wish."

Her mouth tightened. He wasn't giving an inch, was he?

"Breanne, we have hidden for thousands of years. I'm sure you can understand why."

Actually, she did understand. Every other science fiction movie showed what happened when aliens—or anything different—came up against the military or scientists. She nodded.

"Because being revealed would be disastrous to us all, our law states that if a shifter reveals the existence of the Daonain to humans, he is killed." His uncanny eyes darkened to black, the color of death.

"Oh." That wasn't an idle threat.

"Since we usually trawsfur at least monthly to stay healthy, most live in wilderness or mountain towns." He leaned back in his chair. "Shifters do not fare well in cities, surrounded by humans and metal."

But that's my home. Her stomach tightened.

Shay shook his head. "I can't imagine how the noise and smells didn't bother you."

"She wasn't a shifter then." Zeb frowned. "But—you ever hear of a Daonain not shifting?"

"Donal wondered the same," Calum said. "Being surrounded by metal might delay the magic a year or two, but not another decade. You should have died, Breanne."

"I've heard nasty things about city people. Drugs, maybe?" Shay's gunmetal-blue eyes narrowed. "Did you do drugs, little wolf? It's all right—we don't care."

He said drugs as if it were a foreign word, and Bree rolled her eyes. "No, big wolf. I tried some as a teen, but nothing even provided me a buzz. Probably the shifter blood." She gave them a wry look. "The only *drug* I ever took was birth control pills. I've been on those since I was fifteen."

They stared at her like she was naked or something, and she crossed her arms over her chest. "What?"

"Are you still taking them?" Calum asked slowly.

"No. I screwed up, and my refills went to Seattle."

"You think that was it, Cosantir?" Shay asked.

"Very likely. Between the suppression of magic in the city and a medicine that warps hormones, she might have gone into a type of suspended state." He studied her for a minute. "Did you ever experience an overwhelming need to mate?"

"No." Jeez. From the heat in her face, she'd turned the color of a tomato. He was still waiting, so she added, "I've never been interested in sex at all."

Shay's warm hand closed over her cold one. "It's good you

didn't stop the pills before you found us."

"Shifting is that important?"

Calum nodded. "Being descended from the Fae means we're partly *magical*, if that's what you want to call it. The animal form connects us with the source—Mother Earth—and replenishes us. You were dying slowly in the city. And once off your pills, you were well on your way to death."

Shay's hand tightened painfully. His jaw was tight. Zeb looked the same.

"Well, I didn't die," she said lightly.

"No." Calum leaned back. "But I wonder if we have more lost ones in the cities."

"That's not a good thought," Shay said.

"One for another time."

"So how long must I stay here?" Bree asked, returning to her main concern.

"Until your mentors judge you capable of being on your own." Calum tapped his fingers on the table. "Most shifters master everything by five or six months."

Months? "But that's my home." *Not here.* Seattle was home. Friends. Routines. "I have a-a job. How will I live?"

"Ah. Seamus, let us give her free lodging at the Wildwood."

Her jaw dropped. "You can't force Zeb and Shay to put me up. They're running a business, not a charity."

"Quite fierce on your behalf, isn't she?" Calum murmured.

A crease appeared in Zeb's cheek as if he tried not to smile.

Shay grinned. "Thank you, Breanne, but no worries. The Cosantir owns the Wildwood, so the charity will be his."

"Oh." Well. Now she felt stupid. Her gaze slid to Calum. "Sorry." Belatedly she added, "Thank you."

"You are welcome." His eyes held amusement. "It's partly self-interest. An unattached female werewolf would never lack for offers of shelter, but your remaining at the Wildwood will disturb my territory less than other alternatives."

Shay snorted. "Discreetly put."

"As for earning extra income, the Wild Hunt can always use a barmaid on Friday and Saturday nights." His gray eyes were kind. "You've helped Victoria out for fun. Let me pay you for your time."

She wasn't going to win against him. Looked like she'd be here a while. Oh God, somehow she'd have to avoid Klaus. Her heart thumped hard at the blast of fear.

But, at the same time, she didn't have to return to her apartment right away. Like a pendulum of emotion, relief blew through her. Being with Zeb and Shay was...safe.

And yet, she wanted to go home. *My city, my friends, my job.* The need to be surrounded by her comfortable routine shook her.

But until she managed to control the unexpected shifts to wolfy form, she couldn't go back to Seattle. Just imagine her boss's reaction if she suddenly had four feet and a tail.

Just imagine the Cosantir's response. Turning into a wolfy in the wrong place wouldn't just lose her some friends, but would be her death sentence.

THAT EVENING, SHAY finally finished the paperwork. He gave a grunt of exasperation. By the God, the previous owner must have learned bookkeeping from the dwarves, who believed math was invented by demons. After stretching his cramped back muscles, he grabbed a hard candy from the dish on his desk. Maybe he'd help Zeb with caulking the bathtub upstairs.

As he left the office, he glanced over at the library area and paused.

Bent over a wide oak table, Breanne was working on a jigsaw puzzle. Her golden hair spilled over her shoulders, bright against her fuzzy blue sweater. Her lips pressed together as she concentrated.

Playing with a little wolf would be far more fun than caulking. He strolled over. "Can I help?".

She jumped and glared at him. "Would it hurt you to make a little noise? Warn a girl?"

"Ah, but sneaking up on vulnerable females is so much fun." He stood beside her, close enough her shoulder brushed his. When she stiffened, he picked up a puzzle piece. Sky blue—the color of her eyes.

After a few seconds, she relaxed. "I wanted to talk to you anyway." She fit a piece into what might eventually be a log cabin. "I met a woman today. She and her husband run a cleaning business. Jody said the previous owners handled the usual lodge cleaning—like you do—but would call the service for more rigorous stuff."

"Rigorous?"

"Um. Yeah. For when someone drinks too much"—she wrinkled her little nose—"or has a fight and leaves blood everywhere. Do fishermen do that much brawling?"

Shay smothered his smile. *Not fishermen.* The records indicated the cabins filled every full moon with unmated shifters here for the Gatherings. Single males were always fighting, hoping to impress the females. "Hiring her might be a good idea. I'm not the greatest housekeeper in the territory. Not like Zeb."

"You keep leaving the place a mess, and he's going to wallop you one of these days." Her sweet giggle grabbed Shay by the balls and squeezed. "I've been wondering—how did you learn to fight together?"

"You're full of questions these days," he mused. "I should charge you. Collect some thanks."

She gave him a puzzled look.

"I showed you how a female thanks a male." He set a finger

under her chin, lifted, and kissed her. Soft, soft lips. A feminine scent with vanilla and cinnamon and as sweet as any pastry. He felt her stiffen…but not in fear.

SHAY WAS BEING so gentle, Bree thought. His lips brushed over hers, then he licked her lower lip. A shiver ran down her spine and pooled into a warm lake at the base.

"Mmm, more," he murmured. He nibbled on her lips until she opened her mouth, and then swept inside.

He tasted of peppermint and power. As her head spun, she gripped his arms, disconcerted by flexing muscles under her fingers. Anxiety ran through her, and she pulled back.

He smiled and turned back to the table as if he hadn't made the floor shift under her feet.

She stared at him a second, then—heart still hammering—picked up a puzzle piece. It dropped from her shaking fingers.

With amusement in his blue-gray eyes, he handed it to her and answered her question. "I was in the Sawtooth Territory when I felt the pull of Herne, calling me to Rainier Territory. Ailill Ridge has more hellhound activity than here, and they'd lost a couple of cahirs. Zeb had already been there about a month."

"Wait. The pull of Herne. What does that mean?" When he reached for her, she dodged. "Hey, you haven't answered my question yet."

"As a lodge-owner, I've learned to get payment in advance." The sound of his smooth husky voice increased the heat rising in her veins. He slid a hand around her waist and pulled her to him. His chest was big, wide, and she rested her forehead against it, trying to think.

"Breanne?"

When she lifted her head, his mouth claimed hers. No light kiss this time. His tongue swept in, taking possession. His arm around her waist kept her pinned against him, and his other hand squeezed her bottom.

A hurricane of sensation crashed over her. Her arms wrapped around him, and she could only hold on. The place between her legs woke up, tingling, needing.

He finished with a light nip to her lower lip. Before she could get out of reach, he cupped her chin in a big hand and studied her face. His lips curved as if pleased.

"My answer?" she asked, breathless.

"Years and years ago, I vowed to fight hellhounds for the God of the Hunt. Herne." He traced the mark on his cheek that resembled blue-tinted antlers. "Being oathbound creates a kind of trail between him and me. Of course, it's nothing like the highway to the God that the Cosantir has."

"Oh, sure." Her laugh died when she remembered the shimmering air around Calum, how power had flowed into her when he forced her to shift. "Go on."

"Now, Zeb likes to move around. No real direction, just whatever place has hellhounds. Since I'm oathbound, when Herne needs me somewhere, I'm pulled in that direction. I pack up and follow the call until I arrive."

Pack up and leave? Just like that? Years of various foster-homes had taught her what moving was like. Never belonging, always the new girl. And all Shay had to look forward to was blood and death? She wanted to give him a hug.

"When I got to Rainier Territory, the Cosantir assigned me to work with the newest cahir—Zeb. Said he was an evil-tempered wolf."

Bree choked on a laugh. "So true."

"Aye. At first, we fought more than we cooperated." Shay grinned. "He didn't like taking orders."

"And Shay never stopped giving them," came a rough voice.

Bree looked around. Zeb leaned on the wall, his arms

crossed. His hair was loose, a black curtain over his shoulders. He looked angry, sounded angry, but she knew him now. That tiny crease in his right cheek meant he was trying not to smile. "So how did you work it out?" she asked.

"Well—"

"Wait." Shay tugged her hair lightly. "This little wolf is earning her answers with kisses. She pays in advance."

"But…" Her voice faded to nothing as Zeb's eyes darkened. He stalked forward, all predator, making her feel like a defenseless rabbit in an open field.

He was taller than Shay, she realized, when he took her wrists and put them around his neck. His scent was as dark as his deeply tanned face. Studying her with black eyes, he pulled her inexorably closer until she was up against his hard body. His voice was a low rumble. "You will earn your answers." He took her mouth.

Firm, demanding, a little rough, yet gentling immediately. When her lips relaxed, he took more, wet and deep and urgent, until all the blood in her body slid down to her lower half. As her breasts rubbed on his chest, her nipples tightened as if someone were pinching them.

Her arms tightened around his neck.

When he finally pulled back, he had to steady her. Shay gripped her waist to help. Two sets of men's hands were holding her, and somehow she wasn't afraid. All she could see was the fire burning in Zeb's eyes as he looked at her.

"She paid, so answer her question, a bhràthair," Shay said, amusement plain in his voice. His huge hands massaged her waist, and she held her breath, wondering if he'd move them elsewhere.

The gravelly sound of Zeb's voice rubbed over her nerves, like the sandpaper that lights a match. "A hellhound was chasing a little girl. Too close. I emptied my pistol to turn it around.

Figured I'd die. But that idiot"—he glanced at Shay—"shifted to animal form, even though no wolf can win against a hellhound. He ripped at it from the rear."

"No one realized that our fangs could get between the smaller leg plates. I was just trying to keep Zeb from getting killed. Actually getting through the armor was a surprise," Shay said. His arm slipped around her waist, and he pulled her back against his chest. She felt something—he was erect. *Oh my goodness.*

Zeb ran his knuckles over her cheek, drawing her attention. "Before that, he'd tried to talk me into using diversions and teamwork. But I wasn't interested."

"You're more stubborn than a moose in rut."

"But when the demondung went after Shay, I used one of his fancy ideas. Dove, gutted it, rolled out." Zeb stroked his lips against hers again, as if he couldn't get enough. "His plan worked."

Shay snorted.

"So we're partners," Zeb finished. "I still feel like killing him sometimes."

"You and what pack?"

Zeb stroked around her ribs until his knuckles rubbed the lower part of her breasts. Shay's hands were still curved around her waist. The feeling was...indescribable.

With a slight smile, Zeb glanced over her head at his brother and then whispered in her ear, "Ask us more questions, little female."

Chapter Seventeen

EARLY THE NEXT week, Bree scowled as she walked the mile to town. *Walked.* Not much choice since the car made her itch. Shay had laughed and said, "*Shifters and metal don't get along.*" Good to know, but darn it.

Then again, she might as well walk. She sure didn't have much else to occupy her time, aside from wolfy lessons. She'd stopped her target practice. What was the point? Bullets wouldn't kill hellhounds and cost money she didn't have.

Living in the lodge meant she could use the game room, weight room, and TV room, but even those diversions grew old. She was used to working. She *liked* working.

Sure, Calum needed a barmaid for a few hours on the weekends, but that wasn't a career. She lived at the lodge for free, but what about food? Clothes? Even books? *I need a job.*

The few days of warmer weather had melted most of the snow and left the air moist and sweet. As she entered town, she saw a few daffodils were trying to open quickly, as if knowing there'd be more snowstorms before the winter ended. She sighed, missing Seattle.

On the plaza island between traffic lanes, she turned a circle, frowning at each shop in turn, this time with an eye to employment. So few people, such small stores. Maybe the Victorian bed and breakfast needed a maid?

Or... Her eyes narrowed. Next door to the B&B was Angie's Diner. *Hmmm.*

When she walked in, she decided the place was exactly what she'd thought a country diner should look like. With a wooden floor, high ceiling, and square tables covered with blue checked tablecloths, it had a friendly atmosphere. The kitchen was through a door on the left, behind a long counter. The glass-fronted shelves held baked goods. She studied the pastries. The pies, obviously, came straight out of a box. No cake or cupcakes or cookies. *Oookay, here we go.*

A middle-aged woman with faded blonde hair and sharp blue eyes walked out of the kitchen, wiping her hands on a white apron over her jeans. "Would you like a piece of pie?"

She looked familiar. "Do I know you?" Bree asked.

"Not exactly. I'm Angie, and ashamed to admit that I'm part of the pack." The woman's lips drew tight.

Bree's cheeks heated. Had everyone in town seen her naked? Seen her on the ground on hands and knees? Darn it. "You're the one who yelled, '*Leave her alone*'."

Angie shrugged. "Like I did any good. Those two cahirs were a lot more effective."

Thank God for that. "Yeah." Bree stopped, unsure how to move on.

"So, want some pie? Coffee?"

She got a good feeling from the woman. Blunt, good-hearted, self-assured. Bree wiped sweaty palms on her jeans. "Coffee if you'll join me. I'd like to discuss an idea with you."

Angie raised her eyebrows. "Well. Let me get cups."

They settled down at a table close to the counter in case Angie had to get up.

"Do you run this place yourself and make all the meals?" Bree asked.

"Pretty much. You looking for a job?"

"Not exactly." Bree took a slow breath. "I was a pastry chef in Seattle, but Calum says I have to stay here for a few months."

"Long commute," Angie commented in a dry voice.

Bree grinned. "I noticed your pastries aren't homemade. And there isn't much variety."

"I might be insulted, but I think I see where you're going with this. Go on."

"Maybe you'd be willing to try offering donuts sometimes, or cakes, or fresh pies? I'm a really good baker."

"And I hate baking." Angie pulled a pencil and paper from her apron. "No reason not to give it a try. Let's throw some figures around."

An hour later, Bree stepped out of the diner and took a deep breath. Pine from off the mountains, narcissus from the B&B's round planters, coffee wafting from the bookstore's open door. What a lovely world.

She had her first order. The thrill bubbling in her veins mingled with anxiety. She wouldn't have a steady paycheck coming in. *Don't think about that.*

Where to start? *Supplies.* Good, her brain was working…kind of. Flour, butter, fruit, sugar. Given the quantities Angie had specified, maybe the grocery owner would give her a discount. Any little bit would help.

She'd pick up some food for meals as well. The guys sure didn't know how to stock a kitchen. Until now, she hadn't cared. Between healing and long runs as a wolf, she'd been too exhausted to cook more than a can of soup, and sometimes fall asleep before finishing it. But she'd adjusted. Last night, she'd wanted to bake, but hey—no decent fixings.

As she headed toward the grocery store, a gnome peered up from under the curb grill, its stubby fingers waggling impertinently.

Gnomes were so—"Oomph." She hit a body and staggered back, realizing she'd almost knocked a woman over. "Sorry."

"Well, if it isn't our newest member—the baby rabbit who had to be rescued by cahirs." Blatantly sneering, a tall, dark-haired woman stared down her nose at Bree.

Wow. Who spat in your coffee? Bree wondered, then frowned. This was the person who'd shoved her at the pack meeting. Bree tried to shake off her animosity. "Hello." Was there some etiquette for greeting other shifters?

Silently, the brunette walked in a circle around Bree.

Hackles rising, Bree turned to keep her face to the woman. "What is your problem?" Bree finally snapped.

The woman got right up close, her upper lip rising. "Don't get bitchy with me, rabbit, or I'll rip you into stew meat." She shoved Bree.

Without thinking, Bree returned the favor. Her palm impacted the woman's sternum and knocked her back a step.

Shock, then anger turned the woman's sultry beauty ugly.

Great. Way to make friends. "Look, I don't want to—"

"Is there a problem here?" *That voice.*

Bree spun around. Klaus stood in the door of the grocery. When his gloating gaze lingered on the fading bruises on her face and neck, bile rose in her throat. She swallowed hard, then lifted her chin and deliberately stared at his still swollen nose.

Rage flashed in his eyes. "What's up, Thyra?" he asked.

"Did you see, Klaus?" Thyra waved her hand. "She struck me—she disrespected me."

"I saw. You want to call a meeting?"

"Oh, get real," Bree said, dismay edging her voice. "You pushed me, I pushed you back. What are you, a five year old?"

"Insolent bitch," the woman hissed. "You'll learn your place. I'll deal with you at the pack hunt."

"Can't," Klaus said. "Gerhard called off the run since we

just had one."

"Then right now. The park's empty this time of the year." Thyra pointed toward a half-hidden park running along the slope behind the stores. "I'll round up some pack females. Klaus, make sure the rabbit doesn't run."

"Will do." The man licked his lips. "It's always a pleasure when you discipline your females. This one especially should be fun to watch."

As Thyra stalked down the street, Bree's stomach churned like a blender set on high. She started to move away. *Get out of town.*

"Go ahead, rabbit," Klaus said from behind her. "Gerhard hopes you'll screw up and give him a reason to order you out of the lodge. To put you under stricter supervision."

The idea sent a bolt of ice through her. So...what was the worst Thyra could do—yell at her in front of everyone? Straightening her shoulders, she crossed the street.

The little park was cold with mounds of snow under the bare branched trees. The empty swings creaked in the rising wind. Bree shivered, staring at the dull gray clouds over the western foothills. Another storm was coming in.

Klaus stood under a tree nearby. Zeb had called him a scat-head—a shit-head. Very appropriate.

As women trickled into the park, a few greeted Bree with a nod. Most avoided her gaze, and two of the younger ones grinned savagely. When Angie failed to arrive, Bree's last hope of reprieve died.

As the women formed a circle, Thyra sauntered into the center. "Are you ready, rude rabbit?"

Bitterness ran through Bree's veins. Once again, she'd blundered into an idiotic shifter custom. "I'm sorry, but I have no clue what's going on. Would someone explain?"

"The humans must have raised you on stupid pills." Thyra

sighed loudly, getting a laugh from the two younger women. Anger sparked to life in Bree's gut.

"It's like this, rabbit," Thyra said. "I'm the alpha female, which means I'm in charge of the pack females, including you. You do what I say, when I say, and you do it respectfully—or I tear you into pieces. Clear enough for you?"

Where did they get these leaders—*Assholes 'r' Us*? "That's clear. I'm sorry I didn't know who you were." The apology stuck like dry bread in her throat.

"I'll make sure you remember for next time."

Criminy. Resigning herself to a fight, Bree dropped into a defensive stance. From the way the woman moved, she should be easy enough to take down. But a person like this would only get nastier if she lost.

Thyra's lips curved coldly. "Trawsfur."

"What?"

"We fight as wolves, stupid. We're pack." Thyra was stripping as she spoke, and her cold brown eyes raked over Bree. "Shift or I'll take you on in that form."

Fight a full-grown wolf as a human? The memory of the hellhound's teeth ripping into her arm made her stomach clench. Blinking back tears of frustrated anger, Bree yanked off her clothes. At least, her fur would protect her some.

As she shifted into wolf, she felt that wonderful sense of belonging from the earth, but it didn't last.

She looked at Thyra. A heavy-boned wolf with dark fur. A lot bigger than Bree. As her yellow eyes focused on Bree, her lips lifted to show long fangs.

Bree felt the fur on her neck and back rise. Nervously, she moved sideways. Her front legs got mixed up, and a chill slid through her. *I don't know how to fight in this form.*

Thyra charged, snapping at her muzzle. Bree tried to dodge, and the wolf smashed into her shoulder. Bree went down hard.

Scrambling up, Bree tried to defend herself, but the wolf was all over her, biting at her ears, face, and body.

Bree reared onto her hind legs to grapple, but the other's size and weight over-balanced her.

Bree landed on her side. Jaws closed over her throat, the teeth bearing down.

"Kill her, Thyra," Klaus yelled, his ugly voice thick with anticipation.

Bree struggled, paws scrambling futilely. *I can't breathe.*

"What in the Mother's name is going on here?" Angie's firm voice.

The jaws tightened. Darkness edged Bree's vision.

"Thyra, you won. You kill her, and the Cosantir will banish you. Just sayin'."

Thyra growled. After a long second, she let go.

Air. Tongue hanging out, Bree sucked in air. Half conscious, she tried to regain her feet. Tried again. Finally, she stood, wide-legged and panting.

Thyra had already shifted and pulled on her clothes. She glanced scornfully at Bree. "Remember your lesson, rabbit." As she walked out of the park beside Klaus, the other women trailed behind. Only Angie lingered.

Thyra turned. "Leave, Angie. Now."

Angie's jaw tightened, but she obeyed.

Tail drooping, head hanging, Bree stood alone.

After a minute, she shifted to human. An icy wind whipped around her, and she shivered uncontrollably, her insides as cold as her skin. Clumsily, she pulled on her clothes, the fabric painfully scraping bites and bloody spots. A warm trickle ran down her face—her cheek had a long gash. Thyra had been a thorough wolfy, hadn't she?

As the first drops of cold rain fell, Bree walked out of the park on unsteady legs. *I hate this place.*

SHAY JOGGED UP the porch steps and entered the lodge. Despite the pouring rain, satisfaction curled like a satisfied puppy inside him.

Sprawled on the big leather couch in the main sitting area, Zeb looked up from his current mystery. "You been in a farmer's chicken-coop?"

Grinning, Shay dropped into the adjacent chair. "I rented out cabins five through seven for two weeks."

"This early in the season?"

"Some state office in Olympia closed for remodeling, giving their people unexpected time off. A bunch of accountants wanted to get away from the city."

"Good for us." Zeb frowned. "What's booked?"

Shay stared at the ceiling, doing a mental count. "Cabins three and four have two couples here for a long weekend. They leave Tuesday. Ten has the old guy. The fly-tier."

"Scrawny. Beard to his belt?"

"That's him. Like an underfed dwarf." Shay smiled. "You know, the season hasn't even begun. We're going to do okay, a bhràthair." He rose and yanked Zeb to his feet. "Let's get a beer and celebrate. Where's Breanne? I haven't seen her since this morning."

"Sounds like someone's in the kitchen."

"Well, we don't have brownies. Must be her. Cooking." Shay's stomach rumbled with anticipation.

"Speaking of brownies, you think we could lure some here?"

The thought was appealing. The small OtherFolk would keep a kitchen spotless in exchange for cream and sweets. Shay shook his head. "They only move in once a family is stable. We're not."

"Oh. Right." The flash of disappointment on Zeb's face was quickly covered.

His brother wanted to stay in Cold Creek. Guilt settled on Shay's shoulders.

Zeb stopped in the kitchen doorway and glanced back. "Since it's your fault we don't get brownies, *you* should do all the cleanup."

His heart lightened. "Don't even put a paw on that trail." With a thump, Shay knocked Zeb sideways and stepped in first. The kitchen smelled like rich roasting meat, and Shay's saliva glands jumped into action. "What are you cooking, a leannan? Are you going to share?"

"Roast beef." Breanne was bent over, peering into the oven, and her ass in the tight jeans made a shape like a plump heart. Shay hardened as other appetites wakened. His fingers curled, wanting to grip her hips, to hold her for his thrusts. He forced out a slow breath.

Zeb gave him a wry look of understanding and adjusted himself inside his jeans.

Giving a melodic and so-very-female laugh, Breanne poured something on the meat. "Of course, I'm sharing."

I want to share. You. With my brother. Shay closed his eyes. *Bad wolf.*

"Herne help us." Zeb's mutter sounded as splintered as raw-cut wood. "One cold drink coming up."

As Zeb rummaged in the fridge, Shay took himself and his very visible erection over to the oak table. A large salad bowl filled with greens occupied the center. Shay set out the stacked plates and silverware.

She closed the oven door and turned.

Though he knew her face was flushed from heat and not from arousal, the knowledge didn't convince his dick to ease up. And then he saw the long gash on her cheek, mottling her fair skin. "By Herne's antlers, what happened?"

Startled at his loud voice, she startled back and bumped into the oven.

Zeb turned, looked, and snarled. As he stepped toward her, the scent of his anger filled the room. "Who hit you?"

She held her hands up as if to push them away.

They both took a step back, but by Herne, it was difficult, and even harder when Shay noticed bite marks on her wrists and arms where she'd pushed up the sleeves of her sweater. The tip of her ear was ripped. Shay's eyes narrowed. There was a lumpy area—bandages—under one jeans' leg. "Your leg, too."

"And side," Zeb said. "You fought someone."

"We're not angry at you, lass." Shay gentled his tone. "Just tell us what happened."

The unhappiness that filled her eyes wrenched his heart. His instincts couldn't be denied. He took a step forward and folded her in his arms.

After a second of resistance, she melted against him, all soft curves and sweet female.

He closed his eyes as the satisfaction of being needed filled empty places inside him. Unable to let go, he looked over at Zeb and got a wry smile in return.

Want to keep her; can't keep her. Their pack of two must run alone. With a sigh, Shay pulled back and took a firm grip on Breanne's upper arms. She'd stay put until he had answers to his questions. "Talk to us."

Tears sheened her eyes, but she blinked them away. Such a tough female wolf. Such a battered one.

Zeb sat down at the table.

The silence forced her into speech faster than yelling would have. "I met Thyra." A spark of anger showed. "Apparently a pack has an alpha female as well as a guy."

"A female did that?" Zeb asked in disbelief.

"Oh." Breanne sighed. "She certainly did."

Stunned, Shay released her. She took a seat at the table

across from Zeb.

"We should have checked out the females for you," Shay said. "I'm sorry, Breanne."

Zeb's jaw was tight as he echoed, "We're sorry."

"Oh, guys." She reached across the table to pat Zeb's hand, and surprise blanked the cahir's face. Shay almost smiled. The male wasn't used to forgiveness.

"Actually, I doubt a warning would have helped," she said. "If somebody shoves me, I'll push back. That's all it took. She decided I needed to be disciplined."

"She did that much damage? In my pa"—by the God, what was he saying?—"I've never seen an alpha female do more than nip."

"This fucking pack is as warped as a board left in the rain." Zeb's face softened. "How bad are you hurt?"

Breanne shrugged. "You guessed it all. I'm okay."

Her voice sounded hoarse, Shay realized. He grasped her shoulder and tugged her turtleneck sweater away from her neck. Red-purple bruises ran down the sides of her throat.

From across the table came a low growl.

"Didn't you stop fighting when she got your neck?" Shay strove to keep his tone level. Even in male challenges, the victor rarely went that far.

She pulled her sweater out of his grip. "I went limp the minute I felt her teeth on my throat, and after she cut off my air, it wasn't as if I could fight very well."

"Your air?" Another growl from Zeb. "Was she *trying* to kill you?"

Breanne frowned. "I think she got carried away. She let go when Angie arrived and said something about the Cosantir."

Anger burned in Shay's guts, hotter than the oven behind him. He was powerless. What he wanted to do... "Males can't interfere in female business."

"Fuck that. I'll kill her," Zeb rumbled.

Shay gave him a half-amused look, despite his agreement. "You might try. I don't think you could." A male's instinct was to protect the female, no matter how angry he got. Did Gerhard know his alpha female was doing this?

With a sigh, Shay cupped Breanne's face, wincing at the gash. "At least, you'll heal more quickly now than you would as a human."

"That's—Oh, the food!" She pulled away and ran to the oven. "Just in time." She started pulling pans out, and the scents filling the room made Shay moan. "You guys finish setting the table and get drinks while I make gravy."

Gravy? Shay stared as she dished up roast beef, potatoes, and carrots. She pulled something else from the oven, and he recognized a scent from his childhood. "Rolls? You made rolls?" Hell, he'd bare his throat for home-cooked rolls.

He and Zeb barely managed to restrain themselves until she sat down. Then it was war.

Finished long before, Breanne propped her chin in her hand and watched the two of them. "I guess all those muscles burn a lot of calories."

A female noticing a male's body was a good sign. The next step was to get her delicate hands sliding over all those muscles. He cursed under his breath. If he didn't stop thinking like this, he'd be in misery before the full moon.

Breanne would be at the Gathering this time.

The thought of how she'd rub against him, growl her need as he took her, as he'd bury himself so deep inside her slick flesh that—he shook his head—it was going to be a long, uncomfortable week.

CRIMINY, THE GUYS ate as if they'd been starving for a month. Bree loved watching them.

She saw Zeb's surprise when he started to use knife and fork on the roast and realized he only needed the fork. His eyes had half-closed in pleasure with the first bite of potatoes.

Shay had wolfed down five rolls, and his blissful smile was as evident with the last as the first. He finally leaned back with a groan and patted his stomach. "I don't think I've ever had a finer meal. Ever. Your humans in Seattle must be missing you mightily."

Her smile faded as she remembered the regulars who had visited her restaurant. She hauled in a breath. *That's my home. I need to go home.* "I miss them too."

Shay took her hand and kissed her fingers. "Sorry, a leannan. I didn't mean to make you sad."

"Bree." Zeb's black gaze had softened as if he could feel her pain. "Do you want to cook for a crowd?"

"Here?" She glanced at Shay who looked confused.

Zeb leaned his elbows on the table. "Thorson, the bookstore owner, said the Wildwood held a barbeque every other Sunday during the season. All you can eat for a set price. Open to lodge guests and townspeople alike."

"Really." Shay's eyes narrowed. "That sounds like a lot of work for—"

"A barbeque wouldn't be that hard," Bree interrupted. "That must be why that grill out back is so big. If one of you does that part, I can manage the rest of the food."

"I'm good at barbequing." Zeb noted her surprise and added, "The Elder I stayed with…" A flash of grief darkened his eyes and tightened the muscles in his jaw. "Elder Lain only knew how to barbecue."

"Then Shay can handle the people and money." Bree grinned, delight rising in her. A challenge. "It's what he's good at, after all."

"Hey, my fried chicken is fantastic."

"When it's not burned," Zeb said, earning a glare. "The shed's full of redwood tables and chairs. They'll need cleaning and refinishing."

"The grill needs work as well." Shay tapped his fingers on the table in calculation. "It'll take time to get the word out. Let's plan on the last Sunday of the month."

Not quite two weeks. She could figure out a menu, get familiar with this kitchen's quirks, and pick up any equipment she needed, although the kitchen was surprisingly well equipped. Someone here had liked to cook. "That's a workable time."

"Keep your receipts for the supplies. We'll have this business separate from the lodging one, so you can get a percentage of the profit," Shay said. "I have a feeling it'll do well. There aren't many social diversions in town."

"A percentage?" She'd never worked for anything but a salary. Now she had a deal with the diner, and she'd have money coming from the lodge. A business of her own. A thrill like the finest champagne bubbled up. "That will be acceptable," she managed, trying for a blasé tone.

When both men laughed, all she could do was grin.

TWO NIGHTS LATER, Bree dropped onto the shaggy rug in front of the living area fireplace and groaned. Heat radiated from the crackling fire with soothing warmth as she rolled onto her stomach and stretched. God, everything ached.

She heard a thump and a low voice. "What's wrong?"

She opened her eyes.

Zeb knelt beside her, worry on his scarred face. "Are you hurt?"

"Sorry, I didn't see you." His book lay on the floor, the cover showing a blood-drenched body. Why did someone who fought hellhounds want to read gory mysteries? "You are so strange."

His lips quirked. "You're not injured."

"Oh yes I am, you sadist." She tried to sit and groaned, flopping back down. Her eyes closed. "Do you know how many tables I sanded clean?"

A low chuckle. "Sore?"

"You have no idea."

She heard him move, then felt him over her, straddling her, knees on each side of her hips.

Panic blasted through her. She pushed up.

He swatted her butt lightly and growled, "Stay put, little female." As his scent swept over her, reminding her of a shadowy glade she'd found near a stream, she relaxed.

His weight shifted, and his oversized hands closed on her aching shoulders, squeezing and releasing as his thumbs dug into the knots beside her spine.

"Oooooh, yes."

His rare laugh rumbled out. He eased up, running his palms up and down, the warmth loosening more tension. "Did Calum have any news for you from the other territories?"

She felt a twinge of grief and let it go. "Not much. My parents might have lived in Gray Cliff in Rainier Territory, but hellhounds wiped out the town a while back." She sighed. "Did you know there's a shifter on the Seattle police force?"

"Heard that."

Bree smiled at the obvious disgust in Zeb's voice. "He said the summer I was found, the area was full of flooding and car accidents, as well as a few murders and a hellhound. There's no telling what happened to them."

"That bother you?"

"A little. You know, I always thought I'd been abandoned, but Calum said shifters are fanatical about children. That makes me feel better." He pushed on her low back muscles, and she sighed. "What were your parents like?"

The hands hesitated, then continued with long strokes. "No fathers—my littermates and I were full moon bred. My mother died a few years after we were born, and my uncle got stuck with us." His voice was flat.

"Not a good father figure?" Bree asked lightly.

"He hated people. Hated cubs. Didn't talk. Much like me."

"Hardly. You like people. You just don't want anyone to know."

His hands stopped, and she shut her eyes. *Put your foot into it, didn't you, Bree?* But it was true. With that uncle, it was amazing Zeb hadn't turned out a total jerk instead of just rough and gruff.

He was silent, but his hands resumed their work. Within a few minutes, he'd reduced her to a boneless mass of gelatin. She started to drift off to sleep.

"Over you go," he murmured and rolled her onto her back.

Her eyes popped open.

He straddled her, weight on his knees—and before she panicked, she realized he was studying her. Waiting for her to do just that.

"You good?"

This was Zeb. "I think so."

But... He was going to massage her *front*? His hands settled above her breasts. His thumbs dug into the aching muscles under her collarbones, moved toward her breasts, but stopped short. He massaged her upper pectorals and shoulders, then up and down her arms, squeezing right to the edge of pain. Knots dissolved, and blood flowed into the uncramped areas. She sighed.

Finally, when she could swear she was melting between the thin cracks in the wood floor, he lay down beside her.

She opened her eyes.

Head resting on his hand, he watched her.

"Thank you."

He raised one eyebrow as if to remind her of Shay's game, then cupped her cheek. With his thumb on the other side of her jaw, he held her still.

His lips were as warm as his hands. Propped up on his elbow, he lazily indulged in his kiss, teasing and then demanding a response. His hand moved from her waist upward, brushing the side of her breast. With each slow stroke, her skin grew more sensitive, until her nipples were tightly bunched and aching. Her back arched her up toward him.

The thump of footsteps on the porch announced the arrival of Shay.

Bree sat up quickly, staring at Zeb. "Go sit in your chair," she ordered.

A crease appeared in his cheek as he ran his finger over her lips. "You look well kissed, little female, and no wolf could miss the scent in this room."

The scent. A flush scalded her face. As Shay opened the door, Bree jumped to her feet and escaped up the stairs.

Chapter Eighteen

Cold Creek, North Cascades Territory ~ Full moon

"VICKI DIDN'T RETURN today." Shay strode into the library corner of the lodge. His guts felt as if the fly fisherman had tied them into intricate knots. "Calum says she wrenched her ankle. She's staying in Elder Village for a few more days."

Zeb's book dropped to the floor, and dread rolled over his face like black thunderclouds. "You've got to be fucking joking."

"No joke. By the God, Zeb, we have to warn Breanne about what to expect. We shouldn't have put it off." But waiting for Vicki had made sense, since just a year ago, she'd been human, and she could have explained Gatherings.

Now they were caught in their own iron-toothed trap. "Does Breanne have *any* female friends?"

Zeb considered. "A couple of the wolves, but the alpha bitch ordered all the females to stay away until Bree does a public apology. To finish off her *lesson.*"

Pack politics. Shay's teeth snapped together. He'd like to sink his fangs into Thyra and shake some courtesy into her. But only the alpha male could do that. "Nobody else?"

"No females." Zeb scowled. "We should've pushed harder, brawd. Kissing and fondling aren't enough to prepare her for tonight."

"If we'd pushed, she'd have run. At least she trusts us." Shay paced across the room. "She's newly changed. Maybe the heat won't hit her yet."

"Maybe. Or maybe it'll overcome her fears."

Shay kicked the edge of the rug, wishing it were Thyra. "There's nothing we can do."

"Nope." Zeb frowned. "Oh fuck."

"What?" Shay glared. "We don't need anything else."

"Damn fucking right." Zeb scrubbed his face like an annoyed raccoon. "Did you talk with her about lifemating or male-female ratios?"

Shay stared at him, dismay rising. Humans only mated one male to a female, but shifters... "By Herne's hooves, surely she's noticed?"

THE DINER'S CUSTOMERS had cleaned out the pastry shelves, and Angie had reported they'd begged for more. Bree couldn't stop smiling as she trotted up the steps to the lodge.

Her smile faded. Angie had also said she wasn't allowed to chat until Bree publically apologized to Thyra. Angie'd been pretty steamed about the decree, but apparently, the alpha female had the power to enforce her rules.

Mood spoiled, Bree closed the lodge door with a slam. The thought of apologizing to the bitch unsettled her stomach worse than the rat she'd eaten a few days ago. But she couldn't find a way to avoid it. Not if she wanted to make friends with the women in the pack. Thank God, Vicki was a cougar and not under Thyra's control.

After hanging up her coat, Bree took a step and stopped.

Shay sat at the library table where she'd set up a jigsaw puzzle, Zeb in a chair nearby, both watching her with concern.

Worry slickened her palms. "What's wrong?"

"Nothing." Shay rose. "We need to talk to you about something."

"Okay." Did they want her to leave? Her feet dragged as she crossed the room. She sat on the couch next to Zeb's chair. "What's up?"

"It's…" Zeb looked at Shay helplessly.

Shay sighed. "We've been teaching you the way of the Daonain. How to trawsfur. How to be a wolf. But there's more to our customs."

"Like the pack laws?"

"Not just pack," Shay said. "All the shifters—men and woman. I'm talking about mating."

Oookay. Her stomach tightened. "I'm not totally inexperienced, guys." And thank goodness she'd had sex a few times before being raped. "I remember how it goes. A man meets a woman. They like each other. They make love—or mate. Right?"

"Not exactly." Shay joined her on the couch. His weight compressed the cushions, sliding her until her hip bumped against his. "By Herne's antlers, this is hard to explain."

"Bree." Zeb's gaze captured hers. "Each full moon, fertile Daonain females come into heat."

Heat. "Like a dog or cat comes into h-heat?"

Zeb nodded. With a glance, he tossed the conversation back to Shay.

Shay's warm hand closed around Bree's icy fingers. "The full moon is tonight, and your body will want to mate with a male. Will require a male."

A bitter laugh broke from her. "Wouldn't that be a change? That's not—"

"Before, you only had humans around," Zeb said.

Shay agreed. "Daonain aren't attracted to humans."

The idea derailed her growing anxiety for a second. "That's why I never wanted a guy? Because I'm a shifter? That's why with you two, I—" Oh God, what had she almost said?

Darn Zeb for that slashing grin. "That's why."

"Conceited creepazoid," she muttered to her hands. "So I'm going to get all horny tonight and might jump one of you?"

"Not that easy," Zeb muttered.

"By Daonain law, each territory holds a Gathering at full moon," Shay said. "There, each female mates with the males she chooses."

You've got to be joking. Bree swallowed. "What if no one suits me?"

"Your body will choose. Your head will not." Zeb's voice was deep, firm. "And your body will choose more than once."

She yanked free and rose. Her heart hammered inside her chest so hard her lungs couldn't get air. She gasped in a breath. "No. Absolutely not."

"Easy, a leannan." Shay stood, obviously hoping to calm her. "The Law requires only that the unmated spend the night at the Gathering. If you don't want to mate, no one can force you."

"Yeah?" Bree started to breathe again. She could just hang out quietly. Let them have their orgy without her. "Okay then. But I want you to know—this sucks."

"Does, doesn't it?" Shay ran his hands up and down her chilled arms. "Being able to trawsfur into a wolf is a wondrous thing. And the animal nature has benefits—an extra forty years of life, improved healing, better senses and strength. But it also has drawbacks."

"So what's with the law stuff?"

"Our traditions and laws ensure Daonain survival. Our fertility is much lower than humans', and five times more males are born to us than females. The only thing that saves us is that most births are twins or triplets. And the Gatherings."

His matter-of-fact voice soothed. Bree rested her hip on the table. "Am I going to run into more weird laws at this Gathering?"

Zeb thought for a second. "No possessive behavior is allowed." He gave her his half-smile. "Any other time, however—all bets are off."

Shay continued. "Males may fight to win a female's favor, but the Law forbids killing or maiming. The penalty is being cast out."

Was that why Thyra had stopped? "Cast out means you have to leave the territory?"

"Worse." Zeb's voice roughened. "No Daonain will see him, hear him, or speak to him."

She shrugged. "So he'd move somewhere else where no one knew him."

"The Cosantir slashes them." Zeb curved his fingers and drew them across his cheek. "Herne turns the scars black."

Shay added, "If the Mother eventually forgives the crime, the scars turn white, and the shifter can return."

Cold fingers closed on Bree's spine as she imagined wandering a world of people who didn't acknowledge her existence. "That's horrible."

"Many die," Zeb agreed softly.

"Enough of this." Shay rubbed his forehead against hers. "You won't be fighting, little wolf. Tonight is for mating."

I'd rather fight.

Zeb's gaze met hers in perfect understanding.

"The moon rises in two hours," Shay said. "Let's clean up and eat. We'll walk to the tavern together."

She couldn't move. The men there would pressure her to have sex. She knew it. *I can't do this.*

"Little female," Zeb snapped. "A male does not bother a female who is uninterested." A crease appeared on his cheek, and his gaze warmed. "I showed you how we know."

She stared at him, remembering the day outside the cabin

when he'd held her wrist, inhaling the scent. A lick of heat flared in her belly.

The corner of his lip pulled up. "Exactly."

Well, okay. She wasn't interested in any guy, so no one would bother her. *It'll probably be like Amelia's bachelorette party at the strip joint. Lots of drunken horny woman and happy men. I'll sit at the bar and watch.*

BREE STILL HELD strong a couple of hours later as she and the men walked up to the tavern.

Ignoring the "CLOSED FOR PRIVATE PARTY" sign, Shay opened the door and shooed her before him.

One step inside, she stopped. Welcome to Cold Creek's meat market. Women and so many, many men. Turning in a circle, she gawked. One guy wore skin-tight jeans that cupped his ass. A tall blond had skipped a shirt and wore only a vest over a muscular chest. One had a trimmed beard, another a five-o'clock-shadow that her fingers tingled to touch.

The scents were overwhelming. Zeb was right. She could smell arousal. Testosterone had a scent too. Dark and musky. Every inhalation warmed her until she felt as if she'd lowered herself into a hot tub. Her skin felt odd, as if sunburned and sensitive. When she moved, her clothes teased her with new sensations. Her bra rubbed until her nipples tightened painfully.

She tried to ignore it all. Jeez, she wasn't an animal to be ruled by hormones.

"Give me your coat, lass." Shay pulled her jacket off with a smooth tug.

Mmmh, his eyes were steely blue, so intent, and... *Get a grip, dummy.* "Um." Her voice came out disconcertingly breathy, as if she'd jogged over a mountain. "How about a beer?"

Because, darn it, she needed alcohol. Or ice water. Calum

must have set the furnace thermostat at ninety degrees. "How long do we have to stay, anyway?"

Shay chuckled. "Long enough to at least get inside the room."

Snorting in agreement, Zeb set his hand on the hollow of her back and pushed her farther into the room. The heat from his palm, the very feel of his hand was as if he was reaching inside her and stroking her to arousal. *Oh heavens, what is happening to me?*

With a grave look, Zeb studied her.

Bree stared up at him. His hard jaw was incredibly masculine, slightly darker than the rest of his face even though he'd shaved. His lips curved. She remembered the feel of his mouth on hers and wanted it again. She ran her fingers down his chest, savoring the hard bunching muscles.

He made a rumbling noise, and his hand closed around her wrist. He lifted it to his face. Inhaled. "Little female, I don't think you're going to manage to leave."

The sound of his deep, grating voice dragged on her nerves, and she swayed toward him. Then her mind untangled the words. "Leave? Yes, I'm leaving. I'm not staying here, Zeb."

He pressed a kiss to her wrist, sending her senses spinning with the feathery touch, the wash of warm breath. She inched closer to him.

"Good to know." He glanced at Shay. "Commandeer a corner?"

"That's the plan. Gonna be harder than I thought though." Shay's low voice was a smooth stroke of hot silk, pulling her to him as if he'd tugged on a leash.

She stepped closer, breathing the fresh icy scent that was his alone. He smelled like a man. All man. His chest was twice as broad as hers, his shoulders blocked out the room.

His unrelenting stare made her knees weak. "Breanne, come

with us."

River rock. Zeb's voice was jagged granite, Shay's was like river rock, all round and smooth, but still hard.

"Breanne?"

"Oh." She blinked, shook her head. "The corner. Sure. I keep getting...sidetracked or something." Every nerve in her body was firing full-time. "Sensory overload, I guess?"

Shay's fingers curled around her bare upper arm. The abrasion of his calluses was heady, and she moved closer.

"You're killing me here, a leannan," he murmured. As they threaded through the crowd, she caught more scents. Men. Everywhere. They stared at her, their gazes like fiery tickles against her skin.

In the front corner by the fireplace, Zeb shoved tables around to create a blocked off area with a small entrance. "You sure, Shay? Make her start with a stranger?"

"By Herne's antlers, I'm not sure of anything. I just know that if one of us tries and she panics, she'll feel we betrayed her, and she won't have anyone here she trusts." Shay sighed. "If she can handle one or two males, we'll see if she's still interested in two rough cahirs."

"Good enough."

Bree heard their conversation, but their words flowed like water, slipping past her understanding. Yet lovely. Like with wolf song, their voices wove around each other, creating a beautiful pattern.

Zeb stepped closer. He cupped her chin to tip her face up, caught her gaze, and she fell forward into eyes the color of the night sky.

"Fuck." He growled, and the sound shivered through her, making her want. *Need.*

"Bree, listen."

She blinked. "Got it. I mean, I'm listening."

"Shifters will come over. Nice males. *Short* males. If you like one, he'll take you upstairs and—ah—kiss you."

"Okay." She leaned forward and rubbed her breasts against him.

"Fuck." His low growl made her pussy tingle, but then he sat her in a chair.

A chair? She started to get up.

"Stay there, lass." Shay's gaze compelled obedience. "The men will come to you."

As the two men moved away, the air temperature decreased, and her head cleared. Slightly. Taking positions on each side of the barricaded entrance, they waved off man after man until two shorter ones approached. Not small, barely under six feet.

One was lean and rugged-looking with gorgeous turquoise-colored eyes. The other seemed less tough. Sweeter. Not as interesting. After Shay talked with them, they walked into her corner.

"I'm Wayne." The sweet-looking one knelt on her right. His blonde hair gleamed in the light from the wall sconces.

"My name is Evan. I'm from over the border." Taking a knee to her left, the lean one was darkly tanned, his grin almost as bright as Zeb's.

Zeb. She stared at him, at Shay. Why didn't they come to her? She caught Zeb's gaze.

He stepped toward her, then his lips tightened, and he turned his back. When Shay did the same, it felt like a connection snapped.

A hand stroked down her thigh, and she jumped.

"What's your name, pretty one?" Evan asked in a voice that pulled at her, gentle but with a firm base underneath.

"Bree." His face was all angles, cheekbones high and tight. His mustache was the rich brown of his hair and silky soft under her fingers. She traced it twice, marveling at how neatly it curved around the slope of his mouth. "I've never kissed anyone with a mustache," she murmured. Would it tickle? How would it feel against her?

"Do you want to kiss me, pretty one?" He took her hand. His palm was hard, rough, and wonderful, and as he kissed her fingers, his lips were petal-soft in contrast. The mustache tickled her knuckles. When his mouth closed over her fingertips, the wetness of his tongue made her moan. Heat flared into an oven fire inside her, and she leaned toward him.

He pressed a kiss to her wrist, inhaled, and stood, pulling her up with him and against his side. His arm curved around her waist. "Let's go upstairs where it's not so noisy," he murmured. His warm breath brushed her cheek, and she nodded. "Sorry, Wayne," he said.

Had there been someone else beside her? She'd been rude. She tried to turn, but when Evan eased his fingers under her shirt to find bare skin, a rising fire burned the thoughts right out of her head. A pulse throbbed low in her body between her legs.

Somehow, Evan led her up the stairs, but she didn't notice much, never getting past the feel of his hands—one teasing her fingers, the other on her waist. He steered her into a tiny room. In wall sconces, candles flickered with yellow light. Pillows were scattered across a cushioned floor.

Her legs buckled as she realized what the room was for. As she landed up on her hands and knees, a quiver of fear ran through her.

Evan dropped down beside her. "It's okay, pretty one. The cahirs said this is new to you. We'll just sit for a bit, eh?"

His smile was the nicest thing about him, she thought, until he took her hand. Why did the abrasion of his palm make her lower half melt—and flame at the same time.

Watching her with blue-green eyes, he licked her fingers, one, then the next and the next. His tongue was hot and soft but with a little roughness, so different from his mouth.

His mouth. Her gaze fixed on it, how smooth it looked under that silky brown mustache. His lips curved into a satisfied smile.

"C'mere, and you can see if the mustache tickles," he invited, tugging her closer. As she leaned into him, he kissed her gently. The brush of his lips and mustache sent heat streaking through her and tightened her nipples. "Oh, yes," he murmured. "You're a sweet one. We won't hurry."

He kissed her, over and over, nibbling on her lips, sliding his tongue across her mouth until she opened to his demand. He tasted of apples and cinnamon, and when his tongue plunged deep, she needed him so badly that she took his hands and slid them onto her breasts.

As he plucked at her nipples, she whimpered. He cupped her breasts and kissed her more deeply, and the mixture of sensations made her head whirl. Laughing, he rose to his feet to unbutton his shirt and pull it off. As he stepped closer, he loomed over her, a huge shadow backlit by the candles. "I'll—"

"No!" Choking on fear, she scrambled away from him. *No, no, no.*

"Bree. Wait." He stopped, motionless as a predator, shirt still in one hand. His nostrils flared. "By the God, you're terrified."

Trapped in the corner, she panted and tried to draw in enough air to speak, to scream, to fight. Instead, her chest tightened until she couldn't breathe.

He took a step back. "Relax, pretty female. Nothing happens if you're not into it—and, right now, you really aren't."

When he pulled his shirt on, she managed to get a full breath. She stared at him, stomach in knots.

After studying her for a second, he backed farther, all the way to the door.

Evan wasn't going to do anything. He'd only been nice. Shame made her want to hang her head, courage kept it up. "I'm sorry."

"I am too. You're very sweet." His grin was still nice, especially from a distance. "Let me take you back downstairs."

Face all those men. Again? "Can I stay here for a minute? Settle down a bit?"

He nodded. "I'll wait outside and escort you down."

Have him lurking in the hall? A tremor ran up her spine. "I'll do better alone. I really am sorry."

He looked as if he wanted to come forward and reassure her, but he stayed there. "No worries, Bree. I'll be back in the States next fall. If you want, we'll try again, eh?"

He stepped out into the shadowy hallway. As the door closed, she heard someone speak to him.

She was alone. Resting her forehead on her knees, she shuddered. How had she gone from desire to panic so quickly? What was she going to do? She rubbed sweaty hands on her jeans. As her heart rate dropped to normal, the heat inside her grew. Her skin started to tingle, her breasts—

The door opened and she looked up. "Evan?"

Not Evan. *Klaus.* A blade of fear stabbed into her chest.

He closed the door behind him. "Well, if it isn't the rabbit. Having problems?"

"Go away." Her voice sounded thin and weak. As she pushed to her feet, the cushioned floor sank under her weight, and she staggered sideways.

"Nah, I don't think so. Got something to finish." His smile distorted his meaty features into evil. "Not fucking you. But no bitch busts my nose and lives to boast of it."

Her brain froze with the memory of her nightmarish fall, his threats, his fists. She instinctively stepped back. Her lips trembled in spite of her attempt to firm them.

He saw and then slowly inhaled. "Oh, you're scared now." Satisfaction thickened his voice, and his heavy-lidded eyes gleamed with cruelty as he moved toward her.

Terror grew, until she gasped for air, unable to scream. She'd barely fought off one panic attack and had no reserves to handle another. Her fingers went cold. Numb. As her heart ricocheted painfully in her chest, she struggled against the darkness edging her vision. *No, Bree. Must fight.*

He swung, and she ducked, then blocked his follow-up punch. Her return blow to his belly was weak.

His fist hit her cheekbone with an explosion of pain, knocking her back. Her shoulders crashed into the wall, and her senses spun. Leaning on the boards for balance, she front-kicked right into his stomach.

He grunted, hunching over.

Yes! She swung at his temple, but he slapped her fist aside and backhanded her to the floor. Her jaw felt broken. She struggled to sit up. Blood dripped onto her shirt.

As he stood over her, a *monster*, her head reverberated with shrill screams—hers, Ashley's. The walls turned red as if drenched in gore. Whimpering, she fought her terror, trying to regain her feet. The brutal stench of his anger and pleasure filled the room.

Over the shrieking in her head, she heard his gloating laugh. He kicked her in the stomach.

Pain. Oh God. Nausea filled her world and she dry-heaved. Yet it broke her free of the panic attack. Her body took over, responding to years of karate drills. She rolled to her feet. Still unsteady, she staggered back. She glanced at the door. Too far.

He stalked toward her.

Chapter Nineteen

ZEB TROTTED UP the stairs, ignoring curious looks at his unaccompanied state.

With obvious concern, Evan had reported to him and Shay what had happened with Bree. Zeb scowled. If a short shifter didn't work for her, who would? Maybe he or Shay should try, leaving the other for backup in case she panicked. The thought of mating with Bree filled him with warmth. He'd never wanted to be with a female so much.

And yet, if he scared her...*her*...it would gut him completely.

At the top of the stairs, Zeb slowed. First room to the right, Evan had said, and by the God's balls, Zeb didn't want to open the wrong door. Hand on the knob, he sniffed and caught Bree's scent as well as Evan's...and another male's? Even as he smelled aggression and fear, Zeb heard the smack of a blow—so different from the sound of sex. A muffled cry of pain.

His shoulder rammed against the wood. The door crashed against the wall.

Trapped in a corner like prey, Bree faced the alpha's brother. His jaw bore a red mark the size of a small fist, and Zeb's pride flared. The little female was terrified but on her feet and fighting.

Zeb took a step into the room. "What is going—"

She turned and he saw her bloody face. More red was spattered down her shirt. As rage whipped into an uncontrollable storm, he roared and charged.

Klaus jumped back. "It's not what—"

Zeb hit him so hard that at least three ribs cracked, and the male's body dented the wall. Grabbing the scat-head by the neck, Zeb threw him out of the room.

Threw him down the stairs.

Trying to scramble away on hands and knees, the gibbering coward wet himself when Zeb leaped to the bottom of the staircase. With a grip on his collar, Zeb dragged him into the center of the tavern.

A female screamed, shrill and annoying. Shouts. Males closed in. Warily.

"Zeb!" Shay shoved two people aside.

"Bree's upstairs. She needs you. Now."

Shay ran for the stairs.

Zeb fought his instincts, his need to rip apart the male who'd hurt Bree—*my Bree*. His fists opened and closed. *Where's the fucking Cosantir?*

Klaus managed to regain his feet, blabbering at the growing crowd of shifters. "She deserved it. She—"

The memory of Bree's terrified face splintered Zeb's control like an axe against rotten wood. His fist lashed out.

The crunch and breaking of bone was satisfying, Klaus's gut-wrenching scream of agony less so. The asshole sprawled on the floor. He'd never hurt another woman with that arm again.

Anger pulsed in Zeb's head; each beat providing a picture of Bree's face. Blood so red against her whitened face. Terror and courage. Zeb moved forward. *Hit him, over and over.* Be sure the male could never—

"Zebulon." Calum's voice was a winter mist, damping the fire. "Step back. Now."

Zeb hauled in a breath. Finding a space of calm and momentary quiet, he moved back an inch. One more. The red streaking his vision faded, and he received horror-struck stares from the people surrounding him. When he looked at the broken man at his feet, he knew he was doomed.

Gerhard shoved forward, bellowing more like a bull than a wolf. Standing over Klaus, he saw the damage. "He maimed my brother. During a Gathering!" His hand shook as he pointed at Klaus's shattered arm where bones poked whitely out of the skin. "I demand Cosantir's Judgment. I demand—"

"Silence." The Cosantir's command stilled the room, leaving only the clink of a glass and Klaus's sobbing breaths. Calum's gray eyes slowly darkened to the black of the God. "Zebulon. I require an explanation."

Zeb gritted his teeth, fighting the compulsion to answer. He'd broken the Law of the Fight, and he'd be cast out, no matter what he said. Any explanation he gave would reveal why Bree was so terrified—that she'd been abused as no female shifter ever had. She'd shown how shamed it made her. Others, like Thyra, would use it to hurt her.

With no other explanation, the crowd would simply think a mating fight had gotten out of hand. *Leave it at that.* Klaus couldn't harm her anymore. Zeb shook his head. "Just banish me and have this done."

His refusal brought a murmur of shock from the shifters surrounding them.

The Cosantir's unreadable gaze rested on him, then shifted to Klaus. "Explain."

"She wanted me, and she pulled me into the room," Klaus rushed out in gasping breaths. "I was interested, but she started yelling curses against Gerhard. And she hit me. I only slapped her to settle her down; to get her away from me so I could leave."

Zeb shut his eyes, unable to look at the lying scat-head. If only he could block his ears as well. He was the stranger here, always the outsider. No one would believe him over the alpha's brother.

A scent drifted to him, sweet female and vanilla and cinnamon. Bree's hands closed around his arm. Her fingers trembled and yet, she stood beside him. Beside him against everyone. The shock stole his breath, as if he'd fallen from a cliff and landed hard.

Shay stepped up on his other side, his shoulder rubbing Zeb's. Brother to brother. "Cosantir, there's more to this."

Power seethed in Calum, more than could be contained in his body, enough to create waves in the air around him. He didn't speak, merely tilted his head toward the little female.

She took an audible breath. "I... I—"

"No." Zeb put his palm over against her soft lips. "It won't help. The Judgment won't change. Don't do this to yourself."

A huff of almost human exasperation came from Calum, and the black gaze pinned Zeb with the bite of a panther's claws. "*Kneel.*"

Zeb's knees gave way, dropping him to the floor.

Bree gasped and gripped his shoulder with tiny cold fingers.

The Cosantir studied her. "He has bought you the right to remain silent."

"I don't want it. Darn it, Zeb, I won't hide behind you like some—some mouse." She sounded defiant, but her hand trembled without cease. "He..." She pointed at Klaus. "I was in that upstairs room alone, and he came in and shut the door and said h-he wouldn't f-fuck me."

Zeb needed to hold her—protect her—only his legs wouldn't move. Damn the fucking Cosantir anyway. He looked up at Shay and jerked his head toward Bree.

Shay slapped his shoulder and stepped over to wrap an arm around her. "Go on, lass. I've got your back," Shay murmured.

Zeb could only watch, helpless. Of no use to her.

She took in a shuddering breath. "He said we had something to finish. He meant from the pack meeting when he'd knocked me off the trail, and I'd hit him to get him away from me."

Fury raged up in Zeb. Shay growled. She hadn't fallen—Klaus had hit her.

She touched her face and a purpling jaw. "Upstairs, h-he punched me. Kicked me. I fought back—I did!—only I was so shaky and—and that's when Zeb came in. He *saved* me." The soft astonishment in her words was there for everyone to hear.

The Cosantir's gaze didn't waver. "Why was a female in a mating room alone?"

"By the God, you—" Zeb started.

"*Silence.*" As Zeb's throat closed, Calum turned his attention back to Bree.

She swallowed audibly. "I—I'd gone upstairs with E-Evan and I tried to, only I got scared." Her voice faded to a whisper. "I panicked and he was nice and left, but I wanted to—to get it together before I went back downstairs."

Calum nodded and spoke without turning his head. "Owen, please check the room upstairs."

"Aye, Cosantir." The cahir trotted away. Footsteps thudded up the stairs.

"She panicked?" Still beside his brother, Gerhard sneered. "Like anyone'd believe a bitch in heat would panic. She's lying, Cosantir."

Bree gripped Zeb's shoulder as if she needed him to hold her up. "I'm not lying. I was r-raped just before I came here and s-sex… I haven't…" When her fingernails dug into his skin, Zeb risked wrapping an arm around her hip where it pressed against him. Her whole body was shaking.

"Thank you, Breanne," Calum said softly. "As your Cosantir, I cherish the bravery you have shown by speaking when you might have remained silent."

Owen trotted over and stopped on Zeb's other side in open alignment. The anger scent coming from him was so strong it overwhelmed any other. "Cosantir."

"Tell me, cahir."

"The room is scented with the female's blood. And fear." Owen jerked his chin toward Klaus. "No scent of arousal from that one. Just aggression."

Gerhard turned white.

As Klaus cringed, the Cosantir stared at him and finally spoke. "You enjoy causing pain to others. Especially females. During our sacred Gathering night, you attacked a terrified female."

Klaus whimpered.

Calum touched white scars on Klaus's cheek. "You were banished before and forgiven. This time, your banish—"

The air around the Cosantir pulsed...thickened. His voice deepened into the avalanche of sound that heralded the God of the Hunt. *"No banishment. This Daonain is twisted inside. He will not change in this lifetime. Females must be protected."*

Zeb's harsh inhale echoed Shay's. It was a God's sentence. Dread curled in Zeb's stomach.

The black gaze of the Cosantir turned to Gerhard. *"Move away."*

Gerhard opened his mouth, but no sound came forth. Tears filled his eyes as he rose and stepped back.

Klaus had his arms over his head as if to fend off a blow.

The Cosantir's voice was his own when he said gently, "Return to the Mother, Klaus." As he gripped Klaus's shoulder, power flowed.

Life drained from the shifter's eyes. With a long exhale, his body went limp. He fell sideways, and the thud of his body hitting the floor was a blow to the heart. His eyes stayed open, staring at nothing.

The stench of fear filled the room, but silence reigned as if time had stopped. Even if Zeb could have moved, his bones, even his spirit had turned to ice. He would willingly have killed Klaus for what he'd done but this was cold. Fuck, he'd never thought...

Shoulders slumping, the Cosantir sighed, then straightened his spine as slowly as an old man on a winter morning. "Owen, Ben, please help Gerhard with Klaus's body."

"Aye, Cosantir," Owen murmured. Ben nodded. As the two men picked up the dead shifter, people began to stir and voices rose.

The Cosantir pinned Zeb with a long stare. "Rise, cahir."

Zeb blinked at him, unable to comprehend. "But..."

The room went silent again.

"Shut up, stupid," Shay hissed. "Get your ass up and say thanks." He released Bree and jerked Zeb to his feet.

"I—" *I'm not going to be cast out?* "I—"

"Your response was overly aggressive, but understandable. A cahir's instinct is to protect—and to protect females above all else." Calum's eyes were a reassuring gray. He gave Zeb a tired smile. "Perhaps in the future, you will not be so hasty to render judgment upon yourself. It is why they pay me the *big bucks*, is it not?"

Finally, Zeb found the words. "Thank you, Cosantir."

"Truth requires no gratitude, cahir."

Zeb shook his head—he was so wrong—and, at last, turned to Breanne. Wide-eyed as a fleeing horse, shaking like an aspen leaf, tears in her eyes, and totally white-faced. "By the God, little female, you're a mess." The shifters had dispersed, excitement changing to noisy chatter as they rehashed what had happened. The scent of females in heat was filling the room again.

Bree stared at him, pupils dilating, and took a step closer.

She jerked back. "No. No no no." Her nipples tightened even as her shaking increased. "I won't." Her face twisted in horror, her voice broke. "I don't *want* this."

"Fuck." He pulled her into his arms. "Calum, she can't take more."

Calum studied her, then looked around. "Donal, could you join us?"

The healer trotted over. "What can—" He scowled at the bruised and bleeding female. "Dammit, again?"

"Again," Shay muttered, stroking her hair.

Calum sighed. "Donal, please knock her out for the night."

The healer nodded. He tilted Breanne's chin up. "Breanne, look at me."

Zeb felt her shudder as her gaze was caught.

"Sleep, little one," the healer whispered. "Sleep until the sun rises again."

As she crumpled, Zeb scooped her up into his arms. Where she belonged.

BREE AWOKE THE next morning in her bedroom in the lodge. The sun's rays slanted through a gap in the curtains. Music drifted up from downstairs. Country-western, which meant Shay was home. A sense of safety filled her, warmer than the fuzzy blanket someone had tucked around her.

She stretched and winced at the pain in her ribs, then gritted her teeth and swung her legs out of bed. Her jaw ached, and she touched it gently. She must look like she'd been in a bar fight. But the other guy...

Her stomach wrenched. *The other guy is dead.* Surely, they could have just arrested him. But Calum had said he was twisted inside—no, it hadn't been Calum who spoke. She shivered. Their god had passed judgment, not Calum.

After staggering to the bathroom, she checked her bruises in the mirror. No biggie. She'd earned worse in karate matches. What burned was how badly she'd done against the guy. Note to self: *stop having panic attacks.* Or, at least, don't have one on top of the other. Or stay out of little rooms designed for sex.

She watched the mirror as a flush rose into her face. If Evan hadn't scared her… If he hadn't stood over her like that monster-man, she'd probably have screwed his brains out. Her skin started to crawl as if she'd rolled in a sewer.

Desperate to get clean, she yanked off clothes that stank of fear and blood and turned the shower on. Scrubbing helped the memories, but not the facts. She was a neurotic, psychotic mess. Maybe in a kazillion years, she'd be ready to have sex again.

But the men said this *heat* would happen every full moon. She slapped the tile wall so hard her palm stung. Darn this shifter stuff!

Well, if she had to lose control of her body, she'd do it on her own terms. She remembered when she and Ashley had tried tequila. Ash had spent the night throwing up, but Bree didn't remember. She'd passed out.

Before the next full moon, she'd have at least one bottle in her room. *And I'll chug it down until I pass out completely.*

THE UPSTAIRS SHOWER turned off. At the kitchen table, Shay sighed in relief. When he'd heard the water come on, he'd barely kept from rushing up to make sure she was okay.

At the stove, Zeb tilted his head. "Tough, isn't she?"

"Amazing. I'd be hiding under the bed if I'd been her."

"You wouldn't fit." Zeb poured the eggs into the frying pan.

Shay watched him, trying to forget the blinding fear when he'd thought Zeb would be banished. Shay sucked in a breath. By the God, he'd already lost two littermates, damned if he'd lose this brother.

Light footsteps sounded, and Breanne walked into the kitchen.

Shay rose. "C'mere, and let me check your face. Donal was afraid to fix it—said it would wake you back up and you'd probably rather have the bruise."

"He was so right. It's not that bad. Really."

Shay put a finger under her delicate chin and tipped her face up to the light. Over her jaw, her fair skin was swollen. An ugly scab was surrounded by purple-red bruising. Shay clamped his mouth tight against the foul words boiling up. Klaus had paid the price, the ultimate penalty, but seeing Breanne's marred face still sent biting fury into Shay's gut. "You'll live," he said lightly. "Want some ice?"

"Nah." She went up on tiptoes, and her lips brushed over his jaw. "Thank you for the rescue," she whispered.

Surprise held him immobile as she moved away. His skin tingled from her soft lips, and he had to smile. She'd kissed a male without being pushed into it.

By the God, she was so brave. So gentle. She drew him with every breath, and every day, he wanted her more. He wanted to share her with his brother. To see her bloom and fatten with their pups. To hear her laugh, see her big blue eyes in the mornings, hold her in his lap in the evenings. He craved it more than food, than water.

Shay watched as she tugged on Zeb's sleeve. When Zeb glanced down, he got a kiss and thank you also. He muttered something and concentrated on his cooking, undoubtedly to hide the same impossible wish. In this room were the most deadly cahirs in the Northwest, and the little female turned them into fluffy bunnies with a touch. Hell.

"Fuck." Zeb slapped the spatula down, grabbed Breanne's arms, and scowled at her. "Klaus hit you, knocked you down at the pack run. You didn't tell us."

Anger flared in Shay at the reminder. "You let us believe a lie, in fact."

Zeb gave her a tiny shake. "Why?"

She glared at him, then Shay. "What would you have done if I'd told you?"

Ripped his throat out. "Beat on him. Taught him some manners."

"My word against his," she said. "Who would Gerhard believe?"

Shay frowned. "His brother."

"Exactly. If you roughed up his brother without a good reason, wouldn't Gerhard kick you out of the pack? His territory?"

Zeb's jaw dropped. "You lied to *protect* us?"

She crossed her arms over her chest and frowned at them. "Well, duh."

Chapter Twenty

THE SIGN SAID: "COME AROUND TO THE SIDE" with an arrow pointing toward the right. As Zeb finished attaching it to the porch railing, he noticed Bree standing nearby. "Problem?" he asked.

A week had passed since the Gathering. She looked better, finally. He and Shay had taken turns dragging her out of her room and running the mountain trails with her. Not a hardship. He liked having the little wolf at his side.

She'd tried to protect me. Twice now. Fuck, he still couldn't get his teeth around it.

"Do you think anyone will come?" she asked.

Females did like to worry, didn't they? "Relax." He rubbed away the wrinkle between her delicately curving brows, pleased when she didn't retreat. "Calum and his family will come, the storeowners, our guests in the cabins, other cahirs and their families. Enough."

She sighed. "You know, I've put on huge events at the restaurant and never been this nervous. I don't get it."

After a second, the answer came to him. He cupped her face in his palm and almost lost his thought. What was there about her smooth skin that sent lust straight to his groin? "Your Seattle events were for humans. This is for your clan. The stakes are higher."

Her breath huffed out, warm on his wrist. "You're right. Is this how people usually feel then?"

"No clue." He'd never given a party in his life.

As she pulled away, she eyed him. "You're touching me an awful lot."

"I like touching you." He took her hand and breathed in the scent from her wrist. *And you like my hands on you.*

When his eyes met hers, she flushed beautifully and retreated back to the house.

Pink was getting to be his favorite color in the world, especially on a fair-skinned female. What shades would he find elsewhere on her...and how would each taste under his lips and tongue?

BREE HURRIED BACK to the kitchen, her skin tingling where Zeb's hand had cupped her face. When he did stuff like that, she wanted to let him do more. His hands were so skillful at everything. Building and repairing. Fighting and shooting. What about sex?

The thought sent heat right down to her toes.

Get a grip, Bree. Doing anything sexual with Zeb would be *such* a bad idea. What if she reacted as she had with Evan? She wouldn't be able to face him afterwards. Heck, she'd never be able to stay here in the lodge, probably not in Cold Creek.

Nope. Stick to a nice friendly *distant* relationship with the two guys. A no-touching friendship.

She frowned. Considering the way Zeb had inhaled her scent and gotten that barely visible, Zeb-smile, she might have trouble with that plan.

In the kitchen, she checked the baked beans, pleased with the fragrance of ham and molasses. Bowls of potato salad and pasta salad waited in the refrigerator—and now she knew why the fridge was so big. Hors d'oeuvres were ready: crisp vegetables with dip, tiny spinach quiches, and chips for the younger ones. The corn was wrapped for the grill. Drinks were in the refrigerator.

Showtime.

When voices sounded outside, her gut twisted as if she'd swallowed a rat—a live one. *Relax. I know all these people.* Only that made it even worse. After sucking in a fortifying breath, she grabbed an hors d'oeuvres tray and walked out the kitchen door.

As Bree set the tray down on the appetizer table, she looked around. At the vine-covered entrance, Rosie was collecting money from townspeople. The older woman had cheerfully volunteered to serve as gatekeeper and cashier in exchange for a free meal.

To Bree's delight, a few guests were already scattered around the patio. Near the center, Calum sat at a table, laughing at something Zeb had said.

As if Zeb had felt her gaze, he turned, and his black gaze ran like firm hands up and down her body. She flushed, realizing she'd been staring at him. The thoughtful smile curving his lips and molten heat in his eyes said he knew. "Join us, little female."

The rough sound of his voice sent a shiver down her spine. She walked over.

"You look better, Breanne," Calum said. When she stiffened, his smile disappeared. "I regret you suffered at Klaus's hands, but you probably saved others from worse. Another female might not have had a cahir to defend her.

His words eased much of the guilt weighing her down. He was right. Klaus wouldn't have stopped with her.

"He broke the Law, Breanne, and Herne rendered judgment and execution." The haunted look in his face slapped her out of her self-pity. What kind of nightmares must he have? He'd saved her, but at what cost to himself?

"Thank you, Cosantir," she said softly. She bent to give him a swift kiss on the cheek.

Then she shook her head as if it were her fur. Enough of the past. This was *supposed* to be a party. "All right, boys," she said. "I've been wondering, did you two get together to coordinate your clothes?" She tugged on Zeb's T-shirt. "Black and black and—oh, yes, more black. I may have to go shopping so I can join in."

Calum's expression lightened. "It's efficient at least."

Zeb snorted and stepped into her personal space, right into up-close-and-intimate. "Yellow looks good on you, little female. Leave black to the ugly males." He ran his finger along the fancy beadwork on her V-neck sweater, occasionally brushing her skin rather than fabric.

A disconcerting zing shot through her, and her nipples tightened. She took a step back. From the quirk of his lips, she realized she should have worn a more padded bra.

"What would you like to drink, Calum?" she asked hastily. "We have beer, iced tea, Kool-Aid, lemonade, wine, and water."

"An iced tea would be pleasant." Amusement danced in his eyes.

"Coming right up." She chanced a frown at Zeb and saw the same laughter in his eyes.

Men.

In the kitchen, she poured Calum's drink and set sugar, napkin and spoon on the tiny serving tray. After giving him his tea—Zeb could darn well get his own—she made trips back and forth, bringing out the hefty glass pitchers of tea and Kool-Aid and lemonade. Tubs of iced beer set next to the table holding wine glasses and mugs.

Over at the barbeque, Shay raised his eyebrows at her, silently asking if he should start. She assessed at the number of people—people, yay!—and nodded.

The first steak hit the grill with a sizzle, sending out a heady aroma of meat marinated in garlic and butter. *Cholesterol watchers—escape while you can.*

Bree grinned when Vicki entered the patio with Alec. 'Bout time the woman got back. "Hey, you."

As the two walked over, Bree frowned. Alec had curved an arm around Vicki's waist and was stroking the bare skin exposed by her midriff top. Vicki was married to Calum. Didn't Alec realize his brother could kill someone with a touch? Even if he couldn't, messing around with a married woman wasn't right.

"So." She forced a bright note into her voice. "How have you been? Um, both of you?"

Vicki rolled her eyes. "Bree, don't ever play poker."

Bree huffed out a breath. When she'd lived on the streets, she could pickpocket, hotwire cars, and steal as well as anyone. But lying? She screwed it up every time. "I just asked how you were."

"And you were thinking, why's Alec wrapped around me and Calum isn't, right?"

"Jeez, let's just say what we think," Bree muttered, flushing as she darted a look at Alec.

"No, don't involve me. I managed to escape discussing this when Vixen first arrived. I'm sure not going to now." Alec bent and kissed Vicki—open-mouthed with major Frenching—and sauntered over to join the other men.

"Fuck, what that man can do with his tongue," Vicki murmured.

"Uh, Vic? You know what TMI means?"

A snort. "Too much information?" Grinning, Vicki pushed her dark hair back over her shoulder. "What you saw with me and Alec? Shay asked me to discuss that with you."

Why in the world did she need to hear about Vicki's extramarital flings? "This isn't exactly a good time." Never would be the right time.

"True, but I'm leaving in the morning for Elder Village again."

"And hearing about you and Alec is urgent—why?"

Vicki laughed. "Oops, fucked-up communication. I meant, I'm supposed to talk to you about mating stuff."

God, what next? "Still not the time. The guys can explain."

"Get real. Alec—who talks about anything—refused to discuss this with me. Do you think your uncivilized cahirs will instruct you on mating practices?"

"They told me about the Gathering."

"Did they wait until the last minute when they couldn't find anyone else?"

Despite worry burrowing like a worm inside her, Bree had to laugh. "Absolutely."

"Men are such assholes. But considering the way they watch you, you need to know a couple things. Good intel is essential in foreign cultures."

They watch me? Bree glanced around. Zeb was talking to the bookstore owner. But Shay? Yes, he was watching her, and the possessive expression in his face made heat sweep from her toes to her scalp.

"See what I mean?"

"Yeah." Wow. "He doesn't normally…"

"There are other men here, and shifters are territorial about their women."

"I'm not their—"

Vicki interrupted. "Here are the basics: a lot more men are born than women."

"I know that."

"Good. Then you'll understand why a marriage is usually one woman with two or more guys.

The ground rolled as if Bree had stepped on a carnival ride.

More than one man? Like Mormons in reverse? "No way."

"Yes, way. The men are usually littermates, because brothers don't get jealous of each other. But if someone else poaches— it's war."

Wait, wait, wait Alec and Calum were brothers. Littermates. Bree turned. Alec's laughing gaze met hers showing that he knew exactly what Vicki was explaining. "You're married to both of them?"

"And damned pleased about it. Jody's happy with her trio." Vicki nodded to where the short brown-haired women who ran the cleaning service sat at a table with three men. Three husbands? Criminy.

As Bree tried to absorb the shock, Vicki poured herself a lemonade. "I'll return for the next Gather, and we can talk the evening before. With alcohol. You'll need alcohol."

"I need alcohol now."

"Hell, I totally know that feeling." Vicki sipped her lemonade. "My buddy, Heather, sometimes shows up for our Gatherings, and I'll get her to come, in case there's anything I *still* don't know." She gave Calum and Alec a disgusted look. "Between us, we'll get you up to fighting speed."

"You really were a Marine, weren't you?" Bree smiled. "Yes, ma'am. I'd be very grateful." *I have a friend.*

"It's a plan then." Vicki glanced over Bree's shoulder and ordered, "Now, get back to your party."

Bree turned. Holy cow. Her hand pressed over her unsettled stomach. The patio had filled with a myriad of people: the sunburned lodge guests back from fishing and obviously looking forward to a great time; townspeople, including the grocery store owner, Mr. Baty, and Books's owner, Mr. Thorson; a few human college students; families with children scurrying around like puppies.

The wolf pack stood at Rosie's reception table. Bree felt the blood drain out of her face when she saw Gerhard had come too.

Even as Vicki moved closer, Shay appeared. He pulled Bree back against his broad chest, one arm wrapped across her stomach. Setting his chin on her shoulder, he murmured into her ear, "It was Klaus's own fault, a leannan, not yours, and we'll deal with the aftermath as we need to. I won't let anything happen to you."

"I know you won't," she said. He'd defend her, as would Zeb. Klaus's death wasn't her fault. She had to keep telling herself that.

She studied the small crowd of wolf shifters at the entrance. They'd brought their children and were smiling. They wanted a party, not a lynching. The tight ball in the pit of her stomach uncurled.

"All right, little wolf?"

With reluctance, she pulled away. Why did having those muscular arms around her make her bones melt? "I'm fine, big wolf."

He gave her an approving smile.

"I'll get the rest of the food out." She'd also take a moment to recover her balance in the haven of her kitchen. Too many upsets. Not only a pack with a pissed-off alpha, but the real kicker—more than one man to a woman?

Food I can handle; it's the rest of my life that's a mess.

AS BREANNE HURRIED away, Shay sighed. He'd enjoyed how she'd relaxed into him. She probably had no idea how much pleasure it gave a male to have a female accept his protection.

Not that he'd done a very good job. Seemed like every time she was out of his sight, someone hurt her. Of course, if she'd told them about Klaus's behavior at the pack run, the asshole wouldn't have had a chance at her the second time. Knowing she'd tried to protect him and Zeb had sure left them both off-balance.

Nonetheless, the solution to her getting hurt was obvious—he'd just leash her to his side. Yeah. For now, he needed to get back to work.

After returning to the grill, he finished tossing on the steaks, counted the pint-sized bodies, and added hamburgers and hot dogs too.

A few minutes later, Breanne checked the results of his cooking, gave him a pleased smile, and bore the platter away. Her composure was back, and she had a slight bounce in her gliding walk.

By Herne, she was a pretty sight. Her sweater had a folded-over loose neck that kept sliding down, leaving her pale shoulder bare and begging for a male to nibble on the soft skin. If he pushed the fabric down farther, it would expose—frame—a firm, full breast. He'd wanted to nibble on those breasts even before he knew she was a shifter.

His cock hardened. *Bad wolf.* But by the God, he liked watching her.

She was in her element. With laughing firmness, she broke up an impending fight among the teens, then snagged a lost-looking college girl and introduced her to a bunch of youngsters her age, found a chair for an old geezer and plopped down a game that drew several others to his table.

No, more than her element, this was her domain where she ruled. And beautifully.

He should be doing the same, so he turned to the nearby bunch of his lodgers. "How's the fishing, guys?"

"Hey, I caught a couple of rainbow trout this morning." The nerdy-looking twenty-year-old puffed up as if he'd saved the world from famine. "Only I'm not sure what to do with them now."

"Did you gut them?" *Please say you gutted them.*

"Yeah. Devin showed me. But how do you cook them?"

"Easiest is toss some butter in a pan, coat with flour or cornmeal, salt and pepper them, and fry them up. If you want fancier, ask Breanne." He jerked his head toward where she was setting out big bowls of beans and salads.

"Oh, man, I've wanted to meet her. Thanks!" The nerd and his friends trotted off.

Shay growled, then stopped. They were human. Breanne wouldn't be interested.

Yet the irritating anger—*jealousy*—didn't disappear, and he shook his head. His path was supposed to be a solitary one. Yet he'd acquired a brother. Then Breanne. Hell, the whole town. He gave a grunt of exasperation and noticed a girl waiting patiently for his attention. "Hey, you. Burger, hot dog, or steak?"

Golden-haired with a sprinkling of freckles, she reminded him of a teenaged wolf pup, all angles and no grace. "I'd like a hot dog, please. I'm Jamie, and you're Seamus, right?"

Seamus, my ass. "You've been talking to Calum." After tossing on another dog, he stuck out his hand. "Call me Shay, and I'm glad to meet you, Jamie." He frowned. Damned if she didn't seem familiar. He'd heard her name somewhere. "Have we met?"

"No, sir. Not really. You and Zeb saved me and Bree from the hellhound. I wanted to say thank you." To his shock, she hugged him. Him, the terrifying hellhound-killing cahir.

He held his hands in the air for a second, then caved and returned the hug. Damn. "You're welcome, Jamie."

"You got really hurt," she said, her voice muffled by his shirt.

"Not that bad." He eased back, saw tears on her cheeks, and almost panicked. Carefully, with clumsy fingers, he wiped the tears away. "Listen, cub. I can't think of anyone I'd like to save more than you and Breanne. It was my honor. Okay?"

"Okay." She sniffled, and then her smile broke out like sunshine after a cloudy day. As she ran over to Alec, Shay shook his head. Calum and Alec's cub—no wonder she was disconcerting. Even more terrifying, she had the lethal Vicki as a stepmother. Shay picked up his spatula with a smile. The girl was going to play havoc with the males in a few years.

He flipped some more burgers and checked around.

The ping-pong table at the end of the patio had a group of younger guests while the checkers board he'd left out had attracted Thorson and Baty. The trying-to-appear-cool teenagers played badminton and exchanged banter with the opposite sex. Jamie had joined them, he noticed. At the tables, the older people chatted, feet tapping in time to the Beach Boys music on the stereo.

The barbecue looked to be a success.

"Go deal with the guests. I'll do this." Zeb appeared at his elbow. "Avoid the pack; Gerhard's spoiling for a fight."

"That alpha-hole. He knew what Klaus was like. He should have caged him instead of ignoring the problem."

"Too late now." Zeb plucked the long fork from Shay's hand. "No fighting. I just finished the last repairs from our fight at the tavern."

Suppressing a smile, Shay headed off to do the host duty. His brother had lasted longer than Shay'd expected. Even better, he'd lost the deadly expression he normally wore in public. Cold Creek was good for him.

At the drink table, Shay picked up a wine bottle in one hand and the iced tea pitcher in the other and started making the rounds. He got in an argument with Thorson about a controversial book, admired two newborn cubs, and dodged a pack of milling toddlers. He met Jody and her males who ran the local cleaning service and lingered to discuss rates.

At the sound of cheering, he turned to see a delighted look on Breanne's face.

AS BREE BROUGHT out desserts, the hearty applause thrilled her. She'd made cakes with thick gooey frosting and had ice cream to go with them, plus added a variety of cookies for people who wanted less mess.

The plate of brownies was because she deserved chocolate after the lousy week. And, okay, maybe because she loved seeing Zeb's blissful expression when she handed him one.

Even the pack relaxed as everyone enjoyed a sugar rush. Cake in hand, most of the men—including Gerhard—wandered over to watch the badminton game.

Some stayed. When the hair on the back of Bree's neck rose, she turned. Surrounded by pack women, Thyra was glaring at her.

And this is why I wanted you here. Bree squared her shoulders and approached the alpha female.

Thyra opened her mouth, undoubtedly to say something nasty.

"I didn't understand the rules before," Bree said quickly. "I'm sure you know that I didn't grow up knowing about shifters, and I'm still just learning. I hope you will all help me out." She smiled at the other women before looking Thyra dead in the eyes. "Please forgive me for my mistake, alpha." She lowered her gaze, but it took an effort.

Silence.

Bree stared at her feet, her anxiety smothered by a need to laugh. Most of the pack females were here, witnesses to Bree being all humble and polite. With the Cosantir, other non-pack shifters, and a bunch of humans, Thyra could hardly trawsfur to a wolf and beat her up, or even be blatantly rude. *Gotcha, you bitch.*

"Apology accepted," Thyra finally snapped. "Make sure it doesn't happen again."

Bree nodded, keeping her head down. *Don't snicker. Control the face.* She heard the alpha female walk away, followed by most of the pack.

A hip bumped Bree's, and she looked up.

"Good job, girl." Angie's serious expression belied the laughter in her eyes. "Very sneakily done."

"Why, thank you."

"When you bring your goodies in tomorrow, we'll have a nice chat."

Yes! "Sounds good."

Lips twitching, Angie stepped over to the checkers players, "Thorson, when you win, I get the next turn."

Glowing with her victory, Bree went to the dessert table to assess the damage. Shay was still by the ice cream, using the scoop to gesture as he talked with Alec. Most of the cake had disappeared and over half the cookies. Laughter filled the air, conversations hummed.

The barbecue was a success.

THE EVENT ENDED, guests reluctantly left, and finally only Shay, Zeb, and Breanne remained. Shay finished wiping down the grill and shut the cover. By Herne's antlers, he'd have felt less tired if he'd chased a buffalo herd across the Great Plains. Breanne hadn't been the only one worried. "I enjoyed that. Aside from the pack."

Zeb closed up the trashcan. "Wasn't bad."

"Well, don't go chasing your tail with enthusiasm." Shay grabbed a beer from the icy water in the tub and handed another to Zeb. With a grunt of relief, he dropped into a chair, set his aching feet on the table, and sucked down half the can. "First beer I've had all night."

Settling across from him, Zeb raised his drink in a salute. "Likewise."

"Good people here, a bhràthair." Shay tipped his head back. As the sun's glow faded, stars grew in the black sky. An owl hooted nearby. The spruce tree's pixie, who'd watched the party all afternoon, had retired into her nest.

"True."

"You know, I haven't stayed in one place since I was twenty-three or so." Since his brothers had died. He sighed. "I'm tired of moving."

"Pups shouldn't make life-long vows."

Shay ran his fingers over the two marks on his cheekbone. Herne's antlers for the oathbound. The blade of a cahir. Both had appeared with Herne's acceptance of his oath, right before the agonizing changes to a cahir's massive size began. "I didn't see any future for myself. Too filled with anger."

Zeb's black eyes met his in perfect understanding. And regret.

"Hey, guys." Breanne used her hip to knock Shay's legs off the table, then set down a tray. Plates were filled with steak sandwiches and potato salad. "I saw you didn't get anything to eat."

When the scent of meat reached Shay, his stomach growled louder than a bee-stung bear. He picked up a sandwich. "You, a leannan, are a treasure."

"I know," she said. With a heartfelt groan, she put her feet on the adjacent chair. "This is way more work than being a barmaid."

Shay gave her a grin. "But it pays better. We made a nice profit."

"Cool. I can buy some better kitchen equipment. Angie wants to sign a contract." She beamed at them. "I have a business."

"You look happy, lass."

"I am." She ran her fingers through her hair as she confessed, "I hated Calum for making me stay here. I'd never been out of Seattle, and it was my place. My home."

"And now?" Shay asked."

"Little towns are different, aren't they? People stay put, don't move away. It's stable. I really, really like stable." She grabbed a sandwich for herself. "I moved all the time when I was little, and I hated it. This…it might work for me. I'm going to stay here and make this my home."

Zeb's gaze met Shay's. All too soon, they'd be called away. And have to leave her.

Chapter Twenty-One

THERE WERE ONLY four days until the dark of the moon, and the guys were out somewhere, instructing the Cold Creek cahirs in hellhound killing. Keeping the world safe for shifter-kind. After a couple of glasses of wine, Bree had taken a shower—another one—and readied for bed, but the lodge felt too empty.

Abandoning sleep, she padded back downstairs, still in her flannel pajamas. After dropping a pile of soft blankets by the glass-fronted fireplace, she set her glass and bottle of wine on the hearth.

With a sigh, she settled into her nest and poured herself more wine. The level in the bottle was dropping nicely. After Angie's revelations earlier, she'd needed two showers and lot of liquid courage. Would've been nicer if one of the guys was home, but *hey, more alcohol for me.*

The smoke-darkened fireplace glass showed salamanders dancing in the flames, twining together in very sexual patterns. Yeah. Sex. That's why she was drinking and depressed.

With her usual bluntness, Angie had laughed at Bree's plan to drink herself to unconsciousness for the next Gathering. She'd said no matter how plough-faced Bree got, she'd still try to mate. Maybe she'd pass out for a couple of hours, but it wouldn't last all night.

So Bree had visit Donal next. Talk about a humiliating conversation. He wouldn't knock her out without the Cosantir's orders—and Calum wouldn't give them. Not to avoid the Law.

So she was stuck going to the Gatherings.

And dealing with other things as well. She picked up her glass and drank half the wine. *Angie had mated with Zeb at a Gathering.* Bree had wanted to slap the older woman and tell her to keep her hands off, but Angie hadn't done anything wrong. Supposedly, mating during a full moon created no ties.

And...apparently, at Gatherings, Zeb and Shay attracted females like coyotes to carrion. If a guy was God-chosen—like the cahirs, the Cosantirs, the healers, or the blademages—then women wanted their genes.

She scowled at the salamanders. They looked back, unnaturally still, their eyes like shiny black coals in their glowing skins. *Scaring the children, Bree?* She sighed. "Sorry, guys."

Tails swished and they started playing tag, diving into the coals and sending glittering sparks into the air.

Time to face the facts. Gatherings and heats were going to be part of her life, which meant she *needed* to be able to have sex without panicking.

And she wouldn't have oversized babysitters to guard her either. Angie had been impressed Zeb and Shay had stayed with her, but the Cosantir wouldn't allow it for long. Cahir genes were valued in the clan.

Bree smiled ruefully. The two did have great genes. Shay was gorgeous, Zeb deadly, both devastatingly male. She rubbed the cold glass on her cheek. They seemed attracted to her. Were always touching her. Kissing. Hugging. What would it be like to go further?

Which one would she want to make love with? She'd asked Angie about that multiple men/one woman marriage stuff, and the woman had laughed. *"One thing at a time. If you aren't having sex, then the number of men doesn't exactly matter."*

Good point.

The sound of thumping on the porch made her jump. Cool wine sloshed over the sides of the glass, running over her fingers.

The door opened, and Shay stepped inside. White covered his shoulders and hair. As he set his boots in the wooden bin, she realized the noise had been him stamping the snow off his boots. The storm must have hit.

No one else came in. "Where's Zeb?"

Shay threw his jacket on the coat rack. "He lost the toss and has to walk the route with the younger non-cahirs, teaching them tricks to survive."

Oh dear, Mr.-Count-Every-Word would be a grumpy-pants when he got back. She giggled.

Shay tipped his head, his blue-gray eyes penetrating. "I've never seen you drink alone, a leannan. Is something wrong?"

"Yes." She frowned at wine bottle. Not much left. "Angie told me I can't get drunk enough to skip the Gatherings, and Donal won't knock me out for them."

"Ah." He walked over, silent in his stockinged feet, and crouched in front of her. His hard hand cupped her chin, tilting her head up. "I didn't realize you thought you might escape it."

"It sounded like a good plan to me."

When she pouted, amusement filled his eyes. "Got a new plan instead?"

"Yes." If she could get the words out. She swallowed, her throat appallingly dry. "Would you make love with me?"

HER COURAGE TO face her problems was going to break his heart. Shay closed his eyes. This was going to be as dangerous as stealing honey from a bee tree. At least for him. He'd give her what she needed, but...it couldn't be making love, as she'd said.

He mustn't try to win her to be his and Zeb's mate, no matter how much he wanted to do just that. *Don't ruin her life, furface.* He looked into her big blue eyes. "Yes. If that's what you want."

As he knelt in front of her, her scent carried fear, not arousal. At this point, she'd scare herself into backing out before he even moved. "Give me your hand."

She set her hand in his. The pretty fingers trembled in his big grip.

"Breanne, have I ever hurt you?"

"No."

"Do you trust me?"

"I'm not sure." Her brows drew together. "Um. Mostly?"

He barked a laugh. "Well, that's honest." He kissed one finger. "Did that hurt?"

"N-no."

He kissed another, letting his lips caress her skin, alternating kisses with small licks. She tasted of sugar and apples. He moved closer and kissed her wrist, inhaling the beginnings of arousal. There was no scent like it in the world, and on Breanne's skin, it was a heady fragrance. "Did that hurt?"

She choked on a laugh. "Just stop, okay? I see where you're headed with this."

He was close enough to cup her face in his palm and meet her gaze in the dancing firelight. "I know you're frightened."

She tried to pull back. He followed, keeping his hand on her face, his eyes on hers.

HIS HAND WAS hot against her face, his eyes steely blue as he trapped her with his gaze and his touch. "Shay, I—"

"Breanne, let's try something." His slow smile lightened his face. "I have a friend who is into bondage, whips, that sort of stuff. He's weird, but he likes it, and so do his females."

"You're going to whip me?" Her free hand fisted. *I can't—*

His hearty laugh echoed against the log walls. "By Herne's antlers, no. But his mates say a special word if anything is too much—the pain, the ropes, whatever. If he hears it, he stops right away. We'll use *Elvis*." Shay leaned closer, his body almost touching hers. "Say it. What's the word to make everything stop?"

Inside her stomach, a quiver started. "Elvis," she whispered. Her dog that had risked his life to save her. "Elvis."

"Good lass. If you say 'no' or 'stop,' I'll slow down. Elvis means full halt." His eyes were level.

He would stop if she needed him to. A little of the fear drained away.

"Now you've made me anxious, so you should kiss me," he said. "Can you dare that much?"

A kiss. She stared at him.

The sun lines at the corners of his eyes creased as he smiled. He didn't have dimples—his jaw was too strong. He had a little dent in his chin. She'd like to touch it.

Surely, she could kiss him. She had before, just not as a prelude to… She rose up on her knees and was still too short. He didn't move. Her hand shook as she put it behind his neck. His thick hair curled around her fingers as she traced out the lines of muscle. She pulled his head down and lifted her face.

His lips were gentle. Smooth. She brushed her mouth across his lips and started to pull back.

He murmured, "More."

Her heart was beating fast, but she could breathe. His mouth opened under hers, his tongue tracing her lips. She shivered with the sensation. He nibbled on her chin, gently sucked on her lower lip, and swept his tongue inside.

Heat swirled low in her stomach, as he explored and coaxed her tongue into the play. A man's lips felt different from hers.

Firmer. When he rubbed his cheek over hers, his day's growth of beard scratched lightly over her skin.

He lifted his head, his eyes warm. Intent.

Somehow, she'd leaned into him, and her breasts were flattened against his hard chest. She tried to draw back, but he put his hand behind her, stopping her.

"Is something too much, lass? Use your word if you need to."

She stilled.

As he waited, his hand stroked slowly up and down her back. It was comforting, and yet the hardness of his palm through the flannel fabric was…arousing. "Breanne?"

"I'm okay."

"Good lass." The approval in his deep voice warmed her. "May I have a hug now? Can you dare that much?" Even as she was trying to decide, he pulled her arms up around his neck again and inched her closer until her knees rubbed his, and she pressed against him. "You feel good, *mo leannan*." His arms tightened. "Kiss me again."

She managed a shaky breath before tipping her head up. This time he took charge of the kiss, possessing her mouth so completely that her head whirled. His hands moved, down her back to cup her buttocks. To squeeze them through the flannel fabric. Arousal seeped into her blood.

He lifted his head to murmur against her lips, "We're overdressed." Button by button, he undid her pajama top, his gaze on what was being revealed.

As air brushed over her bare breasts, she grabbed his hands, then hesitated. *This is what I want.* "I can take off my clothes."

His heavy-lidded gaze held heat along with a tenderness that turned her body to mush. "Why don't you let me do it instead?" His gaze didn't leave hers as he curved an arm behind her back. His other hand slid under the gaping shirt and over her neck, her collarbone. "You're so pretty, little wolf, and your skin is so smooth." He inhaled. "You smell like vanilla and sugar. I wonder—do you smell like that all over?"

When his palms grazed over her breasts, panic stabbed her. Her breathing hitched, and she tried to pull away, stopped by the merciless arm behind her.

He paused, waited, and stroked her again. This time she felt the warmth of his hand. His palm rasped over her skin, leaving tingling in its wake. Low in her belly, something tightened. Wanted more. Just like she'd felt at the Gathering.

He pushed her shirt off her shoulders. Naked from the waist up, she stared at him.

"By the God, you're beautiful," he said. At the speed of thick syrup, his hands slid over her arms and back to her breasts. Never getting close to her nipples, he caressed the tender undersides in a long, sweet stream of sensation. "Your breasts were made for a male like me with big hands. Touch me back, Breanne. I want your hands on me."

She stared up at him, mesmerized by the sensations rippling through her.

He rubbed his nose on hers and made her smile. "Will you take my shirt off?"

His clothes. Her hands trembled as if she'd chugged a potful of coffee, but she managed to unbutton his heavy shirt and push it off his broad shoulders. She froze. *No, Bree, you've seen him naked lots of times.*

But this was different. He was touching her. She was touching him back.

Feeling as if she wavered on a precipice in a high wind, she ran her hands over his shoulders and down. He hummed with pleasure as she rubbed his pectorals, feeling the flat solid planes of muscles. The crispy hair across his chest curled like froth around her fingers as she explored his nipples—almost flat until they contracted to tiny points.

His shoulder muscles bunched as she stroked over them and down his arms. His rounded biceps were like granite. "You're so hard. Such a guy."

"And you're a soft, soft female." His voice held a distracting growl. When he took her lips again, he pulled her closer, flattening his hands on her back.

When her nipples rubbed the wonderfully abrasive hair on his chest, her head swam with the sensation.

He moved closer, and his erection pressed against her stomach, huge even through his jeans. The jolt of fear made her grit her teeth. A whimper still escaped.

Although he pulled his hips back a fragment of an inch, he kept stroking her back. His fingers made small dips under the waist of her pajama bottoms. "We'll go slow, Breanne. You have a word to make things stop, remember?"

He wasn't going to quit, she realized, with mingled anxiety and excitement. She gripped his biceps as his hands moved over her relentlessly. He kissed the curve of her neck, then her shoulders, and his lips were warm. The air thickened, and her body felt pliant, moving to his touch. She pressed closer.

With a low laugh, he pulled them over sideways onto the soft blankets, then with gentle, firm hands, rolled her onto her back. She stared up at him, her body tensing as she waited for him to fall on her.

Instead, he lay on his side next to her, raised slightly on his elbow. He studied her, his palm splayed open on her stomach. "You still with me here, little wolf?"

Her heart pounded heavily in her chest, and fear wavered like smoke around her, but her skin craved more of his touch. Her nipples were tight and aching. "Yes, big wolf."

"There's a brave female," he murmured. He set his big hand on her shoulder—no worry there—then surprised her by stroking slowly down her front, skimming tortuous paths around the outside of her breast, doing the same on the other side with teasing slow movements.

Only now, every leisurely brush of his fingers sent a sizzle inward from her skin to where hunger pooled inside her. Needing to give him the same sensation back, she ran her hand down his chest and across the hard ridges of his abdomen.

A dangerous heat woke in his eyes. Leaning over her, he took her mouth again. His palm kneaded her right breast.

She gasped. His fingers fondled her, circling first one nipple, then the other. She couldn't think as his tongue filled her mouth. He pulled back to bite her lips insistently, then kissed her even more deeply.

Her nipples ached, needing...and then his fingers closed on one and pulled lightly.

Pleasure blazed straight to her clit. Her fingers dug into his chest. "Mmmmh!"

His laugh was smoky and smooth. He opened her fingers, flattening her hand on his chest again, before returning to torment her breasts. He rolled one nipple between his fingers, and she arched against the exquisite feeling. "Ah, you are sensitive here, aren't you," he murmured. "Then you might like this." Sliding down, he took a nipple between his lips, and the heat of his mouth on her skin bloomed inside her lower belly as well.

His mouth was soft and wet as he swirled his tongue around the aching peak. When he sucked, a stab of lust drove straight to her core. "Oh God."

He stopped long enough to kiss her before he edged down farther. Drawing her pajama waistband down an inch, he licked across the exposed skin. Another inch. His tongue circled her belly button and her skin shivered. Her hips rose slightly. Instinctively. *Do more. No, don't.* "Shay, I...".

Far too easily, he slid her pajama bottoms right off, leaving her bare. Big man, kneeling over her. Horror widened her eyes, and terror turned the heat to ice. "No. No, don't." Panting, she shoved at his hands.

"Breanne. Am I hurting you?"

In control. Firm. Her wolf responded to his voice. Her mentor. Shay. But she couldn't get enough air.

"Am I hurting you? Tell me," he ordered.

He wasn't. He wasn't even touching her. "No," she whispered. A hard-won breath brought her his scent, not foul, but clean and wild. *My Shay.*

Beside her, the fire in the woodstove snapped, otherwise the world was silent. Snow would be falling outside.

His blue-gray eyes studied her, watching her expressions, her breathing. He recognized her fear; would he realize how much she needed to continue?

He stroked a callused hand down her stomach. "Does that hurt?"

"No." *But I'm naked. Scared.*

He did it again, even slower, and this time her skin awoke to the glide of his hand. He ran one finger along the crease between her leg and her hip, and she shuddered against the heavy feeling growing inside her. His hand tingled over her inner thigh, and as he drew closer to her pussy, her insides tightened.

"Ah, there we go," he murmured. "You're with me again." He nudged her legs apart, lowering himself between them until his breath brushed against her curls.

Oh heavens. The surge of need was as hot as at the Gathering and kept increasing as he kissed the delicate skin inside her thigh. He teased closer, just outside her labia. His hot tongue against her skin sent tension seething through her lower half.

When his breath ruffled her curls, her clit gave a demanding throb as if alive. *Touch me.* Her fingers curled in his hair.

He raised his head to look at her. The gaze trapping her own held heat. Pleasure. Understanding. As she stared helplessly at him, the corners of his eyes crinkled. "Ready for more, are you, mo leannan?"

No. Yes. Please.

He slid his powerful hands under her bottom, lifted her slightly, and his mouth came down over her clit.

Hot. Wet. Lightning sizzled through her veins as her insides clenched. "Aaah."

His laugh vibrated against the engorged nub and added more sensation before he murmured, "Nothing in the world tastes as fine as this." His tongue teased around her entrance, over her labia, and circled back around her clit until every beat of her heart made it pulse.

He wedged his broad shoulders down, opening her farther, holding her legs apart.

Panic shivered through her, then he pulled one hand from under her bottom to run his finger between her folds, even as his tongue circled her clit. The trace of fear swirled away under the increasing heat.

Her insides tightened as he licked over the very top of her clit and down the other side. Fingers touched her labia, slick, teasingly circling her entrance, dipping in slightly. And then he pushed one thick finger inside her. Slowly. Firmly.

She stiffened at the agonizing rush of memories. "No, no, please."

He lifted his head, his finger still in her. "Look at me, Breanne."

Panting, despairing, she looked down into his confident...unrelenting...eyes.

"Trust me to take you through this, little wolf," he said.

So much was swirling inside her, heat and fear tugging at her. And he knew. Between one breath and the other, she surrendered to his knowledge, his command. As he watched her steadily, her terror eased back, as if he'd stepped in front of her.

"Brave Breanne," he murmured, kissing the inside of one thigh and the other. He puffed a warm breath over her damp curls, making her jump, then slowly pulled his finger out. Slid it back in. No pain, she realized. She was so wet.

As he moved it in and out, his lips closed on her clit, sending a spear of pleasure zinging through her. This time, his tongue flicked her roughly, and her pussy clenched on his finger, sending tiny cascades of sensation though her. Her fingers pulled his hair.

"Good lass." His voice was deeper than normal, hoarser. His finger moved in and out, slowly, so very slick, not hurting at all. Then he added another. Filling her, stretching her.

Oh God, her clit felt even more swollen as everything he touched turned to seething tension. She was panting, not from fear, but arousal, and the room felt like a sauna. Sweat broke out all over her body.

As pressure coiled low in her pelvis, she moaned, unable to think as her world narrowed to his touch, his mouth.

His fingers moved faster, plunging into her, pulling out. His heavy knuckles added extra sensation. And then he sucked on her clit, rolling the sides between his lips and tongue. As the vise of pressure around the nub tightened so did the one inside her. Every thrust of his hard fingers, every flicker of his tongue, sent brilliant colors shooting through her, and she needed. *Needed.* Every nerve strained to come.

He growled and wiggled his tongue on the very top of her clit, pressing the hood back and forth. Like a fist, her insides gathered tight, tighter, and her muscles turned rigid, as she hovered on the precipice. And then the tension exploded. A million pieces of pleasure burst outward in a storm of sensation. Oh God. Another wave followed as she spasmed around his hard fingers. Another…

Her muscles released suddenly, and her hips dropped to the blankets.

He licked over her one last time, slowly pulling his fingers out, sending a smaller ripple of pleasure through her. The room seemed to shimmer with heat as she tried to catch her breath. Her heart pounded so hard that her breasts shivered with each beat.

Sliding his hands down her thighs, he pushed back to kneel between her legs. "You're a delight, little wolf," he said, smiling slightly, studying her face.

Half stunned, she stared up at him. Was this what normal women felt when they made love? No wonder Ashley had pitied her. Little shudders still rippled her muscles in tiny waves of pleasure. "That was…"

"Next step then, Breanne." He leaned forward, running his hands up her body, and slowly lowering his body onto hers, covering her like a warm blanket.

She had a couple seconds of pure happiness, and then the reality of his weight and size hit. A storm of fear ripped over her, tearing her breath away, her mind…

She shoved against his shoulders, knowing only the weight. "No!"

He rolled off, but before she managed a complete breath of relief, he'd straddled her hips, resting on his haunches, not touching her anywhere. "Breanne. Look at me." He grasped her chin. "*Look* at me, mo leannan."

Filling her vision, his eyes were the color of the tiny lake he'd shown her one afternoon. Under his steady gaze, her panic slowed. Receded.

"Am I hurting you?"

She puffed out a breath, not sure if she was more exasperated with herself or the question. "No."

"I'm going to lie on top of you again. You tell me if anything hurts."

This time, she waited for the panic, but felt only pleasure as his legs fitted between hers and his hot body covered hers.

He took her mouth in a kiss, his lips demanding a response. "There's a lass," he murmured, propping himself up on one elbow. "Now we're at the cliff. I'm going to enter you." His eyes captured hers again. "Tell me if it hurts. What do you say if you want me to slow down?"

He waited patiently as she fumbled for the right word. "No." Oh—she'd already said that, and he'd sat up. Talked. "Thank you."

The corners of his eyes crinkled. "You're welcome. What's your word if you need to stop completely?"

"Elvis." She frowned. "I still need to pay you back for letting me think you were a dog."

"A *wolf*." He gave her a wry smile. "After tonight, I'm not sure who will owe who. I need you so badly I hurt."

Really? The truth showed in his strained expression. Yet he wasn't moving. Warmth filled her chest, not from the heat of sex, but his gentleness. Her heart ached with the need to satisfy him in return. "Can you kiss me and ..." *Go ahead before I chicken out.*

He leaned down, his mouth covering hers, warm against her cold lips.

She felt his cock between her legs. Huge, thick, demanding entrance inside her. Her whimper sounded thin in the quiet room.

"Breathe, Breanne." He reached down, swirling his fingers in her wetness. As he slowly stroked over her clit, sensations started to waken within her. She arched against his hand.

"That's right," he whispered, tracing lines of fire over her clit, and then she felt him entering her. Huge, surging slowly in, deeper. Stretching her...too much like... A vise closed around her ribs. *Can't.*

"Little wolf." He cupped her cheek with one big hand, tilting her face up, forcing her to see him. "Am I hurting you?"

She shook her head, panting a little, balancing on the edge of panic. She felt so full, stretched. Helpless.

His hand swept up and down her body, his hips not moving. Just petting her. Slowly she relaxed, and she realized his groin was against hers. He was all the way in.

"Brave little wolf," he murmured. "You feel good, Breanne. Tight. Wet and hot. You're squeezing me in a way that makes me want to howl."

His fingers ruthlessly stroked her center back into need.

As arousal pooled low in her belly, he pulled out ever so slowly before thrusting in again, each move slightly faster than the one before. Her thighs tightened. Her hips tilted up against his fingers, and he went deeper. Each stroke of his cock, of his fingers, heightened the sensations bombarding her until her hips were bucking under him, her fingers clenching his hips.

His speed increased, and it felt good, ever so good. Each plunge was accompanied by a rough finger teasing her clit—she couldn't tell which was driving her higher.

As her insides clenched around him, she met his thrusts with her own, and then it was too much. She needed more. Something more. She lost the rhythm.

Frustrated, she whined, her hips wiggling uncontrollably—sending his fingers sideways over her clit. "*Oooooh.*" Her core burst into a fireball of sensation that turned the entire room white. Heat surged in waves from her center outward, zinging all the way to her fingers and toes.

He hummed in pleasure. Then his hand slid under her, and he pulled her hips up as he thrust hard and fast, hammering into her. Pressing deep. His low groan and hot release sent her into another spasm of pleasure.

Before she could catch her breath, he rolled them over, putting her on top. He was still inside her and she felt close, so close to him.

As her muscles turned to melted butter, she sprawled across his body, feeling her heart thumping inside her ribs. Her head fit into the hollow of his shoulder. As she inhaled, she could smell sex and their scents mingling together. It made her smile.

With an effort, she pushed herself up, her sweat-soaked hair falling between them.

He ran his finger down her cheek. "Thank you for your trust, little wolf. It's a precious gift." His expression was serious, with not a trace of laughter.

He meant it. The feeling shook her. He'd been incredibly careful with her. And yet, he hadn't let her back out.

And she'd wanted him so much. Had climaxed, and it was amazing. "I never felt that before."

His eyes narrowed. "Felt what?"

"Um. Getting off," she confessed. Even with herself, she'd never been able to, probably because of the pills and a shifter metabolism. *I'm not asexual after all.* The knowledge shifted her emotions as surely as trawsfurring to wolf did her body. *I'm not the person I thought I was at all.*

He gave her a very satisfied, very male smile. "I'm happy to be of assistance." He pushed her hair behind her shoulder. "Maybe we should make sure you've got it mastered."

As he started to harden inside her, she grew very aware of the way his hands were fondling her buttocks.

"By the God, you feel good. You can stay on top this time."

AFTER CALLING IT a night and sending the young males on their way, Zeb walked back to the lodge. When he stepped inside, he stopped, inhaling the scents of wine—and sex. Bree and Shay. Hope and anxiety rose inside him. Was she all right?

He found Shay in the kitchen, eating directly from the container of potato salad.

"Don't let Bree catch you."

Shay only grunted.

Zeb grabbed a beer from the fridge and took a chair at the table. "How'd it go?"

"I've never been that scared in my life."

"And Bree?"

"She'd sucked down a bottle of wine before I got home. When I walked in, she asked me to have sex with her. Like a dream come true." His grin faded. "And then I sent her into a panic attack half a dozen times, even after the first mating."

Zeb winced. "Brave cahir. Did you figure out what sets her off?"

"Some. Don't stand over her if she's on the ground." Shay paused. "That might be what Evan did at the Gathering. She needs to see your face. And she does better if she's on top."

Zeb stared in disbelief. "You let her be on top?" Very dominant wolves rarely permitted that position, and they didn't come any more dominant than Shay.

"Wasn't easy." Shay gave him a rueful smile before his mouth flattened. "I'd have done anything to keep from scaring her again."

"You did well." *And I want her so bad that my bones ache.*

"She's damned brave." Shay put the container back in the refrigerator. "I look forward to sharing her with you."

Together. Like brothers would. Warmth filled Zeb, followed by cold. "No. We won't. She was raised human. One male, one female."

"Now listen, she—"

"Brawd, we can't keep her." No matter how much they

wanted to. His throat tightened as he remembered the way she'd laid her hand over, his to give comfort. She gave of herself so freely, holding nothing back. But she was also fragile. Hurt. "She needs no more upset."

"You've got the brains of a gnome if you think she doesn't care for you."

Zeb's spirits rose at the certainty in Shay's voice. How would it feel to have a female desire him outside of a Gathering night?

"Get some sleep. I'm going to try to crawl back in bed with her without terrifying her." Shay looked at him unhappily. "I'd kill anyone who scared her...only this time it was me."

Chapter Twenty-Two

TWO NIGHTS LATER, Bree roused when the door opened. The draft brought her Shay's scent, so she snuggled back into the covers. Another shifter perk—being able to tell who was who without turning on a light.

He undressed quietly and slid into bed. His legs bumped into hers, and he jerked away. "By the God.

"What?"

The big brute threw the covers back. "You have icicles for feet."

"And taking the blanket will help?" She sat up and grabbed for it.

With a low laugh, he shoved her down and bundled her up with her legs sticking out. Seated at the bottom of the bed, he pulled her feet onto his lap and wrapped his big hands around them.

Warmth surrounded her cold toes. "Oooooh, that's nice."

"You aren't eating enough, mo leannan." His fingers massaged her heels, the arches, her toes. "Your circulation needs better fuel. You cook for everyone else, but yourself."

"Mmmhmm." Her eyes almost crossed with pleasure.

"You shouldn't run around barefoot—we don't keep the lodge warm enough for you to do that."

She snuggled deeper in the blankets, immersed in comfort. He could lecture all he wanted as long as he didn't stop holding her feet.

"Of course, there's a quicker way to increase your circulation." He lifted one foot, and his lips closed over the little toe. His tongue slid over her skin, incredibly hot, and reminded her of how he liked to lick other places. When he moved to the next toe, and the next, sucking on each, arousal flickered to life. Her pussy throbbed, wanting attention.

By the time he finished her other foot, all of her was toasty warm. With ruthless hands, he pulled the blankets away and pushed her legs apart. His fingers opened her, and she saw his grin flash for a second. "This area feels warm enough, but I should check."

"I was asleep, you creep. Aaah!" His light nip on her clit jolted her right into serious need.

"You're not sleeping any more, now are you?" He sucked on her clit, teasing with his tongue until her hands fisted in the discarded blankets. Everything inside her gathered hard and tight as she teetered on the precipice of an orgasm, and then he deliberately pushed her over the edge.

"Oh, God." Pleasure blasted through her, sizzling through her veins all the way to her fingertips.

He laughed and moved up her body, stopping to nibble on her breasts. He rubbed his nose against hers and gave her a light kiss. "I'll just make sure you're all warmed up…inside and out." Pushing her legs apart, he slid in deep and hard.

BREE HEARD THE wind whipping around the lodge as she walked through the sitting area. Clouds had blown in last night, and snow had started falling around noon, but the lodge was cozy. Behind the glass doors of the fireplace, burning logs crackled softly, heating the room. She wiggled her toes and grinned at the blue and green striped socks. Shay had bought her fluffy booties to keep her feet warm.

She glanced toward the tiny office where he was doing paperwork. He could be so sweet. So sexy.

Over the past three days, he'd taken every opportunity to make love to her, no matter the time of day. This morning, she hadn't even been awake when he'd started rousing her, and the second she responded, he'd rolled her onto her back and taken her.

Not the sort of guy to ask permission. She grinned. Even though he always watched to make sure she was 'with him' and enjoying herself, he was definitely in charge. Why that turned her on so much, she didn't know.

I really, really like him. And criminy, she really, really liked Zeb too. Cared for them both and wanted to make love to them both. Everything inside her said it was wrong, but in shifter society, having two men was normal. *Normal. Hah.* She rubbed her hands over her sweater-covered arms, wishing she'd grown up knowing the rules.

This morning, when she'd volunteered to make food for the cahir meeting, Shay had kissed her long and hard and then passed her to Zeb to do the same. Zeb had kissed her so thoroughly her legs had given out. They'd left, shoulder to shoulder, discussing their plans for the day. Nothing changed because Zeb had fondled the woman Shay was sleeping with.

They *shared.*

They'd share *her* if she let them. What would it be like? Zeb was rougher, and yet, not as pushy as Shay. How would he make love? As her lower half melted into quivery jelly, she shook her head. Was she really considering it?

A pounding on the door made her jump. The first of the cahirs must have arrived—no one else rattled the door that way.

Zeb came from the weight room, striding toward the front with his predatory gait. He opened the door. "Ben. Come in."

The other cahir walked in, no taller than Zeb, but taking up a lot more space. Against Zeb's deadly grace, Ben was all power and size, much like his bear form. He took a chair close to the fire and grinned at her. "Breanne, you look well."

"If that's the way you talk to the females, no wonder you're not mated," Shay said, from right behind her.

Bree turned, her heart rate increasing.

"It's done like this, *mo charaid.*" Shay took her hand. "You are lovely this evening, Breanne." His blue-steel eyes trapped her gaze as he kissed her fingers. When he touched his tongue to her palm, she flushed, feeling as if he'd licked somewhere else. Warmth pooled in her depths.

His smile went feral as he inhaled slowly. His grip tightened, and he pulled her out of the sitting area and into the kitchen. Lacing his fingers through her hair, he tilted her head back and took her lips.

He tasted of peppermint and heat, and the thought of resisting never entered her mind. After nibbling her lips, he swept his tongue inside to tease her into responding.

With a low groan, he rubbed his cheek on hers. "Bad move. I'm now as aroused as you are." His erection was massive, pressing against her stomach as he returned to kissing her.

Conflicting sensations shook her like a mountain blizzard: nervousness about being held so firmly, yet delight at how he wanted her so badly. Delight won, and fire melted her insides as he took his time enjoying her, pressing kisses down her neck.

When he tried to pull away, she realized her arms were clasped around his neck. Heck, she was plastered onto him. Shocking—and satisfying.

He was pleased too. "You're getting more demanding, mo leannan. I like it." His eyes were hot with desire as he cupped her butt, rubbing her against his cock. When more voices sounded from the living room, he sighed, grasped her upper arms, and set her back. "I called the meeting. Shouldn't be late."

"Abandoning me for a bunch of cahirs. I hope I'm still in the mood later," she teased and turned away.

She was whirled around so fast her head spun. One hand fisted her hair, his other slid between her thighs to press against her clit. As she gasped, he traced her softness and set her need to blazing.

"I think you will be," he whispered in her ear. After nipping her chin, he walked out of the kitchen.

Staring after him, she leaned against the table for strength. Oh my goodness. She was damp between her legs, and her now swollen clit pulsed with demand. She started to pick up the tray of food and stopped. *My scent.* Every guy in the place would know she was turned on. How in the world did shifter women deal with that?

After eying the giant tray of goodies, she added some extra salami slices. Surely, no one would smell anything but the garlic.

She stopped to listen for a moment. Shay was talking, "...at least one hellhound. With the curfew, all the shifters except us will be safe at home. Basically, we're serving ourselves up as bait. Ben, Owen, and Alec, you'll be together. I'd like to discuss the timing and areas to cover."

As she walked into the room, Zeb glanced at her, inhaled slowly, and a corner of his mouth tipped up.

Darn it. Next time she'd add some Brie. Setting the tray on the coffee table, she tried to forget how Shay had laid her on it yesterday and...

Owen gave her a disgusted look, and her feelings flip-flopped, arousal shifting into shame. It felt as if he knew she was soiled. Dirty deep inside.

She frowned back at him, pushing the feelings away. *I'm not the one with a problem.* She'd met the cahir once before, but his dislike of women—not just her—was very apparent. Cahir-sized at six-five, he was all lean ripped muscle and savage grace, dressing in black, outwardly much like Zeb. Only she'd come to realize that Zeb was immensely protective of women. Owen seemed the type to toss them over a cliff.

To heck with the misogynistic idiot—if he didn't like her, he didn't need to eat her food. She pushed the tray to the other side of the table, far from Owen and in front of Ben who'd suck up food like a vacuum cleaner.

Zeb snorted in amusement, and Shay winked at her.

As the men started discussing their patrols, Bree heard a high-pitched giggle from the back of the lodge. What in the world...? She followed the sounds to the TV room and opened the door.

Tyler and Luke were watching "Lion King." Nora was knitting in the corner.

"Hi, Nora." Grinning at the children's squeals of welcome, Bree knelt to get little boy hugs. "What are you guys doing here?"

Nora's needles clacked lightly as she concentrated on her task. "Bonnie, Brady, and Van are hosting the pack for supper and didn't want the children underfoot. Since Owen was in town, he'd agreed to cubsit. But then Shay called this cahir meeting. I'm just watching the children until it's over."

"Oh." The hurt hit Bree like a slice from a paring knife, not deep, but painful. Apparently, even after apologizing, she wasn't welcome at pack events. Zeb and Shay hadn't been invited either.

"Sorry, dear." Nora gave her a sympathetic look. "Bonnie wanted you and the cahirs to come, but Thyra told her no. Because of Gerhard. Bonnie can't refuse the alpha female's orders."

The alpha bitch seemed as dictatorial as some European chefs Bree had worked with. She forced a smile. "Well, it's nice to see you and the boys." She took the chair next to Nora's. "What are you making?"

"It will be an afghan." Nora held up the to-be-blanket, several long rows of dark blue and white.

"It's lovely." Bree stroked the yarns. "I love the colors."

"Thank you. These are—oh, my, I forgot to change colors here." Tut-tutting, she pulled the stitches out and switched to white yarn. "My brain doesn't work well these days, you know," she admitted, starting to knit again. "Since my last mate returned to the Mother, my body's going downhill. I can't remember where I leave things or what day it is." She glanced at the children fondly. "At least I've never misplaced one of them."

"That's good." Bree took a seat on the wide couch and laughed when the boys jumped up to join her, snuggling like kittens against her sides.

Her mouth firmed. Thyra might be a bitch, but she wasn't going to win. Bree was making her own place here. Making a business. Cooking for the diner and the barbecues was more rewarding than any restaurant kitchen had ever been. And aside from a couple nasty women, everyone else was nice. Angie, Vicki, and Jody were becoming good friends.

Beside her, Nora contently worked on her afghan. She was still useful, a member of a pack.

That's how I want to grow old. Yes, this was her town now—her home.

AFTER THE MEETING concluded, Zeb took Owen to the TV room.

Asleep in the corner, old Nora was snoring quietly. On the sofa, Bree cuddled a child. His little face pressed against her as he contentedly sucked his thumb and watched TV. The other pup was asleep, head pillowed in her lap. Bree was stroking his hair.

Zeb froze, halted by the beauty of the scene. Here was everything he'd sworn to protect. *And more.* A rush of longing shook him. His heart felt like a tree uprooted by the rains, toppling into the river, and being swept away by the rapids. *This is what I want.* Shaking his head to regain his balance, he cleared his throat and said softly, "Bree, the cubs need to leave now."

Nora woke with a snort at his voice, saw Owen, and gathered her knitting.

Bree frowned at Owen, as if she doubted his capability to handle pups, then jostled the children. "Tyler. Luke. Time to go home."

"Let him sleep," Owen said. "My room at the bed and breakfast is quiet enough." He glanced at Zeb. "Next new moon, I'll rent a cabin. You're more my style than that fancy Victorian place."

With unexpected gentleness, Owen picked up the cub that was awake, kissed his forehead, and handed him to Zeb.

Zeb froze, arms cradling the boy automatically. Less weight than a raccoon and infinitely fragile. He tried not to breathe too hard. Sweat broke out on his brow. Carry him to the fucking car. Surely he could do that much.

Owen took the other child, rocking him as the boy blinked and murmured, "Unca Wen, Sim ran 'way."

The man frowned, glanced at Bree.

"Simba ran away," she explained, then smiled. "If Bonnie doesn't have the DVD at home, they can come back and watch the ending here."

Owen nodded brusquely before walking out of the room, Nora on his heels.

As Zeb started to follow, Bree came up beside him, paused

to smooth the child's hair out of his face. "Isn't he adorable?" she whispered.

Zeb bent and brushed a kiss over her soft lips, inhaling the lingering scent of cubs and contentment. *I would give almost anything to keep you.* "You're adorable," he murmured. "And he's way too little and breakable." Then, walking very carefully, he followed Owen and Nora out to the car.

Chapter Twenty-Three

Cold Creek, North Cascades Territory ~ Dark of the moon

WITH THE SLEEVES of her sweater pushed up to her elbows, Bree looked around the kitchen at Angie's Diner for anything else to put away. The room was fragrant with the scent of the spaghetti sauce simmering for tomorrow's special. The counters were clean. No dirty dishes out. She closed the dishwasher. "Do you want me to run this now?"

"No. The noise would make me nervous." Angie hung up her apron and gave Bree a wry grin. "More nervous. I made some chamomile tea while you cleaned. Let's go drink it." Picking up the large white teapot, she nodded toward the public area of the diner.

Bree picked up a couple of cups and followed her out.

She grinned at the empty room. Although the Cosantir had set a sunset curfew for shifters on dark moon nights, Angie had stayed open for human customers. Not any more. According to Jody, Zeb had been furious. He'd told Angie that a hellhound could walk in looking human, then shift…and she'd be the main course.

Tonight—well before the sun went down—she'd put out a "CLOSED" sign and lowered the blinds. Any human wanting a meal was out of luck.

The only light in the room spilled from the open kitchen door, and Angie chose a table in the darkness by the front window. "We can watch the outside from here." She pointed. A gap between the blinds offered a view of the empty street.

Bree rubbed her arms to chase the sudden chill away. The cahirs were out there, patrolling in the cold night. Hunting or being hunted.

"They'll be all right," Angie said softly.

"Of course they will." *Please be safe.* "Thanks for letting me spend the night. The lodge felt awfully isolated."

"I'm delighted you're here. With my daughter out of town, I'd have been jumping at every noise."

As Bree took a seat, the darkness folded around her reassuringly, and the iron bars on the big window were even more comforting. She looked through the blinds. The relentless rain had rendered the old-fashioned streetlights ineffective, and on the center island, the tree branches fought against the gusting wind. "I'm not used to feeling hunted like this. How do you all stand it?"

"It's new to us too. Cold Creek was isolated and safe until that retirement community sprang up less than an hour away. Calum wasn't happy, but it's not in our county."

"So there won't be any end to hellhounds?"

Angie grimaced. "The cahirs may kill one, but another will eventually find us. Or more than one at once."

They both shuddered.

"Thank the Mother, the Cosantir got Zeb and Shay to train our cahirs. I wish we could keep them."

Bree scowled at the cup. "Me too. They look so happy taking care of the Wildwood."

"Calum asked them to stay. But Shay's oathbound, and where one brother goes, the other follows." Angie refilled their cups.

Cold Creek without Zeb and Shay. Bree stared out the window, feeling as if the cold wind was carving a hollow in her chest. Somewhere inside, far away from her logical mind, her subconscious had planned a future. With them. *Not going to happen.* She needed to come to terms with that.

In the street, the shadows wavered.

"Angie, what's that?" Dimly visible in the dark and rain, something moved toward the diner. Bree's heart started to pound, and her hands chilled. "Someone—something is out there."

Angie leaned forward, peering into the darkness. "It has two legs, not four. Must be some idiot human out for a walk in the rain. Hope they're not coming here, expecting to be fed."

"But, they'll be killed. We need to warn—"

"No, Shay said a hellhound in town will scent shifters and focus only on us. It'll treat humans like furniture."

Bree's muscles loosened. "Good. That's good."

Struggling against the sleeting wind, the well-bundled person moved up the street. Awfully small. A woman? When Bree spotted the basket over the woman's arm, she stiffened. "Is that Nora?"

In the rain, the woman lifted her face, pale in the flickering glow of the streetlamp.

Angie groaned. "By the Mother's breasts. Nora…"

They ran for the entrance. Bree flipped open the multiple locks and opened the door.

A shape erupted out of the darkness and wet bony plates glinted. The hellhound hit Nora from behind. Her hands flapped out like wings as she went down with a high scream. Her voice broke off abruptly.

"Nooo!" Bree started out and was yanked back by Angie.

"You can't fight that thing with bare hands!" Angie poked her head out and screamed, "Help! Hellhound! Help! Main

Street."

The monster whipped around.

Angie jumped back, slammed, and locked the door. "Herne help us," she moaned. "Nora—"

"*Bare hands.*" Bree ran into the kitchen. They couldn't kill it, but surely they could slow it down until the cahirs came. A knife lay on the counter. Well, she knew that didn't work. Maybe a loud diversion? With shaking hands, she grabbed an armful of cast-iron pots and pans, the heaviest she could find.

Face dead white, Angie stared at Bree's load. Her mouth firmed, and she nodded.

Bree glanced at the massive pot of simmering spaghetti sauce. "Bring that too." She dropped her load to the right of the front door.

Angie set the sauce beside the pile.

A trickle of fear-sweat ran down Bree's back as she picked up a huge fry pan. "Open the door for me. Close it after I throw."

"Got it." Angie undid the locks and pulled open the door.

Bree forced herself to step outside. The hellhound raised its head from the limp bundle that was Nora. Blood smeared its muzzle as it stared at Bree. She froze, every nerve jittering, panicking, screaming. The ground rolled up and down as if she was drunk, and she felt the skillet slipping from numb fingers.

Won't let it win. Her fingers clenched on the handle. With a grunt of determination, she flung the pan with all her strength. The metal hit the hellhound's skull with a horrible thud.

The monster snarled in fury and charged. Bree lunged back inside. Angie slammed the door and flipped the locks.

A second later, the hellhound hit the wood so hard the tiny glass panel cracked.

Bree's scream caught in her throat, her heart banging painfully against her ribs. Her insides shook as she grabbed a cast-iron pot.

Silence. Had it left?

The monster's long ugly growl raised the hair on Bree's neck. Angie jerked back a step. A second later, the hellhound trotted back to its kill. Bree sagged against the wall, her legs weak. Could they do that again? Was there a point? Nora couldn't be alive, not any longer. Sorrow for the cheerful old woman ached like a pulled muscle as Bree peered through the cracked window onto the street.

"Hey, demon scum!" Ben's loud bellow came from down the street. Bree leaned her head against the wall in relief. The cahirs were here.

Three figures converged on the hellhound. Two men with knives flashing: Alec, his face filled with fury, Ben, a lumbering mountain of muscle. Owen, in cougar form, flashed in front of them and struck the hellhound. Slash, slash to no effect as the cat's claws scraped off the plating. The cougar sprang away, and the futile snap of the hellhound's teeth was louder than the rain.

The two men bore down on the monster, but it didn't wait. The hellhound leaped forward and rammed Alec, knocking him backward before charging Ben.

Ben's downward slice bounced off its shoulder. The creature reared up and its jaws closed on Ben's arm. The man shouted in pain. The shark-like head whipped back and forth, then the hellhound tossed him carelessly away. The cahir hit an iron bench in the center island and didn't rise.

The hellhound stared at Alec as it licked blood from its snout. Bree's insides chilled, ice filling her veins. Those cahirs couldn't kill the monster. They'd get hurt. Die.

Owen attacked from the rear again, rolling onto his back like a kitten. The cougar's front paws fastened around the creature's hind leg; his hind claws scrabbled at its stomach.

Bree's hands fisted at her sides. "Do it, do it, do it," she chanted. *Hurt it bad.*

The monster turned, teeth closing on the cougar's leg, flinging the cat away. As the hellhound followed, Owen rolled. Blood streaked his golden fur. Bree held her breath as he scrambled up and sprang out of reach, his grace gone.

Alec had regained his feet and faced the monster with only a knife.

"He'll die." *Stay here, stay quiet, stay safe.* She couldn't. *Couldn't.* She opened the door and grabbed the pot of steaming spaghetti sauce. So heavy and big, and her legs felt like rubber. Rain lashed her face as she staggered out onto the street. Farther. Her jaw clamped over the screams welling up inside her. *I can't do this.* Two more steps.

Spinning in a circle, she flung the spaghetti, pot and all, at the hellhound. The trailing spray of sauce burned her arms.

With a dull clang, the pot hit the monster's back. Sauce spilled down its sides. As Bree backpedaled, it roared in pain. Alec struck then, rolling under it and jamming his knife upward. The blade scraped off a plate, entering the stomach at an angle.

Releasing another snarl, the hellhound twisted around, knife sticking sideways. Not deep enough.

Alec rolled away and—

Angie stepped up beside Bree and shoved a cast-iron Dutch oven into her hands, then flung an even bigger one. With a high yell, Bree threw with all her might. Both hit, diverting the creature.

Alec lurched to his feet and ran. Ben was up, but one arm hung limply. His knife was in his other hand. A flash of golden, and Owen was there, circling. All of them were hurt, moving badly.

Bree's heart sank.

NO. PLEASE, HERNE, no. Shay's pulse roared in his ears. If Breanne stepped farther out, if the hellhound went for her, he'd have to attack.

To his relief, the demonkin concentrated on the cahirs.

Don't let it look at the females. Shay stalked down the sidewalk, paws silent on the wet concrete, veering to stay behind the creature and out of its line of sight. Recessed in the plating, the hellhound's eyes had a limited field of vision, something he and Zeb had learned to use.

"Try me, you fucking demon-dog." Zeb's gravelly voice sounded over the cougar's snarls. The monster spun to face him.

Like a human gunslinger, Zeb sauntered down the street.

Shay eased up behind the demonkin, timing his attack. *Almost.* As Zeb moved closer, the hellhound's hind end lowered in preparation for a spring.

Shay darted in, snapped his jaws closed on the lower hind leg, biting down, working his jaw quickly until a fang found the gap between the thinner plating. Acrid demon blood burned his mouth. He released instantly, seeing the sag of the leg. The hellhound spun and caught Shay's shoulder. Pain flared. With a snarl, Shay ripped himself loose.

Remembering the other prey, the hellhound whirled around. Zeb stood at just the right angle, only a foot away. He fired two shots.

Black blood splattered outward from a recessed eye. The hellhound stood immobile, a statue of death, then collapsed. As it hit the ground, it shifted into human. Dead and done.

Shay raised his nose and gave a long howl to celebrate the kill. As the sound echoed from the mountains, Zeb's voice, less tuneful from a human throat, joined in, lifting the melody into something strong and beautiful.

When they finished, there was only the sound of falling rain and the rustle of tree branches in the wind.

STANDING IN THE rain, Bree listened to the wolves, their song bold and glorious, filling her heart, pulling her into the melody, telling her she belonged. She was of the pack. Her eyes filled.

Angie wrapped an arm around her and leaned against her side. The feeling was right; she was also pack.

As the song finished, Bree hauled in a breath. Reality returned when her gaze fell on a small basket, colorful yarns spilling onto the muddy street. *Oh, Nora.* Like the pouring rain, grief sheeted over her. With Angie beside her, she reluctantly moved toward the old woman. Her feet dragged as if they'd turned to concrete. She didn't want to see—

Hard hands closed on her upper arms, lifting her into the air. She gave a panicked yip.

"Dammit, female! Are you insane? Trying to die?" Shay's roar filled the street, the town, the entire valley. Naked and furious, he held her a foot off the ground, glaring into her face. He shook her, making her teeth snap together. "What in Herne's name are you doing out here? Don't you ever, ever, ever do something so stupid again." He gave her another hard shake.

Her brains were scrambled forever, she knew it, yet he didn't scare her a bit. All his anger and bellowing came from worry for her, and the knowledge melted her heart.

He dropped her on her feet and yanked her close before her legs could collapse. His embrace mashed her face into his chest, as he tried to squeeze her to death. Her ribs groaned. "By the God, I almost died seeing you out here." He growled and darned if he didn't squeeze her harder.

"Shay, she's a little female. Don't crush her." Anger and amusement mingled in Zeb's rough voice.

The iron bands loosened. Bree sucked in a breath and tipped her face up to say…something, but Shay spun her, none too gently, to face his brother.

Zeb's eyes were like black fire.

Shay gripped her upper arms as he growled in her ear, "Tonight. After I have you in every way possible so I know you are alive, I plan to yell at you some more. A lot more."

Her breath caught at the carnal threat, at the warning.

He pushed her toward Zeb. "Your turn to yell at her, a bhràthair. I'll go tell our cahirs everything they did wrong."

Zeb's hands clamped onto her arms in the very same locations. Painfully. But then he pulled her against him. His embrace was tight. Possessive. He murmured against her hair. The feeling of safety surrounded her, and she sagged.

As adrenaline drained away with each beat of her pulse, cold replaced it. A hellhound. The monster was dead. She was alive. As she burrowed closer, she started to shake.

Silently, he held her as she shuddered against him. The men were alive. But Nora... That sweet, confused old woman. Tears filled her eyes.

His arms gentled as she cried for Nora, as she sobbed away her terror. His hand stroked up and down her back, and his cheek created a warm spot on the top of her head. His breathing, slow and steady, became a recipe for her own until his calm settled into her.

With a trembling breath, she realized her arms were wrapped around him. One hand gripped his pulled-back hair like a lifeline. She didn't want to let him go. "Thank you," she managed shakily.

"Courageous, resourceful female." His raspy voice was as gentle as the warm hand curving under her hair and around her nape. "I have never seen such a thing. Alec owes you a life." He nuzzled her neck and let her loose.

She stepped back, wobbly but upright. She could manage now, and at least he hadn't yelled at her. She needed to check on Nora, check on Angie—

His callused hand caught her chin and raised her face to

meet his gaze. His black eyes blazed with the same fury as Shay's had.

She tried to take a step back and failed. Wow, wolfies got really riled up didn't they?

"Little female." His voice sounded like he'd swallowed gravel. "Be very grateful I have not had you, for I would make you pay for your actions here tonight."

At her startled gasp, a flash of humor lit his eyes. "Sorry, *cariad*—sweetheart. I forget you're not used to a male's response to seeing a female in danger."

He turned her, holding her immovable between his big hands. Growling the entire while, he bit her on the nape of her neck.

Hard.

NOT LONG AFTER dawn, Shay finished showering off the dirt, sweat, and dried blood. After taking care of Ben and Owen, Donal had healed Shay's shoulder, despite his protests that it wasn't worth attention. The healer had laughed, saying Shay and Zeb had collected enough battle marks to impress the females. No need for more.

Shay glanced down at his body. He didn't have as many scars as Zeb, and they didn't stand out as well on his lighter skin, but yeah, he had quite a few.

Breanne didn't seem to mind.

She wasn't in his bed, as he'd hoped. Still not that sure of herself, was she? He stepped into her bedroom. Although she'd returned to the lodge at sunrise, she was already sound asleep. She'd had a hard night, the brave little female.

As the memory of her attacking a demonkin returned, his anger and fear reawakened like flames from smoldering coals. The hellhound could have torn her to pieces.

"Breanne," he growled.

She woke with a start. The second she recognized him, he scooped her up, netting a tiny yip that hardened him past bearing. Soft female, warm and flushed with sleep, fragrant with feminine musk and soap.

Mine.

He tumbled her into his big, littermate-sized bed and followed, pinning her on her back. No fear in her expression, just growing arousal. Her scent drew him down her body. Pulling her legs apart, he exposed her wetness.

"Shay, I—"

"Do not speak to me until I have you at least once," he said. Her eyes widened. "Unless I hurt you." Then, to be certain she wouldn't be damaged, he licked over her female parts, savoring the heady musk, the tremor that rolled through her. His tongue teased inside her entrance, then over the nub, and, despite her squirming, he mercilessly held her open as he drove her over the edge.

Her long moan made him grin. She came so easily now.

Thank the God, because he couldn't wait any longer. Each time he relaxed, he saw her facing a demonkin. Her courage awed him, terrified him. Infuriated him. Throwing pots at a hellhound. Spaghetti sauce.

With ruthless hands, he turned her over.

BREE FELT ANXIETY clog her throat when Shay yanked her up onto her hands and knees. He'd never tried to take her this way, not after she'd panicked the first night.

His huge body bent over her, making her feel too small and powerless. Yet, his hand was incredibly gentle as he caressed her breast and teased her nipple. Her insides felt as if he was turning up the fire under a pot on the stove. He nipped her shoulder and nuzzled the back of her neck.

Her fear was smothered by her increasing need, the warmth of his body, his careful touch. It was Shay. How could she be afraid?

"There we go," he murmured into her ear. "Breanne, I'm going to take you hard. Sing out if I hurt you, but I need to feel you around me, to hear your heart and breath."

He needed her. Heavens, the words simply washed any resistance away. "Take me. However you want."

His growl shuddered through her as he slicked his cock in her wetness. He teased at her entrance for a moment, then sheathed himself in her with one hard thrust.

The shock sent her vagina spasming around him, and she gasped.

"By the God, you feel good, Breanne." His voice was low and harsh as he pulled out and slammed home again.

Her eyes tried to roll back in her head as sensations blasted through her. He felt different in this position. Deeper than normal, hitting new spots.

"Hang on, little wolf." As if following his own orders, his hands closed on her hips in an inescapable grip, and he yanked her back onto his cock with a hum of pleasure. Hard. Fast. Determined. He took her as he'd said, holding her as he wanted. Thrust after thrust.

"More," she whined.

He nudged her legs farther apart, going even deeper, and the relentless rhythm started a pulsing inside her. Pressure built as her center coiled like an overwound spring. She tightened around him, needing more.

He chuckled and slid one hand down over her clit, teasing her with insistent fingers into mindless need. Each plunge of his cock shoved her against his hand.

She moaned and shut her eyes, feeling only his slick heavy erection moving in and out while his firm finger stroked her clit.

As his shaft pushed deeper, as his finger stroked harder, faster, his teeth closed on the back of her neck, and the bite of pain ripped right down to her core. For one second everything inside her balanced on a pinpoint, and then the spring inside her blew. Inescapable pleasure slammed outward in blazing wave after wave, until she wasn't sure where her body began or ended.

He gave a low groan. His grip was bruise-inducing tight, and he held himself immobile as his cock shuddered inside her.

Humming his satisfaction in her ear, he laved the pain of his bite, then he rolled them over onto their sides. He curled around her, her back against his chest.

Her arms and legs melted into the mattress as she rested her head on his hard bicep.

He held her against him, his shaft still deep inside her. "Thank you, mo leannan," he whispered.

She grinned. *No—thank* you. Not only for the orgasm, but also for the discovery that she could enjoy hard and fast sex. "You're welcome." She lifted his hand from her breast and bit his finger. His response was to harden inside her. "Thanks for saving my life."

"It shouldn't have been necessary." He pulled his hand away and set it back on her breast, and she felt her nipple gather into a peak. Funny how stroking herself did nothing, but under his callused palm, her every nerve came alive.

When he rolled her nipple between his fingers, her core clenched around his cock, making him growl in satisfaction. He kissed her hair, pulling her closer. "But you saved others tonight. How did you get so brave? Were your parents warriors?" He winced. "I'm sorry. You probably don't know, do you?"

"No."

"What do humans do with their orphans?" He slid out and turned her to face him.

She nuzzled his chest, breathing in the scent of soap and

their loving. "Don't you ever watch television?"

"No. The males treat their females so badly that I want to teach them manners." His hand fisted, making his knuckles crack. "And everyone is rude."

She tried to imagine Mr. Over-protective Polite Warrior tolerating a sitcom or even something like Die Hard. A giggle escaped her.

"Orphans?" He reminded her.

"Oh. People are hired to care for a batch of children. I didn't talk for a long time, so they thought I was retarded, and I didn't get adopted. I was fostered by a nice couple, but he lost his job and had to move out-of-state. Another one got pregnant, and they didn't want two kids. I moved around a lot. In my last foster home, the guy tried to…"

Shay's eyes narrowed.

Whoa. Not a good story for right now. "Well, I ran away before anything"—much—"happened, and lived with a street gang."

"Gangs are children?"

"Not always, but this one was just a bunch of kids holing up in a condemned warehouse. Scavenging and stealing." She smiled. "I was cute, so I made a good pickpocket and shoplifter. And I was great at hotwiring cars."

"You didn't stay a thief."

Her nose wrinkled. "I tried to lift a wallet from a—well, you'd call him a warrior. Sensei taught martial arts, and instead of turning me into juvvie, he put me to work in his dojo."

He touched her nose. "The courage you already had, but he taught you to fight."

"Yeah." She grimaced. "Although it doesn't do much good against a hellhound."

BY THE GOD, did she have to remind him again? The memory

of her in the street returned, so selflessly brave, trying to save a cahir's life. Herne's hooves, she could steal the heart right out of his chest.

He studied her pale sweet face with the spattering of freckles. She didn't fight with the courage of a warrior but with the fierceness of a mother wolf guarding her young. Shay ran his finger over her cheek. He'd seen her cuddling Bonnie's pups, seen the crayon drawing from another that she'd taped on their refrigerator. She cared. That was her secret: she simply cared. This female had a heart bigger than her tiny body.

And she'd stolen his. He closed his eyes. The inevitability of loving her was like the settling of a mountain. He could tell himself she was merely a lover, and, of course, he would worry over her welfare. But it would be a lie. She meant far, far more.

He sighed, and an odd tightness in his chest relaxed with the admission of what he felt.

Yet…caring for Breanne would create a mess.

Not with Zeb, of course. He smiled and rubbed his face against her fragrant hair. Flowers and citrus; she must have a new shampoo. Zeb was already heart-tied to her, even if he tried to pretend otherwise.

The problem was with Shay. *I'm oathbound.* None of the reasons he'd given Zeb had changed. Moving with him and Zeb would be too hard on her. But what if she cared for them? He thought she did—although he'd be the first to say he didn't understand females at all. What was the correct trail to satisfy both honor and needs?

He'd have to think further. And even if he and Zeb wanted to court her, the Law said a female must attend at least one Gathering first. Females needed to learn to separate physical reactions from her emotional ones.

But all that was in the future, and she was here in his bed now.

She was chewing on her lip, thinking intently. "How come when Zeb used a pistol, the bullets got through the hellhound's armor?"

"What?" His brows drew together as he tried to veer from romance to death.

"The bullets," she said patiently. "How did a pistol kill a hellhound?"

He stared at her. She'd been out there in the street when Zeb shot the hellhound. Her soft little body had been far too close. A memory flashed of his brothers' savaged bodies. A growl rumbled in his chest.

"What? Shay?"

She is alive. He had to keep telling himself that. Proving it. He rolled off the bed, flipped her on her back, and dragged her downward until her sweet ass was half off the edge. "You shouldn't remind a male of how close you came to dying, little wolf."

Her eyes widened as he set her knees in the crooks of his elbows, opening her to his use. *She is alive.* He surged home with one swift thrust.

Chapter Twenty-Four

BREE STEPPED OUT of the kitchen and stretched. All day, she'd been discovering sore spots. Throwing cast-iron pots apparently required different muscles than lifting weights. And sex with an angry cahir...

She put her hand on her stomach. Dear sweet heavens. The sex had been amazing. That he cared enough to be so upset made her all quivery inside.

Don't get attached, Bree. He wasn't after a relationship. As soon as he and Zeb finished teaching the cahirs, they'd be off to a new area. She needed to confine herself to gratitude for having met him. Would she have ever recovered enough to have sex if he hadn't been so understanding and so stubborn?

Yeah, she cared for him, but he didn't need to know. Instead, she'd...somehow...send him off to the wars with a kiss, and not burden him with the knowledge of how unhappy she'd be.

She sighed. As she shook her head to dislodge the unhappy thoughts, she heard soft classical music. Must be Zeb. She followed the sound to the front of the lodge.

In the library area, Zeb was sprawled in a chair, reading. The cover of the book held a dead body and a bloody knife. Crazy cahir.

"Little female?" He patted the arm of his overstuffed chair.

She veered around her jigsaw puzzle table and set a hip on the chair arm. Would he answer her questions? Not if he figured out why she was asking.

Even her few moments of thinking made him frown. "Problems?"

"Did you know you're getting gray hair?" He hadn't worn a leather band. With a finger, she traced one silvery strand through his long, night dark hair.

"Probably from seeing you try to kill a hellhound with spaghetti sauce." His voice sounded like a gravel truck when he finished, and his expression had turned ferocious.

Her heart skipped a beat. Yet, he no longer scared her. And he'd oh-so-conveniently introduced the subject she wanted to discuss. *Go girl!* "Your gun did seem a bit more effective than spaghetti. How come the bullets bounced off before? Did you have a bigger pistol this time?"

"No." He tugged her hand away from his hair and nibbled on her fingers. The teasing bites sent tingles up her arm. "The trick is to hit it in the eye."

Was he insane? "With a bullet?"

"A stiletto works, but they dodge so fast that you'll miss unless it actually has you in its jaws."

She stared at him. In its jaws? She tried to imagine doing anything except screaming. "A pistol's a better choice then," she said hoarsely. "But that's an awful small target."

"Fucking small." He kissed the inside of her wrist, then up her arm. The heat from his lips trickled into her and pooled low in her belly. "Recessed eyes mean you have to shoot straight-on."

"What?" Her skin wakened and her breasts grew heavy. "Oh. Right. Straight-on." She tried to pull her hand away. How was she supposed to keep her mind on——?

He yanked her arm and toppled her into his lap. Ignoring her half-hearted struggles, he arranged her with ruthless hands until her shoulder pressed against his hard chest. His left arm supported her back as he settled her legs over the armrest. With her right arm pinned between them, she couldn't get out of the chair. Her heart rate increased, but she wasn't scared. *Much.*

"Better," he rumbled, rubbing his chin on the top of her head. "I got a kink in my neck with you up there."

Uh-huh. He probably just didn't like anyone above him. Cahirs' attitudes went way past macho.

He shifted his arm behind her back so his palm could curve over her ribs below her breast. If he moved it up…

She pushed at his hand but he laced his fingers through hers. Her every breath rubbed the underside of her breast against his knuckles, and arousal flared inside her.

How the heck could he turn her on when she was sleeping with Shay? Lo—cared for Shay? *Don't go there.* "Uh." What were the darned questions?

"Yes?" His half-smile was filled with satisfaction.

"If hellhounds live in cities, how come the news doesn't report torn-up bodies?"

"A hellhound doesn't leave anything alive. If it only kills one, it'll carry the body away to finish over the course of the night."

Oh God, Ashley.

As she blinked back tears, he hugged her, and the slow thud of his heart was as comforting as his hard arms around her. "I'm sorry about Nora, cariad."

He could be so sweet. She rubbed her wet cheeks on his soft flannel shirt. "How come hellhounds don't overrun the world?"

His right hand stroked across her hip and down her thigh. Warmth followed in its wake. "They're only in hellhound form at full moon. Rest of the time, they're human—and so violent that they tend to get killed by human police."

When he stroked up the inside of her thigh, her body seared with heat. His fingers paused an inch from her pussy to make teasing circles. Even though she wore jeans, she felt exposed. She tried to disentangle her fingers from his other hand, but he merely increased his grip.

"I touch only your leg, little female," he murmured into her hair. "Or is my touch loathsome to you?"

She tipped her face up to answer, and his mouth came down on hers. Gently. Firmly. His tongue swept inside and out before she could adjust. He sucked on her lower lip, then traced it with his tongue.

Oh heavens.

He leaned her back farther, so he could take her mouth more fully, nuzzling and sucking and penetrating.

Her body blazed, as a burning ball of need grew in her lower half. His hand moved up the final inch, palm pressing against her pussy, holding her open, while his thumb rubbed her clit. Exactly where she needed. Wanted. She moaned.

He chuckled, low and deep, and lifted his lips from hers. To her dismay, his hand moved away to rest on her knee.

Her whole body felt sensitive and aching, and she looked up at him, feeling as if she'd stepped into a whirlwind.

His black eyes were hot with hunger, and her hip rested against a massive erection. He kissed her lightly. "I would taste you more...thoroughly, but this is not the time." When he tipped his head, she heard the rattle of a car approaching the Lodge.

"Oh." Oh God, what if it was Shay? Guilt carved a path through her pleasure. "What have I done?" How could she have been such a slut?

Zeb frowned. "What?"

She pushed at him. "I can't believe I let you touch me like

that. I'm sleeping with Shay."

He plucked her hand from his chest and kissed her fingertips. "Brothers share their female. You know this."

"Yeah. Vicki said, but…" But her knowledge—and reasoning—had disappeared under the onslaught of guilt.

"I knew you'd have a problem, little no-longer-human. I'd planned to stay away, but I saw you in danger.

Her mouth went dry. They both wanted her. And she—she wanted them.

With his thumb, he tilted her chin higher and trapped her gaze. "This is not the time for me to take you, but it will be soon. You decide how you feel about that."

He set her on her feet and went to answer the door, leaving her staring at his back. Was that a promise or a threat?

BREE AIMED HER revolver at the target and squeezed off a shot. As a hole appeared in the bulls-eye, the sound rolled through the mountains. *Look at that.* Her month off from practice hadn't messed up her aim. Even better, her weightlifting had improved her muscles, and the revolver felt lighter.

After receiving her part of the barbeque profits, she'd bought bullets. Even if the chance of killing a hellhound was slim, she felt better knowing it wasn't hopeless.

Yesterday, she'd received a notice that her Seattle lease would end in mid-May. The unexpected reminder had led to such a horrible nightmare that she'd taken a shower at three a.m. Her lips curved ruefully. Shay'd thought she was crazy.

As she carefully reloaded her pistol, she ordered her thoughts. She needed to return, pack up her apartment, and move out. But she wouldn't go during the dark of the moon. Nope. She took a shot and nailed the target. And moon or not, she'd be sure she could defend herself.

Aim...fire. She frowned. Her living room was small, and a hellhound would be close. Why was she practicing on a distant target? And an eye was the size of a quarter, not a pumpkin-sized target like what she had now. She needed to rework the firing range.

By piling up logs, branches, and brush, she created something roughly the size of a hellhound. So *big.* Cold slid down her spine. *Stop it.*

She secured two eye-sized targets to her hellhound simulation, then backed up. Not bad. If it came through the glass door, she'd be about...this far away. She assumed the proper stance and fired. Missed the eye.

Again and again. One bullet hit. Zeb had made it look so easy, but criminy, an eye was a small target. Mouth tight, she reloaded.

SUCKING ON A hard candy, Shay strolled down the dirt road toward the cabins at the end. They were the ones in the worst condition. As the previous owner had grown older, he'd maintained only the closest few. After fixing them first, Zeb was working down the line, grumbling as if the disrepair were a personal affront.

Hammering brought Shay to the current project. Taking a comfortable position against a tree, he breathed in the scents of freshly cut wood and damp forest as he watched his brother work.

A chittering sprite perched on a branch, throwing twigs at Zeb. When a tiny missile bounced off his back, he laughed.

Shay smiled. Damned if that wasn't a fine sound. Cold Creek was good for Zeb. So was the brother bond. Then there was Breanne. Scratching his shoulder on the tree trunk, he turned over arguments in his mind. Would his brother agree? And if he did, what would Breanne say?

"You going to stand there all day?" Zeb set down the hammer and turned.

"Heard me?"

"Fuck yeah. You move like a constipated moose."

Now that was an insult. As Zeb shifted his weight to a better fighting posture, Shay considered tackling him. But the ground was muddy and pounding on someone took effort.

When Shay didn't move, Zeb relaxed and leaned a hip on the decrepit porch railing. "What's up?"

"Nothing bad. The Arizona fishermen offered me a big fee to guide them to Eight Lake Valley. We're leaving in an hour, but even if I trawsfur to return, I won't get back before dawn."

"Bree know?"

"Aye." Shay hesitated. "She's had nightmares since Nora died."

"Want me to take the fishermen?"

"Hell no. They were barely brave enough to ask me. Just keep an eye on her."

"Done."

Shay didn't move. How was he going to explain his sudden change of heart?

Zeb's eyes narrowed. "More?"

"I've been thinking."

"There's a surprise."

Not getting any response from Zeb, the pixie edged out farther on her branch and threw another twig. With a quick snatch, Zeb caught the missile and tossed it back. Giving a squeak of surprise, the sprite dodged, then chittered angrily.

"Never seen you play with one before," Shay commented.

A flash of a grin, then Zeb said, "They remind me of Bree when she's startled. Same little squeak."

Shay snorted a laugh, recognizing the sound.

But that introduced the topic he wanted to discuss. "Speaking of Breanne..." He'd decided to voice his hopes to Zeb very slowly. He would ease around to the goal as warily as he'd stalk a badger.

His mouth took over and ruined his careful strategy. "I want to win her. For our mate."

Chapter Twenty-Five

*B*REE *STEPPED CLOSER to the sliding glass door, trying to see through the darkness. Big. Four legs. Coming straight toward the apartment. Glass shattered. A horrible smell. She couldn't move and—*

"Wake up, little female." A deep rough voice. Strong hands pulled her upright and shook her lightly.

She gasped. The foul stench was dispelled by the fresh scents of soap and pine. She opened her eyes. "Zeb."

"Right the first time."

"I had a nightmare."

He briskly rubbed her arms, keeping her in the present. "I heard."

"I made that much noise?" Had she scared every beast in the forest?

"I was awake." He lifted the covers and slid in.

His legs touched hers. Bare legs. Bare chest. "You're not wearing any clothes."

"You're wearing too many." Before she could react, he yanked her T-shirt over her head. "Better."

"Zeb…" No clothes. Big man. Fear slid up her spine. *Don't panic.*

He lay back. After a second, he took her hand and patted it on his chest. "Your head goes here."

They'd just snuggle? She still had her panties on, she realized, and the ripples of fear eased slightly. He wasn't going to jump on her. And she really, really wanted him here. Sweat still chilled her skin from the nightmare. No hellhound would get past Zeb.

"Okay." With a small sigh, she let him tug her down and nudge her head onto his shoulder. He was heavenly warm, all solid muscle and smooth skin.

He drew her closer until her breasts pressed his side. "You fit against me well." With her ear pressed on his chest, his voice sounded even rumblier. "Put your leg over mine."

She hesitated.

He nipped her fingers.

"Okay, fine." She slid her leg over his. When her mound pressed against his hip, she stiffened, but he didn't attack her.

His chest rose and fell in a slow, even rhythm. The coarse hair on his lower legs teased her foot, and she wiggled her toes, earning a grunt of exasperation. "Go to sleep, little female."

She felt tugs on her scalp, and realized he was playing with her long hair. It was as soothing as being petted, and muscle by muscle, she relaxed and dropped off to sleep.

SHE WAS DREAMING, she knew, and didn't care as she ran out into the meadow. The wind from the mountains ruffled her fur, and the sun warmed her. Tall grass swished against her legs. She lay down and rolled, and somehow Zeb was there. His hard hands ran over her.

Warmth pooled in her belly as she wakened to reality and a callused palm stroking up and down her back.

"You are awake, little female. I deserve a kiss for my patience."

She was still curled against Zeb, and all her fears had evaporated during her sleep. "Um."

He didn't wait for permission. His fingers tangled in her hair, tilting her head back, and he took possession of her mouth, going from sweet to outright carnal within a breath.

He growled and a second later, she was flat on her back with him straddling her hips.

"Zeb!"

He paused, and the intensity of his gaze was like the sun. After a long moment, his cheek creased. "You're not afraid." Bending, he nibbled on her lips, then her jawline. He kissed down her neck and licked under her ear to make her shiver. His straight hair fell like a curtain around them, tickling her skin. He bit the muscle at the top of her shoulder and sent heat sliding after it. No, she wasn't afraid.

With one arm under her back, he effortlessly raised her shoulders so he could pull her nipple into his hot mouth. He suckled, teasing with his tongue and rolling the point against his teeth.

Need surged like fire through her body. "Zeb."

He left her breast to take her mouth deeply. As her pussy started to waken, her hips rose involuntarily.

Giving her a light kiss, he said, "I will find my way there, little female. But I have certain other needs to fulfill first."

She looked at him blankly. Other needs?

"To taste your skin." He kissed her neck, then reached under her panties, touching her so intimately that a whimper escaped. Removing his hand, he licked the wetness off his fingers. "To taste *you*."

No, wait. Her legs slid closed, and he shook his head chidingly. With a quick movement, he grabbed her ankle…fondled her foot…kissed her toes.

She tried to pull her leg away, but he held it with an unyielding grip and worked his way upward—calf, knee, tender inner thigh—using teeth and lips and tongue. Each inch made her skin more sensitive and increased the throbbing in her core.

SHE WAS SO still, he would have worried except for the scent of her arousal. Nervous, yes. Unsure, yes. The knowledge deepened his need for her, his desire to bring her satisfaction.

He moved up so he could slide his hands over her lush breasts, fondling her gently. By the Mother, she had lovely, large breasts. And sensitive.

He nuzzled between them, inhaling the light scent of vanilla, then pressed them together so he could lick one nipple and the other, teasing them to hard points.

The thudding of her heart skipped when he nipped a peak. She gasped and fisted the bed sheets.

He didn't take females between Gatherings—without the full moon heat to drive them, females were afraid of him. Too scarred, too big, too rough. He hadn't realized how the lack of a female's urgency would let him slow down and savor everything.

He intended to enjoy all of her. Many times.

Her hand touched his head tentatively, and, when her fingers tangled in his hair, the warmth that filled him wasn't lust. Had he ever met a female so sweet?

Moving down her body, he kissed the curve of her waist, the roundness over her stomach, her small bellybutton. When his lips grazed over the top of her thigh, her leg quivered. He smiled against the warm skin and ran his tongue up the silken crease, then did the same on the other side. Her breathing quickened, but she didn't move.

By now, a female in heat would order him to mount her. Damned if he didn't like this better.

He stripped the tiny underpants from her, ignoring her murmured protest. The crescent moon of new beginnings had set around midnight, and early dawn light shone through the window, glowing faintly on her skin. Her pale pink nipples matched her lips. Shielded by golden-white curls, her female parts glistened with arousal. He'd never seen anything so pretty.

With her pussy uncovered, her scent drew him like a magnet. He breathed in the fragrance of her musk and blew out gently to ruffle the curly hair at the juncture of her thighs.

Her hips tilted up, then she closed her legs as if embarrassed by her response. Fuck, human ideas about sex were strange. He'd not permit her to shield herself from his gaze, his fingers, or his mouth.

He moFved her knees apart and nipped her inner thigh in admonishment. Her muscles quivered under his teeth. Kneeling between her legs, he grabbed the heavy cushions from the chair beside the bed. Setting his hand under her ass, he pushed both tall cushions under her hips. *Better.* Her pussy was not only tilted up so he could enjoy the sight and use his hands, but the position put her cunt even with his cock. He inhaled her heady fragrance and ran one finger through her swollen folds. Her sharp breath was like a fist on his shaft.

Shay had warned that she was still learning about mating. Teaching this little female about her own needs would be a pleasure.

With one hand, he pulled her folds apart, exposing her fully. Glistening and slick. His cock hardened to the point of pain. With a gentle finger, he slid her clit hood upward to display her pretty pink pearl. Still trying to hide from him. How far could he get it to swell?

HEAT ROLLED OVER Bree in a wave of embarrassment and arousal. With huge cushions under her bottom, and her legs splayed to the sides, her private parts were totally on display. Her shoulders were lower than her hips, and blood rushed to her head.

Zeb's ruthless fingers held her labia apart as he ran a finger around her entrance, then spread the slickness over her clit. Slowly. She shuddered helplessly as his finger explored, rubbing and tugging her folds, sliding around her clit, circling her entrance.

Again. And again. Wetness trickled between her buttocks. Her clit swelled, throbbing as he kept her open. She caught the gleam of his eyes and realized that as he touched her, he was watching her face as intently as any predator. "Zeb…"

"Shhh." His finger tapped a reprimand just above her clit, and her whole body jolted.

Another slow circle. Her thighs quivered as the pressure inside her began to tighten.

He bent and his tongue licked her—so hot and soft and very different from his finger. She heard herself whimper when he circled, never quite…there. Her insides coiled with impatience, and her hips pushed up uncontrollably.

I'm ready. Want something inside. She stroked his leg with one foot, urging him to her.

"Uh-uh. This is my trail." With a movement too fast to follow, he snatched her ankle and bit the arch of her foot.

"Ah!" Her whole leg jerked at the feel of his sharp teeth, and the light pain sent heat surging upward.

He set his big hand on her stomach, holding her down as he returned to her pussy. A slow slide up one side of her clit, flickering over the top, slowly down the other. Over and over, until the nub felt swollen and tight, like it might burst. Her lower half ached with need.

He was *teasing* her. She'd never been tormented like this. A whine escaped her. "Zeb, *please.*"

His laugh, dark and low, was one she'd never heard before. "Little female, you taste too good to stop now." He licked around her entrance and buried his tongue inside her.

"Aaah!" She squirmed as he thrust.

His hand pinned her in place. "You will hold still while I enjoy myself."

As her clit throbbed, demanding more, he replaced his tongue with a finger, sliding into her slowly. The nerves inside her flared into life at the ruthless advance. In and out, then two fingers. Jeez. Everything contracted around the penetration, and her pussy flamed with sensation.

Without warning, he thrust hard, pumping his fingers, and her legs quivered on the cushion. Her hips tried to buck; he prevented it. The feeling of being held open, held down, not having any control over what he was doing should have scared her—only it seemed to make her hotter. She felt her insides drawing closer around his fingers as her whole focus turned to only one thing. One spot.

He lowered his head, and his mouth closed completely over her clit, enveloping it in moist heat.

Oh God. Her body tried to arch, and he pressed her flat even as his tongue rubbed insistently over the nub of nerves. One stroke, another, she was so close, almost, almost there… Everything in her tightened. Her breathing stopped.

Then his lips pressed together, flattening her clit, and he sucked as his tongue savaged the top.

"Oooh, nooo." Pleasure fountained upward, exploding through her body in long, hard waves of sensation as she spasmed around Zeb's fingers. Waves of pleasure rippled outward, and her fingers tingled like Fourth of July sparklers.

His laugh held an open delight she'd never heard before. Even as her shockwaves started to ease, he straightened. On his knees, he set one hand on her thigh.

And then she felt his erection at her entrance, teasingly sliding up and down her inner lips, wetting the head. He pressed harder inexorably, working in, stretching her. He was big and thick and much, much longer than his fingers.

Shocked at the intrusion, she whimpered. With her hips positioned high on the cushion, he filled her—too deep, too tight. She tried to pull away as her insides throbbed painfully.

"Shhh, little female. Don't move." His hands gripped her hips, holding her to him.

As she gasped for breath, he leaned forward onto one hand, and she whined as the movement drove him farther in.

Taking her left hand, he kissed and nibbled her fingers, before placing her arm around his neck. He did the same with her right. As he nuzzled her neck and sucked on her earlobe, she felt her body relax around him. His dark forest scent soothed her. Excited her.

He lifted his head, trapping her gaze with his black eyes. His hand closed over her breast, fondling. Then he pinched the nipple, and, as the bite of pleasure zinged through her, her vagina clenched around his cock.

Heated amusement filled his eyes. He switched to her other breast, slowly stroking, and then his rough fingers found the nipple. When he rolled it between his fingertips, it sent a stream of sheer heat straight to her clit, to her pussy, and everything tightened again.

Involuntarily, her fingers tangled in his hair, so silky and long, and her hips tilted up.

He gave a growl of satisfaction, and he pulled out, startling a cry from her, then another when he re-sheathed himself. He continued, increasing the pace until her breath sobbed from her. He was so deep within her, so hard. One of his arms rubbed against her shoulder, like an iron post holding him up. His other hand fondled her breasts, squeezing, gently pulling on her nipples with each thrust until she could no longer keep track of the individual sensations. All of her burned.

But she couldn't quite... She needed to come. "Zeb," she

whispered.

He brushed a kiss across her lips. "Tell me."

"Please. I can't…" Her fingers dug into his shoulders as she surrendered, giving him the last remaining trace of control.

He rubbed his cheek against her. "Cariad, I'll take care of you."

He pushed upright, weight on his knees, his cock still deep inside her. His hands stroked down her stomach until they reached her sex. With her hips on the cushions, he could thrust into her from his kneeling position…and play with her pussy at the same time. Oh heavens.

His fingers found her slick, engorged clit and circled it feather light. Every nerve in her body jumped and sizzled, until the slide of his cock and touch of his finger merged into one exquisite unendurable sensation.

But before she could come, he rolled them over on the bed. She was on top and blinked in surprise at the unaccustomed position.

Patiently, he arranged her legs so her knees were beside his hips and she straddled him. Still fully inside her, in this position, he seemed even longer. Every movement sent shocks of heat through her.

Denied an orgasm, her clit burned painfully, and she tilted to rub it against his pelvis. Oh yes, that was good. As she leaned forward, he took her breasts in his demanding hands. His gaze was on her face, watching her reactions.

Each time he plucked her nipples, she contracted around him, and he growled in dark pleasure. Her breasts felt tight and hot, her clit matching, and she wiggled with ferocious urgency.

"Now, you will move." His hands gripped her hips firmly to lift her off his cock and pull her back down. He was so big inside her that each time she lowered herself on him, she gasped. He directed her movements until she settled into a good rhythm.

With one hand, he returned to fondling her breast, but his other hand slid down to her clit, stoking her hard nub each time she lowered.

More. She moved faster. Faster. Panting with urgency. Her thighs quivered, destroying her balance, and she gripped his hard shoulders, digging her fingernails in. "Oh God, oh God."

"Look at me, little female."

Her gaze lifted to his smoldering eyes. He pinched her clit, as hard as he'd pinched her nipples, and everything inside her boiled over, spilling through her nerves and veins in hot pleasure. Her back arched as more waves hit.

"You're so fucking beautiful," he murmured.

She blinked in surprise. Before she could speak, he gripped her hips, moving her up and down, taking his own pleasure. Her nerves shimmered with his hard thrusts. And then, he growled, low and deep, as he filled her with his liquid heat.

She held herself upright for a long moment, too satisfied to move, before her muscles gave way. As she flattened on top of him, she felt his heart thudding against her breasts.

He wrapped her hair around his hand and used it to tilt her face up so he could kiss her, long and slow and sweet.

The minute he released her, she lay her head on his shoulder, snuggled closer, and fell asleep, wrapped in the safety of his powerful arms.

WHEN BREE WOKE again, bright sunlight streamed in the window. She must have slept like a rock. Yawning, she looked up.

Propped on one elbow, Zeb stared at her. His jaw was tight, his eyes flat and cold.

Her body went rigid. "What?"

He ran his fingers over her shoulder, her arm, her leg, his

gentleness a disconcerting contrast to the granite hardness of his face.

He's touching my scars.

His gaze returned to hers, and he ran a finger down her cheek. "You did nothing wrong, little female. But I would know what has done this to you. This time you will answer me fully."

"I told you, it was an animal." She started to sit up.

One big hand pinned her like a bug to the bed. "Because of your human modesty, Shay and I turn our eyes from your nakedness. But when you and Shay mated, he saw more closely and asked me to look."

Oh-oh.

"A grizzly bear might have a jaw this size," he mused, looking at her shoulder. His black gaze rested on her much like his hand, trapping her. "Did a grizzly bear attack you?"

She licked her dry lips. "No."

"What sort of animal was it?" he asked ever so softly.

"A hellhound." She stared at the wall as shame enveloped her. She felt ugly, filthy. It had pushed inside her, had... "In Seattle, in my apartment."

He curved his hand under her jaw, turning her face toward him. His palm was warm and as unyielding as his voice. "Tell me."

The need to hide was strong, but he wouldn't let her turn away. "It came through the glass door. I couldn't stop it. My friend"—she pulled in a ragged breath—"Ashley was there, and I tried to keep it from her, but the monster heard her opening the locks and it..."

Zeb made a noise, and the lines around his eyes deepened.

"She screamed and screamed, and it killed her. T-tore her... There was blood. Her blood all over." *It licked the blood. Ashley lay so still, her gray eyes unblinking. Wrong.* Zeb's face blurred as tears filled Bree's eyes. *The creature turning into a man. Laughing.* "Th-

that's all."

Zeb's warm hand curved around her nape, and he pulled her against his chest. "Tell me the rest, Bree." His voice was controlled. No shock. No horror.

"I kicked it. Knifed it. Nothing worked. It bit me, dragged me back to the living room. I couldn't get away." *Its teeth ripping into her—the pain.* "I screamed and nobody c-came."

With a growl of sympathy, Zeb wrapped his arm around her waist.

She burrowed closer, a glacier of coldness inside her. His bare chest was slick with her tears. But tears didn't clean her. She felt filth coating her and could smell the monster's foulness on her skin. Her lips pressed tightly closed.

"There's more," Zeb said.

He knew—he *knew*, and he'd still make her say it? Anger flared, fragmenting the ice inside her. A bubble of pain rose, spilling into words. "It changed into a man. It was a man and…it r-raped me. It l-liked my blood." She gagged, remembering. "Said it would be back."

Silence. A sigh. "You had only enough magic in your blood to confuse it. If you'd been fully human or shifter, you'd have died right then." Zeb's muscles around her were like the iron bars over the windows. His embrace was safe, but no longer comforting, no longer gentle, and the loss hurt her inside.

She was ruined and now he knew. She pushed at him. "Let me up. I need to go—" Somewhere. Anywhere but here.

He didn't release her. After a slow breath, he pulled her even closer, smoothing her against him until not an inch of space remained between them. "I would give my life to have saved you that," he murmured against her hair.

He wasn't going to let her run, and she closed her eyes, feeling his breath against her temple. His hard hand stroked down her back. When he finally pulled away to look at her, she couldn't meet his gaze. His fingers tilted her chin up.

"I'm dirty," she whispered, finally confessing the worst of it. "He made me filthy. I smell like him, and I can't get clean."

"Bree." He closed his eyes for an interminable minute. When he looked at her again, darkness swirled in his gaze. "My uncle and littermates were killed by a hellhound." His voice sounded strained, like hers after that night of screams. "My littermates and I had raided the refrigerator, so my uncle confined us to the cabin as punishment. But we were thirteen and just learned to shift. I sneaked out to practice in the starlight by a lake. When I came back, they'd been torn apart."

"Oh God, Zeb. I'm sor—"

"My sister had been raped."

Bree's eyes filled with tears. Littermates—the girl would have been thirteen. So young. And Zeb had seen. Known.

"If you met her now, would you tell her she was filthy?"

"No! Of course not."

"Then neither are you, little female," Zeb whispered, cuddling her like a kitten. "Neither are you."

The sobs took her by surprise, shaking her chest, spilling from her in horrible ugly sounds that she couldn't stop. *His sister. Ashley. Me... So much pain.* Her body shook under the onslaught, anger and grief mingling together. She fought his embrace, needing to get away, to hide, and he wrapped her closer until she could only lean against him and cry and cry and cry.

When she'd exhausted herself, reduced to little gasping breaths, he still held her. Solid, warm, safe.

"I'm sorry," she whispered into his chest. Her head felt heavy as she looked up.

His mouth curved with tenderness, and his eyes were warm with approval. "I am not." He used his fingers to wipe the wetness from her cheeks. "Did you cry for my sister too?"

She nodded, knowing that had started her tears, opened her

to her own misery.

"Thank you, cariad." He shifted so she nestled against his side, her head cradled on his shoulder. "Sleep again. It's early, and I have a need to hold you for a time."

She settled, the rise and fall of his chest infinitely comforting, and discovered she still had a need to be held.

WHEN THEY FINALLY roused, he dragged her to the bathroom for a badly needed shower. She didn't have a chance to over-scrub, since he insisted on washing her himself—so thoroughly that they were both aroused. This time, he set her hands on the wall and took her from behind, hard and fast, an arm across her pelvis holding her hips in place, his fingers on her clit demanding a response. She came, shuddering and crying out, fingernails clawing at the tile wall.

When he finished, he pushed her under the water again.

This time she slapped his hands away, earning herself a low chuckle and agreement.

She followed him down the stairs, her hair still wet, and the air in the cabin cold against her over-heated body.

Shay was in the kitchen when they entered. He ran a finger over her swollen lips and smiled. "You look well taken."

She felt a flush run all the way to her forehead, and both men grinned.

Then Shay's smile disappeared. His brows drew together as he tilted her head to the light. "Your eyelids are as red and puffy as your mouth. By the God, Zeb." Fury hardened his face.

Bree stepped in front of Zeb. "No, Shay. Zeb didn't—"

"The scars are from a hellhound," Zeb said bluntly.

Shay stilled. "A hellhound?"

"Yes." Zeb brushed his knuckles over her cheek and pushed her toward his brother. "She needs to be held. I'll start a fire. It's too cold in here for her."

As he walked out, Bree stared after him. The abandoned feeling shook her.

Shay's arms came around her, holding her tightly against his body. He whispered into her hair the explanation that made her world right again, "He knows I need to hold you, a leannan, and my bràthair is not a selfish male."

AFTER HOLDING BREANNE as long as she'd permit, Shay left her in the kitchen concocting something sweet for Angie's Diner.

Once he'd had the entire story from Zeb, his anger was so deep, his urge to kill so strong that the living room turned red.

With his own fury simmering, Zeb was no help.

"I need to leave," Shay said. In this mood, he'd be no help to the little wolf.

Zeb jerked his head toward the door, and Shay accepted.

As he stalked past the more distant cabins, he spotted a pile of wood, the axe buried in the stump. Something to kill. He set a chunk on the stump, swung, and the wood split, pieces flying in opposite directions. Another. Split it in half. And continued…

Chapter Twenty-Six

THE NEXT MORNING, lured by the scent of bacon, Bree wandered down the stairs and toward the kitchen, pulling a heavy sweater on over her undershirt as she went. The morning air was chilly, although someone had started a fire in the fireplace. Her stomach growled, and she smiled. Her appetite was returning. Good. She'd spent most of yesterday on the edge of nausea and close to tears.

Zeb's questions had brought back all the memories she'd thought conquered, and Shay's fury had topped off the emotional volcano. After Shay had returned, the men had dragged her into the forest to play tag as wolves, wrestling and bouncing and acting like puppies. It had helped. Animals didn't feel dirty.

She'd taken a shower this morning without needing to use up all the hot water. She wasn't completely healed, she knew, but…better.

And she'd slept great. Last night, Shay had curled around her in his big bed. Sometime later, Zeb had joined them. Sandwiched between two cahirs, who could have nightmares?

As she entered the kitchen, Zeb was dishing up bacon and scrambled eggs. *I should sleep late more often.* "You cooked?"

"Only breakfast." He studied her for a moment, and then obviously satisfied, ran his knuckles down her cheek. "One course, no side dishes, no vegetables. Very little to go wrong."

Shay pulled out a chair for her and stroked her hair gently as she took her seat.

They were always careful with her, she'd noticed, but today they acted as if she was something fragile. Okay, yes, their behavior gave her the warm 'n' fuzzies, but good grief, she wasn't going to break. Bree helped herself to the food. "I'm starving."

Zeb's lips quirked. "Considering how little you ate yesterday, I'm not surprised."

"I didn't eat anything."

Shay snorted. "Yes, you did, a leannan."

No, I didn't. After the morning started off with Shay being so angry, she'd never gone back into the kitchen. How could the men think...*oh.* In the forest, she'd gotten hungry, and the big jerks had made her catch her own lunch. She'd only managed to nab a scrawny mouse. One bite—raw. *Ew.* She frowned at them. "I don't like rodent take-out."

Zeb's quick grin flashed.

"You'll have to improve your hunting skills if you want a higher class of dining," Shay said.

As they ate, they discussed the day's projects, reservations for the cabins, new items they'd found that needed repair. The next barbecue was approaching, and they talked over the menu. Zeb, the oh-so-terrifying-cahir, wanted to construct a fenced-off play area for the smaller children. With a handmade jungle gym.

Bree finished her food slowly, unwilling to break the peaceful mood. How odd to be planning the day with two men. Ashley would have been thrilled. The familiar grief washed through her, but it had eased to a dull ache.

After Shay refilled her coffee, he rested his elbows on the table. His gunmetal blue gaze fastened on her in a way that made her insides quiver.

"What?" she asked, wanting to add, *I didn't do it, whatever it was.*

"I've been thinking. You aren't afraid of animals, but you bought a pistol and told me you '*needed*' to practice." His brows drew together. "What are you planning to kill with that revolver, little wolf?"

Her stomach sank. Telling the truth would be like throwing water into a deep fryer; the men's anger would splatter everywhere.

Zeb's eyes narrowed with comprehension. His coffee cup hit the table hard enough to slosh liquid over the sides. "That's why you quizzed me about killing a hellhound with a pistol."

Their intense stares were a heavy weight.

"Well, Breanne?" Shay asked softly.

This isn't their decision, darn them. She raised her chin. "You figured it out. My lease is up, and I have to pack up my apartment. I'm not going to be defenseless." Not this time.

"You'd go alone?" Shay's voice hadn't risen, but his hand fisted so tight that his knuckles cracked with ominous pops. "And expect to stay alive if it comes for you?"

"Even with two experienced cahirs, a hellhound sometimes wins. Against one little female—alone?" Zeb's expression was deadly.

"Hey, I'm not stupid. I won't go during the dark of the moon." She breathed out, slow and even. If they saw how scared she was, they'd lock her in her room.

"You will not do this," Zeb said flatly.

"It's not your decision to make."

Shay shoved away from the table and paced across the kitchen. And back. He set his hand on her shoulder, deliberately looming over her, the brute. "Zeb and I are meeting with the Cosantir this morning. You'll accompany us."

"I don't think so." Her mouth was dry, but her hands shook

too hard to risk lifting her glass.

"Breanne," Shay said in a level voice. "A new shifter must get permission from the Cosantir before leaving the territory."

"I'm just going there long enough to pack." Surely she could rent a truck and have everything loaded in a day or so.

"Nonetheless."

Another freaking rule she'd never heard of. "Fine. I'll go with you."

Zeb took a sip of coffee. His hand was rock-steady, she noticed bitterly. "You will also tell the Cosantir what happened to you. If you don't, I will."

"Oh sure, announce it to the world while you're at it." She glared at him. "You already shared more than enough with—" She broke the sentence off.

Frowning, Shay took her hand. "You weren't going to tell me?"

"I-I… Maybe."

"We're doing more than living together, Breanne. Zeb and I want…" He glanced at Zeb and amended, "This was something I should know." He nipped the edge of her hand hard enough to hurt. "Is that clear?"

Her hand stung. He stood, waiting for her answer. His level eyes held her gaze.

"Clear." She glared at him. *Fine. Yes, I do live here and yes, we're having sex.* But since he planned to leave the minute his pushy god gave a yell, this wasn't what she'd call a serious relationship. At least, not on his part. Darn him. "But I don't live with Calum. He doesn't have any say—"

"He does." Shay said flatly.

God, this was going to be such a fun meeting, wasn't it? She scowled, then decided if they could make her so angry, she could do the same. Time to go and kill some branches.

MIDMORNING, BREE WALKED into town between the two men. Although they'd scowled at her when she returned from her shooting practice—mission accomplished—she didn't give a darn.

It had been a good session, and her bullets were finally going where she aimed them. After moving close enough to Mr. Monster that she couldn't miss, she'd started backing up a step at a time. True, she was still closer than she liked, but she had about three weeks before her lease ran out. She'd be ready.

Pistol or not, the thought of spending hours in her apartment sent a chill through her.

Zeb tugged her hair. "It won't be that bad."

She stared at him in disbelief, then realized he meant the meeting with the Cosantir.

When they reached the diner, Calum waited at a table with a pot of tea in front of him.

With Zeb and Shay behind her, Bree walked past the long counter where an elderly man sat on a blue-topped stool, openly enjoying a piece of the apple pie she'd made yesterday. She'd have enjoyed a second of pride if her stomach hadn't been so knotted up.

Courteous as always, Calum rose and held a chair for her. After everyone had seats, he raised an eyebrow at Shay, obviously expecting an explanation of Bree's presence.

Before Shay could answer, Angie bustled out from the kitchen, three cups in one hand, and a pot of coffee in the other. "Anyone want to order?"

She had no takers.

"I'll leave you the pot then." She patted Bree's shoulder. "Call me if you need anything."

"Thank you, Angeline," Calum said, receiving a pleased smile in return. He turned his attention to Bree. "Can I help you with something, Breanne?"

I don't know him. I can't do this. She tried to push her chair back, but it ran into Zeb's foot.

He jerked his head at Calum in a silent, *tell him or I will.*

She gave him a pleading gaze. *Later. I'll tell him later.*

His return look was cynical; he knew she'd never bring it up.

Fine then. "Before I came here from Seattle, I got hurt. The one who—" She couldn't finish.

Shay's hand closed over hers. "Breanne, he needs to know."

Calum's eyes narrowed.

Gripping Shay's hand with all her strength, she continued, "I was attacked by a hellhound. It killed my friend, before"—would this ever get easier to say?—"before it turned into a m-man and r-raped me."

Calum's eyes darkened. His mouth set into a tight line. "Continue."

"That's all. Except my lease runs out in three weeks, and I have to return to pack up my apartment." She added a hasty, "It shouldn't be more than one night."

"You are not going anywhere near that city," Zeb gritted out.

Odd how he didn't scare her anymore. "I'm sorry, Zeb, but I am."

Shay's grip had changed from gentle to nearly crushing her hand. "Even if it's not the new moon, the hellhound could return for you in human form. Zeb and I will go instead."

"No," she said, despite the warmth filling her. The relief. *Please come with me.* "This isn't your job. I can defend myself."

"Breanne. I'll see what I can arrange to get your apartment packed," Calum said softly.

Someone else could do it? The rush of relief made her dizzy. She'd not even thought of it because, face it, she could barely afford a rental truck. Hiring expensive movers? Hah. But would her apartment manager let a moving crew in? "I—I probably need to be there."

"No." His eyes were almost black, and when his gaze met hers, her throat closed as if a hand had clamped around it. "You may not leave this territory—not for several months—not until there is no chance of you shifting by accident."

His gaze turned to the men. "Cahirs do not fight in human lands. Your gifts from Herne will not be there for you, not in a city of metal, so far from His forests. You are forbidden, cahirs."

Both Zeb and Shay scowled at him.

Bree's hands closed into fists. God, she was tired of being told what to do. "And if I go anyway?"

When his attention swung back to her, her heart stuttered. "The penalty for bringing attention to the Daonain is death, sentenced by Cosantir's judgment, dealt by a cahir's hand. Do not force your lovers to kill you, Breanne," Calum said very softly. His black gaze swept around the table like the hot wind before a forest fire.

She didn't take a breath until he walked out of the diner.

AS HE AND Shay silently left town, Zeb needed to pound on something. Unfortunately, Shay had already split all the firewood. *Fucking mongrel.*

"Well, that went well," Shay muttered.

"Why the hell did you tell him we wanted to go in her stead?"

Shay gave him an are-you-that-stupid? look. "We're supposed to be guarding Cold Creek. Calum might want to know if we weren't."

Yeah, he was that stupid. "Fuck."

"Exactly." Shay scowled. "She doesn't really want to go back. I could see it. I think it'll be okay, don't you?"

Anger had smoldered inside him since he'd realized why she'd bought a fucking pistol—the one *he'd* taught her to shoot. "You're so smart. You figure it out."

Shay growled and shot a fist into Zeb's mouth, knocking him backward.

Pain blasted through Zeb's jaw. He wiped the blood off, lowered his head, and charged. His skull impacted Shay's gut, sending them both to the ground.

The next few minutes were a tangle of blows and grunts and snarls until Shay threw Zeb off. He landed hard and rolled, expecting to get flattened.

Shay hadn't moved. He sat a couple of yards away, sucking in air. Blood dripped down his chin; his jaw had a long graze. As his mouth curved in a rueful grin, he winced and fingered his lower lip. "I feel better. You?"

"Yeah." Zeb stood with a groan—Shay'd gotten in a sneaky kick to his ribs—and pulled his brother to his feet. "Guess we'll just have to keep an eye on her."

THAT WENT WELL, didn't it? Bree thought sarcastically as she walked into the grocery store. Picking up a few items for the barbecue tomorrow had been her excuse to stay in town. Otherwise, she'd have been lectured all the way back by two overprotective, women-can't-do-anything cahirs. She shook her head as fuzzy warmth mingled with frustration. They wanted to protect her. It felt odd…and wonderful.

She nodded at Mr. Baty, who was stocking the soup section. At least Calum had forbidden the men to go to Seattle. Because Zeb was right. Even cahirs could die. The thought of them being hurt made her stomach twist. One friend—one friend was all that creature was going to take.

The Cosantir wouldn't let her go to Seattle either. Overbearing bum. She touched her throat, remembering how she'd choked. Fine, she understood his concern that she'd change into a wolf. But he was used to the new shifters being teenagers. She hadn't had an accident—and didn't that sound as if she'd wet her pants?—a *shifting* accident for at least a couple of days.

She pulled in a slow breath and admitted, *I don't want to go back.* Not for anything. She hadn't even been protesting—not really—when he'd come down on her with his Cosantir crap. She glared at the shelf, then picked up a bottle of almond extract.

Honestly, if he arranged a moving company, and somehow got past her anal-retentive apartment manager, she'd be delighted.

So, yeah, she wouldn't be able to tell people goodbye, except in a letter. She needed to send in her resignation too. She'd stalled long enough.

But... Her shoulders straightened. Although the guys thought they'd won, they weren't going to get everything their way. She sniffed. Her target practice would continue. With any luck, she'd never see a hellhound again in her whole life. But if she ever did, she'd have something in her hand a little more effective than a pot of spaghetti.

THE LAST FEW days had gone well, Zeb decided, as he set out the 2x4s he'd cut for the cabin's stoop.

Last Saturday, after being huffy as a wet bobcat for a couple of hours, Bree had returned to her normal sunny self.

On Sunday, the barbecue had drawn even more people, human as well as shifter. The pack had behaved politely, although Gerhard had avoided any interaction—and Bree had avoided Calum in much the same way.

As Zeb attached the first piece of wood, he smiled, remembering how the tiny cubs had tumbled around the trial play area he'd created. Every evening since then, he'd worked on building a small slide. By the time he and Shay moved on, perhaps he'd have finished the playground he'd conceived. It would be something tangible he could leave behind. There probably wouldn't be much else to show he'd been alive. Cahirs who fought hellhounds rarely lived out their lifespan.

And he would be fighting the demon-dogs until he died.

The wavery old glass of the cabin showed his face. Almost hidden by his dark tan was the new mark he'd discovered yesterday—the blue antlers of the oathbound. *Brothers share*, he thought with a wry smile.

A familiar snapping noise split the quiet afternoon and echoed through the mountains. A pistol.

Zeb's hand tightened on the hammer. By Herne's big balls, Bree was shooting again, even though the Cosantir had refused her permission to leave.

If she were planning to obey, why would she need to practice?

He struck the nail so hard that the board split in half. "Fuck."

A few minutes later, he stepped into the target-shooting area behind the little female. Her fluffy pink sweater made her look feminine and helpless, but the Smith & Wesson counteracted the impression.

She held the pistol with perfect form, squeezing the trigger as gently as he'd taught her. The memory of the example he'd used, *stroking a man's balls*, made him tighten. He still hadn't had time to teach her all the ways two people could pleasure each other.

As he got closer, fury cut so deeply through him he could hardly speak. No round bulls-eye anymore—she'd created a hellhound-sized creation with eyes as the target. "You.

You're…" His voice failed him.

She whirled and took two hasty steps back. "Zeb, I'm—"

"No. No, you will not." *You will not go to Seattle. You will not face a hellhound. You will not let it rip you to pieces.* Growling uncontrollably, he gripped her forearm and peeled the revolver from her grip. "No."

As he left her, cursing him in words no female should use, he knew he'd never get a chance to teach her about loving…but at least she'd be alive to hate him.

Chapter Twenty-Seven

MOST OF THE pack had already disappeared into the forest. Idly scratching his back on a cold tree trunk, Shay waited outside the cave entrance for his brother. Since he'd been stuck dealing with deliveries, and Zeb had been working on the cabins, they hadn't talked all day.

Finally Zeb appeared, still in human form.

The sun had set not long before, and the lower foothills were still silhouetted in pink-gold. To the east, the silvery glow around the white-topped peaks heralded the moon's rising and gave enough light to see the hollows in Zeb's face and the pain in his dark gaze.

"She still not speaking to you?" Shay asked before Zeb could trawsfur.

Zeb shook his head. "Now ask me if I care."

"Hell, I know you care, or you'd give her pistol back." The lodge had been an unhappy place since the blowup. Breanne had spent the last couple of days with Angie in town. Zeb was acting as if he had a foxtail in his paw, snapping at anything Shay said.

Breanne was too sweet to stay angry very long, but time was running out. "Gather's tomorrow."

Zeb gave him an irritated look.

"You think she'll do all right? Are you going to be there?"

The grating sound was Zeb clenching his jaw. "I'll be there."

BREE WALKED ACROSS the parking lot to the Wild Hunt as the moon rose above the mountains. In the quiet night air, she heard the pack heading up the mountain: an occasional howl or bark from a younger wolf, a whine or yip when a more aggressive one chastised another. Wolfy socializing. She sighed. The one pack run she'd experienced had been so wonderful. Surrounded by the other wolves, she'd felt for a moment as if she really belonged. And now, her instincts clamored for her to forget everything and join them.

Her human brain knew that would be the stupidest thing she could possibly do. Zeb would be there. Tears pricked her eyes. That arrogant, over-protective know-it-all. She hadn't been planning to go back to Seattle against the Cosantir's orders, but would he give her a chance to say that? *Nooo.* He'd pissed her off so bad she'd have put a bullet in him—if he hadn't taken her S&W.

She grinned ruefully. Actually, she was awfully close to forgiving him. *It's hard to hate someone who risked his life for me.*

But there were other reasons to stay away from the pack run. Three of them: Thyra, Gerhard, and Dieter. Maybe by the next hunt, some of the animosity would have died down.

For now, her appointment with Vicki provided a good excuse to be absent, and Angie would make her apologies to the alpha.

The cozy atmosphere of the tavern wrapped around Bree as she entered. It looked like a typical Saturday night. Waylon Jennings played on the jukebox with a young couple doing a two-step nearby. One pool table in the alcove had baseball-capped men in flannel shirts and work boots, the other was surrounded by clean-cut college boys in Abercrombie and Fitch.

Most of the tables in the room were filled, and Bree craned her neck, trying to locate Vicki.

Bearing a tray of drinks, Rosie slowed long enough to nod toward the fireplace. "Over there."

"Thanks." Bree made her way over.

"'Bout time, slowpoke. I thought maybe you'd gone with the pack." Vicki shoved a chair out with her foot. "Bree, this is Heather. She runs a software business down in Rainier territory."

"Hi." Bree nodded at the other woman whose lanky frame held more muscles than curves.

"Good to meet you." Dressed in jeans, a white turtleneck sweater, and a turquoise flannel shirt that matched her eyes, the redhead pushed a mug across the table. "That one's yours."

The beer was cold with a nice bite. Bree drank a good third before setting it down with a sigh. "I needed that."

"The Wild Hunt has the best beer on tap." Heather smiled. "I'm not sure if I attend Gatherings in Cold Creek for the beer or the males."

"I thought the guys traveled and the women stayed put." Bree studied the full bar with a quiver of anxiety. How many of the men were shifters that she'd…meet…tomorrow night?

"That's the norm, not the law. I attend Gatherings here, so I can visit my mom up in Elder Village."

"That's where I met Heather, right after I'd learned I was a shifter," Vicki said. "And I was probably as lost as you."

"If you were a late-blooming shifter like me, why do the guys act as if I'm so unusual?"

"I came to shifterhood a different way. Seems that a dying shifter can *gift* his magic to a human. At the time, I thought it was a fucking lousy present." Vicki took a sip of beer. "Poor Heather got recruited to explain the facts of life. Like Gatherings."

Bree snickered. "She probably did a better job than the

guys."

"Males tried to instruct you?" Frowning, Heather turned to Vicki. "You should have—"

"Hey. Not my fault. Calum shipped me off to Elder Village for those damned classes, leaving Zeb and Shay in the fire zone."

"Zeb and Shay—the cahirs from Rainier?" Heather's lips twitched, then she roared with laughter. "You poor pup."

THE WOLVES FOLLOWED their alpha to a small lake deep in the mountains. Near the middle of the pack, Zeb loped beside his brother. The dirt was moist under his paws. The snow-crisp air from the heights brought the scent of a mountain goat. Closer was the fragrance of beaver from a nearby dam. He'd always loved twilight, the time when night took over from the day, when Herne's power pulsed in his veins, and the Mother's love was as heady as her moon above.

In the meadow, surrounded by black forest, the lake was placid, with mist hovering over the surface in lazy tendrils. The moonlight turned Gerhard's naked body to silver as he paced back and forth near the shoreline. Slowly, the wolves lay down around him.

Zeb noted how the wolves divided into groups rather than spacing out evenly. Over on the right were the older, wiser heads—Baty and Angie, along with the three who owned the hardware store. Odd. With a pack this size, shouldn't there be more older ones?

Near the front, the alpha female reigned over the unmated females. Oddly mentorless, a younger pup hovered on the fringes.

To the left were the young aggressive males. Zeb frowned. Wolves didn't have cliques, not in a well-run pack. He glanced at

Shay. From the half-flattened ears, his brawd saw the divisiveness also.

Good thing that Bree hadn't come tonight, although Zeb missed her with an ache like a broken rib. He couldn't remember when he'd been so fucking miserable, but damned if he'd give her weapon back so she could go get herself killed.

"Listen up," Gerhard snapped, silencing the conversations. "We're going that way." He pointed north.

Zeb frowned. He'd visited there a couple of weeks ago. The rugged valley with steep slopes and avalanche debris wouldn't be an easy hunt.

"There should be deer, and we'll bring one down," Gerhard announced. He trawsfurred and leaped forward into a fast run.

Zeb growled his disgust. The moon wasn't even fully risen. The valley would be dark, the terrain difficult, especially for old ones with less keen eyes. Before Elder Lain died, Zeb had learned how fragile elderly wolves became. A pack run was supposed to be for all the wolves, from the newest shifters to the eldest. Challenging hunts were for young males and females.

Ignoring the compulsion to blindly follow the alpha, Zeb turned to Shay.

Shay flicked his ears forward at the older group and looked at Zeb. Zeb waved his tail in agreement.

Then Shay tilted his head at the new shifter, indicating he'd babysit the pup.

Good plan. Zeb waited for the older wolves to move out and trotted after them.

Baty and Angie ran well, muzzles forward, pleasure in their gait. The other three also kept up well for the first part of the run.

The rocky slopes were too much though, and the three fell farther and farther behind. Planning to risk their pride and suggest they head back, Zeb moved closer.

On the talus-covered trail, one male missed his footing. As the debris slipped out from under him, he landed badly and a bone snapped with a gut-wrenching sound. Scrambling uselessly, he teetered on the edge.

Fuck. Zeb leaped forward and clamped his jaws on the old wolf's ruff. Bracing his legs, he held, unable to do more. Any movement would send them over, and the bottom was a fucking long way down.

The other two wolves blurred to human and pulled them both back onto the trail.

As they moved the hurt wolf to a flat spot, tears leaked down the woman's wrinkled face. "I knew we should stop going on these runs. I knew it." She knelt beside her injured mate and asked the other, "Can you tell how bad it is, Quentin?"

Quentin ran his hands over the hind leg as the wolf whined in pain. "Busted it good, Walter. You clumsy idiot."

Zeb padded over. To his shock, the female turned and stroked her hand down his back. "Thank you, cahir, for saving my mate." She glanced over the edge and shuddered. "He wouldn't have survived that fall."

Quentin's face turned grim. "He might not survive the trip out." He set his hand on his hurt littermate. "It's a long way back, brawd."

And too steep for an old wolf using only three legs. Zeb shifted to human form. "Stay wolf, Walter," he ordered. "You'll be easier to carry."

"But…" Quentin started.

Zeb lifted the injured wolf onto his shoulders. "The trip out will be easier for you two as wolves. Shift back."

The old wolves stayed close as Zeb turned back, struggling to keep his footing. A rock scraped his bare foot, and another, and he silently cursed the fucking alpha with every painful slip and slide.

SHAY NOTICED WHEN the older wolves started to fall behind and was grateful his brother was willing to watch over them. As independent a wolf as ever born, Zeb didn't care if he was alone, or with a few wolves, or in the middle of a pack.

Shay was different. Although, over the years, he'd learned to tolerate solitude, being surrounded by packmates filled his soul in a way nothing else did. Like now, as he greedily absorbed the sounds and scents. To his right, a wolf pounced on a rodent, giving a yip of delight. Two young males quarreled in a dominance spat. Other wolves brushed against Shay as they ran. The scents of the females added delight to the evening. Shay let his mind settle and his instincts come forward.

Nonetheless, he kept the youngest female within sight and scent, running slightly behind her, and wondering where her teacher was. A mentor always stayed beside a new shifter until a certain competence was achieved. This pup was quite a ways from that.

She was flagging by the time they reached the bottom of the valley. A giant tree had fallen across the narrow hunting trail, and the wolves scrambled over it. The young female jumped and jumped, trying futilely to get over it. The wolves divided around her, ignoring her, leaving her behind. With her two front paws on the trunk, she looked forlornly over the log as the pack disappeared down the trail.

A few feet behind her, Shay waited for her to notice him and was disgusted at her lack of awareness. She must have a lousy mentor.

She scented him, finally, and spun. Her ears went back. Her tail tucked between her legs.

He didn't move. Had Klaus's influence extended so deep into this pack that a female would be afraid of a packmate? He trawsfurred, pretending he didn't scent her fear. "There are a couple tricks to use when you jump something big. Want me to show you?"

Her ears came forward, and her tail lifted to wave slowly.

Good, she wasn't giving up. He returned to wolf and showed her how to find dents for the front paws, then replace them with back paws for the impetus to get over. She finally succeeded and stood on the top of the trunk, tail wagging furiously, yipping in joy.

Once more, Shay shifted to human. He grinned at her. "Do it two more times, then you'll never forget."

She obeyed, improving each time.

"Well done. Let's rejoin the rest."

When she started to follow the trail, he shook his head. "Use your ears, pup. Where's the pack?"

Her ears pricked forward, back, then her nose pointed to the west.

"Aye. They're circling. We'll meet up with them." A quick trawsfur, and he led the way at an angle.

When they intercepted the pack, and he realized the Gerhard was searching for prey, a snarl of disgust escaped him. Most alphas would scope out an area before a pack hunt. And to keep hunting here? Where was the alpha's nose? The scent of deer was old. There would be no large prey in this area, not when the foothills had greening grass, and new buds on the brush and trees.

With a frustrated growl, the alpha headed back, ignoring the stragglers like Baty, Angie, and a wolf with a cut paw.

Back where they'd started, Gerhard trawsfurred and braced his feet, scowling. "The noise of all you clumsy retards must have scared the game away."

His brother, having shifted also, nodded agreement.

Scenting Zeb, Shay looked around.

"Need help over here." Zeb's voice came from under a sheltering tree. "Walter has a busted leg."

Gerhard and Dieter walked over to look at the panting wolf. "Bad deal, Walter," Gerhard said. "Make sure you take it slow going back down." The two changed back to wolves and trotted away, followed by Thyra.

Fucking lazy assholes. Shay trawsfurred to human and strode over. "How bad?"

His brother's face was streaked with sweat despite the cold air. "Lower hind, but he's got arthritis and doesn't balance worth shit on three legs." Zeb pushed his hair back. "I splinted it, but he looks like hell."

Shay's temper edged toward boiling. This was an elder of the pack, and no one cared. Angie and Baty had hurried over, but they were too old to help.

A young male joined them. "Dad, what happened?" He dropped to his knees, and Shay recognized Warren from the hardware store.

"Angie, where would the closest litter be? Back at town?" Shay asked.

She knelt beside Walter and patted his shoulder. "There's a cabin a quarter mile away. Calum keeps first aid supplies and a litter in there."

"Warren, go get it. We'll start down now, so just catch up."

"Yes, cahir." The young man trawsfurred and streaked out of the clearing.

By the God, Shay was fed up with this lack of pack cohesiveness. He walked over to the young males who were trading stories of the run. "We need help with the older wolf. Put yourselves into pairs of about equal height and line up for the walk down. We'll take turns carrying."

One of the youths sneered. "Why the fuck should we do anything you say? You're not the alpha."

His littermate pulled the same attitude.

Shay stepped closer and unwrapped the dominance he kept buried when in a pack.

They took a hurried step back.

He smiled and said mildly, "You will do the fuck as I say, or I will rip your arms off and stuff your smart mouths with them."

Their faces paled.

"Line up over there."

As they hurried to where he indicated, the rest fell in. Attitude adjustment complete.

Warren caught up them before long, and, with the efforts of Shay's draftees, they reached the Wild Hunt cave without a problem.

Shay picked up the old guy to carry him upstairs.

"Hold up," Walter said. His face was white and pinched with pain, but he raised his voice to be heard. "Thank you all. I wouldn't have made it without your help."

The young males stared at him, as if they'd not realized what they were doing. As if embarrassed to be thanked.

Shay kept his face straight and gave them a nod of approval. "You did well. You should be proud."

As he carried Walter up the stairs, he saw the pups grin at each other and stand taller than they had before.

After settling the old man on the couch in the locked room and sending Warren to phone the healer, Shay pulled on his clothes. Already dressed, Zeb silently struggled to get his socks and boots onto his gashed, bleeding feet.

They met Sandy in the hall. "I don't know how we would have managed," she said, reaching up to kiss their cheeks. "Thank you so much."

As they entered the bar, Shay saw Zeb's face was a dark red—and he could feel the heat in his own.

"Brawd," Zeb muttered, "I need a beer."

"I'll buy."

BREE GIGGLED AS Heather finished a story about her first Gather. Earlier, Vicki had shared her experience with being human, then shifter, then having two mates. They had more beer. Then Bree had talked about the Gathering. That had required another round of drinks.

"A first Gathering is scary enough without adding trauma like you had," Heather said, patting her hand. "Have you been with anyone since then?"

Bree's face turned hot, even as she grinned. "I have."

Vicki laughed. "And you look quite proud about it too. Knowing you, Miss Never-Back-Down, I bet you asked one of the guys to help you out."

Heather's eyebrows rose. "Now that was a smart move. Who'd you pick?"

"Shay." Bree smiled, remembering his deep smooth voice, coaxing her along bit by bit. *"Good girl. May I have a hug now? Can you dare that much?"* "He was wonderful."

"Zeb didn't try to help too?" Vicki teased. "I've seen the way he looks at you."

"Zeb? And Shay?" Heather's eyes widened. "You said you stayed at the lodge, but I didn't realize you were *involved* with them."

Bree nodded.

"I've mated with those males, but only in a full moon heat. I'm not sure I'd dare otherwise." Heather grinned. "By the Mother, you're braver than you look."

Jealousy punched into Bree's chest, and she choked on her beer. Her coughing covered the anger and unhappiness in her voice. "You. And them?" Heather was so striking, so smart, and they'd made love to her? *My Shay and my Zeb?*

"Stop." Vicki closed her hand over Bree's. "You're allowed to be jealous, anywhere except at a Gather. Didn't you notice how the heat affected you?"

Bree bit her lip, seeing Heather's dismay. The woman hadn't meant to hurt her. In fact, she had said she'd mated with the men only during that heat stuff. Zeb and Shay had lived in Rainer territory for a couple of years. They'd undoubtedly had been with a lot—dismay tangled her thoughts—jeez, the guys had moved so often they'd probably bedded every Daonain woman in the western states.

She glanced around the room. How many here had known Zeb and Shay in the biblical sense? Darn them. Unsure if she was more furious at the women or the men, she offered Heather a wry smile. "Sorry. It's a human thing."

Heather shrugged. "Possessiveness is a Daonain trait too, but it's hammered into us that a Gathering is sacred time, so jealousy can't be allowed." She held her hand out. "If it helps any, there was nothing between me and either of those males except a full moon heat."

Bree squeezed the redhead's fingers. "It helps. Thanks." She picked up her mug, but it was empty. So were the others'. "My turn to get the beer."

As she walked across the room, she felt as if her world had tilted, and not because of the alcohol. *I have two lovers who want to share me, and the other two women think that's normal.*

Calum spotted her and held up three fingers in question. She nodded, knowing she'd get the brands that each woman was drinking. The man had a memory like a steel trap. She winced. Perhaps traps weren't the best comparison to use with animal shifters.

A stool emptied, and Bree slid onto the seat. Leaning back against the bartop, she looked around. Full place tonight. The single guys clustered around the bar with a sprinkling of younger women. Older women and mixed groups preferred the tables. Pack members were scattered here and there. Their outing must be over.

A woman's voice, loud and harsh, made Bree's insides curl up into a tight ball. *Thyra*. She glanced over her shoulder to see the alpha bitch and her sidekick, Candice, with a devastatingly gorgeous blonde at a nearby table.

Thyra's sharp voice cut through the chatter. "No, Gerhard is still our alpha. Shay acts as if he wants to take over, but he doesn't have the guts."

Bree stiffened, and her hand fisted.

"He was the same in Rainier." The blonde's laugh was a high tinkle, like the shattering of wine glasses. "Have you had problems with Zeb yet?" Her voice grew louder, as if she wanted to attract attention.

"That cahir." Candice shivered. "He's so nasty looking with all those scars, and he's always starting fights."

"Oh, he does worse than that," the blonde said, even more loudly. People turned to look. "With the females—oh, I shouldn't say."

Thyra leaned forward. "Tell us."

"He's vicious during matings and has even left some females bleeding. Hurt. Crying."

Angry muttering came from the people nearby. Gretchen continued, "He brutalizes every female he mates."

Anger ran through Bree fast and hard. Her hand slapped the bar, and she glared at the woman. "I don't know who you are, but you're a liar."

The blonde gasped. "I am not. I've mated with Zeb and—"

"So have I." Bree tossed her hair back and grinned evilly. "Frequently. And with any luck, I will continue. The man is superb in bed."

"Well, maybe you don't—"

"Poor Gretchen." Angie shouldered her way over to stand beside Bree. "Are you still bad-mouthing any male who doesn't trail after you, sniffing your butt?" Angie curled an arm around Bree's waist. "Having enjoyed Zeb's attentions at a Gather, I'd have to say Bree's entirely correct. The male can win my favor any full moon."

At their table, Heather stood and lifted her hand as if called upon in school. "I agree. He mates as magnificently as he fights."

The blonde's mouth opened and closed.

Bree smothered a smirk. She'd been in enough crowds to know when the tide had turned. She snagged her beer that a tight-faced Calum had set on the bar. "So there you go. That cahir risks his life every month to save ours—and he's darn good in bed." She lifted her beer. "Here's to Zeb!"

All over the bar, glasses were raised, and the roar came back to her, "To Zeb!"

A second later, she realized all attention had focused behind her. She turned and, oh jeez, Zeb stood beside Shay. She'd never seen that unsettled expression on his face before.

Grinning, Shay slapped his shoulder and shoved him toward her.

"A hellhound attack would be easier to take," Zeb rasped as he approached. He nodded at Angie, and she winked at him before heading back to her table. He turned to Bree and studied her with unreadable eyes. "I thought we were fighting."

Bree rose on tiptoe to whisper in his ear, "I hate her more than you."

"Well, then." Tangling his fingers in her hair, he tipped her head back and set his mouth on hers in a demanding, possessive kiss. With an iron-hard arm around her back, he yanked her against him, and continued—taking it deeper. Wetter. By the time he finished, heat ran like boiling oil through her veins, and the entire bar was whooping and cheering.

He nipped her earlobe, adding a sizzle of pain, and whispered, "You may enjoy my attention any time your heart desires. My door will be open."

After setting her on the bar stool, he jerked his head at Shay and headed for the exit, suffering the hands that slapped his back and the lifted toasts.

Chapter Twenty-Eight

Cold Creek, North Cascades Territory ~ Full moon

TO A CHORUS of greetings, Bree entered Heather's room in the Victorian bed and breakfast. Angie was painting her toenails, and Heather was at the mirrored, antique dresser, curling her hair.

Vicki popped out of the bathroom, dressed in skin-tight jeans, a low-cut knit shirt, and makeup that made her dark eyes look huge. "Hey, Bree."

"Wow—look at you. I thought lifemated people didn't attend Gatherings?"

"We don't." Vicki tossed her long hair back over her shoulder. "But my guys take turns supervising the tavern, and I want to make sure they don't think they're missing anything. Too many gorgeous women come to the Gatherings here."

"I've never seen Alec or Calum give anyone a second look," Bree said.

Heather shook her head. "I keep telling Vicki that lifemating is more than a bracelet and a vow. It's called *life*mating because it goes to the center of you."

"Oh, yeah." Vicki set her hand over her chest. "It's got the pull of a magnet, only it feels like a glowing light." Then she grinned and pulled her shirt down to expose more cleavage. "But

I've seen a damned lot of married men screwing other women in humanland."

"I'd feel the same way." And it would be hard seeing Zeb or Shay with someone else. Her mouth turned down.

"Whatcha got in the backpack, girl?" Angie asked.

"I brought clothes." Bree dropped her backpack on the floor. "I remember women dressed sexy at the Gathering, but it's kind of a blur." And face it, her attention had been on the men. "Can you help me figure out an outfit?"

"No problem," Angie said. "Show us what you brought, and I hope it's better than the uninspiring clothes you're wearing."

So maybe business casual clothes weren't that glamorous. Bree glanced at the dressy—loose—slacks she'd packed. Guess those wouldn't work. She pulled out a pair of jeans, ones with the higher waistband since the low-cut styles pushed up her flesh until she had handles on each side.

"They might be tight enough," Heather decided. "Let's see."

After tugging them on, Bree dug in the backpack and held up her selection of tops. A long-sleeved white shirt was booed down. A cowl-neck sweater was pronounced the right color, but Angie said the tavern got overheated, so it went back in the bag. Her last choice—a green silky top—was rejected for the high neck.

"You don't own sexy clothing?" Heather asked in disbelief. "You're worse than Vic was."

"I have pretty clothes. Just not let's-get-it-on clothes. I never wanted to attract anyone before." *Not sure I do now, if they're not Zeb or Shay.* The sinking in her stomach was dread, not arousal. What if Zeb and Shay didn't choose her even once? There'd be lots of other women…and they'd already mated with her. She bit her lip, feeling like an unwanted mongrel.

Heather studied her. "Hmm. I have a peasant top. It's sexy enough on me, but on you—with your breasts?"

"Men's tongues will drag the floor." Vicki snickered.

"Lose the bra." Heather handed over a rich blue floral top.

"But—"

"Your girls don't sag," Angie said. "Be practical. Taking a bra off when you're ready to mate is a pain in the tail."

The nods were unanimous. She dropped her bra on the floor and donned the royal blue top. It had an elastic neckline and didn't seem all that sexy until Angie pulled the gathered sleeves down, baring her shoulders.

Hoots and clapping made it sound like there were a hundred women in the room.

Bree checked the mirror. "Oh my heavens." The neckline showed a...lot...of cleavage, and the clingy thin fabric didn't hide her braless state. Every time she moved, things wobbled.

"Donal might have to deal with some heart attacks," Angie muttered.

"Perfect," Heather pronounced. "Now, let's see what we can do about your totally inadequate make-up job."

Bree turned wide eyes on her.

Vicki snickered. "She's a lot like my first drill sergeant."

"Are you an alpha female in your pack?"

"The Mother forbid." Heather grimaced. "I'm too busy for more responsibilities. Besides, the alpha male makes me want to puke."

Bree frowned. An alpha female had responsibilities? Thyra never seemed to do anything. And why did alphas have to like each other? Thyra and Gerhard didn't live together. More questions to ask the guys or Angie. *I need to make a list.*

"I'm going to add a line to my resume," Heather said airily, pushing Bree down in front of the mirror. "Humans taken by the scruff and oriented to shifterland. Catchy, eh?"

SHAY SAT AT the bar. The conversations in the tavern had the added intensity of aroused shifters: lowered masculine voices, breathy feminine ones. Various scents drifted past, an older female, a young one, then an aggressive, familiar scent. *Thyra.*

Despite the three males competing for her attention, she gave him a long speculative look.

Not interested, alpha bitch. His cock didn't even twitch. Deliberately rude, he resumed scanning the crowd. He'd pick a female and go upstairs eventually, because it was required, but he wanted—needed—to make sure that Breanne would be all right.

Although seeing her with another male might kill him. The jealousy pissed him off good. Shifters didn't get possessive, not on Gathering night. Why did it feel as if someone had changed the rules on him?

Beside Shay, Zeb wasn't in a happy mood either. His top lip drew up in a silent snarl. "I feel more like fighting than fucking, but if we disrupt a Gathering, Calum might claw our balls off."

Nasty thought. He'd seen the Cosantir in cougar form, and he wanted those lethal long claws nowhere near his pride 'n' joys. "No fighting," he agreed.

"Want to go pretend to patrol?" Zeb asked.

"Yes." Hell, he wasn't even hard. "But let's make sure she'll manage first."

Zeb nodded to the entrance. "She's here."

Breanne stood in the doorway with her back to the room, speaking to someone outside. Her long waterfall of blonde hair reached almost to the jeans that curved under her lush ass. She turned.

May the Mother save me. Her eyes were bigger somehow, her mouth shiny and red. And all he could think was how those glossy lips would look around his cock. He inhaled slowly, since the air in the bar had turned to steam. Her blouse exposed her shoulders, smooth and pale, and her breasts... Shay's cock not only stood up but tried to bust out of his jeans.

Zeb straightened. "Males are looking at her." His tone held the growl of imminent attack.

Shay slapped a restraining hand against his brother's chest. "She's not ours. It's Gathering Night." He heaved in a strangling breath of air. "She'll mate with other males."

"*Not. If. They're. Dead.*" Zeb stared at her and stood. When Shay snapped, "No," Zeb gave a shake, as if flinging water from his fur. Jaw tight, he leaned back against the bar.

"We stay long enough for her to pick someone," Shay gritted out. "We make sure she returns safely. Then we leave until later. Until she's had a chance to be with others."

ENTERING THE TAVERN was like stepping into a sauna—one filled with overwhelming scents and sounds. After stalling at the door, Bree managed to edge farther into the room.

As Heather followed, Bree saw her face flush.

Bree's probably looked the same, since her nerves felt as if they'd had been abraded into a hot sensitivity. On the walk over, her breasts had wobbled with every step. Now they swelled until she felt as if she still wore a bra—one a size too small.

A flash of panic hit, and she froze. A breath, another, and she managed to relax. True, her hormonal faucet was cranked wide open, but, after being with Zeb and Shay, she could deal with the sensations of arousal.

And I've had sex. I'll be fine.

She took in a slow breath and checked the place out. Although Vicki had left to join Alec in their home above the tavern, Heather and Angie stood nearby.

Bree smiled. It was good to have friends. But they needed to be off and doing—mating. "I can handle this. Go play." She gave them a firm nod.

The two women grinned, headed into the room, and parted to each establish a small territory of her own. Men followed in their wake, and Bree laughed to see Owen trail after Heather as if pulled on a leash. *Go, Heather.*

"You're a pretty female." A mild voice.

Bree glanced up to see a slim man. Her interest-o-meter didn't even bleep, so she smiled politely at him and shook her head no.

He looked disappointed but slid back into the crowd.

Hey, it worked. Her momentary delight disappeared under another swell of heat. *Criminy, I need a beer.* She worked her way toward the bar. Her body felt hot, needy. The scents of the men around her were heady at first, then smelled wrong. Warring sensations whiplashed through her.

A man touched her arm, and the graze of his callused palm melted her insides, but when he said something, her mind cleared. Her body cooled. He withdrew.

"Breanne." Calum stood at the end of the bar—apparently there wasn't much call for his bartending skills tonight. His gaze took her in, and a glint of worry appeared in his eyes. "Can I get you something?"

"I really, really want a beer."

He gave her a faint smile. "I can do that."

Another man appeared—bear-sized Ben. He grinned at her. "Want to go upstairs with me?"

She giggled. "Aren't you supposed to...oh, be polite and flirt or something?"

"Some do. Some don't." He pushed her hair away from her face. His hand was as big as Zeb's. "I'm no wolf to want to play first."

She liked him. Could she go to bed with him? He was nice. "Well—"

A thump on the bartop announced the arrival of her beer.

"Breanne," Calum said. "If you don't have an overwhelming need to go upstairs, then you politely refuse." His smile flickered. "When the right one appears, you won't be able to say no."

"Oh." She bit her lip and glanced up at Ben. "I guess I can say no."

"Guess you can." His smile was charming. "And it's sorry I am, although it'll probably keep me from having my throat torn out."

"Huh?"

He nodded toward the other end of the bar where—

Furious black eyes trapped her gaze.

Everything inside her flared up so hot that her legs gave out. With a barking laugh, Ben grabbed her arms and halted her fall.

A low snarl sounded. *Zeb*. Her heart rate increased at the deadly—erotic—sound.

Ben released her, pushing her toward Zeb. "Have fun, sweetie."

Fun wasn't what she needed as the air throbbed with the heat pouring off her body. With every step, the peasant shirt brushed over her loose breasts. Her nipples hardened into peaks that ached for a touch…a callused hand. Hands.

She approached him, vaguely noting how people moved out of her way. He sat on a barstool, one elbow on the bar as he watched her with burning eyes that reached into her core and pulled.

He inhaled, and a shudder ran through him. "Little female, I'm trying not to grab you."

His voice rasped over her, setting every nerve tingling with need. "Grab me." She pushed his knees apart and stepped between them. When his legs closed, trapping her with his thighs, she shivered with pleasure.

"Breanne, this isn't wise." Shay's voice surrounded her, submerging her in velvet. His scent caressed her with the fragrance of the wind off the glaciers and a hint of the hard peppermint candy he liked so much. She clenched his shirt, and the flannel teased her fingers with softness. She pulled him down to lick across his lips. So firm with the tiny taste of mint.

He growled. His hand fisted in her hair, tugging her head back as he took her lips and possessed her mouth.

Zeb's legs tightened, holding her up. He rumbled a strained laugh as she moaned.

"She's going to fuck both of them right here?"

The voice made anger flare inside her, and she stared at the gorgeous blonde, Gretchen.

The blonde motioned to Shay. "Take him upstairs and mate up there like you're supposed to." Her gaze turned to Zeb—thick with lust.

"I will." Bree's lip lifted in a snarl. She didn't release her hold on Shay's shirt but wrapped her other hand around Zeb's wrist. Her fingers traced the thick cords, the tiny scars. So hard and... *Upstairs.* "I'll take them both."

"Breanne." Shay went silent as she pulled him forward. She switched her hold to his wrist as well and towed her men after her. *Mine.*

At the top of the stairs, she stopped. How did a person choose a room? Were there rules?

With a snort of amusement, Zeb stepped forward and pushed open a half-ajar door.

Good. Not releasing their wrists, she led them into the room. A tiny fireplace held a snapping fire. A sea of silky green cushions covered the floor. She had a flash of fear, a memory of being hurt, and then arms enfolded her.

Shay's deep voice whispered, "We're here, a leannan, no one else." He pulled her against him, her back to his chest, and his erection was hard and all for her. She rubbed her backside against him, and he groaned.

Every nerve in her body demanded that he take her. *Now.* She turned. His chest was so, so wide, the muscles flexing as he moved. She unbuttoned his shirt, needing her hands on those muscles. He laughed and helped her.

Hands cupped her breasts. Zeb's scent. He leaned against her from behind to press his cheek against hers. His palms were warm as he weighed her breasts, molding them. His thumbs teasing her nipples caused a simultaneous tugging in her groin.

More. She pulled free and whipped her shirt over her head. After resuming her place, she put his hands over her breasts again.

A laugh rumbled in his throat. "The little female has a demanding side. I like it."

"But she shouldn't have it all her own way," Shay said. He turned her around to face Zeb, then embraced her, pinning her elbows to her sides. "Get rid of her jeans, a bhràthair."

SHE HAD A second to feel Zeb unzip her jeans before Shay kissed the curve of her neck, his mouth hot and his lips like satin. Her pants were yanked down. Shay simply lifted her up enough that Zeb could remove her shoes and jeans. Cool air bathed her over-heated flesh.

"Fuck," Zeb said in a strained voice. "Shay, her scent is… Open her for me, brawd."

What?

Shay pushed his knee between hers. Setting his boots between her bare feet, he nudged her legs widely apart.

Callused hands cupped her bottom, squeezing and making her shudder. A hot breath washed over her mound, and then Zeb licked the crease at the juncture of her hip and thigh in a slow stroke of liquid heat.

Her back arched, and she gasped at the sensation.

Laughing in her ear, Shay shifted and curved his hands over

her breasts. The graze of his palms over her nipples made her breath hitch, and somehow the heat washed straight to her core.

Zeb's tongue teased over her mound, dipping down to just above her clit. Hot and wet and wonderful. Her head spun, and she wiggled uncontrollably as the ache inside her kept growing. "I need…"

"We'll get there, a leannan," Shay said, pinching her nipples.

Electricity zapped right to her clit—she could feel blood engorging it. "Oh please."

Zeb sighed. "All right." He started to stand.

"No, Zeb. Enjoy her for a bit first," Shay ordered. "She's not going anywhere."

Zeb sat back on his heels, and his black gaze stroked her with the same heat as Shay's hands on her breasts. "She isn't, is she?" His eyes met hers, and a crease appeared in his cheek. "I've never had the heart to torture a female in heat. This might be fun. I can go as slow as I want."

"You do that," Shay agreed.

"Jeez, you can't." Bree struggled. "Take me, please, I can't—"

Merciless fingers pulled her labia apart, exposing her completely. Air tickled the wetness at her entrance. Her clit felt oversized as his lips closed around it, and her knees buckled at the rush of sensations, of pleasure and needs and…"Ahhh, ahhh."

His mouth released her, and his tongue circled her tight, hard nub. Her hips strained toward his touch, and her core ached with emptiness, demanding something to fill her.

With an arm around her waist, Shay held her up. His other hand caressed her breasts, rolling the nipples between his fingers.

She shuddered as her body tried to process the sensations. He bit the muscle of her shoulder, and Zeb's teeth grazed her clit.

"Oh please." The air thickened as she panted. Zeb's finger eased into her entrance, pushing and waking her nerves. Stretching her. She shook uncontrollably, making whimpering noises.

"Get her off, a bhràthair. I want to be inside her," Shay said, his voice raw.

"Fuck yes." Zeb thrust his fingers in, setting up a rhythm. She arched at the burst of sensation, and then his mouth closed over her swollen clit. Her breathing stopped.

As he swirled his tongue over the top, he made long pulsing sucks that dragged every nerve in her body to lodge all in one place—right there.

Her pussy tightened around his fingers. She tried to move, but Shay's arm held her immobile. Her fingernails dug into his forearm, as everything coiled tighter, tighter…

Zeb increased the speed, sucking, thrusting, driving her higher, until nothing could stop her. Pressure built to an excruciating edge—and shattered. Her back arched as pleasure tore through her body in vibrating shudders.

Even as she gasped for breath, Shay pinched her nipples roughly. Oh God! Her vagina clenched convulsively around Zeb's fingers, shooting more pounding waves of sensation through her.

Her legs gave out, and only Shay's arm around her waist kept her from falling.

"Fuck, that was fun." Zeb sat on his heels, absently sucking on his fingers. "We should have done this before."

Bree leaned against Shay, telling her legs to work. *God help me—they'd have killed me dead.*

ZEB GRINNED AS Bree tried to glare at him and failed. Her eyes were heavy-lidded, her mouth soft. Funny how a good orgasm could drain the fight right out of a female.

Her muscles quivered as he ran his fingertip up the inside of her thigh where the skin was almost as soft as the undersides of her breasts.

He saw pleasure in Shay's eyes. Sharing with a brother. Could anything feel more right?

But now what? How did two males share? A flash of pain darkened his mood. His brothers had died at thirteen, before they'd ever had a chance to mate. His throat tightened as he tried to explain to Shay. "With my littermates, I never…"

Shay kept an arm around Bree, but reached forward to squeeze his shoulder in understanding. They stayed like that a second before Shay's lips curved. "I think that means I get to give all the orders—as is only right." His smirk wiped the grief from Zeb's heart. "Strip down, a bhràthair, then you can play."

Shay nuzzled Bree's neck and teased her breasts until she was squirming and making cock-hardening squeaks. Zeb hurriedly pulled his clothes off, tossing them to one side.

"Ready? Here you go." Shay pushed the rubbery-kneed little female forward.

Zeb wrapped his arms around her, burying his face in her hair. By the God, she filled his heart.

When she wiggled closer, her soft belly rubbed his cock, driving him to the cushions. He pulled her down beside him and took her mouth. Velvet lips, warm and giving. Her fingers tangled in his hair, giving tiny tugs as she kissed him back. She was delightful in her urgency. Strong too, with distractingly firm muscles under the smooth female padding.

Finished stripping, Shay dumped his clothes beside a pile of pillows. "Ready for more?"

As Bree sat up, her gaze took in his rigid cock—then Zeb's. Her eyes widened. "Um."

Zeb brushed his knuckles over her cheek and studied her expression. Undoubtedly, her heat had receded with the orgasm, leaving her brain in charge. The little female was having second thoughts about taking two males at once. As she should. If she knew the carnal dreams he'd had about sharing her with Shay, she'd probably flee the room. But Shay would figure out how to handle all their needs. Somehow.

As if in answer, Shay pointed to the pillows in the corner beside his clothing. "Zeb, sit over there."

The cushions sank under his weight. Zeb leaned back, feeling as if he'd taken a throne.

Shay scooped Breanne up and followed, taking a moment to nibble on her breasts.

Zeb grinned. His brawd was definitely breast-happy.

"Legs apart," Shay said to him, then set Bree on her hands and knees between Zeb's thighs.

Zeb tensed. Surely, Shay didn't plan…

Without speaking, his brother moved her up and adjusted her so her chin was directly over his erection.

Rather than objecting, she smiled. Her delicate hands closed around Zeb's cock, and her breath washed over the sensitive head.

Fuck. He inhaled hard and fought for control. He'd only mated females during Gatherings, and, when in heat, a female wanted only one thing—a cock inside her. She wouldn't waste time sucking off a male.

"You're used to giving. Now, you'll be on the receiving end." Shay grinned. "You'll enjoy this…if we can keep her from biting."

Bree's color deepened, and her scent grew more compelling. The feeling of her tiny hands around him made him throb. Her golden hair spilled in a silky, cool waterfall over his groin when she looked over her shoulder. "Shay?"

"Breanne, I want you to suck Zeb's cock until he gets off. Clear?"

Her big blue eyes took in the erection in her hands. As she

licked her lips, Zeb couldn't look away from her tiny pink tongue. Her breath hitched once, and she wiggled her ass. "I'll try, but..."

But a female in heat needed a cock. "It's all right, cariad. I don't—"

"Yes, you do," Shay interrupted. He knelt behind Bree, closing his hands on her hips. "I'll give you what you need, mo leannan, and you will give Zeb what he needs."

"Okay," she whispered. She turned to Zeb and tightened her grip on his erection. After a second of study, she gave him a radiant smile and licked the base to the head, her tongue hot and wet.

Oh fuck. Zeb's breath strangled in his throat. Her hands tightened, making him throb with every heartbeat. By the God, he might not last.

As her mouth slid over his cock, he could feel the slight graze of her teeth, the way her lips closed around him. When her tongue rubbed on the underside, the diversity of sensations made his eyes cross. His fingers tangled in her hair, and he forced himself to let her do as she wanted. She sucked him down, deeper.

Shay grinned, waiting patiently. After a second of foggy thinking, Zeb realized he was giving her time to get used to sucking a cock before taking another from behind.

She was so sweet. Giving. Any other female would demand to be fucked right now, but Bree was concentrating hard, trying to please him despite her own urgency.

Had he ever met anyone like her before? The heat of his cock didn't even come close to the warmth inside his chest. Zeb ran a finger over her pink cheek. *Ours.*

Chapter Twenty-Nine

SUCKING A COCK was amazing. Bree tongued the thick winding veins on Zeb's shaft—tight, yet elastic. *What else can I do?* She tried alternating licking and taking him deep in her throat.

When his hand tightened in her hair, she had a second of panic. Her head jerked up, and, even as his grip released, she met his eyes. So black. Yet, despite the aroused flush in his face, he was watching her carefully, making sure she was all right. She smiled. Heavens, she loved doing this for him.

She paused to nuzzle the hair beside his cock. Here, his dark forest scent was muskier, richer. As she inhaled, her pussy thickened with blood, pulsing with hunger.

She tried to push her need aside, but it was sweeping her away, blurring her thoughts. Shay moved closer. His hands ran over her bottom, and his body heated the back of her thighs. As fire sizzled through her veins, she groaned.

Zeb jumped and sucked in a breath. Shay chuckled. "Do that again, a leannan. My bràthair likes it."

Really? She groaned again. Hummed. Growled. And this time when Zeb's fingers fisted in her hair, she didn't panic. She giggled.

"You're killing me, little female." Zeb's voice had gone an

octave lower, sending tingles across her skin.

Rather than answering, she started bobbing her head, sucking with each upstroke.

"Very nice," Shay said. His resonant voice filled in all the gaps that Zeb's had left, as if adding the other melody to Pachelbel's Canon. He clasped her hip with one hand, using the other to guide his cock to her entrance.

Oh please, now. She choked, lost her rhythm, and Zeb's hand guided her back into it.

"Breanne, whatever you do to Zeb, I'll do to you." Shay slowly pushed inside her, filling her, stretching her.

Her whole body shivered in delight, in growing need. *Deeper. Pound me. Take me.*

"If you want slow, then slow down," Shay said. "You stop. I'll stop. Suck him deeper, and I'll go deeper." His cock pulled out until it was only an inch inside her. Not moving.

Nooo. She wiggled to no avail before realizing her lips were closed lightly over the head of Zeb's shaft. Not moving. Oh. As she lowered her head and sucked his cock into her mouth, Shay's erection pushed back inside her, rolling a wave of heat before it.

She lifted her mouth off the shaft in her mouth. The shaft in her pussy pulled out.

A shiver ran through her. Need more. She took a firmer grip on the base of Zeb's cock, and Shay's hands tightened on her hips. As her lips closed over the velvety head, sweat trickled between her breasts. The room seemed to have turned into a sauna. Her pussy throbbed...almost matching that of the erection in her hands.

She ventured a look at Zeb. His lids were half-closed as he watched her. Glancing over her shoulder, she saw Shay's jaw was tight, and his muscles almost vibrated with his desire to pound into her. Had she ever felt so needed? Wanted?

But he didn't move. He was waiting for her. Her lips curved.

Sneaky Shay. *We're all going to enjoy this.*

She pulled Zeb into her mouth, so fast and hard that he groaned.

Shay thrust into her so deep and hard that electricity ripped through her body.

Work it, Bree. She did, bobbing and sucking and doing her best to deep-throat. Faster and harder. Shay pounded into her, faster and harder, exactly matching her movements. Her thoughts whirled away as the need inside her grew, as she clenched around the cock inside her.

When she lifted her head, Zeb's fingers in her hair tightened, not painfully but firmly. His thighs pressed against her sides, the muscles rigid. He was close.

The base of his cock thickened, and with a desperate growl, he tugged her back onto his shaft. She relaxed her throat, taking him deeper…and he came. Startled but delighted, she swallowed frantically, and the salty, musky taste shoved her arousal to a higher pitch.

Eyes closed, he groaned in satisfaction. A glow of joy ran through her. *I put that contented expression on his face.* Smiling, she licked him gently as he softened.

Shay had paused.

"Fuck, Bree." Zeb opened his eyes. His hand cradled her face. "That was beautiful. Thank you." His surprised gratitude brought tears to her eyes. Did no one ever put this man first? He ran his thumb over her lower lip. "Your turn, little female." He glanced at Shay.

Shay's hands tightened on her hips. "Hang on, a leannan, I'm going to take you hard."

Rather than frightening her, the thought was perfect.

SHAY GRINNED AS the little wolf pushed back onto his cock, and her musky aroused scent urged him to action. Despite the heavy ache in his balls, Shay felt contentment warm his soul. Watching Zeb get Breanne off and then her do the same to him had been a joy. Memories of his brothers—their voices and scents—as they shared a mating swirled around him, then dissipated, overcome by the reality of this female.

And this male. Zeb was a worthy brother. Breanne would be a worthy mate, but would she agree? There were too many reasons for her to say no. Shay pushed the thought away. *Live in the now.*

Zeb eased sideways to a position where he could play with Breanne's breasts. When he took a nipple in his mouth, she gave a startled exhalation, and her cunt tightened on Shay like a vise.

By the God. "Good, a bhràthair," Shay said. "Keep that up."

Zeb growled his pleased agreement.

Running his hands over her back, her sides, and her lush ass, Shay savored the satiny feel of her skin. With a low whine, she wiggled, needing more. Needing to be fucked.

Grinning, he released his animal, the one that drove him to take her hard and deep, to give her his seed, and make her scream with pleasure. He pushed her legs farther apart, enjoying the sight of his cock thrusting in and out of her slick pink tissues. *Ours.*

He pistoned into her, and the slap of flesh was accompanied by her pleased grunts and the rumble of Zeb's enjoyment. The sounds of their pleasure added to his own. As Breanne's cunt tightened around him, pressure built low in his spine and every thrust built it higher. He gritted his teeth. Not yet.

Her legs quivered as her ass lifted higher in the air. Convenient. He grabbed the lube packet from the pile of clothes beside the pillows and ripped the top off with his teeth. He had a feeling the little wolf would enjoy this. Someday, he and Zeb would enjoy it more.

HEAVENS, SHE NEEDED to come, Bree thought. Come *again*. The slide of Shay's thick cock was the most exquisite of sensations. Simultaneously, Zeb sucked and pinched her nipples, creating a line of fire from her breasts to her clit. The combination was so, so good.

She was close, desperately close. Her fingers tightened on the cushions as she teetered, unable to reach the pinnacle. "I can't."

Shay gave a low laugh. "Oh, you will. Hold still, little wolf."

Liquid dripped onto her bottom and trickled between her cheeks, startlingly cold against her overheated skin. She tried to move forward, away from it but Shay wrapped his hand around her thigh.

His thrusts had slowed, and she whined.

"A bhràthair, together now. Use your fingers on her." A deep chuckle. "I'll use mine on the backside."

A pause, then Zeb rasped a laugh.

What does he mean?

Zeb's hand touched her mound. Her clit gave a giant throb.

"Oh, pleeeeease." It was just what she needed. Her clit was painfully swollen and tight.

Then Shay's finger slid between her butt cheeks to circle her slickened asshole. She jerked in surprise and tried to tighten her buttocks to keep him away.

His knees nudged hers even farther apart. And his fingertip pushed in just a fraction. Into a place that…

Zeb ran his finger over her clit, and she gasped as her insides started to gather.

"Hang on, lass. This will feel strange," Shay said. He worked his finger in, slowly, steadily, burning as he stretched her. Strange sensations tangled together in her center.

"Oooh, don't," she moaned. He slid his finger out—then back in—and the feeling was so, so different. Wrong. *Erotic.*

"Don't do that."

Even as he pulled his finger out of her backhole, his cock thrust into her pussy. Oh god. All her nerves merged, firing in odd sequences.

Zeb chuckled. "Her nipples are like tiny rocks." His tongue left a trail of fire around one.

"Does it hurt, Breanne?" Shay asked.

It did. Didn't. Not right. "No. But I don't want…"

Shay wiggled his cock side-to-side, hitting every nerve inside her as he continued sliding in and out of her asshole. "It's different, but I think you'll like it. I'm adding a finger. Can you dare that much?"

The same words he'd used the first time they'd made love. "*Why don't you kiss me? Can you dare that much?*" He'd been so careful, and with every step had led her further from her fears. This weirdness didn't really hurt. "I guess…"

"Good lass." His approval sent warmth through her. His cock plunged slowly in and out, his finger in her asshole kept the same pace. Zeb rubbed one side of her clit, then the other. Not fast or hard, just unrelenting stimulation.

Her insides gathered, pushing her toward an even higher precipice.

"Zeb, now," Shay said.

Zeb sucked roughly on one nipple, even as his finger slid directly over her clit, rubbing insistently. Shay slammed into her with his cock, hard and deep.

Her muscles went rigid as the seething tension coalesced for one interminable, incredibly overwhelming second…and then it all exploded. She shuddered as waves of pleasure blasted through her, one after another.

As the sensations slowed to ripples, she managed a breath—and then Shay shoved two fingers into her asshole. The rim stretched and burned, nerves flared, and she came again, so brutally hard that she screamed.

Her vagina clenched like a fist around his thick cock, her backhole contracted on his fingers. It was too much; she was too full—yet everything inside her kept spasming in bursts of pleasure.

When he withdrew his fingers, she gasped at the emptiness. Body shaking, she panted for air.

"I'm going to take you hard now, mo leannan." Shay gripped her hips. "Brace yourself." He pulled his cock almost out of her pussy and drove back in so deep that more aftershocks tremored through her system.

As her arms turned to rubber, Zeb pulled her head down onto his chest to support her.

Shay leaned forward, his chest hot against her back, one arm curled around her waist. The two men pinned her, holding her tightly, as Shay hammered her with short, fast strokes.

He pushed deep, deep into her, and his teeth closed on her shoulder as he came.

BY THE GOD, she was killing him. Shay's pulse roared like a firestorm in his head as he emptied himself over and over in hot jets. The feeling created a primal longing that his seed—and Zeb's—should find a home.

Reluctantly, slowly, he pulled out and dropped onto the cushions beside her.

Her forehead was against Zeb's chest, her body motionless, as if unsure whether to move. Or too exhausted to try.

"Time to relax, little female." With a smooth move, Zeb rolled her onto her back beside Shay.

They both moved closer to her, the scent of a satisfied female the finest fragrance known to shifters.

Lazily, Zeb nibbled on her fingertips; he'd never looked so content.

Shay propped up on an elbow and smiled at her. Face flushed, lips and nipples red and swollen. "You look well mated, a leannan." He cupped the breast closest to him. So heavy and full and soft. And the silken feeling of a nipple... He ran his finger around it.

She gave him a laughing look. "My friends used to talk about their boyfriends. One was a 'breast' man. That's so you."

"True." From an after-climax softness, the nipple started to pay attention to his touch. Tiny bumps gathered, and the peak lengthened.

Eyes closing, she sighed like a contented pup with a full stomach. "What happens now?"

"We'll rest for a bit." Zeb sucked on her finger. "Then I want to see if you're as good at licking Shay."

Her eyes popped open, and she stared at Zeb in disbelief. "More?"

"Fuck, yes."

Shay recognized his brother's expression and laughed inside. A male's instinct to give a female his seed was as strong as her heat. Shay ran his finger down Breanne's flushed cheek. He had to admit: when the male cared, that instinct grew until it was impossible to fight.

AN HOUR OR so later, Bree was back, sitting on a barstool in the tavern. After the guys had kissed her as if trying to brand her, Shay had pushed Zeb to the end of the bar, leaving her stranded like a mouse in a roomful of cats.

"I brought you a fresh beer." Calum set a glass down in front of her.

The beer was cold, and the light bite teased her tongue and soothed her dry mouth. Too much panting. Screaming. She frowned. And *begging*. Zeb really, really liked to tease.

She took another sip, trying to concentrate on the taste. It didn't help. In despair, she felt her body waken again. The heat rose, demanding satisfaction.

Without thinking, she turned toward where Shay and Zeb sat, their eyes on her. *My Shay. My Zeb.* But they said mating with her again tonight was against the rules of the Gather. Stupid shifters and their stupid rules.

God, they were big. Wonderful. Gorgeous. And she loved them. Both of them. So, so much. She wanted them to touch her, to take her, to—

"Breanne." Calum tapped the glass on the bartop. "Look at me."

The power in his voice broke the hold. She shook her head to clear it and frowned at him. "Calum?"

No humor showed in his face. "Breanne, you are perilously close to forming a bond with Zeb and Shay. Be certain it is what you desire."

I love them. "Don't they want me?" Lord, didn't that sound pitiful?

"That's not the problem. You need to understand that the oathbound cannot lifemate." His brows drew together. "Humans have priests? Those who live apart, promised to your God? Shifters who are vowed to Herne can live with someone, but the final step—lifemating—cannot happen."

Well, Shay sure wasn't celibate. Her smile faded as she caught Calum's point. "Since Shay is committed to Herne, he can't...marry."

"Exactly." He patted her hand. "Usually, the oathbound are older and past the time they would lifemate, or they've lost their mate. I've not run into this dilemma before. I don't want you to get hurt, Breanne."

Too late. She pulled her hand away and gave him a stiff nod. "So, I should..."

Calum tipped his head toward the shifters who had ranged around her in hopes of attracting her attention. "Choose from those who can give their hearts or, at least, divert you from wasting your life on two males you can never possess."

Her heart ached, but she saw the wisdom. Shay had said they'd leave Cold Creek. He certainly hadn't made her any promises. She involuntarily glanced at him, and everything inside her melted. Skin taut over his high cheekbones, he stared at the bartop with the same tortured expression as Zeb's. Her fingers remembered how thick and soft his hair felt. *His jaw will be scratchy now and...* She slid off the stool.

Calum leaned forward and grasped her upper arm. "Breanne."

"Oh. Right."

"I'm ordering them out to patrol. Find a male here who pleases you."

They'd leave her? Desolation swept through her, removing every trace of heat. Nonetheless, she turned and looked at the men around her. Tall and short. Dark and pale. Older, younger, and just her age. She forced her lips into a smile.

Even without looking, she knew when Zeb and Shay left the bar.

THE MOON SLOWLY crossed the sky toward the western mountains. Zeb's feet hurt—he didn't usually patrol in human form for an entire night—but neither he nor Shay were willing to risk what their animal instincts would do.

Now it was time to check in with the Cosantir and take Bree home.

She'd have mated with other males. He'd smell someone else's scent on her. Zeb's jaw tightened, and his teeth ground together as he fought for control.

But she'd finished her first Gathering, leaving her free to make her choices. Even if they couldn't lifemate with her, they could ask her to come with them when they left.

And their time here wouldn't be much longer. He'd been feeling a deep inner pull, tugging him east. The God's call.

Would Bree want to stay with them? Fuck, they had so little to offer her.

With Shay behind him, he walked into the tavern. In the swirling scents, he caught Bree's unique fragrance...and the lack of any arousal. Shay's frown mirrored his as they walked to the bar.

The Cosantir was talking to the old bookstore owner. He motioned them over. "Cahirs."

Zeb concentrated on Calum, not looking elsewhere. Fuck, his control had never been this shaky. If he saw a male touch Bree, he might easily destroy the tavern.

"You been stuck down here all night?" Shay asked Calum.

"No, Alec monitored the Gathering for a while. I came down to speak with you before Thorson takes over."

Zeb nodded to the bookstore owner. The werecat was old, but Zeb'd think twice before taking him on. Good choice to supervise the Gathering, and Calum would have a chance to join his brother and their mate. "Speak to us about what?" Zeb asked.

Calum mouth flattened to an unhappy line. "Breanne has refused every single male in the room. She's not afraid. She simply has no interest."

Zeb felt as if the Cosantir had stopped his heart. "Only bonded females act that way."

"Indeed."

Zeb met Shay's gaze, seeing his concern. Even if she'd bonded to them, they couldn't complete it. Couldn't lifemate with her. "What will this do to her?"

"With sufficient distance, her tie to you will eventually fade. Otherwise…" Calum frowned. "I'm not sure."

"By the God," Shay said in a hoarse voice. "What have we done?"

"You're not to blame for this," Calum said. "Perhaps if I'd pulled her away from you when we learned she was a shifter, it might have been prevented. Then again, she might have died with her first trawsfur, having no one in whom she could trust."

Shay's voice was tight. "We should never have mated with her."

"Maybe." Thorson's voice was as scarred as his arms and face. "But if you hadn't, she'd be in here, deep in heat and panicking. She'd have no ties to anyone to keep her from going feral."

Fuck. Zeb went rigid. Daonain with no loved ones to draw them back to human form could slide into madness, living only in their animal form, unable to return. Twisted inside, preying on their own community. Ferals had spawned most of the grisly legends that terrified the humans.

Thorson nodded. "You do the best you can. Only Herne knows all the trails in the forest."

"What should we do?" Shay asked Calum. "We'd planned to ask her to stay with us, but I can't lifemate her."

"Seamus, she's attached already. It's not a true bond—not without the Mother's blessing—but you can't change it."

Zeb bowed his head, anger and grief roiling inside him. He'd have stayed miles away from her if he'd known. Yet, as Thorson said, perhaps that would have been a worse choice. She was alive.

He and Shay wanted her with them. Even if they couldn't lifemate her, she'd have all their love, their caring. Would it be enough?

THE FIRE IN the bedroom woodstove crackled happily, sending welcome warmth through the room. Bree snuggled closer in Zeb's arms. Shay pressed against her back, his arm heavy over her hips. Her breasts were sore and tender, her pussy even more so, and that other spot, her anus ached. She felt her face heat. That had been amazing.

Gatherings aren't that bad after all.

After Shay and Zeb had brought her home, they'd made love to her again, this time so tenderly that she'd cried. How could she ever survive their leaving? She pushed the thought away. Live for today.

"Breanne," Shay said. "Let's talk a bit." Lying on his side, Shay raised up on his elbow. On her right, Zeb slid back and mirrored his position.

Talk? That usually meant a nasty revelation or an odd shifter law. She rolled onto her back and looked at him. When no laughter lit his eyes, dread ran a cold hand up her spine. "Wait."

She grabbed the pillow on Zeb's side of the bed, stacked it on hers, and squirmed until she was propped up with her head even with theirs. "Okay, tell me."

"I don't know how to say this." The lines beside Shay's mouth tightened. "You know I'm oathbound. Did you realize I can't lifemate?"

It hurt. Hurt when she thought about it; hurt worse when he said it. "Calum told me." To keep him from abrading her heart further, she did it herself. "I realize you'll leave when Herne calls you." *I don't like your arrogant God. Have I mentioned that?* She thought she was holding up well, until she saw Zeb's gaze on her clenched fingers.

"I can't see the trail we should follow, but Zeb and I decided you have a right to know everything. To decide for yourself." Shay uncurled her fingers and wrapped his hand around hers.

"We lo—" He stopped and started again. "We care for you. Both of us."

The words made the blood dance in her veins like water down a rocky streambed. "Really?"

Zeb took her other hand. "Fuck, yes."

A spurt of laughter caught her. "So poetic."

"We want you to stay with us. Live with us," Zeb said.

Stay with them. Her heart lifted, soared into the sky—*yes yes yes*—and then fell like a rock. "But...but you won't stay here." She swallowed hard. "You want me to go with you?" *Leave Cold Creek?* "And move every few months. You don't have a *home*."

She'd gone from foster home to foster home, school to school, never keeping friends, never knowing people with whom she had a history. To stay with the guys, she'd have to abandon her brand new friends and her budding business. Her throat tightened.

And if she did make friends elsewhere... "You go where the hellhounds are. Where shifters get killed." Even if she found other friends, they might get slaughtered. Like Nora. Like Ashley.

"Aye." Shay's eyes were level. He knew what he was asking.

"You'd fight monsters." Month after month, she'd be terrified, waiting to hear if they'd been killed. If they'd been torn apart like Ashley.

"Yes." Zeb's eyes filled with pain. "Little female, we want you"—his mouth tightened as if he were trying not to say more—"but it's not a happy way of life, especially for a female."

"And yet..." Shay kissed her fingers. "You care for us."

"I do," she whispered. Her heart felt swollen with pain. "But I don't know if I can do this." Ash had called her a homebody. Each move—during childhood and after—had ripped away pieces of her soul and left them behind. Could she survive that again?

Don't ask this of me.

But how could she let them leave when she might be with them? Tears pooled in her eyes as she scrambled off the foot of the bed. Her chest felt as if a giant oak had fallen on her, crushing her ribs, bruising her heart.

"I don't—" Her voice cracked, and she fled the room like the coward she was.

Chapter Thirty

ZEB LEANED BACK against a tree, watching silvery undines swirl in the shallows. The mountain lake was turning an ominous gray as dark clouds filled the sky. A freshening wind whipped the tiny waves into white tips.

In wolf form, Shay lay on his belly, staring at the water. His thoughts looked to be as ugly as Zeb's.

Neither of them had wanted to talk about the wretched end to the night. He swallowed. Why the fuck had he let himself hope?

And what had they been thinking? Fuck, she'd just lost her best friend to a hellhound, and they wanted her to undoubtedly see them suffer the same fate. He and Shay were the stupidest shifters ever birthed.

This morning, after Bree had retreated to the kitchen, cooking as if the world was about to end, Zeb had dragged Shay up to the lake. Somehow, they had to fix this for the little female. A few minutes ago, he'd come up with an idea.

He nudged the wolf lightly with his foot.

Shay snapped at him.

"Trawsfur, brawd. Time to talk."

The wolf's lip curled up as the wind ruffled his fur, but he shifted to human. Sitting up, he shivered and glanced up at the clouds. "We're going to get wet."

"Life's tough. We need to talk about Bree."

"I know." Shay's face tightened. "By the God, there's nothing I want more than for her to be with us. But we shouldn't have asked."

Zeb nodded. He'd never seen her more miserable.

"You haven't taken a vow, a bhràthair. You could stay—brothers don't always live together. You deserve someone to love as much as she does."

The blow was brutal. Shay didn't want to remain brothers? Then Zeb saw the desolation in his eyes—stupid, self-sacrificing mongrel. "There's so fucking much wrong with your idea that I don't know where to start."

"Like what?"

Zeb held up a finger. "She loves us both, not just me." Second finger. "We're brothers. Only death breaks that bond." Third finger. He hadn't planned to mention this, hoping Shay wouldn't notice. "I can't lifemate her any more than you can."

"Number three—I'm missing something."

"Apparently." Zeb fingered the cahir scar on his right cheekbone and the new one below. Since his dark tan rendered the mark almost invisible, he turned his head and let the thin sunlight illuminate it.

"What the…!" Shay grabbed his chin and ran his fingers over the faintly blue antlers of the oathbound.

"No matter who makes the oath, brothers share," Zeb said. The appalled guilt in Shay's face was exactly why he hadn't mentioned the scar before.

"Zeb." Shay dropped onto the grass. "By the God, Zeb, I'm sorry. I didn't—"

"I didn't foresee it, but I wouldn't have stepped away if I'd known."

Shay was silent for a minute. "I've screwed up everybody.

I'd ask to be released from the oath if I thought it would do any good."

"Never heard of Herne releasing anyone."

"Me either."

"I'm feeling a pull. Like something trying to drag me some-where." Zeb gave Shay a steady look. "Is that the call?"

"Aye. Me, too." He studied his hands. "It'll get stronger."

Sorrow was a lead weight in Zeb's gut as he cleared his throat. "I've heard the Mother can erase a bond if she hasn't blessed the lifemating yet."

It took Shay a minute. "You want us to ask the Mother to remove the bond Breanne formed for us."

"Fuck no, but I can't think of anything else to do. Bree can't survive going from town to town, waiting for us to die. That's not right, brawd. She deserves better. Lifemating. Children."

"By the God, it hurts to think of her with someone else."

"Yeah." More than pain. Zeb felt as if his soul was slowly being torn into pieces.

A FORMAL CALLING upon the Gods, requesting attention and action, wasn't something a Daonain did lightly. The Cosantir had an open line to Herne; everyone else had to work to be heard. The Elders said the soul's desire must be great enough to overcome the needs of the body: hunger, thirst, exhaustion. The trappings of civilization had to be worn away.

And so they ran.

Hour upon hour. No food, no water, no shelter. Open to the elements. Slowly as Shay's weariness grew, his mind quieted. The spirits guided his paws. His fur was matted by the pouring rain, his ears deafened by the thunder rumbling through the passes.

Zeb kept pace, a dark shadow on his right.

Just before dawn, the clouds started to part, showing the full-bodied moon. He halted on a rain-dark ridge of rock, an island in the glaciers creeping down from the peaks. Moonlight glimmered over the white expanse. Forest covered the valley below, and the scents of pine and cedar, wet granite, and distant deer drifted upward. Zeb's shoulder pressed against his in a small patch of warmth.

Through his paws, he felt the sweet touch of Mother Earth and a low hum like the thunder that had passed, marking the presence of Herne.

He formed his desire slowly. The thought of losing Breanne and Zeb made cuts in his heart and soul, but he steadily held his wishes up to the God and the Mother both.

Not Zeb's wish—that the little wolf be set free to seek love elsewhere. She wouldn't be happy. She'd be alone, and he couldn't stand thinking of her alone. Or of seeing the grief in Zeb's eyes when they left her. Of forcing Zeb into a life he hadn't asked for.

No, Shay had made the vow. He should be the only one to have to walk the trail to the end.

Please. Remove the brother bond—and the oathbound one—from Zeb. Let him be free to lifemate Breanne. Let her love him alone so neither will grieve when I follow the path of the God that is mine alone.

Zeb's wishes would contradict Shay's. Neither request might be granted.

Herne's presence increased, overwhelming the Mother's soft touch, and the sense of her faded away completely. The thunder rolled through Shay's heart, then disappeared. He'd been refused.

Despair filled him, and his mournful howl echoed back from the cliffs.

With a low whine, Zeb nudged his shoulder.

No point in remaining. Shay led the way back down the

mountain. Each mile seemed longer than the last, and they had hours yet to go.

Dawn broke over the white peaks. Exhausted to his bones, Shay stumbled to a halt by a gurgling creek. The icy water soothed his raw throat.

Finished drinking, Zeb shifted and rose to his feet. "Sorry, brawd. Guess asking the Mother for help was a fucked-up notion."

The pain in his voice pulled Shay from his dark thoughts. He looked up. The light of the morning sun shone on Zeb's strained face.

Shay backed away and shook, as if the action could get his mind—or his eyes—to work. A trick of the light? He traws-furred. "Zeb."

"What?"

It had worked. The Gods had answered his request. Zeb was free. Misery squeezed his heart, and his throat tightened until his voice came out hoarse. "Your mark—the antlers are gone."

Expression blank with shock, Zeb touched his own cheek. "Herne's mark?"

Shay could feel the hollow place where their bond had been.

"Why the fuck…?" Zeb's face darkened. "You asked for that. That our brother bond be dissolved. That you be left alone."

"Aye. Breanne needs you," Shay whispered. "I'm sorry, a bra—

"*Fuck* you."

The fist cracked into his face, knocking him on his ass. He wiggled his jaw—the throbbing pain couldn't compete with the one inside. "Dammit, I—"

"Fucking shut up."

Shay braced himself for another punch.

As Zeb glared down, the fury in his black eyes drained away.

And then he laughed. "Feel your cheek, *brawd.*"

Shay touched his face with chilled fingers. He traced the slightly raised cahir scar and beneath it...nothing. "Herne's mark is gone."

The bond that he'd lost wasn't the brother one—that tie remained, a golden rope between him and Zeb. Instead, there was a lightness where the weight of the God of the Hunt had rested within him. Shay studied his oversized hands. "He left me a cahir."

Zeb's grin was a white flash in his dark face. "Guess he'll let us fight for him. But we can form another bond. A lifemate."

"I—" Shay's throat closed. The future spread out in front of him, almost appallingly open, as if he'd veered from a narrow mountain valley onto a plain. He could see from horizon to horizon; his feet could take him anywhere he wanted.

"Well, now we know why the Mother refused. They had other ideas. Wonder if they fought about it." Zeb's eyes glinted with amusement.

Shay sank to his knees, despite the freezing ground. "I need a minute." How many years had his vow dictated his life? How could he get his mind around this?

Zeb squeezed his shoulder. "Shift back, brawd, before you freeze. While you think, I'll hunt us some breakfast." He shifted and sniffed the air, before loping into the forest.

Shay stared after him. Eventually, growing aware of the chill under his bare knees, he trawsfurred to wolf. As the clouds drifted across the pale blue sky, he watched the increasing glow of the sun in the east.

Chapter Thirty-One

SINCE THEY'D FOUND no prey on the last run, Gerhard had called for an extra pack hunt. Unable to think of a good excuse, Bree had gone this time. For a while, she'd run beside Jody and Bonnie, then joined Angie. Although Thyra had bit her once for being "*too clumsy*", she hadn't had a bad evening, aside from missing Zeb and Shay like someone had removed a body part…maybe her heart.

Bree slowed, letting the wolves run past her.

Yesterday morning, she'd been relieved they'd left her alone to think and stew. And cry. Yeah, she'd done quite a bit of that. She'd written out reasons why she should or shouldn't join them. The answer had been an overwhelming no. All her life, she'd looked for a home, and here in Cold Creek, she'd found her place.

Like a flowing stream, the pack ran across a meadow, and moonlight dappled their fur as if glinting off water. But there was no huge silver-gray wolf with a dark deadly brother beside him. As despair stabbed into Bree, her legs tangled, and suddenly she was on hands and knees in human form. Tears pooled in her eyes as she pushed to her feet, shivering in the cold wind.

Zeb and Shay hadn't returned last night. Hadn't returned today. What if they'd been hurt in that terrible storm last night?

Caught in a flood? Guilt was a knife slash to her belly as she remembered how miserable they'd looked yesterday morning. As if they already knew her answer. She'd made them so unhappy.

Like I'm a happy camper? She stared up at the moon, and the glow seemed to illuminate her heart. Honestly, even if she gave up Cold Creek and her friends, could she be unhappier than she was now? All the self-preservation in the world didn't help when everything inside her wanted to be with her men.

But they'd probably die—horribly. Her throat tightened. Every month, she'd risk them, knowing she'd end up mourning them, as she mourned Ashley now.

But... The wind whipped through her hair as she gave a rueful laugh. *Would I really want to give up a moment of the time I had with Ash?* Even if she'd known how Ash would die, would she have backed away?

No. Everyone died. Her men might suffer an ugly death sooner than others, but they were doing something important. Saving lives.

But this is my home. Here. But was it? If Angie and Vicki and Calum and her other friends weren't here, would Cold Creek feel like home? No. When Shay and Zeb left, would she really have a home here? Was this what Ashley had tried to make her see? *Home isn't a place; it's people.*

And she darn well knew who her people were. She scrubbed her hands over her face, wiping away her tears. Guess she'd be dragging her suitcase back out of her closet. And she'd need to tell Calum to hold off on arranging for people to pack up her apartment. No need to move everything twice.

Leaving Cold Creek wouldn't be easy. She swallowed hard, thinking of her friends. Her arrangement with the diner. She'd be homesick. *Must remember to stock up on chocolate chips.* But this time when she moved, she'd take her home—her family—with her. Now if they'd only get their butts back so she could tell them.

Smiling, Bree trawsfurred back to wolf. The moon lit the entire sky as she loped across the mountain meadow. The soft new grass released a fragrance that made her paws dance, and she spun in a circle, chasing her tail. Then with a yip, she caught up to the pack.

AN HOUR OUT from Cold Creek, Shay raised his weary head and sniffed. Wolves. Smelled like the entire pack. Zeb's upright ears showed he'd caught the scent as well.

Would Breanne be with them? Probably. She'd missed the run the other night. A surge of sheer need washed through him. By the God, he needed to see her. To hold her and tell her what had happened.

As he and Zeb emerged from the trees into a long mountain meadow, yelling drowned out any other sounds. The scents were ugly. Aggression and fear. By the God, now what? He was too tired for games; all he wanted to do was hold Breanne.

As they reached the pack, he saw Gerhard yelling at a young male. Nothing new.

Jody spotted them and walked over. "Hey. Bree just said you're all leaving soon. Do you know who'll take over the lodge? Can you give our cleaning service a recommendation?"

Breanne said what? Shay shifted, Zeb a second behind, so they rose and stood, shoulder-to-shoulder.

"We're *all* leaving?" Zeb repeated in a raw voice. "Bree, too?"

"That's what she said." Jody's mouth pulled down. "I'm going to miss her—and those fattening cherry pies."

Exhilaration bubbled through Shay's veins. Over everything else, she'd chosen them. "Well." His voice wasn't steady.

Zeb's gaze met Shay's. "Well." His voice wasn't all that

even, either.

"No!" Breanne's voice—the furious one she'd used when Zeb had used her fancy fillet knife to whittle wood. Shay grinned and looked to see who'd earned her wrath.

His smile died. *Gerhard.* The alpha had changed to wolf and was stalking the younger male. He struck and the pup yelped. Growling, Dieter circled, ready to join in.

Breanne marched closer to the alpha. "Stop it. He's just a kid!" Dieter blocked her path. Dammit, didn't she ever learn? Yet Shay's heart quickened at her courage.

Two other females followed her, then some males. A murmur swept around the meadow like a whisper of wind. More shifters stepped forward.

Gerhard didn't notice, too intent on savaging the cub.

Notice this, *alpha-hole.* Shay bellowed, "What's going on here?"

People jumped, and the fight broke apart.

As Gerhard trawsfurred, Breanne and Angie ran past him to care for the young wolf.

"Stay out of this, cahir," Gerhard snapped. "That clumsy fool lost us the kill tonight."

"Then teach him. Don't punish him." The careless savagery sent anger searing through his veins. He tried to tell himself that the alpha had the right to decide discipline—even if wrong. But the idiot was constantly wrong. His decisions weren't made for the good of his wolves, but because he enjoyed the power.

Shay frowned. An alpha's over-riding instinct was to protect, but Gerhard didn't. Klaus must have been dominant enough to influence his littermate, and his sick desires apparently lingered. Gerhard might have been a good alpha once, but he was no longer fit to lead a pack.

Shay clenched his jaw. If he, Zeb, and Breanne stayed in Cold Creek, they'd be constantly battling the alpha.

Taking Shay's silence for acceptance, Gerhard shifted back to wolf.

Breanne went white, but she placed herself in front of the youngster. Her balance shifted, and Shay knew her first kick would probably take out Dieter.

By the God, he loved her. And he'd die before those misborn mutts laid a fang on her. When Shay snarled, loud and long, the wolves froze. "I challenge."

Gerhard's head whipped around, yellow eyes blazing in shock.

"You can't," someone in the crowd stuttered. "You're oathbound to Herne."

"He released us," Shay said, tilting his face to the moonlight so they could see his unmarked cheek.

Gerhard exposed his fangs.

"Let's do this, you gutless mongrel," Shay said. "I don't want to waste the moon."

RELEASED? BREE'S HEART soared high enough to join the stars in the sky. *They can stay with me? We can—*

The pack formed a wide circle around Gerhard. A fighting ring. No, oh no. Off to one side, Zeb and Shay were talking.

What have I done? She grabbed Shay's arm. "Don't do this. I can—I'll apologize to Gerhard. You don't need to fight."

He put his hand over hers, his gaze steady. Warm. "Mo leannan, the day I let you apologize to that weasel is the day I return to the Mother." Crinkles appeared around his eyes. "And that won't be today."

"Don't. *Please.*" He was going to get hurt. Bad.

"So little confidence in me?"

He made her want to hit him. She turned to Zeb and saw the same determination. Were both of them going to be thrown out? Her eyes started to burn. This was all her fault.

Shay curved his hand over her nape and pulled her to his chest. "Don't cry, little wolf. This was inevitable if we stayed."

She wrapped her arms around him. *I love you so much*. She bit back the words. He didn't need a distraction. Instead, she squeezed as hard as she could, trying to shove extra strength into him. He kissed the top of her head and handed her to Zeb, who kissed her long and slow.

Before she could argue further, they shifted, one tall dark wolf, one heavy-boned, silver wolf. As the shifters opened a path for Shay to enter the circle, Zeb slid through the crowd and stopped beside Gerhard's brother. Guarding Shay's back.

Bree pushed her way to the front. A cold hand slid into hers, and the young shifter, Lacey, gave her a terrified look. Angie and Jody joined them.

Shay stalked into the center, curling his lips to expose his fangs. He and Gerhard stalked around each other, ears sharply forward, both holding their heads high. The raised hair down Shay's back made him look huge.

HE'D BEEN AWFULLY young the last time he'd challenged an alpha, Shay thought. Not any more. He moved slowly, assessing his opponent. Gerhard was a damn big wolf. Confident and experienced. But a good part of a fight for domination was in the mind, and the alpha-hole lacked the bone-deep resolution he'd need to win.

It showed. Unable to wait, Gerhard charged first, snarling, snapping at Shay's nape.

Shay rose onto his hind legs, knocking him free. He tried a slashing bite. Gerhard stood to meet it. They grappled. Shay evaded the front paws and bit at his opponent's neck.

Gerhard shoved away, and they circled, clashed. Circled, clashed. Over and over. They were too evenly matched, Shay realized, at least today. Although adrenaline had revved him up briefly, he'd spent the night running deep into the mountains and had spent today returning. His paws dragged as if they were covered in heavy mud.

Gerhard charged again. His fangs ripped Shay's shoulder. Pain flared. Shay's bite caught him below the eye. Blood spattered, and the weasel broke free. They backed away from each other, snarling.

Gerhard's legs lowered slightly, ready to attack. Shay braced himself. Breanne's voice: "No!" Something moved to one side. Without looking, he dodged. Teeth snapped on air—and Gerhard attacked, taking advantage of the distraction.

Snarls sounded behind him, then a high yelp. People shouted. Shay put it out of his mind; Zeb had his back.

Up on hind legs, Shay pushed Gerhard sideways, taking any opening to bite. Fresh blood filled his mouth, and Gerhard snarled. A return slash sent pain flaring down Shay's side. He bit at his opponent's neck, but heavy fur and loose skin limited the damage.

They fell sideways, rolling and biting. He ripped at Gerhard's muzzle. His opponent's teeth clamped on his leg, sending a flash of pain through him, and he struggled to keep from being overwhelmed by fury. *Balance, furface.*

He broke off and circled. Another charge. Shay twisted aside and set his paw on the other's shoulders, trying—Gerhard went for his other paw, and Shay dodged.

On their hind legs, they grappled. Gerhard's fangs slashed his neck. Shay shoved, overbalancing Gerhard enough to catch the loose fur of his nape. He jerked his head sideways, tossing Gerhard down. He followed. His jaws closed on Gerhard's throat, and he clamped down, fighting the drive to rip the flesh away.

Gerhard went limp. Shay didn't release. The weasel whined. His tail curved between his legs in surrender.

Shay let go but maintained his stance, his teeth bared over the other's neck, reinforcing dominance. A second. Another. He closed his jaws over Gerhard's muzzle. Gerhard didn't move, whined again.

The need to kill still raging in his veins, Shay turned away as if in indifference, ears swiveled in case the male had no brains in him. But the movements behind him were slow.

He heard the wolf retreat, running across the meadow.

And then Breanne landed on her knees next to him. Her arms wrapped around him so tightly he could hardly breathe. "You did it. I'm so proud of you. I was so scared for you. Don't ever do that again." The words turned incoherent as she buried her face in his fur.

Her scent surrounded him, warming him as his battle-anger dimmed and disappeared. He twisted far enough to lick her neck and buried his muzzle in the fragrant hollow at the base.

"Well done, brawd." Zeb lifted Breanne up and slung an arm around her as she tried to burrow into his side instead. "Took you too long though."

Shay snapped his teeth in a token reprimand, then traws-furred. "Thanks for the backup. Who was it?"

"Brother." Zeb jerked his head toward the wolf following Gerhard. "Chad tried to help Dieter. Stupid, but I think he'll learn."

Shay turned. A youth in human form held his bloody ear, while Albert Baty yelled at him.

"Good enough." Shay looked around. As the pack—his pack—drew closer, their wide smiles startled him. They were pleased? He turned in a circle, looking at each, before checking the sky. "You have until the cloud clears the moon to talk, then I want you all in wolf form."

He gave Breanne a hard kiss, fighting the need to mate her here and now, to mark her with his scent. Instead, he stepped back with a sigh. "Shift, little wolf." If they were to have a future in Cold Creek, somehow he had to meld this bunch of wolves into a true pack.

A few minutes later, he took his wolves into the forest. His ears turned toward the rear, hearing the soft thudding of paws, breathing, rustling, and quiet snarls as the younger ones jostled each other for positions. *My pack.*

As they streamed up the mountain behind him, something inside him eased and an unrecognized ache drifted away like mist off the mountain.

THE MOON WAS heading toward the west when the wolves returned to the caves under the tavern. Bree followed, staying near the rear.

She felt the satisfaction in the wolves near her. After running for a while, Shay had stopped in a clearing and talked about the changes he planned to make. He'd given people a chance to talk as he wandered around and spoke to various groups.

Then he'd taken them on a hunt. The old ones had been able to keep up, the younger daring ones had been sent off behind Zeb to flank a herd of deer and drive them toward the rest of the pack. The chase after an older stag had been thrilling. Everyone had dined well.

Shay—and Thyra—had eaten first.

Shay—and Thyra—led the pack. Even now, they ran side-by-side, brushing shoulders occasionally—deliberately on Thyra's part.

When Bree had tried to stay close to Shay, Thyra had attacked, biting and driving her to the rear with the old ones.

Shay'd turned and knocked Thyra away from Bree, but the mess had brought the entire pack to a stop. The second time it happened, Bree'd given up and stayed at the back.

When Zeb wasn't taking the younger wolves on an extra jaunt, he'd run beside her. And Bree noticed puzzled looks from the wolves. Zeb was the beta—the second-in-command—and his place was just behind the alphas.

Now, as they reached the cave, Shay and Thyra shifted first. Thyra gave a fake shiver, the bitch, and snuggled against Shay, running her hand up and down his chest. With a cold look, he pushed her hand away and headed for Bree. Thyra stared after him.

Mine. See? He's mine. Only she could feel a tie between him and Thyra in the same way she sensed the one between him and Zeb. What did that mean?

"Breanne." Shay hugged her. His body was warm and hard, his arms comforting as he kissed her. But something had disappeared, and her worry drained the pleasure away.

As he released her, whispers skittered around them, matched by more confused expressions from the pack members. Near the cave entrance, Thyra stood, her glare hot enough to burn skin.

"I'll talk to you in a bit, lass," Shay said. She'd never heard him sound so miserable. Shoulders slumped, he walked into the tunnel.

Bree turned to Zeb. "What's going on? I thought—"

"We didn't. Think. Fuck, but Shay didn't think at all." He leaned his forehead against hers. "Let's leave, then we'll talk."

But the minute he stepped away from her, he was surrounded by the young guys, so Bree took her time getting dressed. Dread was a cold lump in her belly.

Eventually, she went upstairs, through the private room to the hallway. When she entered the tavern, it was nearly two a.m. and only a few non-pack shifters remained. Near the fireplace, Thyra stood beside Shay, and Bree recognized the posture of a queen beside the king.

But...isn't he mine? She bit her lip and looked for Zeb.

He stood by the bar. Young males around him were boasting about their parts in taking down the deer. Fighting for his attention.

At a table nearby, Angie sat with Albert, saying, "Wasn't that wonderful? I haven't had such a great time in years."

He nodded. "Everyone was satisfied. I hadn't realized how badly Ger—" He pressed his lips closed and shook his head.

"Bree!" Lacey ran across the room to give an exuberant hug. "Did you see me? I helped take the deer down. Was that cool or what?"

"You did good. Was Jody with you during the run?"

"Yeah, Shay asked her to be my mentor. Candice had been but"—Lacey grimaced—"it didn't work out. Jody's crazy bold. She's just great."

With a final squeeze, Lacey darted away, leaving Bree standing alone. Now what?

Now nothing. She wasn't about to join the crowd around Shay…and Thyra. To heck with that.

She slipped outside. Clouds were slowly covering the moon, dimming its glow. In the forest to the east of the tavern, an owl hooted and hooted again, waiting for a response that didn't come.

The door opened. Thyra stepped out, dressed in skin-tight jeans and a crepe blouse that showed off her breasts. "He's mine now."

No need to ask who Thyra meant. "That remains to be seen."

"You really are stupid." Thyra lit a cigarette. "Do you even know what being alpha male and female means?"

"You lead the pack, take precedence with food. Stuff like that." Bree forced a casual tone, despite her heart rate increasing.

"Alphas are paired, dummy. He's mine—and since Zeb's his brother, he will be too." After flicking her cigarette into the damp gravel, Thyra walked off into the night.

After a while, a long while, the glowing stub burned away into ash and darkness.

SHAY LOOKED AROUND the room. Where was Breanne? At the bar, Zeb was trying to escape the young wolves vying for his attention. He finally succeeded, perhaps not as politely as he might have, but Shay felt the same urgency.

"I'm sorry, people," he said to the wolves packed around him. "I need to talk with someone."

The group let him through and he headed across the room. What a damned mess. Why hadn't he considered the consequences of being pack alpha? He caught up to Zeb at the door of the tavern. "Where's Breanne?"

"Outside." Zeb scowled. "Where's the alpha bitch?"

"She left a few minutes ago, thank the God. A bhràthair, what have I done?"

Zeb shook his head, not answering.

Outside, Shay spotted Breanne, leaning against the wall. The dimmed moonlight shadowed her expressionless face. Her posture spoke of despair.

All he'd ever wanted was for her to be happy, and he'd destroyed that completely. He pulled her into his arms. So small and fragrant, smelling of vanilla and the lingering wildness of the wolf. "Breanne. I—"

"No, Shay. I couldn't let the youngster get ripped-up." She buried her face against his shoulder. "And neither could you. It's not your fault." She hugged him, settling his world...and showing him everything he was losing.

His arms tightened, then he released her with a sigh and let Zeb take his turn. His brother needed her comfort.

For a few short hours, the world had been right. His heart had been singing on the way down the mountain. He'd planned out how they'd ask her to be their lifemate. Planned to visit the local blademage who'd make their bracelets. *I destroyed everything.*

After a long hug, Breanne kissed Zeb's cheek.

As they walked down the trail toward the lodge, she said, "Thyra told me alphas are paired. How far does that go?"

Far. Shay scowled. The bitch had probably rubbed Breanne's face in it. Anger smoldered in his gut.

Shadows darkened Zeb's face. "Not sure. I've stayed on the outskirts. Brawd?"

Shay walked in silence, searching for the words. "It's another kind of a bond. Like between mates, only different."

"Before when you led a pack, were you paired with the alpha female?" Zeb asked.

"Aye. She was older—forties, maybe—but a good competent alpha." When he looked back now, he saw how lucky he'd been in his pack, in his mentors. The female alpha had taught him everything. "We had nothing between us except the alpha bond, but I liked her." Thyra wasn't fit to lick her paws. "Breanne, I'm sorry."

"It's like the tie with Herne, isn't it? If you have that—or something with the alpha female—you can't bond with another woman." She inhaled slowly before looking at Zeb. "Being brothers, you're tied to Thyra too. I understand. It's nothing that you wanted." Her face smoothed of all expression.

The only sounds were their footsteps on the path and the rustling of night creatures. Every time he looked at Breanne or Zeb, Shay thought his heart would crack open. *This cannot happen.*

But all night, he'd fought against the bond with the alpha female—without success. When the pack was near, the tie to Thyra was a constant hum, like a magnet that had been turned on. He'd move away from her, but the minute his attention wavered, the bond pulled them together.

How could he fix this?

Chapter Thirty-Two

THE NEXT MORNING, Bree knelt behind the diner counter, filling the pastry goods shelves. The sweet scent of the pies and cakes made her empty stomach churn with nausea.

How could everything have gone so wrong? She'd had one soaring moment last night where she'd had a family and a home and then she'd been blown out of the sky. And she'd hit hard. Her whole body hurt.

As Angie bubbled cheerfully about the new pack leader, Bree fought against screaming in anger—at Thyra and her gloating, at Angie and her happiness, at Shay for his blind honor. Heck, she wanted to yell at their stupid gods, as well.

It's not *fair*. Her hand fisted, crushing a strawberry-filled scone. As she opened her fingers, letting the red goo and worthless crumbs fall onto the tray, she realized Angie had fallen silent.

"Bree?"

She looked up at the older woman. "Thyra said she and Shay were…were like mates now. Zeb too. Shay tried to explain, but is it true?"

"Well, by the Mother's love!" Angie's brows drew together. "I hadn't thought about Thyra being alpha."

"But?"

"She's right. If an alpha male or female is already lifemated, those bonds can't be broken, and the alpha's mate becomes the new alpha female. Unfortunately, Shay isn't lifemated, so pack instinct takes over, and the alphas become a couple. It's a bond they can't fight." Angie rubbed her hands on her apron. "He really can't, Bree."

A couple. A bond. The words sliced into her chest. "And Zeb?"

"They're brothers. Zeb will feel the bond through Shay." Angie's eyes filled with sympathy. "I've seen them with you. This must be ripping them into pieces."

"I know." She'd seen the desolation in Zeb's face. Shay's guilt...and grief. She wasn't the only one hurting. Silently, she wiped the scone off her hand. Well, she had her answers now. Fine. She could handle this. Hey, she'd never believed she'd end up with the men. Or a home.

Would Thyra move into the lodge? The thought was horrendous. She blinked back tears. "I can't stay there."

"Come here," Angie said instantly. "There's only me and my daughter these days. I've got an extra room."

A friend. Bree pulled in a slow breath. Even when everything else turned black, she'd always had friends. Maybe they were the gods' gifts to make up for everything else. She rose and hugged Angie hard. "Thank you. I'll get my stuff."

SHAY WALKED INTO the kitchen, and his hunger disappeared as the emptiness struck him again. Breanne's absence was a reverberating ache inside him. Sometime earlier, the little wolf had collected her belongings while he and Zeb weren't in the lodge. Her note said she'd moved to Angie's.

He'd hurt her, dammit, hurt her badly. How fast could he fix this? He'd decided to ask the Cosantir to help him find a strong wolf from out of the territory. One who could hold the pack. Shay shook his head in bitter amusement. How many alphas could say they'd given away two packs?

He'd have to leave the territory, of course, since staying would undermine the new alpha. But he could be happy anywhere if Zeb and Breanne were with him.

Footsteps sounded, and Thyra waltzed into the kitchen as if she owned the place. "Shay, I want you to take me out to eat tonight. The diner is having an Italian night."

"No." The pull wasn't gone, dammit, and never would be, but as long as the pack wasn't around, he could keep a distance.

"What do you mean?" With a baby-like pout, she ran her hand up his chest.

He felt himself respond in spite of his annoyance.

"Shay, did you get—" Zeb took in the sight and scowled. "Never mind."

"No, don't go, a bhràthair. Thyra is leaving." Shay set her to one side.

"I'm not," she said. "I want to—"

"I'm not going anywhere." Shay crossed his arms. "I can't change the fact we're both alphas. Or that we have to be together during pack times." The next part made his gut tight. "And we'll probably end up mating." As the moon waxed, so would the bond between them. His jaw tightened. "But I don't want you around here."

"Shaaaay."

The whine made his teeth grind together. He started to tell her what he thought of her and refrained. They needed to be able to work together for the good of the pack. "You aren't my type, Thyra," he finally said. "We're the alphas. There's nothing more between us."

After a moment, her mouth twisted into something ugly. "Who the hell would want you for anything else? I was just trying to make the best of this." She shoved Zeb out of the way and stalked out of the kitchen. A few seconds later, the lodge door slammed so hard the building shook.

Zeb let out a laugh. "Got quite a way with the females, don't you, brawd?"

The feeling of his fist against his brother's jaw didn't help at all.

THE TINY MEADOW was quiet with not even a breeze to ruffle the dead grass. If Bree pushed the brown stalks apart, she could see green blades poking up from the dirt. New life.

But not for me. She felt dead inside and out.

She'd left the guys a note after she packed. Cowardly, for sure. But she couldn't face seeing their distress again.

Last night, Zeb had wanted to talk, but, for the first time, she'd locked her door. Wasn't that funny? Even when she was half-afraid of him, she'd never thought of locking the door. No...that had waited until she loved him.

She tilted her head back. Overhead, a vulture circled, lazily riding the warmer air currents. It reminded her of Thyra.

Later today, she'd visit Calum. Surely, the Cosantir would find her new mentors and a different territory. With a sigh, she tossed a twig into the calm lake. It hit with almost no splash, and the ripples faded away before reaching the shore. Like her time in Cold Creek, she'd created a slight disturbance, then would disappear.

In contrast, the effect of the men on her? Oh, now that was more like an avalanche, tearing up the mountainside, leaving black treeless rock behind. Sometimes nothing ever grew there again.

And, jeez, wasn't she getting maudlin?

With a disgusted growl, she rose, picked up a massive

branch, and threw it into the lake. The splash made a mini-tidal wave that tore away parts of the shore. She set her hands on her hips. *So there.*

Pulling in a long breath, she gazed at the mountains around her. She'd miss the peaks, the forest, the creeks. Undoubtedly, Calum would help her find somewhere nice to live, but still…this had become home.

I don't have a home. Or a family. Again. Her chest hurt as she headed for the trail down the mountain.

Three wolves eased out of the forest, eyes focused on her. Her heart thudded hard before she caught their scent. Shifters. Angie, Jody, and Bonnie, the sheriff's dispatcher.

Somehow, she doubted they were merely out for a run. Had Angie told the others about what had happened? Would she have humiliation added to her misery?

"Ladies," she said evenly.

They shifted. Angie smoothed out a place on the softer grass by the bank and eased down with a groan. "I ran more last night than in the previous month. This change of leadership is going to be the death of me."

Jody dropped down beside the older woman. Bonnie took the other side, picking a shady spot to protect her fair skin. All three looked up at Bree.

Three naked women. Life sure could get bizarre. "What's up?"

"Sit," Angie said testily. "You're giving me a crick in my neck."

Bree settled down where she could see all three. Unfortunately, that left her feeling like her versus them. Definitely outnumbered.

"Bree," Bonnie started off in her soft voice. She was Tyler and Luke's mother and awfully gentle to be raising those little rascals. "Angie told us about your questions."

I knew it. Bree glared at Angie.

"Ah, no, don't blame her," Jody said, amusement in her rough voice. "Bonnie and I were having breakfast in the diner. We saw you leave."

Bonnie shook her head. "Last night, we saw how hard Shay fought the alpha bonding. Alphas always stay together, but he kept moving to be with you. Zeb too."

"Oh." Bree felt the prick of tears and blinked them away. "That's nice to hear. But you don't need to worry. I'm leaving soon, and they'll be okay."

"By the Mother's breasts, you got it all wrong. Listen, we talked and"—Jody shoved her short brown hair behind her ears—"I don't know how to ask this politely. Would you be willing to fight for your males? To challenge the alpha female and take her place?"

"Fight Thyra?" Were they insane?

They all nodded.

"You might remember that she ripped me to pieces?" Bree said politely. "Or weren't you watching?"

"Oh, I remember." Jody grimaced and fingered a scar on her shoulder. "Been there, done that. I challenged her a couple of years ago. And lost."

Bree blinked. "But you're still here? I thought losers had to leave." Gerhard and his brother had already moved out of Cold Creek. No one seemed unhappy.

Jody shrugged. "Males tend to move away, but they have that whole testosterone thing going. Females are more practical."

"You weren't keen on being alpha either," Angie pointed out. "It wasn't like Thyra destroyed your ambitions by winning the challenge."

"True. I just hate taking orders from a dimwit, and, since I'm lifemated, I wouldn't have had to mate with Gerhard." Her nose wrinkled. "Be like fucking carrion."

Bonnie choked on a laugh. "Bleah, Jody. Breanne, when you fought Thyra, you'd only been a shifter for all of—what—two weeks?"

"Uh." Bree tried to do the math. It seemed so long ago. "A little less."

The women waited.

"You're thinking I was too new to win a fight with her?" Bree thought about how clumsy she'd been. How shocked stupid. Heck, she'd never even seen a dogfight. *Not my best performance.* "True, I made it easy for her. But she's also twice as big as me and a lot heavier."

"More experience, yes. And bigger." Angie's gaze was direct. "She *counts* on being bigger."

Bree opened her mouth. Closed it. Turning, she stared at the lake. She'd had years of street brawls and karate tournaments. Bigger and heavier didn't ensure a victory. She'd actually won more contests against large opponents than those her size. "Are you saying she doesn't fight…smart?"

Angie smiled like a teacher when a student finally caught on. "Vicki says you fight as well as she does. That kung fu stuff or whatever."

Yeah, I'm just awesome with karate. The momentary hope died. Fighting with teeth and paws rather ruined any skill in kicking and punching. "I don't think karate quite translates into a wolf style."

"Speed and cunning do, though," Bonnie said. "I watched you with Lacey last night. You might be little, but you're really strong and so fast that she looked as if she was standing still."

"Speed doesn't go far without experience," Bree said. "Without skill, you lose to size every time."

Jody leaned forward. "We can't fight for you, but you can use us to practice on. Between us, we've watched and fought a lot of challenges. We can give you tips. Point out where you could do better."

Darned if hope wasn't rising again.

Bonnie chewed on a lock of hair before admitting, "It wouldn't be easy."

None of the women matched Thyra's size or weight, but they were all fairly large. Bree knew how to hone her body into a weapon, how to fight through pain and keep going. Was it enough?

Did it matter? Could she give up Zeb and Shay without trying?

"No," she said decisively and saw three faces fall. "I mean, *no, that bitch won't take my men.* Not without a heck of a fight."

Bonnie let out a yip of joy.

Angie grinned. "I knew it. Let's get started."

Chapter Thirty-Three

THE YELP OF pain filled the sunny clearing.

Bree released her hold immediately. After shifting to human, she knelt beside Bonnie. "Oh God, I'm sorry. I didn't mean to—"

The fluffy blonde wolf snapped her teeth in Bree's face, then trawsfurred. Sitting on her heels, Bonnie scowled. "*Bad* wolf. Don't you ever stop fighting because your opponent screams. Honestly, Bree, you did that karate stuff before; you're supposed to know better."

"I do, but I *bit* you. I can't stand hurting you guys. You're my friends." And they were filling the hole Ashley had left in her heart.

Bonnie examined the red marks on the pale skin of her foot. "You didn't even draw blood, and that's another problem. Somehow, you need to practice ripping without maiming."

"That just sounds ugly."

"You think Thyra will tuck her tail for a puppy mark like this?"

"I'd bite harder if it was her."

Bonnie shook her head. "You need to—" As something crashed through the brush uphill, she jerked around. "Who—"

A tawny cougar bounded into the clearing, sending both

Bonnie and Bree to their feet.

Bree stepped in front of Bonnie, then relaxed as Bonnie laughed and said, "Hey, Vicki, what've you got there?"

The cat stalked over and dropped a small deer on top of Bree's feet.

"What, do I look hungry?" Bree asked.

Vicki shifted and stood. "Nope. But Angie told me you don't know how hard to bite. Alec said young males sometimes practice on dead animals." She motioned to the deer. "So I brought you a toy to play with."

"That's clever." Repressing her need to say *eeewww*, Bree added, "Thank you."

"You're welcome." Vicki took a seat beside Bonnie.

Great, an audience. Bree shifted, backed up a few feet, then sprang at the deer. *Pretend it's Thyra*. Grabbing a hind leg, she bit down, released, and darted away. After turning, she trotted back and checked the leg. Heck. No blood.

"Nice dent marks, killer." When Bree flattened her ears at Vicki, she only snickered. "You gotta do better than that, wolf girl."

FOUR DAYS LATER, Bree walked down the stairs into the cave under the Wild Hunt. People milled around, undressing, and shifting into wolf form. Shay had ordered weekly runs, setting a time soon after sunset so the young ones had time to party afterwards and the mated ones could get home to their children. Another example, Angie said, of how good Shay was at being alpha.

He was, and she was so very proud of him. He needed to stay here and lead them.

No matter what happened tonight.

The scents and the noise were too intense, and her stomach

roiled as if she'd eaten something rotten. She shoved her clothing in a niche and hurried outside, staying in human form. The cold air hit her bare skin in a welcome slap.

Her instructions from Angie filled her head, "*It must be done in front of the pack. Be loud. Be aggressive.*"

The sun had set minutes before, and a light mist swirled in the breeze. Grass alternated with mud that squished coldly between her toes. She looked around.

Zeb was already in wolf form. He caught her scent and started toward her.

Shay and Thyra hadn't trawsfurred yet and stood together on one side of the clearing. Thyra kept rubbing herself on him like a starving farm cat, following when he'd step away.

Jealousy—and anger—surged through Bree, lighting up her nerves. Biting the bitch was *so* not going to be a problem. She walked into the center of the small clearing.

This was it. Showtime. Her hands felt sweaty and her stomach churned unhappily. Too bad, body, she told herself, no time to puke. She straightened her spine.

"Thyra." Her raised voice echoed from the mountains. "I challenge."

Surprised whispers ran around the clearing like a gust of wind.

Thyra peeled herself off Shay. Her snooty expression just begged to be slapped off. "You? Get real!"

Concern filled Shay's face. Zeb tilted his head, ears forward.

Bree set her focus on Thyra. "Do you concede?"

"To a scrawny rabbit like you? Hell, no." After stretching for the benefit of the men, she said, "Don't worry, my alpha. I'll win." She rubbed her breasts against Shay.

He put his hands on her arms—whether to pull her closer or push her away—Bree couldn't tell.

Thyra put her arms around his waist. "After this, we'll laugh about her silly lovesickness for you...like we did last night."

The verbal blow shoved Bree back a step. Had Shay really laughed?

As the pack—human and wolf—formed a circle in the center of the clearing, Bree lost sight of Shay and tried to put it out of her mind. *No emotions. The fight is all.*

Thyra stepped into the circle. "You're obviously too dumb to learn anything, rabbit. This time I'll leave scars."

Fights are won in the head, Sensei would say, and Thyra had already used Shay to score a point. No more of that. Bree gave her a pleased smile. "That's fair since I intend to do the same. When I'm done, gnomes will look at your face and puke."

Oh, snap. Worry flickered in Thyra's eyes, before turning to sheer hate. She shifted to wolf and snarled.

Bree trawsfurred quickly and checked the air. No scent of fear from Thyra, but plenty from Shay and Zeb. For which woman were they concerned? She stomped on the thought. Not her concern right now.

In wolf form, Angie had positioned herself next to one of Thyra's buddies, who'd also shifted.

An elusive scent drifted past—a cougar. Vicki was probably perched in a nearby tree. It was good to have friends.

Bree shook herself, settling her fur, settling her mind. Females didn't play the same dominance games as the males, and she had no wish to prance around as the men had. She wanted to get down to business.

With a snarl that exposed her sharp fangs, Thyra lowered her shoulders slightly.

Bree lifted her upper lip to show her own teeth, then snapped her jaws—something that had always goaded Bonnie into attacking.

Thyra sprang.

Bree dodged, twisted quickly, and bit the bitch's hind paw

hard enough to get a yelp and the taste of blood in her mouth. She darted away and Thyra's jaws snapped on emptiness.

They circled. The alpha's gait was uneven. The scent of blood on the grass sent wildness raging through Bree, and she struggled not to lose control to her animal instincts.

Again, Thyra charged—the danger would come if she stopped—again Bree evaded, snapping this time at the large muscles on the same leg. *Score.* Bree danced away, feeling the scrape of Thyra's fangs against her back leg, followed by burning. A line of blood trailed down Thyra's leg.

Enraged now, Thyra stalked her around the clearing, and Bree let her, moving only quickly enough to escape the constant attacks. Another and another…

With a snarl, Thyra lunged again. Dodging, Bree slipped in the mud. The huge body struck, knocking her down. As she rolled to her feet, teeth slashed her shoulder. She yipped at the blast of pain.

She darted away. The fire in her shoulder streaked her thoughts with red, and each movement of her front leg brought a stab of agony. *Block it out.* Fear sparked alive in her gut.

Thyra headed for her. Feinting a dash away, Bree charged instead, ripping at Thyra's ear on the way past. A horrible snarl followed her.

She spun and braced for the next attack, pain and exhaustion weighing down her legs.

Thyra was panting and limping too, but she was so darn big. After taking a step toward Bree, she stopped and stood. Not moving.

Bree's heart sank. The alpha bitch had kept up her stupidity longer than Bree'd figured she would. Long enough to exhaust herself. But now she'd wised up. As Jody had pointed out, Thyra could stand there all night, and she'd win. It was up to the challenger to take the alpha down. Darn it.

Before Thyra could realize the tactics had changed, Bree charged her straight on. At the last second, she veered to slash and—*Crack*! Pain burst over her left eye. A blizzard of white filled her vision, and Bree staggered, blind and dizzy.

With a terrifying snarl, Thyra was on her, knocking her over, snapping and biting.

Bree couldn't see, pain screamed everywhere. She tried to fight, to get up. Couldn't. Teeth dug into her throat, cutting off her air. Panic filled her, and she started to go limp.

Zeb's furious yell and Shay's bellow broke through the roaring in her ears.

My men. Fight. Ignoring her need to breathe, Bree frantically clawed at Thyra's belly with her hind legs. The bitch winced. Moved. Bree ripped away, tearing the skin at her throat. Pain burned down her neck, but she was free.

No more running. Bree spun and attacked, trying for Thyra's neck. Missed. The bitch twisted, but Bree's fangs caught the skin under her eye and raked downward. The taste of coppery, hot blood filled her mouth.

Thyra yanked free, but her high yelps chilled Bree, and she hesitated. She didn't want to hurt—

"Get in there!" Jody's yell.

No pity. Bree used all the power in her muscular legs to slam into Thyra. It felt like hitting a wall, but the alpha staggered. Bree snapped her teeth upward onto the exposed throat. Thyra tried to break free.

Bree shook her head, the movement driving her teeth deeper. She tightened her jaw until blood ran into her mouth.

Snarling, shaking, clawing, Thyra went mad.

Bree held. *Can't kill her, can't maim her, can't let go. Tightrope.* She gripped harder, terrified she'd hit the jugular.

Suddenly the wolf went limp, dropping to the ground. Bree followed, holding, holding, holding until the whining sounded sincere, and Thyra's tail curved between her legs in submission.

After releasing her grip, Bree raised her head two inches and waited with teeth bared. Growling.

Thyra stayed put.

A second later, sound erupted around the clearing. Jody's, "Wahoo!" Bonnie screaming, "Bree, Bree, Bree!"

Exhilaration hit like a blast of internal fireworks. *I did it! Holy moly, I'm the alpha female now.* Riding on the victory, she stood in the center, head and tail high—Miz Dominant Bitch—waiting until Thyra staggered out of the circle and her scent wafted away.

Two women were shouting.

"I'm sorry. I didn't mean it!" Screaming shrilly, Thyra's friend, Candice, fled from the crowd.

"You like throwing rocks? Me, too!" Jody yelled. Two hard-flung stones hit Candice on her naked butt before she disappeared into the tunnel.

A stone. No wonder my head hurts. Bree looked at the milling shifters, trying to locate Zeb and Shay, and her heart started pounding harder than it had in the fight. Were they upset? Did Shay really want Thyra? Would he—

A hard body hit her from the side, rolled her completely over, and she snarled. Then the scent of Shay engulfed her, as the huge wolf placed one paw on her ribs and proceeded to lick her muzzle enthusiastically. Lovingly.

God, she wanted him. Fire swept through her.

The pack took up a chant: *alphas, alphas, alphas.*

Bree whined up at him, accepting his ministrations, ready and willing to accept much, much more. From his bone-shakingly carnal growl, he could smell that on her.

Zeb shoved him aside, nipped her ear gently, and licked her nose. His deep growls sounded like a cat's purring.

No, they weren't unhappy. Her heart filled until it felt as if joy was fountaining all around her.

A second later, they both stepped back. Bree rolled, scrambled to her feet. Waited.

With a long howl of delight, echoed by Zeb, Shay led the pack out of the clearing. When Bree caught up, he moved over. New alpha female on one side, Zeb on the other.

The three of us. For a second, Bree tried to remember if she'd ever been so happy, then gave up and ran the mountain. *My men. My pack.*

THAT NIGHT IN the tunnel entrance, Shay stood beside Breanne—carefully not touching her—as the pack members bowed slightly to him. He was delighted when they did the same to Breanne. The older ones had begun using the gesture of respect soon after he'd become alpha, then the younger ones had taken it up. No one had ever bowed to Thyra.

Shay's mouth tightened. There was yet a lot to fix with the pack. His thoughts broke off as Zeb walked up, the last to leave.

He stopped in front of Breanne, gripped her bare shoulders, and gave her a hard shake. "Little female," he growled. "You fucking scared me to death."

She opened her mouth.

"No," he snapped and took a breath. "I'm damned proud of you, but do not ever do that again."

After releasing her, he shot a glance at Shay, and his lips quirked. "Have fun, alpha."

As Zeb headed up the stairs, Shay looked around. He'd seen... Ah, there it was. Taking Breanne's hand, he tried to ignore the way the alpha bonding soared between them—as it had every time they'd touched during the run.

Control. Maintain control. He grabbed a blanket from a rock shelf and pulled her out of the cave.

"Shay." She tried to drag her heels.

Zeb was right. She was a little female, and she had no chance against his cahir-size and weight. Ignoring her protests, Shay walked across the clearing and down to a level area on the stream bank. He flipped the blanket onto a patch of soft grass and turned.

"What do you think you're doing?" Her eyes flashed in the starlight.

By the God, she was lovely and she was his. With a sigh of relief, he gave in to the pull. Within a heartbeat, he was harder than granite. Growling, he yanked her into his arms, startling a yip out of her before he kissed her. He took and took, tightening his embrace until there wasn't a smidgen of space between her soft body and his.

Her stomach pressed against his erection and, with his tongue deep in her mouth, he tucked his hands around her round ass and squeezed.

HER HEAD SPUN. He hadn't stopped growling even as he kissed her so thoroughly her knees buckled. The growly noises of her own grew as he rubbed his cock against her and she felt how hard he was.

When he tried to raise his head, she grabbed his hair and dragged him back. Not leaving her—no, he couldn't. He kissed her again, exploring her mouth, fondling her bottom, before he pulled away with a tight chuckle. "Lay down, mo leannan."

When she didn't move, he swept her up and sat her on the blanket. Standing over her, he stared down, his face in shadow. His musky scent was like a blast of testosterone and lust. "Roll over."

With a shiver of need, she complied, lying facedown on the rough fabric.

"Spread your legs."

The air chilled her exposed private parts as he knelt between her legs. He gripped her hips and yanked her onto her hands and knees. She fisted the blanket as his knees pushed hers outward, opening her more.

One hand tightened on her hip, and he slid his erection through her increasing wetness. Up and down, brushing over her clit, teasing until every part of her swelled with need. She whined and tilted her bottom up.

With low snarl, he sheathed himself in one hard thrust. She gasped. He was huge, thick. Her insides convulsed around the intrusion as his groin pressed on her buttocks. With his shaft deep inside her, he lowered himself until his chest rubbed her back.

"Shay?" she whimpered, not knowing what she wanted. More, she needed more.

He gave her more. Even as his teeth closed on her shoulder, his fingers tugged and rolled her nipple. The pains were sharp, sending heat straight to her groin. Her pussy clenched on his cock, and he groaned.

His first movement, sliding out, moving between her slick puffy tissues made her gasp. He bit her again, pinching her breast at the same time. Electricity shocked through her as if he'd nipped her clit instead.

He pulled his cock out. Thrust it in, inch by inch. The slow slide was so exquisite, she moaned.

In, out. *Need more.* She throbbed, her nerves screaming for speed. She rocked against him, trying to direct his movements. His free hand curved over her hip, forcing her into his rhythm, his control.

"Nooo," she moaned, "I want more." Her core coiled like a fist, each relentless stroke sending more urgency through her.

"Stay with me," he rumbled in her ear. Thrust after thrust. He grew even harder inside her. Bigger.

She panted, almost sobbing, fighting his grip. Her thighs

quivered. Her clit was so tight. *I can't take this.*

With a low laugh, he nudged her legs apart farther, opening her to his touch. His fingers settled right next to where her need was the greatest, and he traced circles around her clit. She wiggled uncontrollably. But his arm pressed against her side, and his teeth gripped her shoulder, holding her in place for his thrusts. Harder, deeper.

His fingers worked her clit, ruthlessly driving her upward. He growled when she whimpered. The pressure in her lower body increased, and with each slide of his finger, her clit grew more swollen, more sensitive.

Everything inside her tightened, then clamped down on him. Her whole body turned rigid, poised on the edge, and waiting for…just…

His cock slid deeper, a sensuous impalement, and his finger flickered against the ball of nerves, directly on top. Somehow, she tightened even more, and a fireball of pure sensation blasted through her body. *Oh God, oh God.*Pleasure boiled through her veins, sending every nerve ending to tingling. Smaller explosions kept her spasming around him until he finally came himself with a low roar.

As the aftershocks receded and he softened inside her, her head drooped between her quivering arms.

After easing out, he rolled onto his back and settled her beside him. She pillowed her head on his chest, enjoying the springy hair under her cheek. His arm was tight around her, and she slung one leg over his and pressed herself closer. Contentment seeped into her like the steady inrush of the tide.

He touched the gashes on her neck, shoulder, and forearm. "It's good that we're shifters, *mo chridhe*. You'll heal fast."

Good, since she was starting to hurt. After the fight, the bleeding had stopped quickly, and the excitement of her victory and the run had kept her from feeling much of the aftermath.

She'd undoubtedly feel every bite tomorrow.

"When you challenged Thyra, I feared for you." He snorted and added, "By the God, you terrified me. But like my brother, I am very proud."

She was proud too, but mostly just happy. The men were hers now. *Mine to nibble on, to kiss.* She licked his shoulder, tasting salt, and he hummed his pleasure. The scent of sweat and musk sent a thrill through her. *Mine.*

He paused. "I've never seen such canny fighting though. Where did you learn that?"

With her fingers, she circled his pectorals, then the tiny nipples under his golden chest hair. "Angie, Jody, and Bonnie gave me lessons. Oh, and Vicki brought me a deer to practice on."

"Even without being alpha, you'd won over the top females in the pack."

The satisfaction in his voice warmed her, yet still… Worry kept bubbling up. "Did you mind losing Thyra? Would you rather I hadn't fought?"

When his other arm came around her and crushed her to his side, she wouldn't have traded the uncomfortable position for any other in the world.

"I don't like Thyra," he said bluntly. "But the ties binding the alphas—you've felt them now."

"I understand. You didn't have any choice." She tried to keep the jealousy out of her tone and didn't succeed.

"Just so you know, the bond is much stronger between you and me. I never mated her, Breanne." He laughed under his breath. "But with you? No power in this universe could have kept me from taking you tonight."

He rolled his heavy body on top of hers, pinned her hands over her head, then nipped her chin. "As no power will keep me from having you again."

Chapter Thirty-Four

BREE WAS LATE getting to Angie's the next day and a bit grumpy as well. She might heal faster, but between the lack of any sleep and all the bites and slashes and bruises from the fight, her body felt as if she'd been dragged down a mountainside.

The last of the breakfast crowd was leaving as she walked in. "You gonna make the cherry chocolate cake today?" one old-timer asked.

She looked at his hopeful face and revised her menu. "Sure."

He gave her a grin displaying a gold center tooth and hurried after his equally decrepit friend.

"In the corner," Angie called from behind the counter. She picked up two cups and a pot of coffee.

Bonnie and Jody were already at the table. Dressed in office clothes, Bonnie was probably on break from her dispatching job. Jody was in her usual jeans and T-shirt, smelling faintly of cleaning solution.

"I didn't see you two," Bree said, hugging them tightly.

"You won!" Bonnie squeezed her hard. "I'm so proud of you."

Jody studied Bree's face and laughed. "You have a bite mark on your chin, beard burn on your cheeks, and you look like you didn't get any sleep."

Bonnie giggled. "I take it Shay was pleased with the new alpha female?"

"That's quite a blush," Angie commented, pouring two cups of coffee and sitting down. "Must have been some night."

Bree settled at the table, took a sip of coffee, and admitted, "I didn't realize how strong the bond is between alphas."

Angie leaned back. "Shay wouldn't have tolerated Thyra for a second unless something was compelling him. I'm sure he's wagging his tail today."

"We both are. All three of us, actually," Bree amended, thinking of Zeb's extremely carnal kiss when he'd found her in the kitchen.

She looked across the table at her friends. *Friends*. "It wouldn't have happened without your help." Her eyes filled with tears. "Thank you so very, very much."

"Oh, hell, don't do that." Tough Jody was the one whose eyes turned shiny.

They all turned to their drinks for a moment.

"Okay, now that I'm alpha-girl, what in the world am I supposed to be doing?" Bree asked lightly. "I know Shay has certain jobs as alpha. Do I have some?"

"Yep," said Jody. "Not that Thyra ever bothered."

"Shay tends to the whole pack, with extra attention to the males. Your job is the welfare of the females and children." Angie motioned to the women at the table. "For example, you can assign females to help out new mothers and with watching over the pups."

"You make sure the cubs are safe during pack activities," Jody said. "In my other territory, the children came to everything, and wolves would share the cubsitting." She sighed. "I miss having pups in my life."

"It reminds us of our purpose, that there's more to the pack than just hunting and howling," Bonnie said softly.

Bree nodded. "Keep going. I want to hear it all." She saw what Shay had been saying; the pack lacked its center. *I can help fix this.*

ANXIETY BURNING A hole in his gut, Zeb followed Shay into the Wild Hunt. The tavern was quiet before the evening rush started. A lone dwarf at the corner table gave a spare bow. The two foresters playing pool nodded.

Carrying dirty mugs and humming to George Strait, little Jamie grinned at them, then two-stepped her way to the kitchen. She was sure a bouncy cub.

Behind the bar, Calum looked up. "I hear you have a new alpha female. Congratulations."

"Thank you." Shay slid onto a stool.

Unable to relax enough to sit, Zeb stood beside him. Would the Cosantir agree?

"Can I get you a drink?"

"No." Shay leaned an elbow on the bartop. "Cosantir, we want to run something past you."

"Go on."

"My brother and I want to stay in Cold Creek," Shay said.

My brother. Hearing it still warmed him, Zeb realized. Would that someday he'd hear *my mate*, from a little female.

"Nothing would please me more," Calum said, dragging Zeb's attention back. "You'll continue with the Wildwood?"

Zeb nodded. "We will."

"And more. We're no longer oathbound, but Zeb and I feel as if we're leaving a job undone. The demonkin are everywhere, and cahirs will die trying to kill them."

Zeb figured it was his turn to step in. "Together we've taught cahirs how to fight the hellhounds in Rainier Territory and now here."

Calum nodded. "You both are remarkably good instructors."

Having expected an argument, Zeb could only stare at him in surprise.

"So," Shay said, "would you allow us to teach out-of-territory cahirs how to fight hellhounds?"

"We could house them at the Lodge," Zeb said. "And use the forest for a training ground."

Calum said slowly, "That's an excellent idea. The techniques you've acquired so painfully can save lives." He nodded. "The idea will be welcomed by other Cosantirs—and you have my support."

In the parking lot a few minutes later, Zeb exchanged a grin with Shay, feeling lightheaded. "That's that, then."

"Aye. We're now in the training business as well as lodge-keeping." Shay rubbed his face. "I'm headed for town to get that hardware order. You going home?"

Zeb nodded.

As Shay headed for his pickup, Zeb turned toward the lodge. Toward the female they hoped would be their mate. His stride lengthened as he took a deep breath of air, scenting the coming of spring.

FLAT ON HER back on the weight bench, Bree pushed the bar up and groaned. "Nine." One more rep. She could do it, darn it. She might be the littlest alpha in wolfy-land, but she intended to be the strongest.

And hey, she'd already had her aerobic exercise for the day, thanks to her stupid, unreliable car.

Arms trembling, she lowered the bar to her chest—she shouldn't have added the five-pound weights—and inched it back upward. Halfway there, her muscles wimped out, and the bar stopped as if someone had sat on it. She pushed, feeling her face turn purple.

Criminy, the guys would find her someday, dead on the bench with the bar across her chest.

When scarred fingers wrapped around the middle of the bar, Bree startled.

Zeb lifted the bar a fraction of an inch. "Push, little female."

He made her work, easing only enough of the weight so the bar kept rising, inch by inch. When she finally dropped it in the rack, all of her was shaking. Her arms flopped off the bench. "I don't know whether to thank you or curse you."

He chuckled and walked around to kneel beside her.

She started to sit up, but he put a big hand on her chest, right between her breasts.

"I like you on your back." His dark eyes heated as he looked her over...slowly.

A flash of heat ran through her, and the thin tank top didn't conceal her tightening nipples.

A crease appeared in his cheek.

"Uh." She tried to sit again, but he effortlessly held her down. She sputtered a laugh, despite the way his strength sent a glow right into her belly.

A thought sobered her. "I know you and Shay are brothers, but...I just want to make sure. Now that he's alpha, are you still allowed to share?"

He took her hand and nibbled on her fingers before giving her a predatory smile. "Yes. Which is a good thing because if I were not his brother, Shay would rip my throat out for what I plan to do to you now." The carnal look in his eyes sent a streak of heat straight to her center.

"Well, okay then." Her voice came out breathless. "Where..."

He slid her tank top up, baring her breasts. Cool air wafted over her damp skin. "Here."

"B-but—"

He bent, closing his lips around her nipple. His hot tongue circled the peak, and her back arched, pressing her farther into his mouth. He palmed her other breast, fondling it until that peak was also rigid. Electricity sizzled from her breasts to her core, and she dampened.

Lifting his head, he surveyed his work with half-lidded eyes. Her nipples pointed upward like mountain peaks, one a rosy-pink from his teasing. "Pinker looks better." And he took the paler one into his mouth, using his tongue. When he nipped her, the jolt of fire almost sent her over.

He was still fully dressed when he yanked off her sweat pants, then replaced her legs, one on each side of the weight bench, opening her to his gaze. Cupping his hands under her buttocks, he slid her down until her butt rode the edge. "Better." He went down on one knee, between her legs.

When he trailed a finger through her curly pubic hair, she flushed. "Zeb, this is… What if someone comes back here?" Words failed her, and she struggled to rise.

"If you try to sit up again, I'll put that weight back on your chest." The look in his dark eyes showed he meant it. "You're wet, little female, and hot." His finger pushed inside her an inch, setting off disconcerting detonations of nerves. She was still sore from the night before, her tissues sensitive enough to protest his thick knuckle as he pressed farther in. And yet, heavens, the sensation. Her hips lifted.

"By the God, Gatherings are over-rated," he muttered. "I like this better." He slid his finger out, leaving her shivering from the loss.

"Zeb…" Her body was starting to ache. To burn.

Eyes narrowed, he studied her breasts, then her pussy.

"Your pink bits don't match. I like things orderly." With merciless fingers, he drew her inner folds apart, letting air to the hot wet areas.

She tried to close her legs and received a bite on her thigh that made her squeak.

"You will stay open for me." His black eyes met hers, reinforcing the command, and her gaze dropped.

"Good wolf," he said softly. His mouth settled on her, his tongue licking up one side, then the other, ever so slowly, over and over. He never quite reached the area where her nerve endings were most sensitive.

Desperately, she pushed her hips up, her thighs quivering with the need clawing at her center.

His finger slid back inside her, and the feeling was perfectly exquisite. When she moaned, he laughed against her, and the vibrations against her pussy made her moan again. As he added another finger, his lips reached the place she'd been waiting for.

"Oh, Ooooh…" So close. Her whole body focused there as his tongue dragged over the top of her clit, then teased with flickers. Her lower half was simmering, trying to reach boiling. Her breathing slowed to infinitesimal as her body tightened. She tried to lift her hips, and his forearm pressed her flat. "Zeb, please. Please."

With a growl of agreement, he lightly scraped his teeth on each side of her clit.

Fire blasted through her. Everything inside her came to a boil, erupting over the sides of the container into fiery pleasure. Spasms shook her as he wiggled his fingers inside her and mercilessly licked her clit over and over.

"Ooooh. Oh, that was wonderful." She tried to move, but her body had melted into a puddle on the bench.

The sound of a zipper.

She opened her eyes. His belt was loose; his jeans unzipped.

His erection was huge.

His hard palm pushed her legs farther apart as he leaned over her, setting a hand beside her shoulder. The head of his cock entered her, and she winced, still sore from last night. He paused, and his black eyes trapped hers. He watched her as he rocked his hips, slowly and relentlessly impaling her. Her vagina spasmed around him, protesting the entry yet sending waves of pleasure through her.

When he was completely in, she fought for breath. He lifted himself up higher to look down on her, and she felt as if he'd spread her out on the bench like a feast for consumption. His cheek creased as he pulled her nipples back into tight peaks. Each tug of his firm fingers created ripples inside her, around his cock, as if her pussy and breasts were connected.

He slid his cock out, then in. So very slowly, as if he savored the feeling and was unwilling to hurry. Lowering his head, he licked across her lips, then took her mouth. As he stroked his tongue inside her mouth in time with his cock, her whole body pulsed to his rhythm.

She felt lost, unable to control her own reactions. She shivered. "Zeb. I can't—"

"Little female, I want more from you. You will give me more." He reached down, and his fingers slid through her wetness, drawing it up over the hub of all her nerves. His eyes never left hers as he stroked her, as need again began to pulse in her blood stream. Her eyes closed as his cock thrust in against one side of her vagina, slid against the other side. Her feet pushed to her toes, driving her hips upward to meet his.

"Good wolf," he murmured, and the sound of his deep gravelly voice broke something loose. Her core tightened and then spasmed in sheer pleasure, shuddering under his fingers, around his hard cock. A scream echoed in the room, high and wild. The voice was hers.

He brushed his lips over hers in approval. His hand slid under her bottom, and he lifted her hips to meet his as he thrust harder. Deeper. Faster. With a harsh sound, he pressed deep, and she could feel his cock jerking, flooding her with his essence.

His forehead rested against hers, his breath warm on her lips. She felt the trickle of his seed, and she wrapped her arms around his neck, holding him closer.

Eventually, he smiled at her.

She smiled back, wondering if she'd ever manage to stand again. Her legs had gone as limp as overcooked noodles.

His powerful hand under her bottom held her to him as he pushed them both up and off the bench. As he straightened and stood, she realized he was still inside her and growing hard again.

"My need was too great to take my time, but now—now, we'll use the incline bench."

THE KITCHEN WAS fragrant with the yeasty scent of hot rolls as Bree finished making gravy. Needing to celebrate—in a way other than sex—she'd prepared fried chicken. That should divert the men.

She smiled. Her favorite entertainment was watching them fight over helpings, but she wouldn't indulge tonight. Either Zeb or Shay had cleaned her kitchen, even removing mineral stains from the sink, and that guy would get the biggest serving of everything.

When the two walked in, the pleased grins on their tanned faces made her heart turn over. Heavens, she loved them. Both of them.

Shay kissed the top of her head and Zeb her cheek as they walked past to wash up, jostling each other like little boys.

"I didn't think you were here," Shay said, drying his hands.

"Your car's gone."

"The engine wouldn't start after I got to town. Contrary thing."

"Want me to take a look?" Zeb asked.

"No. Kevin Murphy was in the diner. He said it's the alternator, and it'll be a couple of days before he gets the part in." She sighed. That was the downside of living in a tiny town. A city garage would carry more stock.

She handed Zeb the milk to pour and Shay the silverware. When she set the basket of rolls on the table, she laughed at the greedy expressions. Was anything better than cooking for hungry men?

Well. Maybe having sex with hungry men. She was already looking forward to tonight in Shay's big bed where they all fit so well.

As the men set the table, they never missed a chance to touch her. Shay slid a hand down her back as he moved paperwork onto a chair. Zeb curled an arm around her waist as he sampled the salad dressing she'd made. A kiss here, a nibble there. Would she ever feel as free to touch them in turn?

Or was she being stupidly shy? Fair was fair.

Taking a step forward, she looped an arm around Zeb's hard waist, snuggled close, and ran her hand over his butt. To her surprise, he growled, yanked her into his arms, and took her mouth in a hot, wet kiss. The room rolled under her feet when he set her down. "Ah—"

He trailed a finger across her chin and tilted her face up. "I like your hands on me." His gaze intensified. "Bree, I..." His mouth closed and he stepped back.

Somehow, she felt as if he had her in his arms.

When they were seated, Shay reached for the chicken platter.

"Oh no." Bree held up her hand to stop him. "Whoever cleaned the kitchen gets the first helping."

The two exchanged confused looks.

"You didn't?" Bree stared at them. "Then who did? I left it a mess this morning."

"Did you?" Zeb straightened. His gaze roved, stopped, and he pointed to where a softball-sized hole showed in the corner baseboard. "Looks like we've got brownies."

"Well now." Shay smiled slowly. "We'll need to put cream and a pastry out for them each night."

A brownie? OtherFolk? Bree stared at the hole.

A small wrinkled face peeked out. A pointed chin and sharp nose. One long pointed ear was bent at the tip. A *brownie*—and they only came if the people there had made a home. Like a family. *We're a family*. Hugging herself, Bree savored a moment of sheer happiness.

Chapter Thirty-Five

S HAY GLANCED UP when Breanne came into the office. Her lips were swollen, her neck and cheeks scratched. She looked beautiful...and tired. He and Zeb had kept her awake the last two nights, ensuring she had no doubts that they loved sharing her.

Actually, he had trouble letting her out of bed at all. He'd wanted her before, but with the new alpha bond, he hardened whenever he caught her scent. Like now.

"You're hitting the paperwork early." She smiled at him. "Couldn't it wait until this evening?"

"Nope." Since she'd arrived, they'd developed a routine. He'd do his paperwork in the library area where Zeb would be reading and Breanne working on a jigsaw puzzle. As Shay worked, they'd discuss business, make plans, and order from the catalogues. Breanne and Zeb would argue over upgrading the cabins and lodge.

How the design of a doorknob or kitchen latch could be important, Shay didn't know, but he never tired of listening to them. "It's new moon, so Zeb and I have to patrol. Will you stay with Angie?"

Her face paled until her freckles stood out in tiny smudges. "I forgot. I wanted to forget. You'll be careful, right?" Her eyes showed her fear for them and warmed his heart.

How long had it been since someone worried over him? "We will." He walked around the desk. Drawing her in, he molded her soft body against his, until their breathing rose and fell in unison, and their hearts beat together. "*A chuisle mo chridhe*," he murmured.

She rubbed her forehead on his chest. "You and your Gaelic. Translation?"

"Mmmmh." *You're the pulse of my heart.* "Something like sweetheart." He kissed her, wanting to say the words. But he must wait. Zeb would visit the blademage today, and then they'd do it right.

Breanne deserved everything done right.

"So what're you guys planning for this afternoon?"

He smiled, enjoying how she kept track of them. If they were working near the lodge, she'd bring them treats warm from the oven. "Zeb walked to town to help Jody put bars on their office building. He'll be back this afternoon. I have an appointment downtown with a supplier in"—he glanced at the clock—"fifteen minutes."

"Okay. I'll cook something early for you tonight." She started to leave, then stopped. "Oops. Here's the mail." She dropped a pile onto his desk.

He glanced through the letters and held up an envelope. "This one's for you."

"Really?" With a pleased expression, she glanced over the letter. "It's from Eric—that little boy I told you about. I wonder if I get a new picture."

Their refrigerator was crowded with artwork, and not only Eric's. In the past couple of days, the pack pups had added more. They adored Breanne.

Shay had to smile. She never turned down a chance to cuddle a cub...and each time, the awed expression on Zeb's face

WINTER OF THE WOLF   427

was heart-rending. From the tidbits Zeb had mentioned, he'd never been snuggled.

Wouldn't Breanne look lovely with his and Zeb's babies in her arms?

As she perused her letter, he leaned a hip against the desk and opened his own. Junk mail for the Lodge, bills, a request for reservations. Something in Breanne's silence had him looking up.

Her face had gone white, matching her knuckles that clenched the paper.

"Little wolf? What's wrong?"

"J-Just"—she cleared her throat—"bad news. A friend died."

"I'm sorry, mo leannan." He hugged her, wishing he could do more. To keep any sorrow or disappointment from ever touching her.

She clung for a minute before her spine straightened. "I'm okay. You need to get going, or you'll be late."

"I can cancel."

"Go. I'll see you later."

BREE DROPPED ONTO her bed and unfolded the letter again.

At the top of the page, Eric had written, *"I love you, Bree."* The "B" had been erased and reprinted so many times that the underlying paper was almost gone. "I love you too, Eric," she whispered.

Her gaze slid to the bottom, and a note from his mother.

"I miss you, Bree, and Eric asks every day if you've returned yet. But I'm glad you're not here. Truly, you shouldn't come back to the complex. Something horrible is happening. Devon, in the apartment next to yours, disappeared the first week of March. His car was still parked in the stall. None of his stuff was missing and

there was blood all over his place."

Bree saw where the words, "*like yours*" had been scribbled out. The note continued.

"*Then the first week in April, Marylou in the apartment across from yours, also disappeared. Same thing—blood, nothing missing, no body. The cops don't know what to do. Jim wants to move, but we can't afford it yet.*

I hope you're doing well. Please write and let us know how you are.

Love you,
Diane"

Bree felt as if someone had punched her in the stomach. Devon'd just started his first job after college and had never been away from Nebraska before. He'd come over, wanting to know how to make meat loaf. After that, she and Ash had often invited him for a home-cooked meal.

Marylou was—had been—divorced. She'd cried when her new man-friend had sent roses for her birthday.

How could they be gone?

It's because of me. The knowledge welled up, ugly and sharp. The hellhound had said it would return. Since Bree wasn't there, it was murdering others. Guilt tightened her throat, even knowing she couldn't have prevented the deaths. If she'd hadn't left, she'd have died, and the monster would still be killing.

Understanding didn't lessen her shame. She'd been here, falling in love, making a new home, while her friends were dying. Her hand felt heavy as she laid the letter on the nightstand. What was she going to do?

Outside the Lodge, Shay's truck started with its distinctive roar, then the noise faded as he drove down the lane toward the highway. The lodge was empty.

I have to go back. Bree swallowed against nausea. She was the only one who knew how to kill it.

Couldn't she call the police? Tell them about the hellhound? *Sure, Bree. Did that work out well for you the first time?* Even if the cops believed her about a monster—and they wouldn't—then once spotted, they'd try to shoot it and get slaughtered.

Shay and Zeb could kill the hellhound. They'd help save her friends. They'd insist. She stood and sank back down.

The Cosantir had said no. *"Cahirs do not leave the territory to fight. Your Gifts from Herne will not be there for you, not in a city of metal, so far from His forests. You are forbidden, cahirs."* The Cosantir had executed Klaus for breaking the "Law". She could never, never risk Zeb and Shay that way.

Only—if she lived—when she got back, they'd be furious that she didn't tell them. They'd...

I'm forbidden to go too. The Cosantir had looked at her, the black of the God in his eyes. *"Do not force your lovers to kill you, Breanne."*

The men would never hurt her, but if they didn't obey the Cosantir, they'd be exiled or executed as well. Her insides chilled as her bones turned to ice. Once she left, she couldn't return to Cold Creek. Ever.

She pulled in a shuddering breath. Just a few days ago, she'd planned to leave the men and move. So why did it hurt so much more now, as if someone had opened her chest and poured acid inside?

Swallowing, she tried not cry. She'd never hear Zeb's rough voice calling her 'little female'. Never wake to Shay's kisses. Never see the surprise in Zeb's eyes when she baked something just for him. It *hurt.*

They'd hurt too. But they'd be alive.

And she had no choice. Tonight was new moon, and the hellhound would be at the apartment complex. Someone would die.

She raised her chin and straightened her spine. No human would die. Just the creature. *The monster won't get you, Eric. Or Diane. It won't get anyone else.*

Rubbing the ache in her chest, she dragged her suitcase from the closet. She wouldn't be coming back. If she lived, she might as well have her own clothes.

As she haphazardly packed, she considered. It was a few hours drive to Seattle. Better leave now and have time to coax Diane and Jim to stay elsewhere. Maybe a hotel.

After securing her suitcase, she grabbed her purse and...*My car.* She didn't have a working car. And Cold Creek had no car rental. Stunned, she stopped in the middle of the room.

Borrow a vehicle? Hah. Neither Zeb nor Shay would offer, not to let her go to Seattle. Her eyes narrowed. Zeb had walked to town as usual. His truck was parked outside the lodge. He'd have his key, but hotwiring old Fords was as easy as boiling water.

Hey, what was one more crime in the grand scheme of things?

She picked up her suitcase. Dropped it again. *I need a pistol.* Darn Zeb anyway, the overprotective butthead. A wave of grief thickened her throat. Blinking hard, she strode down the hall to his room. Where would he have hid her gun?

She found his pistol in his nightstand along with one of his knives. He was never without the other knife, she knew. She stared at his weapons, wanting everything she could get her hands on.

But this was new moon. What if he had to fight a hellhound here?

She'd just have to search for her own pistol.

Twenty minutes later, she found her S&W inside the closet, duct-taped over the closet door. She'd never have spotted it if she hadn't had to climb a chair to check the top shelf. The man could give paranoia a bad name. He'd unloaded it, but she had boxes of bullets in her dresser.

After setting his room back to rights, she paused to hug his pillow and breathe in his lingering scent. He hadn't slept in his room for a couple of nights. No, they'd been in Shay's giant bed. All of them.

She wistfully replaced the pillow. If she left now, she'd be in Seattle in good time.

ZEB RETURNED TO the Lodge in a piss-poor mood and slammed the door behind him. *Fucking pup. My fucking bad temper.*

At the reception desk, Shay looked up from the registration book. "Problem?"

Zeb tried to nail his anger down. "Chad mouthed off and pushed that new wolf, Lacey. I shoved him face first into a wall to show him what it felt like."

"Sounds good. So?"

"I should have talked first, disciplined later." Zeb rubbed his face. Him and his fucking temper.

"Normally." Shay tapped his fingers on the desk. "But not yet. Because of Klaus, the Cosantir's watching the pack—and he won't tolerate any more females getting hurt. If we don't come down on that behavior hard and fast, that pup will get himself banished."

"Well." He hadn't messed up?

"You know, eventually, the cubs will absorb your attitude."

Zeb snorted. "My attitude?"

"Yeah, a bhràthair, that over-protective one that Breanne bitches about. And the pack will benefit from it."

The glint of pride that edged Shay's grin made Zeb blink.

"Go get a sugar fix. Breanne left us some pie."

"Cherry?" Zeb's stomach growled. He'd missed lunch, and he loved cherry pie.

"And apple too," Shay said smugly.

Zeb was halfway to the kitchen when he stopped. There'd been only one truck in front of the lodge. He reversed directions and opened the front door. "Where the fuck is my pickup?"

"What?" Shay joined him. "Who'd steal that POS?"

"That piece-of-shit is mine, and I'll gut whoever took it," Zeb growled. He patted his pocket. "I have my keys. Where...where's Bree?"

"Don't know. I can't feel her through the bond, so she's not close." Shay turned slowly. "She said once that she'd learned to hotwire cars in the city."

"Guess she had something to do. But I didn't see my truck in town."

"You think...?" Shay's jaw tightened, then he relaxed. "No. She wouldn't return to the city on a new moon night."

Uneasiness twined up Zeb's spine like a strangling vine. "Check her room."

Shay beat him up the stairs. "Her suitcase is gone."

Fuck. What was she doing? Zeb found his pistol still in the nightstand. His knife too. He opened the closet and slapped his hand above the door. His palm hit the wall, and a piece of duct tape dropped to the floor.

TEN MINUTES LATER, Shay pulled his truck into the Wild Hunt parking lot. Every cell in his body ordered him to head straight for Seattle. But they couldn't.

Calum wasn't in the bar.

Rosie jerked her thumb upward. Calum, Alec, and Vicki lived on the second floor with their daughter. The men went around to the backyard and ran up the steps. Shay pounded on the door.

Jamie opened it, took one look at their faces, and yelled, "Daddy, I think they need you bad."

Calum walked out of the kitchen followed by Alec. "Come in, cahirs," Calum said. "Sit."

Shay stepped inside far enough to let Zeb move up beside him. He felt urgency burning in his brother as hot as his own. "Breanne took her pistol and headed back to Seattle to kill the hellhound."

"That's purely suicidal." Alec's brow creased. "Why?"

"The hellhound that attacked her is stalking her apartment complex. Probably looking for her and settling for humans." Shay handed Calum the letter he'd found in her room.

Calum skimmed it before handing it to Alec. "I understand her concern. But new shifters are forbidden human cities. If she's hurt or scared—"

"Can you widen the patrols to cover our area?" Shay asked Alec.

Understanding softened the sheriff's face. "We'll handle Cold Creek."

Darkness moved in Calum's eyes. His voice was soft. "You also have been forbidden, cahirs."

Zeb spoke finally. "Kill us later, Cosantir. After we keep our female from being slaughtered."

They didn't wait for his answer.

As they rounded the corner, Shay heard Alec call, "Best hurry, cahirs. It's not that long before sunset."

By the God, he knew that all too well.

SHE MIGHT AS well have driven her own car. Criminy.

As fine mist dampened her hair and face, Bree paced outside the auto repair garage, unable to sit. She could just slap Zeb for not keeping his pickup in better shape. She should have expected this. He loved working with wood, but he absolutely hated metal and engines.

How could this happen to her? Now, of all times.

She looked inside. The hood of Zeb's truck was open, and a mechanic worked away at its innards. Turning, she stared west. Through the gray clouds, the setting sun glowed a sullen red behind Seattle's skyscrapers and the Space Needle.

Her hands fisted in her jacket pockets. "Can't you hurry? Please?"

"It'll get done when it gets done, lady."

Chapter Thirty-Six

Seattle ~ Dark of the moon

"WATCH OUT FOR that red car. The driver's drunk." Zeb gripped the door handle. He'd thought itching was the worst part of being in a vehicle. Fuck, was he wrong.

"I see him." Shay's jaw clenched so tight that the muscles stood out. He slowed his truck. "Hope her hellhound shows up," he muttered. "I need to kill something."

"How can there be so many people in one place?" Zeb stared through the windshield into the misty twilight. In the three lanes in front of them, taillights streamed forward in steady lines, sometimes flashing the brighter red of brake lights. On the other side of the divider, three more lines of glowing headlights zoomed past. Horns blared. The car in front had the bass turned up far enough to reverberate in his bones. Disgusting music. "You hear the words to that song?"

"Would be a pleasure to meet the singer, teach him how females should be treated and spoken of."

"We've had rotten Daonain too."

"Yeah, and look how Klaus ended up." Shay's face chilled as the music continued. "I could ram the asshole hard enough to crush the radio."

"Tempting," Zeb admitted. He checked the map. "That's

our exit."

A few minutes later, he snarled. "How many fucking lights can one town need?"

"It's a city." Shay brought the truck to another halt. "You never been in one before?"

"Never even interested."

"I tried Portland as a cub. Thought it would be exciting." Shay absently rubbed his chest and set off Zeb's urge to scratch.

Fucking metal. "Was it?" Zeb caught glimpses of red outlining the Olympic Mountains. The sun had set. His hands fisted. Was she even now facing a hellhound?

"By the God, no. I only lasted two days. Humans are insane." Squinting at the street sign, Shay turned right. "Some own mansions. Others live in cardboard boxes."

Zeb stared down a block filled with big square structures, all eerily identical. "And some live on top of each other. You're right, brawd. They're insane." The numbers on the buildings increased slowly. "Another. One more. Stop."

Shay pulled the pickup to the curb outside a huge, boxy building. "She lived in something like that?"

Zeb double-checked the return address on the envelope. "Correct street. Right number." He jumped out. "Let's go."

No doorbell. Shay knocked on the dark glass door.

No one came.

Impatiently, Zeb yanked the door open and found a long hallway with numbers on each door. That explained the extra number in the address. Maybe if he watched television now and then, he'd figure out human customs. "Look for two-two-five."

"Right." Shay strode down the hall. "None here."

Could they have the wrong building? Zeb scowled, and then remembered how high the box was. More doors would be upstairs. "There were stairs at the front." They ran back to the entrance, and Shay led the way up.

These apartment numbers were in the two hundreds. Midway down, Zeb stopped. "Here." *Don't scare the humans.* He let Shay knock.

The door opened, and a human male in his twenties looked at them warily.

"Hi," Shay said. "Are you Jim?"

"No solicitors." The man started to close the door.

Shay set his hand on it, holding it open. "Wait. We're friends of Breanne."

A female stepped up beside Jim. Probably the Diane who'd written the letter. "You've seen Bree? Is she all right?"

"She's fine." Shay smiled at them. "All healed-up."

The humans relaxed. His brawd could be fucking charming when he wanted.

"She was headed here," Shay said, "and we're worried about her. This isn't a safe place, as I'm sure you know."

"I haven't seen her," the female said.

Zeb interrupted. "What's her door number?"

"One-sixteen," Jim said. "Downstairs."

Shay turned to Zeb and said under his breath, "Go. I'll talk them out of this trap."

Back downstairs, Zeb trotted down the hall. *One-sixteen.* The door was locked, of course. He tapped. No answer, no sound of anyone inside.

Where the hell was she? She should have arrived hours before. The sun was already down. His gut tight with dread, he pounded. Nothing. The door was cheap wood and hollow. After checking the hallway, he tipped his body to try to muffle the sound and rammed his fist into the wood next to the handle. Took more effort than he'd figured. Definitely hurt more.

Reaching through the hole, he unlocked the doorknob and the deadbolt above it, and entered. After a quick sniff, he knew he had the right den. The stuffy air said the place had been empty for some time. He glanced around. Pretty with soft colors and fabrics. The kitchen held a myriad of cooking stuff: copper-bottomed pots, more knives than any female should possess, herbs running the length of one wall. Yes, this was his little female's den.

He frowned at a sliding door made of glass. By the God's balls, talk about being unable to defend your cave. Zeb turned to leave.

Glass shattered.

He spun. A hellhound charged across the room.

Zeb flung himself sideways and over the couch. He hit the ground hard, rolled to his feet, and reached for his knife. The hellhound crashed into him, knocking him on his back. As fangs bit deep into his knife arm, pain seared through him. He kicked out uselessly.

Fuck, he was dead.

THESE HUMANS WERE incredibly stubborn. Shay tried again. "You don't understand. There will be someone killed here. Tonight."

"How do you know that?" Jim's eyes narrowed suspiciously. "I can't afford to take my family to a hotel for weeks until they catch this guy."

"Just for tonight." Shay caught sight of a cub, all freckles, and big eyes.

"You're really big," the boy said.

"I'm from the mountains. We grow bigger there."

A flash of humor showed in the father's eyes.

"You're Eric, aren't you," Shay guessed. "Are you the one that gives sticky hugs?"

Beaming, the boy grinned, displaying a missing tooth.

By the God, he couldn't let the hellhound have this family.

Shay pulled the father into the hallway. "Listen. That's a fine son you have. Don't risk him."

The man shook his head again. "I can't—"

"The hel—the murderer attacks on the new moon."

Shay got a blank look.

"The night with no moon. One night a month. After the sun sets. Tonight."

As comprehension filled the man's eyes, his color drained, leaving him almost gray. "Diane, bring Eric. We're going to visit Shawn and Susie."

"Jim." Diane glared at Shay. "We can't just up and leave. I have work tomorrow."

Sighing, Shay prepared to start over again.

GOD, COULD ANYTHING else go wrong tonight? Bree tore into the apartment building from the rear parking lot and ran up the back stairs to the second floor. It was after dark. If the hellhound had already visited her place, it would now be looking for other prey. She had a vision of Eric, torn apart like Ashley, and she shuddered. *No, don't go there.* She needed to get them out. *Now.*

THE HELLHOUND WHIPPED its head, flinging Zeb across the room. He skidded into a chair. Mind fuzzing, he staggered to his feet. What the fuck was wrong with him?

The demon-dog took a step, ran its tongue over its bloody muzzle, and stopped dead. Its rust-colored eyes focused on Zeb with new interest.

Yeah, I got magic in my blood. And oh fuck, the magic was why he was fucking weak. *"Your Gifts from Herne will not be there for you, not in a city of metal, so far from His forests.*" Damn the Cosantir for being right.

He kicked a chair into the hellhound's path and pulled his knife, feeling the weakness in his torn muscles. He might not have the strength to shove the blade through its leathery belly. Could he use his other hand quickly enough?

He was slower too. Hell, he'd probably be slaughtered trying to reach the creature, especially with no diversion. Where the fuck was Shay?

In this piled-upon place, a yell wouldn't be heard upstairs. But… He yanked his pistol from his left-hand-holster and aimed at the hellhound. Wouldn't work, but the noise might.

THE SOUND OF a handgun sent fear ripping through Shay. *Zeb or Breanne.* He shoved Jim to one side and ran down the hallway. He took the stairs, jumping down them four at a time. On the ground floor, he checked doors as he ran. Number one-sixteen had a fist-sized hole in it.

"Zeb!" he roared. Couldn't strip fast enough to trawsfur. He drew his knife. As he charged into the room, he caught the scent of blood and pain, and the foul stench of demonkin.

Small place. Too small. Cornered by a hellhound, Zeb had a knife in one hand, a chair in the other. As Shay charged across the room, the beast started to turn, ruining his chance at the belly. Shay lunged in to slash at its hind leg. The knife scraped off, not getting between the plates. Fangs worked better, dammit.

The hellhound snarled and snapped at Shay.

Shay dodged and slashed toward its eye, but it was old enough, smart enough, to turn its head so the blade stabbed only the facial armor. Its jaws almost caught his arm, and Shay evaded, banging into furniture.

It kept coming.

He desperately dove over the coffee table and landed on his side, knowing he'd not get out of this one. The room was too crowded.

"Fuck, no!" Zeb hit the hellhound from the rear as Shay staggered to his feet.

The hellhound spun, and Zeb jumped away, hitting an end table. He fell in front of the door. The hellhound went for him.

No! Shay ran forward—too late, too late.

THE SHARP RETORT of bullets had turned Bree around as she reached the second floor. Now on the first, she burst out of the stairwell to the sound of thuds and snarling. Her place. Someone was in her apartment. Being hurt.

The hellhound must be there. Her pulse increased, roaring in her head loud enough to drown out every other noise. A voice inside her screamed, *Get away. Run!* Pulling her pistol from her purse, she forced her legs to keep moving. Toward her apartment.

The door was open, red splatters on the carpet. And...the *monster.*

Its stench hit her, and she froze. *Ash's screams, blood, teeth ripping into her. Pain, pain, pain.* Her world narrowed, turned gray. Sounds receded. Paralysis gripped her until she couldn't move.

"Breanne, no!" Shay's voice came from far, far away. "Run!"

Blood covered the monster's muzzle. Pink frothy saliva ran down its jaw and dripped off, drop by slow drop. Her gaze followed the liquid as it seemed to float in the air, descending and landing on a person. A man. Zeb.

It stood over *Zeb.*

The world snapped into focus. Sounds blasted into her ears: shouts, snarls, growls.

As the monster turned toward Bree, her hand came up, her form exactly correct. She pulled the trigger gently—*just like stroking a man's balls.*

The red-brown eye splattered.

THE HELLHOUND DROPPED onto Zeb, knocking the air out of his lungs. *Again.* With a groan, Zeb tried to shove it off. Got nowhere. "Fuck," he gasped. "Why am I always on the bottom?"

"Because I'm the alpha?" Shay asked in a strained voice. He grabbed an armored leg, and then Bree was there, pushing from the other side. As the demon-dog changed to human and Shay tossed it aside, Bree fell to her knees.

"Jeez, Zeb!" She wrapped her arms around his neck, trying to fracture his spine.

He pulled her closer. Warm, soft female, leaking tears all over his chest, smelling of fear and vanilla. Sweet, sweet Bree. Her heart was pounding so hard, his ribs would probably have bruises. As he buried his face in her silky hair, for a second, his world was just right.

"*Mo chridhe*, you're going to strangle him." The amused tone said Shay wasn't seriously injured, not that the mongrel would let anyone know.

After a gentle touch of her lips to Zeb's forehead, she jumped up and did her best to choke Shay instead. Shay wrapped his arms around her, set his cheek on the top of her head, and looked at Zeb. His mouth formed one word. "Ours."

Oh yeah. Pain flared like wildfire in his arm as he sat up, but Zeb still managed to smile. "Ours."

Chapter Thirty-Seven

R AIN BULLETED THE smeary windshield of Zeb's truck. As
he wrenched the steering wheel to the left to enter a motel
parking lot, his arm flared with pain. It felt as if the fucking
hellhound's teeth were still embedded in his flesh. He pulled up
beside Shay's truck, letting the engine run as his brother disappeared inside the office.

In the passenger seat, Bree stirred. "Where are we?"

"Motel." Not his choice of places to stay, but at least they'd
driven long enough to get away from all the metal and concrete.
He wasn't sure what Shay had in mind though—Cold Creek was
to the east, not south.

"Oh. Good. We need to patch you up." Bree frowned at the
blood-soaked dishtowel he'd wrapped around his arm. "You
should have let me drive."

"Uh-huh. Hold your hands out."

She gave him a dirty look, not even attempting to prove she
wasn't shaking like an aspen in a high wind.

In the apartment, when she'd seen what her bullet had done
to the hellhound's face, she'd turned green and dashed for the
bathroom. But she'd returned on her own two feet and, hearing
sirens, had led them out of the building. By the God, she was a
strong female.

Shay appeared, carrying a sack, and jumped in his truck. Zeb followed to the rear of the motel and parked, nodding approval. The line of small cottage-like buildings was much better than the huge building in front.

Their cottage was at the end. After slinging an arm around Bree, Zeb went inside. The room was clean and decorated in pleasant green and white colors. One side held a token kitchen area containing a round table and chairs. A microwave, tiny refrigerator, and coffee pot sat on a counter. The center had a small couch and television.

Near the far wall was a bed only slightly smaller than the one at their lodge. No—not their lodge any more. At the best, they were now exiled from Cold Creek; possibly, they'd be outcast completely.

He took a slow breath, pushing away the ache of loss. The sweet female cuddling against his side was enough recompense for any male. "What you got there, brawd?" he asked as Shay set the sack on the counter.

His brother pulled out several microwavable soups and hot chocolate packets, plus some white T-shirts boasting pictures of the Space Needle.

"You wanted souvenirs?" Bree asked in disbelief.

Shay laughed. "After Zeb takes a shower, I'll wrap his arm up with special Seattle bandages." He patted the T-shirts.

"Good plan." Zeb frowned at the guilt on Bree's face and kissed the top of her head. "Make me some soup, little female?"

She gave him a wavery smile and nodded.

THE GUYS HAD taken quick showers, and Bree had been grateful to go last so she could take her time. Finally feeling clean again, she donned one of the oversized Seattle T-shirts and stepped out.

At the table, Shay was ripping up shirts while Zeb drank a cup of soup. Both men were shirtless, wearing only their jeans.

Shay smiled at her. "C'mere. I need to hold you before I yell at you."

As his arms closed around her, she breathed in his masculine scent of snowy mountains—the fragrance of safety, comfort, and love.

"I understand why you thought you had to come back here." His voice turned to a low growl. "But if you ever do something so dangerous again, you'll find that Gerhard's discipline was nothing."

She rubbed her face against the crisp hair on his chest. "Uh-huh. And you'll do what?"

He nipped the top of her ear in a stinging reprimand. "I'll bare your ass and pound on it."

"Sounds like fun." Zeb leaned forward and swatted her lightly. "Can we practice first?"

"There's a thought." Shay's big hands massaged her bottom, lighting a warmth inside her. "Maybe after I rest a bit."

"You too? Guess the Cosantir was right about being weaker in a city. And slower, dammit." Zeb turned his arm over, examining the bite.

She stared at the torn flesh. "There's no healer here."

"Not the first time." Not looking up, he poked at a spot, trying to shove the skin together. More blood trickled down his forearm.

He'd been hurt because of her. "I'm sorry," she whispered, blinking as tears welled in her eyes. "I'm so sorry."

"What are a few more marks?" He picked up a strip of T-shirt.

She couldn't stand to look, to see what she'd done to him. He'd been hurt so many times before. She turned her back, and a sob escaped despite her efforts.

Zeb made a low noise of pain, and his chair scraped on the linoleum. Stepping in front of her, he set a finger under her chin and lifted her face. His eyes were dark and intent. "Do the scars bother you, little female?"

"Of course not," she choked out.

"Then why the tears?" With his thumb, he wiped them from her cheeks and released her.

Didn't he understand anything? "It's my fault. And—" Horror rose inside her as she realized something else, remembered why she hadn't told them anything. "Are you in trouble because you followed me?" She looked at one man, then the other. *Have I ruined their lives?* "You can go back, can't you?"

"No, mo leannan. You don't defy a Cosantir and expect to live in his territory." Shay folded a piece of shirt into a square. "I called while you were in the shower. Rosie will watch over the lodge until we return and make a formal break."

The corner of Zeb's mouth lifted. "We'll wait a few days to let his temper cool so maybe he won't drop us dead in our tracks."

Bree's breath caught. "Don't go back."

"That wouldn't be honorable." Shay shook his head. "No, I think he'll just kick us out of his territory. Zeb was mostly joking about him killing us."

"Mostly?" She shuddered, remembering the life draining from Klaus's eyes. "I'm sorry. I didn't want either of you dragged into this."

"Looks like you'd have done all right without us. You killed yourself a hellhound." Shay gave her a thoughtful look. "Knowing you, you had a plan."

"Yeah, I was going to stack up furniture so when it broke through the patio door, it would have been funneled toward me in a straight direction. I figured that way I'd get a clear shot at its eyes."

Zeb brushed his knuckles over her damp cheek. "Good plan. Fair chance of working."

"Only I wouldn't have had time to set up, not after the pickup broke down. So I'm glad you were here, but now the Cosantir will—"

"Eric's a cute kid," Shay said, interrupting her. "And he might have been the next victim. Or you. We were where we needed to be."

Zeb nodded agreement and handed her a cup of soup. "Drink that while Shay wraps my arm."

Trying not to cry, she forced herself to sip, as the men argued amiably over ways to tie the bandage. She'd totally destroyed their lives. The pack would lose Shay as the alpha. Zeb wouldn't get to finish the cabins. The little brownies had just moved into their lodge, now they'd have to move out again. Misery enveloped her, compressing her chest until she found it hard to breathe.

Laughing at one of Shay's insults, Zeb glanced at her. His brows drew together. "Bree. What?"

"I'm sorry. So, so sorry." She sniffled. How could she have hurt the people she loved best in the whole world? "You can't go back. I've ruined everything—the pack and the town and the brownies."

"By the God, you're a mess." Zeb started to rise and stopped at a gesture from Shay.

Shay put his foot up on a chair and leaned on his thigh, contemplating her. "You're not going to forgive yourself, are you?"

"How can I?" Under his steady gaze, she had to look away. "I should leave. Maybe if I go, then Calum will—"

A hand hit the table, making her jump. "No," Zeb said in a deadly voice. "Don't even consider it."

"Look at me, Breanne." Shay waited until she complied. "It took me years to forgive myself for the mistakes I made as a pack leader. Finally someone asked me how many people I had to save before I thought I'd evened the balance." Shay rubbed his face. "I would have suffered anything, to escape that guilt."

Mouth tight, Zeb nodded in understanding.

She understood. She'd ruined their lives, and she'd live with the remorse forever. "I'm sorry," she whispered again.

"You should be. Because I'm furious." Shay's hand closed into a fist, and the knuckles cracked. She felt the pull of an alpha as his anger reverberated through her. "Not for trying to save a child, but that you didn't trust us to help."

What could she say? She couldn't let them get hurt. But—

"You feel bad because Zeb was hurt and the Cosantir might banish us, but that's not why we're angry. Not even close." He studied her. "Until you get past the guilt, you won't understand the rest."

What did he mean? "I—"

"A good parent—or alpha—disciplines to teach," Shay said. "As a cub, I didn't understand how punishment could lessen anger and guilt. Or how after a punishment is done, the trail is wiped out. No tracks remain."

She remembered the pain of Thyra's discipline. Would they really attack her? Savage her as wolves? But if it would make them feel better... She pulled in a breath. "Okay. I can take it."

Zeb straightened. "Shay, are you insane? You'd bite her?"

A grim smile flitted over the alpha's face. "Bite? No. This is going to be difficult though—I've never struck a female." He sat on the bed. "Come here, Breanne."

She hesitated. But whatever he wanted to do to her, she'd endure. When she stood beside him, he gripped the front of her T-shirt and pulled her downward over his hard thighs.

He shoved the hem up to her waist and rubbed her bare bottom. Only then did she realize what he planned. *Spank me?* Humiliation swept through her. "No!" She struggled.

He pinned her shoulders down. "Yes. I don't want to do this, but you're mired neck-deep in guilt. And not hearing what we're saying." His hand hit her lightly.

She heard Zeb growl.

"*Dùin do bhuel.*"

"Fuck your *shut up* and—"

"A bhràthair, she needs this." Shay brought his hand down. Hard. The slap echoed against the walls, and her butt stung. "I wish someone had beaten the guilt from me back then." Another slap, this time harder. And another.

"No!" When she kicked, he ruthlessly trapped her legs with his, then started spanking her in earnest. Blow after blow, one cheek, then the other. The stinging on her skin turned to burning, then to fire. It *hurt*. "You butthead!"

As she fought back, she heard his voice, "...this is for not telling me. This is for not sharing the letter. This for lying to me. This is for not letting us protect you..." The red-edged pain grew and grew, and she started to cry. "This is for not allowing us to decide what we would risk or what we find to be important."

When something jostled the bed, Shay paused.

Oh, thank God. Choking with sobs, she tried to rise up. The ruthless hand on her back flattened her. She saw Zeb's legs. He'd joined Shay.

"I get it now. But if I use my arm, I'll start to bleed again," Zeb said.

"I'll hold her for you, a bhràthair."

Zeb, too? His betrayal made her sob harder.

"I hate seeing you cry, Bree." Zeb pushed her hair from her wet face with a gentle hand. "But I'm angry too. And I want you to understand why. Maybe this will take away your guilt, so you can hear what we're saying."

He didn't wait for her agreement but moved to Shay's other

side.

He hit her. His palm was fully as hard as Shay's and more abrasive. Fresh pain firestormed over her skin. *Left, right.* When he slapped the tops of her thighs, her fingernails dug into Shay's jeans.

Slowly, Zeb rasped out what he was mad about: not coming to him with the problem, not calling when his truck broke down. Each blow seared her skin. "We're together. All of us." *Slap.* "Even if we take on the fucking world, we do it together." Another blow. "We're family, and you'll fucking understand that."

Family. They weren't angry because they'd been hurt or would be banished, but because she hadn't treated them as family. *Us against the world.* Something inside her cracked, then blasted open, and warmth poured into places that had been cold and empty.

She could probably do anything to Zeb, and he wouldn't care as long as she loved him. Calum had told her that Shay had planned to give up the pack for her. Because he loved her. *Family.*

God, she had a family. "We're family," she whispered, and somehow they heard her.

"Aye."

"'Bout time." Zeb's voice sounded like ground glass.

Shay sighed and rubbed her burning bottom, making her hiss at the sting. "You'll have trouble sitting for a day or two." He pulled her up to sit on his lap. She jumped as the coarse material of his jeans rubbed her raw skin. "Easy, mo leannan." He wrapped his arms around her.

She sagged against his chest, hating him. Hating them both for the pain—and she loved them more than life itself.

Eyes worried, Zeb cupped her face with his hands and kissed her damp cheeks. "Are you all right, little female?"

His uncertainty helped. She hated them anyway, and she glared at him.

"Do you still feel guilty?" Zeb's grin flashed unexpectedly. "Or should we pound on you longer?"

She bit back the rude word she'd learned from him. His hands framed her face in warmth, keeping her from looking away.

"Breanne?" Shay prompted.

Darn them. Both of them. She pulled in a breath and paused. The tightness was gone from her chest, and the heavy weight of guilt had lifted. Not all, but enough that she could accept she'd done the best she could. And hey, how could she know they felt so strongly? Not as if the terse cretins had ever told her.

Family.

She looked Zeb in the eyes. "It's better." And criminy, her butt hurt. Her brows drew together. "I'm not going to thank you though."

Shay snorted. "I didn't think you would. I never thanked an elder for a punishment when I was a pup." A laugh rumbled through his chest. "But we're not finished. Completely."

She yipped in alarm as he tumbled her onto the bed. He rolled her onto her back and pinned her down with his hands on her shoulders. "Do you remember what happens to shifters when their female is in danger?" Shay's eyes heated. "Zeb and I need to reassure ourselves that you're alive."

As Bree started to realize their intent, Zeb stripped off his jeans.

Chapter Thirty-Eight

S HAY'S HAND BURNED from the spanking, so he could imagine how Breanne's delicate ass felt. Guilt scraped his guts at having hurt a female. *My female.* But as he studied her, he saw her reddened eyes were no longer muddied with unhappiness.

He rubbed his cheek against hers, and she curled her arms around his neck. Thank the God, she was willing. Seeing her facing the hellhound had left him with an unfightable need to be inside her.

Bree pushed to a sitting position, pulling the shirt down to cover herself. That wouldn't last long, but he liked the way her full breasts moved under the thin fabric.

"Now, we'll finish your punishment, Breanne," Shay said, sitting beside her.

Her eyes widened, and he grinned.

Zeb merely raised an eyebrow, willing to follow Shay's lead.

"What?" Her voice was husky from crying, but he could smell the beginning of her arousal.

"You will give in to whatever Zeb and I ask of you tonight. Having nearly lost you, we're going to be very, very demanding."

She swallowed, and her nipples contracted. "I...that's fair."

"Good. Let's lose the shirt."

Zeb's grin flashed, and he yanked her shirt off and tossed it on the floor.

Shay knelt on her other side and pushed her flat. By Herne's balls, Breanne had gorgeous breasts. He ran his fingers over them, and she inhaled sharply. How soon could they have her moaning? He pinned her hands beside her head and took her mouth, gently at first, then hard.

He felt her jerk and squirm from whatever Zeb was doing. She moaned and sucked on his tongue, teasing him with her own until he pulled away. By the God, he needed to taste her elsewhere, to have her scent on him. "A bhràthair," he said, his voice strained. "She needs something to suck on. Help her out."

Zeb moved up on the bed and turned her face toward him. "Little female, I want those lips around my cock."

Shay chuckled, delighted at how sweetly she opened her mouth. Zeb slid his cock in deep, his groan low and raspy.

Our mate. Shay ran his hands down her body, teasing her nipples. Already reddened—Zeb had played with them. What male could resist? He brushed his hand down the slight roundness of her stomach to the springy white-gold curls over her mound. Pushing open her legs, he inhaled her musky scent. His cock hardened painfully.

Zeb's nostrils flared. "I think you enjoy this, cariad."

In answer, she sucked so audibly hard that Zeb's hand fisted in her hair.

Shay grinned.

BREE'S URGE TO drive Zeb crazy was siderailed by the way Shay stroked her body. He'd been so harsh during the spanking and was so gentle now.

He slid his hands up the insides of her thighs, pushing her legs farther open. But, jeez, his fingers stopped short of where her clit had started to throb.

Concentrate. She kissed her way up the taut velvety skin of Zeb's cock. As she used her tongue to tease the engorged veins, his breathing deepened. When she scraped her teeth lightly over the head, his low growl was a song of pleasure and need.

A sharp nip on her mound made her jump, and Shay laughed. He wedged his shoulders between her thighs, and she paused in anticipation.

His breath brushed over her pussy. "She's all puffy and wet for us." His finger touched on top of her clit, and she gasped, her hips jerking up.

Zeb pulled on her hair and slid his cock out of her mouth. "I'm too tired to take you several times tonight." His black eyes burned into hers. "So I want to be deep inside you when I get off." He ran his knuckles over her cheek. "Of course, you're female. Doesn't matter if you're tired."

Shay chuckled. "We've been too easy on her. Let's get nasty."

"Agreed."

Oh heavens. Her nipples tightened to aching. She swallowed, tasting Zeb. "I don't want you to be nasty." *I think.*

"Really?" Zeb ran his finger in a circle around her bunched nipple, and his cheek creased. "I'm not smelling fear, little female. Just arousal." He mercilessly pinned her hands over her head. "No human worries allowed in this bed." His rough kiss silenced any protest.

Even as Zeb kissed her, Shay teased her pussy, making the humming sound that meant he was pleased. He licked and nipped her folds, sending jolts of light pain searing along her nerves. Deep inside, pressure started to coil.

"Ah, I forgot. Fast and hard," Shay muttered. His mouth closed over her clit, engulfing it in heat and wetness, a match for the kiss Zeb was giving her.

When Shay sucked lightly, her hips bucked uncontrollably.

He laid an arm over her pelvis, holding her immobile as his tongue stroked over and around her clit. He sucked again. Licked. Sucked. Her world spun.

Zeb pressed a light kiss to her lips and cupped his left hand over her breast.

The next time Shay sucked, Zeb pinched her nipple hard, and the sensations zinged back and forth, blooming into heat in her belly. She needed to touch so she squirmed and pulled at her arms to get free. Zeb held her wrists ruthlessly; Shay pressed down on her hips.

She was trapped between two men—each trying to drive her crazy. "Oh *God.*"

With a rumbling laugh, Zeb switched to her other breast. Shay sucked harder.

The increasing pressure of impending climax made her body tighten. Every nerve was burning to come. She closed her eyes.

"No, cariad, look at me," Zeb said in a strained voice.

She looked at him blindly, and then Shay sucked her clit hard and his tongue lashed over the top. Everything inside her contracted with a grip as hard as Zeb's, released all at once, and exploded outward in a wave of sheer sensation.

Her hips tried to buck and got nowhere as Shay held her down, his tongue working her until the slightest touch was too much and even the brush of his breath made her shiver and spasm.

When her eyes cleared, Zeb was still watching her, his dark eyes softer than they'd ever been.

"I've never seen anyone so beautiful when they come." He ran his knuckles over her flushed cheek, then rose. "My turn, brawd."

"Aye." Shay walked away from the bed.

When he glanced back at her, she realized her legs were splayed wide open. She struggled to sit up.

Zeb pushed her down. "Stay where we put you, female," he growled. With one hand, he pinned her wrists over her head as he fondled her breasts. "You're ours tonight. Say 'yes'."

She shivered, excitement rising, even though she'd just gotten off. "Yes, Zeb," she whispered.

"Good answer."

Shay returned from the kitchen and handed Zeb something that made him laugh. She raised her head, trying to see. As Shay replaced Zeb at her side, he set his hand on her forehead and pushed. "Stay, little wolf."

Zeb lifted her hips and shoved a pillow under her, making her squeak as the fabric rubbed her tender bottom. Both men laughed, the brutes. She glared at them. Yeah, her guilt was definitely gone. How could she have let them spank her? Then again—she saw Shay's smoldering blue-gray eyes—how could she not? She was free of the guilt. Free to think how much she loved them.

As if he understood, he whispered, "*A chuisle mo chridhe*," and kissed her fiercely.

"What does—"

With firm hands, Zeb bent her knees and settled between her legs.

She tried to move and realized Shay's hand was still on her forehead, holding her down.

His eyes laughed into her hers when she scowled at him. "Just think of yourself as a meaty bone for a couple of wolves to play with. Chew on. Nip. Tug." He pulled on her left nipple. Her breasts were swollen from Zeb's attentions, and the feeling of Shay's callused fingers made her startle.

She heard something tear, but Shay kept her head pressed down so she couldn't look. The feeling of helplessness in the face of their strength made her quiver. "Just take me."

"Oh, I don't think so." The corners of Shay's eyes crinkled.

"Darn you." Heat flared under her skin, and it felt frightening, as if she'd been caught in a current and couldn't break free. She shoved at Shay's hand on her forehead.

Zeb gave a snort of laughter. "She's always trying to push me away too, brawd."

Shay gripped her wrists, setting them over her head. "You keep your hands right there, or I'll tie them." He smiled slowly. "And I'd enjoy it too."

"Good idea," Zeb said, and Bree caught her breath at the dark dangerous look in his eyes.

Criminy. The thought of being tied down while the men did...things...to her sent heat searing through her body. Was she getting warped or what?

Shay circled her nipple with a finger. "Look how hard these are. We're not the only ones who'd enjoy it."

Zeb studied her, his gaze going from her breasts to her face. The corner of his mouth tipped up. "Let's see if she does." He fetched a long strip of T-shirt from the table.

As Shay held her in an unbreakable grip, Zeb wrapped the shirt around and around her right wrist, then knotted it. After running the other end of the cloth through the slatted headboard, he secured her left wrist, tightening the strip of fabric so both arms were restrained over her head.

A surge of heat blazed up at the fire in his eyes. She pulled at the T-shirt binding, realizing if she really, really needed out, she could pull her hands free...although it would take work and time. What were they going to do to her?

"I gave you a word to use if you ever got scared. Tell Zeb what it is." Shay brushed her hair from her face.

The edge of fear disappeared, leaving only nerves and anticipation behind. She licked her lips and tasted Zeb. "Elvis."

Zeb actually laughed. He nuzzled her neck, his day's beard growth rough against her skin compared to his soft lips, then walked to the foot of the bed.

When Shay's hands closed on her breasts, she jerked. The helpless feeling increased as she tugged on her bonds.

As Shay watched her struggle, his lips curved. "I hadn't realized how much fun this could be." He rolled her nipples between his fingers. The feeling was indescribable, and her back arched up, pressing her breasts into his hands.

Zeb pushed her legs up, tipping her knees outward. The pillow lifted her bottom, so the position exposed…everything.

He looked down at her pussy, pleasure in his face. After running his fingers between her folds, he pressed a finger inside her. She shivered as her vagina added to the clamor of sensation streaming upward. "She's very wet," he said softly.

"Um-hum." Shay's gaze stayed on her face as he pinched her nipple lightly, and sheer heat sizzled straight to her pussy.

Zeb said, "Whatever you did, she just clamped down on me. Do it again."

Shay's smile widened. "My pleasure."

Bree tried to move as Shay's head lowered, but her arms jerked futilely on the restraints. Zeb pressed another finger inside her, sending warring sensations through her.

Shay licked a nipple, then sucked lightly. The sensation squeezed something deep inside her, and she felt her peak swell. He gently nipped the very tip.

Her gasp choked her as the tiny pain ripped downward, and her pussy responded.

"Nice," Zeb growled. When his mouth settled over her clit, the room blurred. His tongue, oh God, his tongue. Rasping and soft at the same time, so wet, and—

Shay switched to her other nipple, and she moaned as desire became a terrifying vise. Another bite on her breast.

As she clenched, Zeb thrust his fingers in and out of her in a demanding rhythm. Her insides tightened around him, and she felt her climax building from her toes north. He sucked her clit, strobed it with his tongue, then stopped before she could come. She moaned, and a *please* broke from her.

He chuckled. "No, little female, not yet." He pulled his fingers out, leaving her empty and aching inside. Her clit felt as if it might split from the blood pouring into it.

"Need an extra hand here," Zeb said, and Shay slid one hand down to her mound, teasingly flicking his fingers as if he was playing a keyboard. She trembled.

"Open her more," Zeb directed, and Shay fanned his fingers, pulling her labia apart. Cool air brushed like a kiss over her clit, as if it stood out all by itself, and the firmness of Shay's pull made it tighter.

A hand closed on her bottom, squeezing slightly. She flinched, her skin still hurting from the spanking, and started to straighten her legs.

Zeb pushed her knees higher. "If you move, I'll swat your pretty pink ass."

God no. She stopped fighting, too aware of how the pillow lifted her pussy upward, keeping her more available.

Shay blew across her nipple, making it bunch tighter.

"Don't move, little female," Zeb cautioned, and then she felt—*oh my heavens*—his finger slicking her anus and pressing in. Like what Shay had done at the Gather and a couple of times since.

Oh God, what were they planning? "Wait…"

Both men chuckled at the same time, murmuring something comforting. The finger slowly advanced, then slid all the way in.

"Shay…" she whined, before realizing he was the one who'd bought the lubricant.

"You enjoy a couple fingers there." She felt the determination of her alpha as he said, "You'll try a cock tonight." He kissed her.

She felt a touch of coldness, then Zeb pushed a second finger in. More burn. She tried to wiggle away, and he made a warning sound.

She froze.

Zeb rumbled something. To her surprise, Shay released her arms from the restraints and lifted her up. "Your arm can't support you. Means you get the bottom," Shay said to Zeb.

Zeb snorted. "As if you'd allow anything different." He took Bree's place, on his back with his knees hanging off the end. Shay set Bree down, straddling him. Her dangling breasts rubbed his chest.

Winding his fingers in her long hair, Zeb tugged her close for a gentle kiss, then smiled into her eyes. Her heart ached for the pain she'd given him yet expanded at the love in his gaze, as if she were a treasure he'd found.

Although his erection bobbed against her mound, he just played with her breasts, saying, "I like when they hang down into my hand."

Behind her, Shay rubbed his erection against her sore bottom. When she winced, he chuckled. "Poor little wolf. A sore ass will make this more interesting. For you."

Interesting? She closed her eyes as he parted her buttocks and applied more cold lube. He slid his finger into her anus, making her jerk.

She shivered. "You're too big. Way too big."

"Let's find out." Shay added another finger, stretching her, before pulling out. More lube. Her eyes opened wide when she felt a cock slide between her buttocks. "Nooo."

Shay swatted her bottom lightly, making her squeak. "If you hate this, we'll stop, mo leannan. But you come harder with fingers, so I think you'll like it. I'll go slowly."

He was huge. He went slowly as promised, easing the tip in and out, even as Zeb ran his finger over her clit, sending waves of sensation through her.

She squirmed, all her senses jangling from the need to come and the need to get away from the cock trying to push into her. Shay's hands gripped her hips, keeping her still. He pushed harder, and she whimpered as he stretched her until her anus burned as badly as her bottom.

Zeb pinched her clit, and the sensation consumed the pain. *I need…*

Her hands closed into fists, and then the head of Shay's cock went in with a soundless plop. "There you go. It'll be easier now, lass." He rocked, each time advancing more. Cold made her jump as he added lube and slid more easily. Slid too far.

Burning and too full and…

"I'm in," he said. His thighs bumped her sore bottom, and she squeaked, trying to pull away but getting nowhere.

Zeb pinched her clit, and she wiggled.

Shay growled, low and dangerous. "Breanne, the way you feel around me…" He leaned forward, nipping her neck, kissing her shoulder, and the movement drove him deeper.

She whined.

SHAY STILLED, ALTHOUGH his cock was pulsing, demanding that he take her hard. But if she was in pain, he needed to stop. Yes, many females seemed to like this, especially with another male involved, but he'd had one female who hadn't. "Does it hurt?" He slid in and out, and her body quivered. So soft. So female. *Mine.*

When he'd been young, he hadn't thought of females except in terms of sex. Not for friendship and love. Then, once oathbound, he'd tried not to think of all he was missing.

But now… "Breanne." He ran his hands up and down her sides, massaged her hips as he thrust gently. "You're more than I ever dreamed of," he murmured and laid his cheek on her hair.

"Hell, you made her cry again." Zeb's voice sounded exasperated, but the rasping sound said he felt the same. "I think she needs a diversion. We're supposed to be nasty, remember?"

Breanne's entire body stiffened with alarm as Zeb started to work his cock into her cunt.

Shay put one foot up on the bed, his knee against her thigh, stabilizing himself. He tightened his hands on her hips. The pressure around his cock increased as Zeb carefully filled her.

"Oh God, I can't breathe." She leaned her forehead against Zeb's chest, her voice shaking.

Zeb froze.

But she was breathing just fine, Shay realized.

Zeb lifted her face and studied her for a moment. He smiled and glanced at Shay.

"Too much to process?" Shay said lightly. "Let's add to it." He nodded at Zeb who put his hands on her breasts.

Her insides clamped down so hard that Shay almost came right then. He groaned and pulled out slightly, waited for Zeb to slide out before he pushed back in. As always with his partner— his brother—their movements came together, and within a few strokes, they were in a perfect rhythm.

Breanne's whole body trembled, but he caught no scent of pain or fear. Still, he wanted her to come with them, all of them together. Shay straightened slightly so he could reach around her side. There was the little nub of nerves. She was so wet his fingers glided easily over her clit.

She made a heat-inducing mewl, and her ass contracted around him. As he continued, her hips bucked, making his head spin. Damn, she was tight, especially with Zeb at the same time.

Zeb's eyes met his, and he nodded. They could keep this up longer, but she'd be too sore to walk. The joining in this way was what he'd wanted, celebrating that they were alive and together.

Zeb picked up the pace, and he followed, using his fingers

to tease her clit back into hardness. Zeb did the same with her nipples, and he could only imagine how overwhelming it all would feel. Her legs quivered.

"Oooooh, God." She'd braced her forehead, and her back arched. Shay felt her asshole tighten at the base of his cock, and then her climax hit, rippling around him, battering his shaft softly. She let out delightful high yips as she came.

He grinned at Zeb, sharing the joy of having satisfied their female. Then Zeb thrust faster; Shay followed. Zeb came first, the cords on his neck standing out as he pushed deep.

Shay gripped Breanne's hips, plunging deeper. His own climax dug claws into his spine, flooded through his balls, and through his cock as he filled his female with his heat. He held on for a moment: thrusting gently, emptying fully, and savoring the feeling of being clasped.

When he finally pulled out and released her hips, she collapsed with a groan. Laughing, Zeb wrapped his arms around her, keeping her against him and filling the need females had of being held afterward.

Shay shook his head—as if males didn't need it also. He cleaned himself and washed her as well.

Finally, he slid into bed. Zeb was curled around Breanne from the rear, sound asleep. She roused long enough to give him a sleepy kiss and an "I love you" before fading away.

He stared at her. She'd said it. She loved them—oh, he'd known it—but she'd actually said it. His heart felt full enough to overflow. He pushed closer, enjoying her softness against his chest and the scents of their love-making in the air.

There they were: his mate and his brother. In his bed. Sound asleep. He settled beside them with a long sigh of perfect happiness.

Chapter Thirty-Nine

Olympic National Forest

IN THE FAINT moonlight, Zeb crouched on the creekside in the Olympic forest, enjoying the show.

Bree was trying to fish. Her tail would wag hopefully as she spotted one of the shy trout, and then she'd pounce. Water would splash, the fish would slide through her paws, and she'd snap futilely at the escaping prey.

Hopeless. Just as well he'd stayed as a wolf, or he'd be strangling with his attempts not to laugh. Her soft blonde fur was drenched and dripping, but she hadn't given up. Not Bree—she never gave up.

Stubborn and brave and loving.

They'd spent the last four days and nights in the Olympic Mountains as wolves, hunting and playing and piling in a heap to sleep. Occasionally, they'd trawsfur and make love in the lush grass of the meadows. Afterwards they'd bask in the sun and talk.

He'd learned more about his brother and Bree. Like him, they were survivors of pain and death, still fighting back. Fuck, he loved them. Each night, he thanked the Mother for her gifts: for his brother, for finding this little female, for her love for them in return. For being alive.

Bree missed another fish. When she looked at him, Zeb put his chin on the ground and covered his eyes with a paw.

She gave a tiny growl and snapped her jaws at him for the insult.

Truly, it was good he'd stayed wolf.

As the moonlight glimmered over Bree's damp fur and danced along the splashing water, Zeb caught Shay's scent. 'Bout time. Before dark, he'd gone back to the truck, evading Bree's questions as to why.

He broke from the forest, and Zeb saw metal gleaming on his leg. Anticipation swelled within him. Last night, the moon had been a sliver, almost too small to be seen. Tonight, the crescent of a waxing moon showed clearly. It was a time for new beginnings.

As Shay reached the bank, a flopping, fat trout landed in the grass. Bree bounded over, tail high in victory.

Zeb's ears went back. Neither he nor Shay had thought she'd succeed. Hell, they'd never hear the end of this.

As if she'd heard his thoughts, she shook hard, splattering him and Shay with cold creek water.

Zeb growled, looked at Shay.

Shay dipped his front quarters, darted around Bree, and flattened on the ground beside her.

Zeb charged, shouldering into her on the opposite side, knocking her off-balance. She tripped over Shay and fell. Her breath grunted out and then they were both on her, nipping at her belly and flanks. With one on each side, she couldn't roll over or escape. Soon her paws scrambled in the air as if trying to run.

When her tail slapped her belly, Zeb changed to nuzzling her neck and licking her nose. Setting a paw on her chest, Shay did the same.

She shifted. "Sadistic cretins," she sputtered between giggles.

She brushed dirt from her shoulders in a way that made her breasts bounce enticingly. "I'll get you back, I swear."

Zeb trawsfurred and couldn't keep from laughing. Fuck, she was the cutest female he'd ever met.

After Shay changed to human, he studied the moon in the dark night sky and nodded at Zeb. It was time.

Zeb's hands went cold. He and Shay thought they knew how Bree felt about them, but she'd been raised human. And she was female. He'd never understood either. What if they were wrong? Would doing this mess everything up? Pull them apart? His body felt awkward, as if he'd shifted into skin that was too small.

By the God, how did males ever manage to do this? As his courage drained away, he needed to touch her, to feel her against him. He pulled her to her feet. "Bree, I need a kiss."

STANDING CLOSE ENOUGH to feel the heat radiating from Zeb's body, Bree looked up at him. His eyes were shadowed in the dim moonlight, his jaw muscles tight. He'd been laughing a moment ago. She laid her hand on his cheek. "Is something wrong?"

"No, cariad. I just need a kiss. Now, please." His vocal cords sounded as if they'd shattered.

What had happened? On tiptoe, she curled her arms around his neck. Her fingers tangled in his straight black hair as she pulled him down to her mouth.

He kissed her hard, pulling her to him tightly, and she felt his cock lengthen against her stomach. She had a momentary wonder of how quickly these guys hardened before he kissed the thought right out of her.

Giving a low sigh, he set her on her feet. Shay pressed against her from behind, his hands cupping her breasts. She looked back at him, and he took her mouth in a plundering kiss as intimate as Zeb's had been.

When he released her, her body hummed with need. She

staggered a little, feeling the breeze cold on her bare skin where a second before two male bodies had been. She shook her head, trying to get her bearings. "Guys, what is…?"

They were kneeling in front of her, side-by-side, Shay's huge body next to Zeb's leanly muscular one. Light and dark, day and night. Both deadly. And wonderful.

"What's going on?"

Zeb glanced at Shay with the expression that meant, you do the talking.

The moonlight made Shay's eyes glimmer like jewels. No laughter showed in his face. "You know that some brothers lifemate—marry—the same female, sharing her for all their lives."

Her breathing stalled, and she wrapped her arms around herself, trying to hold down rising hope.

"Zeb and I…we love you, Breanne. We want you to be our female. Our lifemate." On his palm was a bracelet, the tiny silver discs lit by the moonlight. A bracelet like the one she'd been found with. Zeb opened his hand to show one as well.

"I—" Her throat closed off, and she couldn't get the words out. Oh God, was this really happening? They were serious; they really wanted her. Forever. "I…"

A frown started on Shay's face.

Zeb's free hand fisted, and he scowled at her. "The answer is yes, little female."

As laughter welled up in her, she could finally speak. "God, I love you," she said to Zeb, "you domineering brute." She turned to Shay. "And you're just as bad, Mr. Alpha, and I love you just as much."

She'd frozen them in place. Now that was new. Her lips curved as the word came easily. "Yes."

Shay sprang to his feet. He carefully slid the bracelet onto her left wrist, then his hands closed around her upper arms and he lifted her up onto her tiptoes for a long, wet kiss. "*Tha gaol agam ort.*" He crushed her against his massive chest. "By the God, I love you."

The words turned everything inside her to pudding, and she blinked back tears. She saw Zeb waiting, his face expressionless, but his eyes…his eyes burned. Shay released her, and she took a step toward him.

Zeb slid the bracelet over her hand. "I never thought I'd do this." He pulled her into his arms, holding her as if he thought she wasn't real, was afraid she'd disappear. With a shuddering breath, he started to let her go, then snatched her back to rumble in her ear, "Our mate. I love you."

When he finally released her, she was light-headed from being squeezed so hard. "Well."

Shay smiled and held out two bracelets. "These are for you to put on us."

She remembered seeing the one on Calum's arm and grinned. *My men—marked and everything.* She put one on Shay's big-boned wrist and the other over Zeb's corded wrist, and nothing had ever looked so beautiful. "They'll shift with us?"

"That's right." Zeb ran a finger over the metal discs on her arm, leaving a trail of tingles behind.

When she looked up, the two men were smiling at her in a way she'd learned to recognize. One that sent heat streaming to her lower body. Excellent idea. She stepped forward and rubbed her breasts against Zeb's chest. His face darkened with hunger.

Shay stopped her. "Not quite yet, *a chuisle mo chridhe.*" His eyes were half-lidded. "We're going to run while the moon is up, so the Mother can bless her new bonds." He cupped her breast, his thumb teasing the nipple and sending heat through her. "Trawsfur."

Now? But the moonlight shimmered around her like warm rain, and when she shifted, she felt it more clearly—the Goddess's approval and love.

The other two trawsfurred as well.

Shay loped away from the creek, through the forest, moving higher into the mountains. When they reached a tiny meadow burgeoning with silky-soft, new grass, he stopped.

Bree stared up at the black sky. Stars had been scattered with a liberal hand, and the crescent moon in the west lit the white-topped mountain peaks with gold. What a world. And so very, very beautiful in this form.

When she looked for her companions—her mates—Shay stood close, mouth open in a canine grin, bowing his front quarters down, butt in the air. It was an invitation to play, and she reacted instinctively, springing forward to nip at him before darting away. He yipped happily and sprang at her, even as Zeb did the same, and they played in the moonlight. Danced.

The dancing slowly changed. The males' nips changed to licks over her nose and chin, then to nuzzling along her body...everywhere.

Oh Lord, her body went on alert. Need pooled inside her and unfamiliar instincts had her brushing against the wolves, enticing them to chase after her. Zeb slid up beside her and set a big paw on her back. He mouthed her nape, sending shivers through her. His musky wolf scent washed over her, and she whined, her fur feeling as if it had grown nerve endings.

Although he jumped down, her paws seemed stuck to the damp meadow grass, not letting her move. As Zeb came up behind her, her tail went sideways in a strange manner. Her nerves flared with heat; her mind was smothered under the rush of instincts. She started to pull away.

A wolf blocked her. Shay. As he licked her nose in reassurance, the power of the alpha ran through her.

She shivered. Zeb's paws held her shoulders, his heavy weight anchoring her in place. His cock pressed against her, seeking entrance, and she instinctively lifted her hind end higher to give him access.

He slowly penetrated her, and his shaft grew longer and thicker with each thrust.

She trembled, the sensation different, primal. His paws curved in front of her, holding her as his thrusting grew harder.

Then, she felt the shimmer of change and realized she was on hands and knees in the soft grass, her bracelet sparkling on her wrist. Zeb slid one palm around to cup her breast, his bare chest rubbed on her back. "Our mate," he growled in her ear and plunged deep. His arm lifted her hips up to him before he moved his hand lower.

Oh God. His fingers slid over her mound and pinned her clit. Her center balanced on a razor's edge and burst in a blast of pleasure. He laughed, hammered deeper, and his cock jerked with his own climax.

Good grief. Her arms trembled, and her head hung down as she panted.

He bit her nape, making her shudder before he kissed the tiny pain away. "I love you, little female," he whispered into her ear, sending warmth of a different sort through her.

As he pulled out, she whined, wanting to be taken again. The cool air against her heated sweaty skin made her shiver, and she started to stand.

He set his hand on her shoulder.

"What?" she asked.

Lifting her chin, he ran his finger over her lips. His dark gaze met hers. "Trawsfur."

Again? But his eyes held her pinned, and she couldn't deny him. The door to her animal shape hadn't completely closed, and she slid into wolf without thinking. Happiness radiated through her as Zeb stroked her fur and tugged on her ears.

He stepped away, and she glanced around for Shay. *There.*

The rush of lust startled her, but God, he was beautiful. He stood in the center of the meadow, ears forward, tail raised high, the moonlight gleaming on his silver-gray fur. Her heart swelled with love as she trotted over. A second later, Zeb joined them, his dark fur rustling against hers.

Shay barked once and loped through the silky grass, startling rabbits and mice as he led the way out of the meadow.

Bree followed, paws hitting the soft grass, tail high. The feeling of running with her mates was heady. Powerful. She could remember the slow decline in her health, her exhaustion at the end of each day, and her loneliness. Now she was healthy, loved, and mated.

With every footfall, she tried to give the Mother her gratitude.

The trail wound upward and upward until they came out onto a grassy-covered knoll, high above the valley where they'd been. The moon lingered over the mountains, her light a soft caress. Dark forests and white covered peaks surrounded them.

Zeb went to sprawl in a grassy spot. As she started to join him, Shay moved closer to her. His body was huge, radiating heat and power. He circled her slowly, sniffing, licking her nose and chin. His scent was musky and heavily masculine, waking everything in her to a searing need. And then he was behind her, his breath on her hidden areas. She moved her hind paws apart, her tail easing to one side.

With one lunge, he was on her, far heavier than Zeb. She was slick and ready as his cock slid into her, and with each thrust, it thickened until it was almost more than she could take. His front paws pinned her as he pounded into her, and her head spun with the joy of being taken, of being wanted.

God, she loved them both so much.

His teeth closed on her ruff, sending a shiver down her spine. Then everything blurred, and she was human again. Her arms gleamed white in the moonlight. She saw Shay's tanned, thick forearm next to hers for a second before he gripped her hips. He lifted her higher, yanking her back onto his shaft, and she gasped at the sensation.

Her arms turned rubbery, and she dropped to her elbows as his rhythmic pumping took over her body. The pressure inside her grew, higher and higher until an overwhelming eruption ripped through her, sending pleasure flowing along her veins as if she'd absorbed the moonlight itself.

As she panted, Shay's hands tightened painfully, and he thrust deep and hard. He came with a low growl that changed to a croon of love as his forehead leaned on her back. "*Tha gaol agam ort*, little wolf."

He rose and pulled her to her feet. Wrapping his arms around her, he molded her against him. In his usual embrace, he fondled her ass as he kissed her thoroughly. With a pleased sigh, he passed her to Zeb.

After Zeb finished kissing her, he pushed her sweat-streaked hair off her forehead. His teeth flashed white in his dark face. "You look confused, little female."

Who me? She shivered at the memory of paws on her furry shoulders, of the scent... "We were wolves. I mean, we made love and—"

As Shay nuzzled her neck, Zeb ran his knuckles over her cheek and said, "Under the Mother's moon, lifemated shifters of the same animal can mate in both forms."

"It's another blessing of the Mother." Shay looked at the moon, barely over the top of the mountains. "Let's sing her down." He shifted, shook his fur out, and paced to the edge of the knoll over the meadow. Zeb stood next to him, dark fur next to the light, and then Bree.

Shay barked three times, lifted his nose, and gave a long lonely howl. Zeb joined him, lower and rougher. Then Bree added hers, and their voices twined together, filling the valley with a primitive melody as beautiful as the world around them.

They sang until the last glimmer of moonlight disappeared from the mountaintops.

Chapter Forty

Cold Creek, North Cascades Territory

U NWILLING TO BE apart, they'd all piled into Shay's truck for the final day of their trip back. As Shay drove, Zeb stared out the windshield, trying to ignore the ache in his chest. The trees on each side of the road whipped past, too quickly for his liking. Bringing them to the end. Overhead, the sun broke through the morning rainclouds like a beacon of hope. *A beacon of hope.* Zeb snorted. *As if.*

Bree sat between him and Shay, and her eyes glistened with tears. Zeb took her hand and squeezed gently.

Last night, they'd crossed into Calum's territory. The welcome from Herne and the Mother that every shifter got when returning to their home territory had been wrenchingly strong. Although the Olympic forest had been beautiful, everything inside Zeb reverberated with the knowledge that the North Cascades Territory was where he belonged.

Bree hadn't been ready—hell, neither had he. He'd never felt such a sense of coming home before.

She'd cried. His sweet female who faced everything head-on had wept so hard that she'd broken his heart. She'd never had a home—and she knew they hadn't either. Between her feelings of loss and her guilt about them, she'd made herself sick. They'd ended up camping right there in the forest.

Undoubtedly, Calum had felt them enter his territory, but Bree couldn't have known or she'd have been more nervous. At least, the Cosantir hadn't sent a cahir to hunt them down last night. Zeb wasn't sure if he was relieved or not.

Shay put his hand on Bree's knee. "We'll speak to the Cosantir, then pack up and leave. Quick and easy."

"Of course." Her chin came up as if she weren't leaving the first home she'd known.

Zeb's lips tightened. Not fair. She hadn't done anything wrong. But sometimes that was where the trail led. "We'll be together," he said roughly.

"Thank the Mother for that," Bree murmured.

"Finally got your gods sorted out?" Shay asked with an amused look.

"Yeah, well, after this last week, it's hard to deny Her."

Shay drove through Cold Creek and turned onto Main Street. "Uh-oh."

Two sawhorses blocked the street by Angie's Diner. A sheriff's car was parked to one side with Alec leaning against it. People—mostly shifters, some humans—lined the sidewalks.

In front of the sawhorses, alone in the center of the street, the Cosantir waited, arms crossed over his chest.

"Guess we're expected," Zeb muttered. His stomach tightened. He and Shay had assured Bree that Calum wouldn't drop them dead in their tracks, but the Cosantir had the power and the right if he chose to do so.

"Looks like an old-fashioned hanging." With a scowl, Shay parked on the side of the street. He gave Bree a lingering kiss before getting out.

Zeb did same. Before he closed the door, he ran his knuckles down Bree's soft cheek, needing to touch her one last time. Just in case. Then he tapped her chin. "Stay here. Do *not* get out of the truck." *No matter what you see.*

He caught up to Shay, then shoulder-against-shoulder, they approached the Cosantir. His eyes held the black of the God, and Zeb felt his heart sink.

Calum glanced behind them, and his brows drew together ominously. "Did you tell her to stay in the truck?"

Fear burst in Zeb's stomach. Did the Cosantir plan to punish her as well? He swallowed. *Beat me, kill me, don't hurt Bree.* "Yes, I did. Cosantir, please..."

The Cosantir smiled faintly. "It didn't work."

A second later, he heard pattering footsteps, and then Breanne shoved between him and Shay. "Cal—Cosantir. It was my fault they left, all my fault, so if you need to kill someone, it has to be me."

"Indeed."

CRIMINY, THIS ISN'T going well. Bree shivered as Calum's eyes, a black without any glint of light, held her gaze. The power in him was a rumble of thunder in her bones.

"Were you seen by any humans?"

"Only in human form to warn them about a murderer in the area," Shay replied. "We didn't trawsfur at all."

The black gaze wandered across their bodies, lingering on the Zeb's arm even though his sleeve covered the wound. "The hellhound?"

"Dead. We left its body in Bree's apartment," Zeb said.

"We wiped her revolver clean and tossed it into Puget Sound," Shay added. "The humans might be confused, but nothing will point to the Daonain."

"Cosantir," Bree said. The guys had assured her they'd be all right, but she could tell the Cosantir was going to make them pay. She had to get her men out of here. "I had to go back. It was killing my neighbors while searching for me." She put her arms in front of her men, as if she could block him from hurting them. "Zeb and Shay were just trying to keep me safe. It's not their fault."

His expression didn't change. She'd never realized how cold his face could be. "Breanne. Since your actions did not expose the Daonain's existence and as you are a new shifter, you are forgiven."

She felt the men relax and knew the dummies weren't worried for themselves, just for her.

"Thank you, Cosantir," Shay said, echoed by Zeb. The gratitude in their voices made her growl. They stepped forward, pushing her behind them, as if scared he'd change his mind.

"*Kneel.*"

The men dropped to their knees as if their legs had given out.

A chill ran through Bree as the memory of how Klaus had died filled her. "No!" She went around them, dodging Zeb's grab for her. Stepping in front of the Cosantir, she pressed her hands together on her chest in a plea. "Cosantir, please, they were only—"

With a werecat's uncanny speed, Calum grabbed her left wrist and held it up in the air. Her silver bracelets gleamed in the sunlight. "Breanne, are Zebulon and Seamus your lifemates?"

Her eyes rested on the two gleaming bands, her heart too full to keep the joy from spilling into her words. "Oh, they are," she whispered.

The flash of satisfaction in Calum's face disappeared too fast for her to be certain of what she'd seen. He released her arm. As the blackness in his eyes turned silvery-gray, he pulled the sawhorse barricade to one side.

Bree stopped breathing, hearing only the pulse of her pounding heart. No one moved.

"Cosantir?" Shay asked after a long moment. He was so

brave. "Are we forgiven then?"

"You are." Calum's lips quirked. "Herne won't step between a female and her lifemates. The Mother would have his…antlers." His mouth curved into a real smile. "Cahirs, Breanne, welcome home."

As relief ripped through Bree, she staggered. "We can stay? Really, really stay?" She wrapped her arms around Calum and hugged him tightly. "Oh, thank you."

He chuckled, hugged her back, and pushed her gently through the sawhorses. She heard Jody's whoop of delight, was caught in hard hugs from Angie and Vicki, and kissed on the cheek by Bonnie. A second later, Bree was engulfed in women.

SHAY GRINNED AS the females surrounded their alpha, and their happiness flowed into him like a bubbling creek. Standing quietly, the males of his pack waited, and their support and pleasure at his return were a low hum in his bones. *My pack, my mate.* The hard shoulder rubbing against his completed his world. *My brother.*

As he rose to his feet and yanked Zeb up, he noticed the storeowners were bringing tables and chairs out. Bowls and platters of food appeared from various cars and stores.

After checking the Cosantir who'd moved aside to talk with his littermate, Shay lowered his voice, "A bhràthair, either Cold Creek likes watching their Cosantir kill people or—"

"Or the fucking feline set us up," Zeb muttered. "Again."

"Did you know about that lifemating thing?" Shay said under his breath.

"Fuck no." Zeb lowered his voice further. "I wonder how close we came to getting fried?"

Calum turned and gave them a grim smile. "Very, very close."

Shay winced. The Cosantir definitely had a mountain lion's

hearing.

Calum added, "If anything had gone wrong in Seattle, the Mother wouldn't have been able to intervene. It helps that Herne favors his hellhound fighters—he was pleased to go easy on you, especially since you killed another demonkin."

Shay eyed the Cosantir warily. What kind of a person has conversations with the God and the Mother?

Alec punched Calum in the shoulder. "Nobody pissed themselves, dammit. You're losing your touch, brawd."

Amusement lit Calum's eyes. "I will endeavor to meet your expectations next time, sheriff." His gaze returned to Zeb and Shay, and darkness flashed again. "Do not let that next time be either of you."

"No, Cosantir." Shay gave a slight bow and heard Zeb's grunt of agreement.

As Calum strolled toward the crowd and the beginning of a celebration, Shay's eyes narrowed. All those preparations already made. Just when had the Cosantir had that little chat with the Gods?

He rubbed his chin, remembering where they'd camped last night. He turned to Alec. "Calum already knew we were lifemated, didn't he?"

"Aye. He said you were so well-mated that you lit up the edge of his territory like a fireball. He was damned pleased. As am I." Alec stuck out his hand. "Good job, cahirs."

They shook hands with him and ventured into the press of people. Slaps from the pack males, hugs from the females, congratulations from the townspeople.

When they were finally permitted to rejoin Breanne, Angie pushed glasses of champagne into their hands. As the noise died, everyone looked at them expectantly.

When Breanne looked confused, Vicki said, "With the—in Cold Creek, the newlyweds make the first toast."

Shay didn't even have to think. He stepped forward and raised his glass. "To our friends."

Zeb's shoulder rubbed his as he said in his rough voice, "Our family."

Breanne squirmed between them, her gentle voice filled with joy, "Our *home*."

~ The End ~

Daonain Glossary

The Daonain use a conglomeration of handed-down languages from the British Isles. Some of the older villages still speak the Gaelic (Scots) or Irish Gaelic. Many of the more common (and mangled) shifter terms have descended from Welsh.

Errors and simplification of spelling and pronunciation can be attributed to being passed down through generations...or the author messing up. Below are a few of the more common words and terms used by the shifters.

a bhràthair: brother

a chuisle mo chridhe: pulse of my heart

a leannan: sweetheart, darling

a mhac: son

brawd: brother

cahir: warrior

cariad: lover, darling, sweetheart

cosantir: guardian or protector

dùin do bhuek: shut up

mo bhràthair: my brother

mo charaid: my friend

mo chridhe: my heart

mo leannan: my darling / my lover

tha gaol agam ort: I love you

trawsfur: transform or shift

Ready for more? Then try,

Eventide of the Bear
The Wild Hunt Legacy: Book 3

Available everywhere

Get *Eventide of the Bear* Now!

There's a reason why Cherise Sinclair is on my auto-buy list: she writes fantastic erotic romances with great stories and wonderful characters.

~ Rho The Romance Reviews

She risked her life to save a human child. Pain was her reward.

All her life, Emma longed for someone to love. Instead, disaster sees the brand-new bard banished from her people for long lonely years. Injured saving a child, the werebear has to steal food from humans, breaking shifter Law. The territory's Cosantir and his lethal grizzly warrior catch her in the act. To her surprise, she's healed and welcomed. Obviously, they don't know her past. But oh, she can't resist being around other shifters—especially the captivatingly powerful warrior. Maybe she can stay...just a little while.

As a grizzly warrior, Ben is ordered to house the pretty werebear until she heals. His littermate abandoned him, his home is empty, and he's been alone for a long time. Intelligent and sweet and lushly curved, Emma is a delight...even if she is oddly reticent about her past. Although having sworn off females, he's sorely tempted by this one. Damned if he doesn't want to keep her, secrets or not.

Females were trouble. Years past, one split Ryder from his littermate. Now the panther shifter is returning to Ben, bringing his cub with him, a four-year-old he stole from the abusive female. To Ryder's annoyance, his brother is sheltering a wounded bear. A *female*. Even worse, she's beautiful and gentle and loving—damned if he's going to fall for that act again. But when the dark of the moon arrives and death reigns supreme, he'll discover that not all females are alike.

In a world filled with hellhounds and pixies, can three lonely shifters and one silent cub create a new family together?

Whether you are interested in erotic BDSM, sci-fi or paranormal, Cherise Sinclair is always my top pick and number one suggestion.

~ You Gotta Read Reviews

Excerpt from

Eventide of the Bear

T HE SCENT OF cooking meat drew Emma back to the human campground. With every step, her broken leg caught on brush and downed logs. Pain stabbed into her over and over, and the agony was getting worse.

The knowledge she wouldn't last much longer was actually a relief.

Since her injury half a moon ago, she'd been unable to hunt. Even going to a stream for water was almost impossible. Under her brittle, dull fur, her muscles sagged from dehydration and weight loss. She was finding it harder and harder to move. But in bear form, her animal nature wouldn't quit, no matter the inevitable conclusion.

Regret for a life cut short curled through her like wood smoke rising from a fire. She'd had so many dreams—loving mates, cublings, pleasing her clan with her songs and stories. Instead, she had caused Gary and Andre's deaths. On the other hand, she'd rescued children from a hellhound. Maybe the Goddess would find it an adequate balance, and if not…Emma was content.

Under cover of the forest, she surveyed the clearing. Two large men sat at a campfire. A hint of a familiar, wild scent caught her attention. She sniffed, but the elusive smell disappeared under the heavy odors of wood smoke and grilling meat.

Meat.

Despite the driving hunger, caution lent her patience. She

was too weak to fight, too weak to run. Yes, patience would gain her all.

Unhurriedly, the two men smothered the fire, cleaned up, and stored their food in a bear-vault. Rather than erecting a tent, they simply stripped and climbed into sleeping bags.

Long and long, she waited. An owl hooted from nearby. She caught the scent of a skunk, probably a scavenger like her. A weasel passed by, probably after the tiny shrew in the leaf litter.

The men's breathing slowed. They were asleep.

Slowly, she entered the clearing, holding her injured rear leg up to eliminate any noise. Step by step, she advanced.

The container lay on its side under a tree. She hesitated, fighting the fiery throbbing in her leg and ache in her left forepaw. Where was the coin or key to open the metal-sided canister?

A pile of copper pennies caught her eye. Now she needed fingers. All she had to do was be human.

As she visualized turning in a circle, a door glowed—so very dim—in the rear of her mind. The magic was dying. She was dying. She opened the door and stepped through. Magic ran over her skin in a glorious tingling that, for one wonderful second, wiped out her pain.

One breath later, she stared at her fingers splayed on the sparse grass. Dirt and pine needles ground into her bare knees. Unable not to look, she tipped her head to look at her lower leg and flinched. The oozing, gaping wounds exposed the muscle and the jagged ends of bones in a horrifying, agonizing mess.

As she reached for the food container, her shattered leg grated as if massive nails were being hammered into the bones. She clenched her teeth as tears flooded her eyes and dripped onto the dead leaves and into the dirt.

"Child." The low voice came from behind her.

No, no, no. The men were *awake.*

She jerked around. Her broken leg caught, twisted. *Oh, Goddess.* As agony overwhelmed her, she lost her grip on her shape and fell through the door to the wild. Her flesh blurred, transformed. Fur. Fangs. Claws.

As the pain ebbed, horror filled her. She'd *trawsfurred* in front of humans.

Too late. She spun around.

A man stood in front of her. Olive skin. Dark hair. No weapon. His dark eyes were turning black and—

Bear instincts took over. She rose, trying to balance on one leg, and let out a roar of anger.

Run, human. Please, run.

Instead, an answering growl came from the side. Another bear.

She dropped to all fours and tried to flee, but her bad leg hit the container. The flare of agony shot red-tinged lightning through her. Her eyesight fuzzed and—

Slam.

The bear hit her shoulder and knocked her off her paws. Before she could move, the massive grizzly flopped across her, driving the air from her lungs.

Caught. Trapped.

Panicking, she struggled, grunting and growling.

Fearlessly, the human went down on one knee beside her head. He caught her muzzle in an unbreakable grip and forced her to meet his gaze. His eyes had turned black as a winter's night.

"*Trawsfur.*" His voice held the power of the God.

A force in her head pushed her through the door to human and locked it behind her. Her fur, her claws, her size melted into a human frame. He'd forced her to shift. How could he…?

New fear struck. She couldn't *breathe*.

The man shook his head. "Remove yourself, Benjamin, before you suffocate her.

With a growling snort of amusement, the grizzly rose, shook out its fur, and changed to human.

They weren't humans; they were shifters. That was the familiar wild scent she'd caught.

As Emma's leg throbbed with pain, she stared at them through tear-blurred eyes.

The werebear's cheekbone held a blue scar shaped like a knife. He was a cahir, sworn to protect the clan.

And the other male? Only one type of Daonain held the power of transformation. He was a Cosantir of a territory and Herne's representative on earth.

Her doom had found her. She closed her eyes and inhaled, knowing her breaths could now be counted on one hand. And despite her pain and sorrow, the air was sweet, fragrant with evergreen and wood smoke, and the scent of other shifters.

Truly, she was blessed. Her death would be quick at the hand of the Cosantir, and…she wouldn't be alone.

She met the Cosantir's gaze. Black for the God's presence. "Send me back to the Mother," she whispered. "I'm ready."

To her surprise, he shook his head. Silver-gray was breaking into the darkness of his eyes. "I fear I am not."

He glanced at the huge bear-shifter who was pulling on a pair of jeans. "Benjamin, get some information. I'll bring the first-aid kit from my pack."

She struggled to sit up as the werebear approached. The male—Benjamin—was huge. Over six-five. His straight brown hair was cut to ear-length and shorter than most shifters preferred. Curly chest hair made a triangle over his thick pectoral muscles. His angular features were big-boned, his jaw square and strong. Not handsome, but oh, far too compelling.

"I'm Ben." His deep voice held a Texas drawl. "Got a name, girl?" *"Got a nayum, gurl?"*

"Emma. Why didn't he kill me?" she whispered. "I broke the Law."

"Pretty name, darlin'." He took a knee beside her. "The Cosantir takes his time before dispensing judgment."

Should she...could she...run?

She glanced at Ben's jeans. Clothes would be a handicap if he shifted back to bear. He'd have to remove the jeans first or be tangled up until he could rip them away. She was naked, so she could *trawsfur* to bear and try to escape. Without thinking, she edged slightly away.

Ben's laugh was the rumble of rocks avalanching down a cliff. "You can't move fast enough to get away, li'l bear. Not from me and not from Calum. He's a cat."

A mountain lion? The chill came from more than the frosted grass under her body. On three legs, she couldn't escape a lion. Or the grizzly, either. So she'd die. Please, let her at least maintain some dignity. But fear and pain were tearing at her resolve. Averting her face, she blinked back tears.

With a grunt, Ben settled next to her, his body near enough to impart warmth to her bare body. One big hand curved over her ankle below her wound. His brows drew together as he took in the extent of the damage. "Those are bite marks. What in the Hunter's lands happened to your leg?"

"Indeed, I have the same question." The Cosantir's resonant voice held a faintly clipped British accent, a marked contrast to the bear's slow drawl. He carried two straight pieces of wood, each covered with a ripped-up T-shirt.

He set one on each side of her broken leg.

"You call that first aid?" Ben protested, although he held the braces in place as Calum secured them with more strips of cloth.

Her whole leg felt submerged in fiery lava. As the bindings tightened, her agony grew. Hands fisted, she fought back scream after scream. Finally, the pain receded enough she could hear the

Cosantir.

"I am disinclined to attempt anything other than conveying her to our healer. That"—he indicated her leg—"is as bad a fracture as I've ever seen. Anything we do here is liable to make it worse or restart the bleeding."

"But…" She'd been banished and was to be shunned by all Daonain.

Why were they even speaking to her? She touched the raised parallel scars along her jawline. Didn't they see the marks? Know what black scars meant? This Cosantir had surely banished people before.

She struggled to sit up.

"Stay put, li'l bear." Ben set his huge hand on her shoulder, and the warmth of his palm seared her frozen skin.

"Aren't you going to kill me? I don't understand."

The Cosantir rose, his face unreadable. "You broke the Law by raiding human campgrounds. However, I've heard no reports of a shifter, merely speculation about clever bears or vagrant humans." He paused for a long moment. "There will be consequences, but death will not be one of them."

Not die? Her breath caught on the influx of hope.

The Cosantir glanced at Ben.

The grizzly shifter's square jaw went tight. "Brace yourself, darlin'. This is going to hurt." His hands slid under her body, and he lifted her into the air.

The pain rose to intolerable, and she screamed before blackness took her away.

Get *Eventide of the Bear* Now!

Also from Cherise Sinclair

About Cherise Sinclair

A *New York Times* and *USA Today* Bestselling Author, Cherise is renowned for writing heart-wrenching romances with devastating alpha males, laugh-out-loud dialogue, and absolutely sizzling sex.

I met my dearheart when vacationing in the Caribbean. Now I won't say it was love at first sight. Actually since he stood over me, enjoying the view down my swimsuit top, I might have been a tad peeved—as well as attracted. But although we were together less than two days and lived on opposite sides of the country, love can't be corralled by time or space.

We've now been married for many, many years. (And he still looks down my swimsuit tops.)

Nowadays, I live in the west with this obnoxious, beloved husband, a puppy with way too much energy, and a cat who rules us with a fuzzy, iron paw. I'm a gardener, and I love nurturing small plants until they're big and healthy and productive…and ripping defenseless weeds out by the roots when I'm angry. I enjoy thunderstorms, collecting eggs from the chickens, and visiting the local brewery for the darkest, maltiest beer on tap. My favorite way to spend an evening is curled up on a couch next to the master of my heart, watching the fire, reading, and…well…if you're reading my books, you obviously know what else happens in front of fires.

~ *Cherise*

Connect with Cherise in the following places:

Website:
CheriseSinclair.com

Facebook:
www.facebook.com/CheriseSinclairAuthor

Facebook Discussion Group:
CheriseSinclair.com/Facebook-Discussion-Group

Want to be notified of the next release?

Sent only on release day, Cherise's newsletters contain freebies, excerpts, and articles.

Sign up at:
www.CheriseSinclair.com/NewsletterForm

CPSIA information can be obtained
at www.ICGtesting.com
Printed in the USA
LVHW031859210821
695820LV00006B/252